D0849116

Her, Too

ALSO BY BONNIE KISTLER

House on Fire

The Cage

Her, Too

A Novel

Bonnie Kistler

HARPER

An Imprint of HarperCollins*Publishers*

FIRST U.S. EDITION

Designed by Emily Snyder

Library of Congress Control Number: 2023934929

ISBN 978-0-06-308920-4 (pbk.)
ISBN 978-0-06-308924-2 (library ed.)

23 24 25 26 27 LBC 5 4 3 2 1

For all who were silenced, and all who refused to be

Every word has consequences. Every silence, too.

—JEAN-PAUL SARTRE

Her, Too

1

THERE IT WAS: THE RUSH, the thrill, the exhilaration coursing through her veins like molten gold. It hit her the moment she swept through the courthouse doors. Other lawyers felt that rush when they rose to open, or to close, or at the moment the jury returned its verdict. But for Kelly McCann, it was this moment, the victory lap, her triumphal chariot ride around the coliseum while the crowd roared in the stands. It was better than drugs. Better than sex—at least what she remembered of sex. After all, an orgasm was only the payoff of maybe twenty minutes of effort. Whereas this—*this!*—was the reward for weeks of trial, months of prep, years of sacrifice.

The crowd thronged the pavement in front of the courthouse and spilled out into the street. The reporters had pushed their way to the front; at the back were the TV news vans with their rooftop dishes pitched to the sky like SETI satellites searching for intelligent life. A burst of camera flashes met Kelly as she stopped at the edge of the stairs. Before her was a sea of upturned faces and microphones on poles that stretched like cranes' necks over their heads. The media was there—her team saw to that—and the protesters were there, too—the media saw to that—with their hand-scrawled placards raised as high as the cameras and microphones. #MeToo and JUSTICE FOR REEZA and TAKE RAPE SERIOUSLY and BELIEVE REEZA. Some of them had been there from the first day of jury selection, and their signs were now tattered and rain-streaked, a proud emblem of their endurance.

On the other side were the counterprotesters, in equal numbers. They held up their own placards: JUSTICE FOR GEORGE, DON'T CANCEL DR. B, and, most prominently, SAVE OUR SAVIOR—hyperbolic perhaps, but not the first time he'd been so dubbed. After all, he was the man who may have cured Alzheimer's.

Kelly paused to allow the photographers their shots. She was dressed severely, in a black suit and white blouse, tortoiseshell glasses, her blond hair sleeked back in a tight French twist, her only jewelry a wedding band. On her feet she wore not the expected sensible flats but black pumps with four-inch heels. At only five foot two, she needed that extra height.

This had been her signature look ever since her early days in the DA's office when she learned her colleagues were calling her the Cheerleader. The nickname was probably unavoidable, even if they'd never unearthed her high school history. She was, after all, a petite blonde with a southern accent, a penchant for bright colors, and a tad too much enthusiasm about her work. She couldn't do anything about her height, and not much about her accent, but she ditched the bright colors immediately. As for her enthusiasm—that died a natural death even before she went over to the defense bar.

Her courtroom team fanned out in a V-formation behind her, like geese flying south. First was her associate, Patti Han, a brilliant young lawyer whose talents were wasted riding second chair beside Kelly. Striding up next was Kelly's assistant, Cazzadee Johnson, a long-legged beauty whose competence and composure were likewise indispensable to Kelly's success. Two men brought up the rear: the Philadelphia lawyer serving as her local counsel and the suburban lawyer serving as her hyper-local counsel—both men, both white, and both so nondescript that Kelly routinely confused one with the other. They were indispensable, too, but only because the local court rules required them—a way of protecting the hometown bar from marauding out-of-state lawyers like Kelly. The final member of her team was Javier Torres, her investigator. He was there, too, but not on the courthouse steps. He was on patrol, moving through the crowd like a panther, silky smooth and stealthy.

"For ten long months," Kelly began, her voice ringing out down the steps and over the street, "Dr. Benedict has borne the awful weight of a false accusation. His reputation has been sullied. His family traumatized. He's received hate mail and even death threats. And his work—his vital, critical work—has been horribly hampered. That's the awful power of a false accusation. And perhaps worst of all is that he had to bear all this in silence. The reality of our legal system meant that he couldn't say a word in his own defense."

Of course, it was Kelly herself who forbade him to speak, but the crowd didn't need to know that.

"Today, at last, twelve good men and women spoke up for him. They put the lie to that awful false accusation." She allowed a smile then, a big beaming smile that broke out like a sunrise over the crowd. "The jury returned a unanimous verdict of not guilty on all counts!"

Her declaration was greeted with boos and hisses from the protesters, but she heard only the applause and whistles from the counterprotesters. Like any good cheerleader, she knew how to whip up her own side to drown out the other side. The technique still worked today. She raised both arms in triumph, and Team Benedict roared its approval and sent the blood singing through her veins.

This moment was her compensation for all she'd sacrificed and all she still endured. For ten years she'd done nothing but defend men accused of sex crimes. Athletes and musicians were her bread and butter, along with the occasional CEO. It was sordid work. The accusations themselves, of course, but also all the borderline-dirty tactics it took to defeat them. All the unreasonable ways of creating reasonable doubt. It left her feeling soiled sometimes, as if her hands were stained with the damned spots of complicity. But this moment scrubbed those spots away. It was like tossing a match on tinder and watching the flames erupt. She was purified by fire, silver in the refiner's crucible.

She liked to win. She *lived* to win. It was the entire secret of her success. Her courtroom victories weren't due to any great brilliance on her part. She had no more talent than the average lawyer. What she did have was this abiding lust for victory.

Early in life she realized that she was never going to be more than a runner-up in either athletic or academic competitions, so she found other ways to use her competitive drive: cheerleading squad, drama club, debate team. Law school was a natural progression, and criminal trial work the natural culmination. Most of her cases she settled swiftly and quietly, but two or three times a year she took them all the way to trial. Always in the best interests of her clients, she maintained, but admittedly it was also to preserve her reputation and keep her profile high. And *high* was how she felt right now.

"I want to thank the jurors for their service," she shouted. "They sacrificed more than three weeks of their lives; they had to endure endless hours of testimony and several more hours of thoughtful deliberation. But in the end, they delivered justice for Dr. Benedict. And with it they restored hope for all those people around the world who depend upon Dr. Benedict and his lifesaving work!"

The cheers came even louder then, loud enough to drown out the groans that came from the protestors.

"And now, thanks to those jurors and their outstanding service, Dr. Benedict no longer has to remain silent. Doctor?"

George Carlson Benedict, MD, PhD, shuffled forward to take Kelly's place at the edge of the stairs. He was fifty, a gray-haired, bespectacled man in a slightly rumpled gray suit. His shoulders were stooped, no doubt from years of hunching over a microscope.

He didn't look like a multimillionaire, but as controlling share-holder of UniViro Pharmaceuticals, he surely was. He didn't look like an international celebrity either, but he was that, too. It was rare for any scientist to achieve such status, but Dr. Benedict had done it. He was the man who maybe, hopefully, had cured the most-feared disease in the world. He'd already been awarded the Presidential Medal of Freedom. The Nobel Prize in Medicine was surely on the horizon.

Kelly stepped aside as her client cleared his throat and droned out his thanks to the jury in his usual low-pitched monotone. The cameras flashed again, and Kelly smiled blindly into the starbursts of light.

When her vision cleared, a face in the crowd leapt into view as suddenly as if she'd zoomed in on it. A glamorous brunette of fifty, tall and handsome, even with her striking eyes narrowed and her mouth twisted with disgust. Kelly froze on that unexpected face for a moment before her vision panned camera-like to the right and zoomed in on another face twenty feet away. It was a young woman this time, quietly pretty with short brown hair and, behind her glasses, deep-set eyes that still looked as haunted as the day Kelly met her. Then her vision-camera panned left, pulled back, and a third face came into focus at the rear of the crowd. Another woman, this one very young, a skinny blonde with timid, bashful eyes. Three different faces, three different women, three different cases with only one common thread.

Dimly, Kelly heard her name spoken. It was Dr. Benedict, thanking her in his robotic voice for all her hard work.

She hadn't expected to see these women, here or anywhere, ever again. Their cases were done and dusted, checks delivered and cashed, papers signed and sealed. She searched for Javi Torres in the crowd, found him, and raised an eyebrow. He nodded to acknowledge that he'd clocked them, too. As of course he would.

He would know their names, too, while all Kelly could remember were their jobs and the dollar amounts: chief information officer, $2.5 million; research scientist, $500,000; office cleaner, $20,000. Money paid to them in exchange for their nondisclosure agreements. The NDA women, she called them.

Her heart started to hammer with a second spike of adrenaline. They shouldn't be here. They mustn't be here. This could only mean trouble. She forced herself to take a breath and study each of them in turn. They weren't holding placards, she noted. They didn't seem to be part of any group. They weren't looking at one another. They didn't even know one another. They couldn't. So they mustn't be here to make a scene. They wouldn't dare.

She searched out Javi again, and he met her eyes and gave a shrug. This was nothing, his shrug said, and her pulse slowed.

Now Dr. Benedict was thanking his wife, Jane, who stood the requisite three steps behind him. She was a plump, rosy-cheeked woman with a mobcap of gray curls, and she gazed on him with eyes aglow behind her glasses.

A disturbance sounded from around the corner as he was thanking the board of UniViro for standing with him throughout this ordeal. A shout rang out, then a chorus of shouts, and part of the crowd broke away and scrambled for the rear of the courthouse. Most of the cameras and microphones followed. Kelly knew what that meant: Dr. Reeza Patel, the alleged victim, was trying to sneak out the back door. But no such luck. The crowd and the media would be there to catch her in the agony of her defeat, this sad perversion of the walk of shame.

A man stepped forward to escort the Benedicts to their waiting car. He was Anton, Benedict's ever-present shadow. Whether that was his first name or last was never clear to Kelly, nor was his exact job description. He was a towering hulk of a man, bald, with deep forehead wrinkles, like a Shar-Pei.

Kelly signaled her own team to huddle at the far side of the courthouse plaza. She demurred at the fawning congratulations from her local counsel and got down to business. There were housekeeping matters to attend to. Reminders to submit their final statements as soon as possible. The logistics of packing up her files and shipping them back to Boston. There was transportation to arrange, and her assistant, Cazzadee, was already on the phone booking their flights. The Philadelphia lawyer offered to drive them back to their hotel in the city. Kelly declined—she needed an hour to herself—but she pointed Patti and Cazz to the man's car and promised to meet them at the airport for their flight home.

Patti hesitated and threw an anxious look around the courthouse plaza.

"Don't worry," Kelly said. "He'll make his own way home."

Patti blushed and ducked into the car. She was in love with Javier and thought no one knew it, while the sad truth was that everyone knew it but Javier.

IT WAS TWENTY minutes before Kelly's Uber arrived, and she sank into the back seat with a long shuddering sigh. "Tough day?" the driver asked.

Tough day, month, decade, she thought, but she didn't answer. For three weeks she'd been onstage, her manner and dress and expressions scrutinized by dozens of people. Every word she spoke was consequential. Any slip of the tongue could have been fatal. Any unguarded reaction a signal to the jury that she didn't want to send. After all that, she was determined for at least the next hour not to perform, and certainly not for the benefit of an Uber driver. He took the hint of her silence and didn't speak again as he drove away from the courthouse.

In minutes the brick storefronts of the county seat gave way to the gentle hills of open country. It was late September, the last gasp of summer, and the scrolling landscape looked dry and brittle in the late-afternoon sun.

She closed her eyes and leaned back against the upholstery but soon got a crick in her neck. She shifted left then right in search of a more forgiving position, but it was no use. Here was the trouble with the purifying fire of acclamation. It burned out when the acclamation ended, leaving her with cinders in her hair and soot on her hands and the taste of ashes on her tongue.

This case had been particularly sordid. Reeza Patel was a PhD virologist who'd worked on Benedict's research team. One day last year she'd dared to correct one of his comments, and worse, she'd done it in front of other people. If she were to be believed, he raped her in retaliation. A violent, sickening rape that she described in lurid detail.

But she wasn't to be believed. The quicksand in the evidence was the fact that Benedict fired her only days before the alleged attack. That could have been the sum and substance of his so-called retaliation, while her cry of rape could have been her own retaliation for having been fired. These circumstances gave Kelly a lot of material to work with. Under cross-examination, Patel dug herself in deeper and deeper until she finally sank. The jury didn't believe her story, and they acquitted Benedict.

Kelly's phone was singing in three-part disharmony as alerts for calls, texts, and emails streamed in. She couldn't turn the phone off—it might be Todd or the children—and she couldn't ignore it either. Like Pavlov's dogs, she was conditioned to respond to every ping and chirp. She opened her eyes and opened the phone. Already there was a deluge of emails from reporters, and she deleted all of them without reading.

There was a voicemail from Harry Leahy, her all-but-retired senior partner. Plenty of other septuagenarians had embraced texting over voicemail, but Harry seemed to delight in being a dinosaur, and, sadly, one to whom her fortunes remained tied. "Call me," his voicemail message said, as if that conveyed anything more than a missed call alert would have.

She didn't call him. There was time enough for that tomorrow. Instead, she sent messages to Todd and the kids letting them know she'd be home that evening. Todd replied instantly with a thumbs-up emoji, followed by a party-hat emoji, followed by a "whew!" emoji. She couldn't blame him for that last one. They'd worked out a good division of labor over the years, but when she was out of town, he had to shoulder all the care responsibilities on his own. He deserved a break.

She looked up from her phone and out at the roadside as it blurred past the car windows. The open country had funneled them onto an eight-lane superhighway, flanked by office parks on one side and housing developments on the other. The UniViro campus was somewhere to the left, along with the headquarters of a dozen more pharmaceutical, biotech, and medical device companies. This stretch of suburban Philadelphia was the headquarters of Big Pharma. An employment magnet for bioscientists, it was responsible for much of the brain drain from South Asia, including, Kelly recalled, the parents of Dr. Reeza Patel. The industry had long been tarnished by price-gouging scandals and the opioid epidemic, but thanks to George Benedict, it was suddenly basking in the heavenly glow of public esteem. Science was good again. Drugs were great, and vaccines were miraculous.

She shifted position again. Her right leg had fallen asleep, and she had to shake it out to restore feeling. This had been a recurring problem during the trial. Too much time sitting motionless in courtroom and conference room. She needed to find time for a long run tomorrow.

Her phone buzzed. This was the call she'd been waiting for. "Javi," she answered. "Anything?"

"Nothing," her investigator said. He was a former cop, but there was never any bully or bluster in his manner. He reported to her in an even-tempered tone. "They peeled off in three different directions. No phone calls. No signals to each other I could see. They didn't even glance at each other."

"Okay. Good."

"I followed one of them, LaSorta . . ."

"Remind me—?"

"The tech lady. Hey, guess what she's driving. A brand-new Porsche."

Kelly remembered her now: $2.5 million.

"I followed her to see if she was gonna meet up with anybody after, but she headed straight for New Jersey. That's where she's living now. I left her at the bridge."

"Good. Thanks, Javi."

"I'm gonna hit the road now. I'll swing by the hotel and pick you up if you'd rather drive than fly."

She laughed. "Six hours in a car with you? Pretty irresistible." But even as she said it, she knew there were countless women who would find him irresistible in any setting.

Her phone buzzed in her hand. Another call was coming in, and at the sight of the name, she let out a startled *"What?"*

"I said, unless you need anything?"

"No, no. Safe trip." She connected the incoming call. "George?"

Dr. Benedict's dry voice sounded in her ear. "You didn't think you'd escape me that easily, did you?"

In fact she did. Their business was over. It was like she always instructed her team: Move on. Don't look back. No regrets. No recriminations.

"Come to dinner tonight," Benedict said. "We're having a few people over to celebrate."

"Thanks, but my flight leaves at eight."

"Reschedule for tomorrow."

"Sorry, no. I need to get back tonight." She'd been away for three weeks without even a quick trip home on the intervening Saturdays. Lawyers didn't get weekends off during trial. That time was for witness prep.

"Tell you what," he said. "I'll have the chopper fly you home."

"Oh, thanks, George, but I really—"

"I must insist. For Jane's sake. She wants to thank you in person."

She hesitated at the mention of his wife. His bride, he called her—an affectation perhaps, but in this case it was literally true: they'd been married only a short time. And she was such an unexpected choice for a powerful man to make in a second wife. Wife Number 1 had been a brittle blonde who favored short skirts and tall heels, while Jane could have played the sweet-natured grandmother in an old black-and-white movie. She was an RN who'd cared for George's mother in her final illness.

Kelly considered her their best witness at trial, even though she did nothing but sit silently behind her husband throughout. Her appearance did all her talking for her. She looked like a woman for whom sex was only a slightly embarrassing memory, which had to mean that her husband was the kind of man who didn't really care about sex very much either. No, he must value companionship, friendship, good character, or why else would he choose a woman like this?

Kelly always wondered what their deal really was. "Well—"

"You'll be home before midnight, I promise."

She laughed, a feeble sound of defeat, and accepted his dinner invitation, along with his offers of a car to pick her up and a helicopter to take her home.

Her next call was to Cazz. "Change of plans," she sighed.

2

BACK AT THE HOTEL, KELLY packed up her room, arranged for her bags and file boxes to be shipped home, and changed into a plain black dress that would have to pass as evening wear.

Benedict said he'd send a car at six thirty, and at six twenty-five, a baby-blue Bentley cruised into the entry court of the hotel. Benedict's man Anton climbed out from behind the wheel and straightened to his full height like a telescopic crane. Without a word, he opened the rear passenger door, and, without a word, Kelly got in. Anton made her nervous. She could never get a handle on what his role was in Benedict's life. Sometimes he seemed to be his executive assistant, other times merely an errand boy, and always his driver. Lately he seemed to be his bodyguard, too.

He pulled out from the curb, and she took in her surroundings—the quilted leather upholstery, the burled wood tray tables, all the other luxurious trappings of the car. Benedict was sometimes referred to as a billionaire, though he wasn't yet. Soon, though. Once the FDA approved his vaccine, the price of his UniViro stock would skyrocket. And once the vaccine went into production, his license agreement with the company would give him a cut of every sale. People around the world would be lining up for that shot. He'd be a billionaire many times over.

They rode in silence as Anton navigated the clogged streets to the expressway. It was thick with rush-hour traffic fleeing the city, and cars were slaloming across lanes and jockeying and jostling on all sides for any advantage. Kelly's armrest held some kind of control panel, and she was studying the buttons when Anton looked in the rearview mirror and said, "You want privacy screen, yes?"

It seemed rude to say yes, but she said it, and as soon as the translucent panel clicked into place between them, she took out her phone and called home. Six thirty was when she called home every day when she was away, when the kids would be finished with dinner and, she hoped, homework.

"Hi, Mommy," Lexie answered.

"Hi, honey! I'm coming home tonight!"

"I kno-ow," the child said.

"How was school today?"

"Fi-ine." Lexie was using her sulky voice.

"What's wrong, sweetie?"

"Courtney's here."

"Oh?"

"She's in with Daddy."

"That's nice."

"It is not! She doesn't even talk. She just *looks* at him!" Her voice rose, from sulky to indignant.

"Still. It makes him happy."

"I hate her."

"Don't say that. She's your sister."

"Ha-alf." She pronounced the word with enough syllables to make her southern relatives proud.

Kelly changed the subject. "How was your vocabulary test today?"

"Okay, I guess. Hey, Mommy? What does *complicit* mean?"

"Wow. That's a pretty big word for fifth grade. Well, it means helping somebody do something bad."

"Then—what does *traitor* mean?"

"Oh, honey, you know that one. Like Benedict Arnold, remember? Somebody who hurts his own side to help the other side."

Lexie was silent for a moment. "I don't get it. How you could hurt your own sex?"

Kelly felt a flare of panic that her little girl was talking about some kind of injury to her genitals. Then she realized. "Oh. Did Courtney say *traitor to her sex*?"

"Yes! About you! So what does she mean?"

"It means she disagrees with one of my cases. That's all. It's no big deal." Again she changed the subject. "Where's your brother?"

"In his room. Probably texting with his girlfriend."

Kelly didn't rise to the bait, because she didn't believe it. Justin was only fourteen, for one thing, and for another, he was undeniably a nerd and proud of it. Awkward and bespectacled, his only interests were science, math, and video games. Which was fine with her. The football-player types peaked early and fizzled out. Nerds grew up to run the world.

"I'll call him and tell him to come out. And when you wake up tomorrow, guess what? I'll be there! We'll have pancakes, okay?"

"Okay." Lexie's tone now was grudging, a slight improvement over sulky.

Kelly rang off and placed a call to Justin's phone.

"Yo, Mercy!" he answered.

"Hey, there, Doomfist," she said.

These were the names of two of the characters in *Overwatch*, the video game they played together almost every night. It was the one game Kelly was willing to play, since the violence wasn't too bad and there were no hypersexualized female characters. She couldn't stop him from playing those other games on his own time, but she could let him know she disapproved, which was the only real power the mother of a teenager had.

"How was chem lab today?"

"Awesome! We stunk up the whole science wing! It smelled like farts."

She tried not to laugh. "How's your *Gatsby* essay coming along?"

He let out a groan, and all his enthusiasm went with it. "I don't get it," he said. "The dude's uber-rich, right? He can have any girl he wants. So why's he so hung up on this Daisy chick?"

"Because she's unattainable. You know how he gazes out across the water at her house? So close, yet so far? He can see her but he can't touch her, and that kind of longing and frustration leads to obsession."

"Huh," he said, and Kelly could almost hear the wheels turning. "Yeah. I can totally see that."

She smiled. It was nice to know her scientist son could grasp emotional subjects, too. "Listen, do me a favor and keep Lexie company until Courtney leaves?"

"Yeah, yeah." His tone changed abruptly. Now it was as grudging as his sister's.

ANTON TOOK THE Gladwyne exit off the expressway, and the noise level inside the car dropped to a hush. Gladwyne was a suburban enclave five miles from the city and one of the wealthiest zip codes in America. The roads here were narrow lanes over gently rolling hills, and they were lined with grand old manor houses of gray stone with slate roofs. The late-summer burn hadn't touched this landscape. The lawns were lush and green, tastefully irrigated by subterranean sprinklers.

Kelly checked her email before putting her phone away. There were more reporters' requests for interviews, and she deleted them one after the other. Except for carefully crafted press releases and her verdict-day pronouncements from courthouse steps, she refused all contact with the media. That was her steadfast policy ever since a disastrous interview she gave three years ago following the acquittal of a rap star client. It should have been a softball question: *Had she herself ever been the victim of a sexual assault?* She should have refused to answer. *This isn't about me*, she should have said. Instead she'd replied: *No, but then I was never much of a party girl.* All she meant was that most acquaintance rapes—which, after all, are most rapes—occurred at or after parties. That was a statistical fact. She almost never went to parties, ergo, she was statistically unlikely to be assaulted. She never meant to suggest that women who went to parties were asking for it.

But that was everyone's takeaway. Overnight she became the internet's favorite punching bag. She was called victim-blamer. Slut-shamer. Protestors marched outside her office. Hundreds of women came forward on social media with accounts of attacks they'd experienced in venues other than parties. The workplace, of course. Public transit. Shopping malls. Even church.

She tried to defend herself. The reporter had asked only about actual assault, not other forms of sexual abuse. She'd endured plenty of that. But dirty jokes and leering looks weren't in the same universe as forcible rape. Those protesters at the courthouse with their #MeToo placards? They were like patients complaining of a hangnail in a cancer hospital.

And now, after all that, here she was, going to a party anyway, and for no reason other than curiosity about Jane Benedict. It was a mystery to her why such a good woman would want to marry that kind of man. Unless she honestly didn't know what kind of man he was. Kelly had done a pretty thorough job of suppressing that truth.

ANTON SPUN THE wheel to turn onto a long drive that curved around a grove of trees that cast deep shadows into the car. Dusk was creeping into the evening. He circled past a pond covered in lily pads, then around a formal knot garden. One last turn revealed the Benedict mansion.

Institution would be a better word for it. With Greek columns on the portico and an actual rotunda on the roof, it could have been an art museum or the Federal Reserve. And unlike its gray stone neighbors, Benedict's mansion was built of limestone blocks. Their smooth ivory surfaces were now washed pink in the glow of the setting sun.

The cars of other guests were parked in a cobblestone courtyard, and tucked discreetly around the side of the mansion was a caterer's van. Anton stopped at the front stairs as the Benedicts emerged from the Palladian double doors. Mrs. Benedict gave a hearty two-handed wave when Kelly stepped out of the car. She'd dressed in somber tones throughout the trial, but tonight she was wearing a rose-colored suit and a pussy-bow blouse. Dr. Benedict wore his usual thoughtful frown and the same rumpled gray suit he'd worn in court that day.

"Welcome, welcome!" the woman cried as she took Kelly's hands in both of hers. Behind her glasses, her eyes were soft and gentle. "Thank you so much for coming, and for . . . for everything!"

"Thank you for having me, Mrs. Benedict." Kelly had to suppress the urge to call her *ma'am*; she reminded her so much of the church ladies back home.

"Jane! Please! We'll never be able to thank you enough for all you've done." Jane's voice held all the inflection that her husband's lacked. It rose up and down like a singer practicing scales. She'd once been an oncology nurse, and Kelly could easily picture her bustling into a hospital room with a cocktail of chemicals and cheerfully exhorting her patient to *sit up now, there you go, nice and easy, now swallow these down.* "Oh, what am I doing? Let me hug you!" Jane said and clasped Kelly to her pillowy bosom.

"Let's take this inside," Benedict said.

His wife drew back, still beaming, and took Kelly by the hand to pull her into the entry hall, a vast cylindrical space capped off by the dome of the rotunda. From somewhere beyond it came the sounds of party laughter and light classical music.

"I'm sorry your husband couldn't be here, too." Jane's sing-song voice echoed across the marble floor. "He's home in Boston, I imagine?"

"Yes. Yes, he is."

"Is he a lawyer, too? I've been wondering."

"Yes. Yes, he is," Kelly said again.

Benedict cleared his throat. "Jane, dear, why don't you rejoin our other guests? Kelly and I have some business to attend to."

"All right, but don't you linger now." Jane laid a fond hand on his arm, and once again Kelly wondered what held them together, this kindly woman and this humorless man. "Everyone's dying to meet her!" With a wag of her finger, Jane hurried off on her low-heeled pumps.

Kelly raised an eyebrow at Benedict. "What business?"

"The little matter of your success fee."

"Oh. Yes." Harry Leahy managed the financial side of their business, and this time he'd negotiated a bonus for an acquittal. Normally he had to hound clients after trial to collect it. He'd be thrilled to learn that Benedict paid the success fee on the same day as the success. It might even keep him from hounding her about the next big case for a week or two.

"Let's go to my study," Benedict said. He ushered her through a doorway on the left that opened onto a long gallery, with a wall of windows on one side and a wall of art on the other. She studied the paintings as she followed after him. They were mostly oils, and mostly featured groups of men stroking their beards or checking their pocket watches while standing beside an examination table where a patient lay supine.

"I see a theme," she said to Benedict's back.

He didn't react. He continued to the end of the gallery and

opened a set of double doors. Inside was a stark white space that looked more like a laboratory than a study. The walls were lined not with the expected bookcases but with white library cabinets. The floor was gleaming white marble. The desk was a long slab of thick beveled glass. Opposite it were two white upholstered chairs. Even without windows, the room was dazzlingly bright.

"Have a seat." He sat behind his desk and opened his checkbook.

Her heels clicked across the marble floor as she made her way to a chair. She was sitting down when the cushion suddenly stirred. She let out a startled "Oh!" and jumped clear as a sleek white cat sprang to the floor.

"Meet Jonas Salk," Benedict said.

"Hello, Jonas." She held out her hand, but the cat lifted his nose in the air and stalked away. She moved to the other chair. There was a strange smell in the room, like disinfectant. As if every surface had been wiped down with rubbing alcohol.

"Harry Leahy told me the story, you know." Benedict didn't look up from the check he was writing.

"What story?"

"Of how he lured you over to the dark side."

"Oh. That." She gave an awkward laugh.

"You were with the DA, he told me, prosecuting sex crimes. Prosecuting his clients, in fact, and winning every time. He tried again and again to hire you. He knew a woman could better defend those cases than he could, than any man could. The optics are so much better. So he offered you more and more money, even a partnership, but you refused him every time. You wanted no part of it. He said you didn't want to dirty your hands—"

"No, it wasn't that—"

"—with clients like me." Benedict looked up then and held her gaze as he tore the check out. It sounded like a bandage ripped from a wound.

She blinked first. "None of his clients were like you, Dr. Benedict."

With a mirthless smile, he passed the check over the glass slab of his desk. She swallowed her gasp at the amount. It was for $200,000. Their final bill would be a multiple of that figure, but that number reflected actual hours of hard toil by her and her whole team. This check was pure gravy.

"Let's have a drink to commemorate the moment, shall we?" He stood and opened one of the cabinet doors to reveal shelves of glasses and bottles and a small refrigerator below. "What can I fix you?"

She looked up from the check, still a bit dazed. "Oh, gin and tonic, I suppose. But only a splash of gin. Really, just a tiny splash."

He reached for a bottle but checked his hand before he touched it. "Why don't you fix it yourself? You can make it the way you want."

She nodded, rose, and walked over to the bar, much more comfortable with that arrangement. She opened the seal on a new bottle of gin and tipped a small amount into her glass. A fresh bottle of tonic was in the mini-fridge, and she unsealed that, too, and topped off the drink. He poured himself a dram of Scotch and held his glass up to hers. "To one more success in your career of so many."

She shrugged as she took a sip of her drink. "I've had my share of failures."

"Not this time, I'm happy to say."

She returned to her chair, and he took the chair beside her. Jonas Salk leapt from the floor to the desktop and from there another six feet through the air to land on top of a cabinet.

"Speaking of failures," Benedict said as Kelly sat back and crossed her legs. "Have you ever heard the story of one of the biggest pharmacological failures of all time? Curare?"

"I don't think so, no." She took another sip of her drink.

"This was back in the 1940s. Curare was a paralyzing poison that primitives used on their arrowheads. When Western medicine discovered it, they thought it would make a fine anesthesia. Unlike a lot of other drugs used at the time, this one rendered the patient completely immobile. The last thing a surgeon wants is for the patient to flail or even to twitch while he's got that scalpel in his hand. Curare paralyzed the muscles, you see."

"Uh-huh." Her right foot started to buzz once again with that sensation of falling asleep. She uncrossed her legs. She really needed a long run.

"Only one problem," Benedict was saying. "The patients were still conscious. They could hear everything. They could feel everything. The agony of every slice through their skin and into their organs. And they couldn't even scream."

"Oh my God! How awful!" Her other foot was asleep now.

"I've developed my own formula," he said.

"Really?" She stood up to get the blood flowing to her feet. "Whatever for?"

"For situations like this," he said and caught her as she fell.

The glass slipped from her fingers and shattered on the floor.

"It was in the tonic, you see." He lifted her in his arms. "One more thing your partner told me. You always order a G and T."

The horror spread through her as fast as the paralysis. She started to scream, but the air died as a gurgle in her throat. She tried to hit him but now her arms were asleep, too.

He laid her out like a corpse on the glass surface of his desk. "You muzzled me," he said. "For ten months, you muzzled me. You treated me like a fucking dog." His robotic voice was gone. Now he spat out his words in a guttural spray. "Like a little lapdog. Sit here. Stand there. Wear this. Don't do this. Don't do that. Stay. Heel. Sit up and beg. Like you were the alpha and I was your fucking bitch. Me! The man who cured Alzheimer's! I'm gonna win a fucking Nobel Prize, and you treat me like that? Like a piece of shit you can't wait to scrape off your shoe? Well, guess what, Counselor? Now you're *my* fucking bitch."

She was frozen, an iceberg floating in a cold sea under a blindingly white sky. She could feel his hands on her. She could feel him turn her on her side. She could hear the metal scrape of the zipper sliding down the back of her dress. She could hear the clunk of her shoes hitting the floor. He rolled her back, and his face loomed over hers. He pulled her glasses from her face, and she tried to squeeze her eyes shut. She couldn't.

"What luck," he said. "That's perfect. You need to see. You need to see all of it."

The paralytic had reached her eyelids at the worst possible moment. Her eyes were wide open, fixed and staring straight up at that white ceiling.

"Shall I tell you the best part of this?" he said as he yanked off her dress. "I don't have to worry about DNA this time." He took off his suit jacket. "I don't have to pay any hush money. This one won't cost me a thing. Because you won't dare report this. You'll never speak of this to anyone. Not a soul," he said as he slithered off her underwear. "Because everything you proclaim, everything you stand for would be ruined if you admit that one of your clients is actually a rapist. Your reputation would be trashed. You'd be humiliated as badly as you humiliated me. No more high-profile, big-money clients for you." He spat that out as he unhooked her bra. "Your high-flying career would be over. And the DA would never take you back after all the things you've done. Even if you could afford to go back, which you never could, not with the exorbitant costs of running your household. So you see, *Counselor*"—he sneered the word—"that's my revenge against you. Now you're the one who's muzzled."

His face hovered over hers, twisted and ugly in his hatred. She tried with every ounce of strength she had to close her eyes and shut it out. But she couldn't.

She could see everything.

She could feel everything.

From his perch on top of the cabinet, Jonas Salk tucked his front paws under his chest and watched what happened next.

3

Reeza Patel

I WAS IN A CAR accident last March when my little Honda was rear-ended at an intersection. It wasn't entirely the other driver's fault (a fact he was quick and loud to point out when he jumped from his car). I'd failed to proceed after the light turned green. I'd simply idled at the intersection, staring at the windshield in a blind fog.

That fog had descended often in the days immediately following the Incident. (The Incident was how I referred to it even in my own mind. Anything more descriptive than that might make memories erupt.) But the Accident happened months after the Incident and wasn't triggered by anything I could identify. I was simply driving home from the store. Then suddenly I wasn't. Driving, that is. I was sitting at a green light on a busy road. And was slammed into from behind with a force strong enough to propel me into the intersection, where I collided with another car and my airbag deployed.

My symptoms arrived with a fury the next day: back and shoulder pain, a pounding headache that began at the base of my skull and traveled up over my cranium, and a neck so rigid it felt like my cervical vertebrae had been welded shut. My doctor dismissed my condition as *merely whiplash* and prescribed Tylenol. When the symptoms grew worse, he sent me to physical therapy. When that didn't help, when the pain was so crippling I could barely see, he suggested it was psychological. (This is often the case with soft-tissue injuries; in the absence of readily ascertainable physical evidence, medical science defaults to *all in your head.*)

(The same proved to be true in the legal world. In the absence of solid forensic evidence, did it really happen? Or was I only imagining it? Or worse, making it all up?)

It took persistence in both cases. I returned to the doctor again and again with the same complaints until he finally relented and prescribed an opioid (albeit in the lowest possible dosage). And I returned to the district attorney again and again until he finally relented and obtained a grand jury indictment against George Benedict.

I fought hard for both outcomes. But while the oxycodone gave me some relief, the law gave me none at all.

THERE WAS NO mystery as to why I was remembering the Accident today. My drive home from the courthouse took me through that same intersection. The force of that rear-end collision in March felt like an assault—as if an enemy force had charged up behind me with a battering ram. And it felt like an assault today, too, when the jury foreperson stood up and pronounced, "Not guilty."

It was exactly like the car that hit me. I never saw it coming. I believed justice would prevail, right up until the moment it didn't. Maybe it was the courthouse picketers who gave me that false hope. All those women waving signs that said BELIEVE REEZA and END SEXUAL PREDATION. (Many of them said #MeToo, but I was less grateful for those. *You, too?* I wanted to say. *Then press your own charges and stop freeloading on mine.*)

It wasn't even a case of "he said, she said," because he didn't say anything at all. He didn't take the witness stand; he didn't raise his hand and swear an oath to tell the truth, the whole truth, and nothing but the truth; he didn't endure three days in that box as I did with back and neck pain so severe it brought tears to my eyes.

No, it was only a case of "She said, but she's lying." And "Where's her evidence?" (As if the words from my mouth didn't count as evidence at all.)

I did have some DNA evidence, but not enough. Because I showered right after the Incident. I knew that was stupid. I was a scientist—a biologist, no less—so I knew not to do that. But the need to clean myself was a physical imperative akin to vomiting; the body had to purge itself.

As a result, there was almost no forensic evidence that Benedict had even been to my apartment. There was no semen. He wore a condom, and he must have taken it away with him, for I couldn't find it afterward. The police found some of his hair on the couch, along with fibers that matched the tweed jacket he'd been wearing. But his lawyer waved that away. After all, she forced me to admit, I'd worked closely with the man, often standing side by side with him in the lab and at lecterns. His hair and jacket fibers could have gotten on my clothes a hundred times, and I could have been the one who brought them into my apartment.

Then there was the fingerprint evidence, or lack thereof. If he'd actually been in my apartment, he would have left his prints on the doorknob, the counter, anywhere. His lawyer hit hard on that point, probably because my explanation made me look like either an idiot or a liar: Benedict arrived at my door wearing latex gloves and kept them on throughout. *Why would I let a man into my apartment wearing latex gloves?* his lawyer hounded me. *It didn't strike you as odd,* his lawyer said to the jury. (She did that throughout her cross-examination—pretend to ask a question of me that was really only a speech to the jury.) But it didn't strike me as odd. He wore gloves almost every time we were together. So did I. We worked in laboratories. Gloves were like a second skin to us. We were scientists. But no one on the jury was.

Of course, the bigger question was why I'd opened the door to him at all. He'd fired me; I'd already hired a lawyer to sue him; we were clearly enemies by then. It simply never occurred to me that he posed any kind of physical danger. As a little girl I'd learned to be on guard against men who were too friendly, but not against a man who patently hated me. Nobody ever warned me about a man who looked on me with disgust. I'd thought I was safe from a man who felt that way about me. I'd thought rape was a sex crime, not a hate crime. (Now I knew it was both.)

(Many of my thoughts came in parentheticals these days. The twin arcs of the punctuation marks seemed to encapsulate my most dangerous ideas. That way they could be dispensed in slow-release dosages and absorbed with caution.)

I WAS ALMOST home now, and the pain was gnawing through my spine like a caged rat. The pain triggered my asthma (something else my doctor suggested was psychosomatic). I could feel my bronchioles constrict. I could hear the whistle in every breath, and I groped for the albuterol inhaler on the passenger seat and took a puff.

In my field, in all the sciences, there was accountability. If something went wrong—for example, a sample was contaminated—we traced back every step in the process to determine where the fault lay. Something went very wrong in court today, and on my drive home I thought about where to place the blame.

1. On myself, obviously, for failure to preserve the evidence.
    (Or for opening the door in the first place.)

2. On the prosecutor, for his lackluster performance at trial. (Worse than lackluster. He seemed absolutely cowed by Benedict's lawyer.)
3. On the jury. I hated to play the race card, but here were the facts: Benedict was a white man, and I was an Indian American woman. The Constitution guaranteed a jury of one's peers only to the defendant, not to the victim. This jury comprised six men and six women, nine whites, two Blacks, and one Latinx. No Asians. (Do the math.)
4. On Kelly McCann.

I could stop right there. This was all her fault.

Kelly McCann. Impeccably dressed every day. Abundantly self-assured. Never a blond hair out of place. Perfectly shaped eyebrows that she deployed as supertitles to the words coming out of her mouth—one brow lifted in skepticism, two in surprise, both furrowed in a frown. Glasses Reeza felt certain were more for show than for vision. Thin, cruel lips that pulled apart into a simpering little smile that sent my mind tumbling back to prep school.

My parents sacrificed to send me there, and it was the school that later got me into Harvard. But I hated it. It was full of simpering white girls exactly like Kelly McCann. The cheerleaders, the athletes, the popular girls, all of them so confident that they were liked and admired that they never needed to be nervous about anything. Doors would automatically open for them. Their chairs would be pulled out, by magic or divine right. Girls who never deigned to notice the brown girl in their midst until I won an academic prize—*Oh, Reezy, wish I had your smarts!* they'd say, in a way that made it sound like intelligence was something rather quaint. Or until my asthma kicked up—*You poor thing*, they'd coo, then exchange glances that said, *Sure glad I'm not defective like this one.* (I'd been stupidly flattered when they called me *Reezy*—a nickname was a sign of affection, right?—until I realized it was only so they could rhyme it with *Wheezy*.)

In fairness, those girls came by it naturally, since their mothers maintained cliques even more exclusionary than their daughters'. I used to watch them gossiping in the school parking lot, in their golf sweaters and tennis dresses, standing in tight little circles to keep others out even while their voices projected far beyond their boundaries. My own mother would walk by in her sari and sneakers and wish them a good morning, and they'd answer her with little nods and smiles, then burn holes in her back as she walked away.

My parents begged me not to press charges. It would follow me the rest of my life, they said. All my degrees, my academic honors, my research breakthroughs, my publications—all that would be forgotten. Everything I (and they, of course) had worked so hard to achieve, would be erased. I'd forever be known as the woman who accused a great man of rape. They didn't doubt me, they swore they didn't. But I needed to get past this, and the only way to do that was to let it go.

They chose not to attend the trial. They didn't want me to be embarrassed, they said. (I knew it was their own embarrassment that kept them away.)

He wasn't a great man, but he was a great scientist, and I was thrilled to be working alongside him. So thrilled that I not only tolerated his abusive behavior, I made excuses for it. Of course he was a harsh taskmaster. A genius couldn't be expected to be a gentle, nurturing kind of boss. Of course he shouted and cursed and once threw a glass beaker at a lab tech. A genius couldn't be expected to tolerate fools. (And he did pay for her plastic surgery afterward.) Of course we must keep our phones on at all times. Of course we should sleep with them on our chests. He might have an epiphany at any moment, and we should all be alert to receive and applaud it.

I had no objection to any of that. Working at UniViro was a privilege, and worth every indignity. I mean—my God!—we were on the brink of curing Alzheimer's. (Though we weren't there yet, notwithstanding the company's PR spin. We still needed to prove that correlation was also causation, *i.e.*, that the virus didn't merely coexist with the beta-amyloid proteins in the brain but that it caused the buildup of such proteins. I'd designed a study aimed at answering this critical question. The funding committee was still considering my proposal when I was fired.)

(And of course there remained the overarching question as to whether the amyloid hypothesis was even valid, i.e., was the accumulation of beta-amyloid proteins the actual cause of cognitive decline? Medical science took that as a given, but it wasn't, not yet.)

Science was more than a career to me. It was my vocation, and I meant that in the same sense that clerics did. Science was more miraculous than any religion. Over the last century, the average human life span had doubled—doubled! Partly due to industrial safety and better obstetrics, but mostly due to antibiotics, vaccines, pasteurization, and disinfectants. That was science at work, and no calling could be any more important than mine.

But science demanded accuracy. I had no choice but to point out his error when he misstated a key finding of our research. My mistake was doing it while we were onstage in the UniViro auditorium. *Excuse me, George*, I said. (That was my first mistake. He allowed me to use his first name in private, but in public, I should have said *Dr. Benedict.*) *Excuse me, George*, I said, *I think you meant to say—*.

Ah yes, thank you, Reeza, he said for the audience's benefit. But the look in his eyes was lethal. By the time I returned to my office, our HR director was waiting with my termination notice and a guard to escort me from the premises.

(I couldn't even take my lab notes with me. My own notes.)

ANOTHER FIVE MILES to go, and my wheezing was getting worse. My tongue felt swollen in my mouth, and my pulse was fluttering. I knew I was heading into anaphylaxis, and I pulled to the side of the road and grabbed the EpiPen from the passenger seat and jabbed myself in the thigh.

Relief came at once, but I forced myself to sit there and try to relax while the traffic zoomed past so close and fast it rocked my little car on its axle. I'd been relying on the EpiPens too much these last few weeks. My skin was covered in so many pinpricks I looked like a plucked chicken. If I were to die today, the coroner would think I was a junkie.

(If I were to die today. Now there was a dangerous thought that definitely demanded a parenthetical enclosure.)

Don't cancel Dr. B, his groupies chanted at the courthouse, but what about Dr. P? I was the one who'd been canceled. Blackballed from every other virology research job in the country. Unemployed now for nearly a year. Unemployable. Declared incompetent by the great Dr. Benedict. Declared a fantasist by everyone else. Deep in debt and living off a small stipend from my parents that they couldn't sustain much longer. Oh, his lawyer made a generous settlement offer, but there were strings attached: I'd have to sign a nondisclosure, nondisparagement agreement and publicly recant my accusation. Those strings formed a noose, and I refused to put it around my neck.

WHEN MY BREATHING returned to normal (what passed for normal in my life anyway), I pulled back out onto the highway and drove the rest of the way home. But my musculoskeletal condition hadn't improved. I reached my exit, and the simple effort of turning my head to check for traffic at the bottom of the ramp sent hot needles of pain stabbing the back of my neck and across my shoulders.

I couldn't wait to get home and take a pain pill. For three weeks I'd been under orders from the assistant DA who tried the case (the government's lawyer, not mine, he often reminded me) not to bring any Oxy with me to court, because defense counsel might ask about it and make me look like an addict before the jury. At the time that struck me as a remote risk. But now—now I wouldn't put anything past Kelly McCann.

I made the final turn into my apartment complex, and my neck screamed in pain when I saw the reporters gathered at the entrance to the elevator lobby. They'd haunted me at the courthouse, but this was the first time they'd dared to come to my home.

So here was one more humiliation for me to endure today. I got out of the car and walked stiffly to the door, eyes straight ahead, brushing past outstretched microphones, holding my head up high despite the blinding flash of the cameras and the blinding pain in my neck.

How do you feel? they called out. (*In agony*, I might have answered.) *Are you disappointed by the verdict?* (I wished I could answer: *Duh*.) One intrepid reporter asked it better: *Are you surprised by the verdict?*

(Yes. More the fool, I.)

It felt like the longest trek of my life, but at last I was inside and in the elevator, and finally in my apartment.

The prescription bottle was on the kitchen counter. I grabbed it and shook out a tablet and held it in my hand.

I wondered what to call this latest mile marker on the road to my ruin. First came the Incident, then the Accident. And now?

The Verdict.

How do you feel? the reporters cried.

Assaulted. By the Incident, the Accident, and now . . . the Verdict.

I threw the pill to the back of my throat and gulped it down.

4

D R. BENEDICT KEPT HIS PROMISE. Kelly was home by midnight.

Anton had to carry her from the mansion to the Bentley, and from the Bentley to the helicopter, and even from the helicopter to the taxi in Boston. But her motor control was returning by the time the cab pulled up to her house in Weston, thirty minutes away. She paid the fare with fumbling fingers and climbed out under her own power.

"Hey," the driver called with a chuckle. "Take it easy next time, huh?"

"Right," she croaked. Her throat muscles were still tight.

She walked on wobbly legs up the brick path to the front door. The house was a white clapboard Colonial with black shutters and a red front door—a classic New England look—but tonight the glossy red paint swirled luridly in her vision. Todd had left the porch light on for her, but she was barely able to stab her key in the lock to let herself in.

Inside, she managed to enter the security code before the alarm sounded. She turned off the porch light. Darkness descended, and she descended with it, sagging against the wall and sliding down until she landed on the floor in a heap.

The house was dark and quiet. Not a lamp on anywhere. No rumble of the heater and no hiss of the air-conditioning either, not this time of year. Not even a distant hum from the refrigerator. It was a relief not to see, not to hear. She tried to imagine herself in a sensory deprivation tank, closed off from everything. But it was no use. She could still feel, and she could feel everything.

It hurt to sit. She hauled herself to her feet. It hurt to walk, too, but she navigated by memory through the darkened house, down the center hall and through the kitchen to the mudroom bath. She took off her shoes and dress and peeled off her underwear. When she unhooked her bra, something fluttered to the floor. She stooped to pick it up. It was Benedict's check for $200,000, but not the one he gave her earlier. That check dissolved into pulp after he stuffed it in her mouth. *Now you're muzzled, bitch.* This check was crisp and neatly folded, still for $200,000, but instead of Leahy & Mc-Cann, the payee was Kelly McCann. A mindfuck to go along with all the rest.

The only light in the room was a utilitarian fluorescent tube. She laid the check aside and blinked at herself in the mirror. In the harsh light she could make out the bruises forming on her neck and arms, and on her ribs and shoulders. There was a bite mark on her right breast. No marks on her face. He was careful about that. Her eyes, though—they were sunk deep into her skull as if trying to retreat. The mirror didn't capture anything lower than her waist, but she could look down and see the rest for herself. Bruises were rising on her hips, and her thighs were streaked with blood and with the viscous sludge of Benedict's semen.

She knew all the protocols. Even if a woman chose not to call the police, there were certain steps she should take. Later she could decide what she wanted to do, but meanwhile she had to preserve the evidence. She had to bag up her clothes. Take swabs and bag those as well. Photograph herself from all angles and save the photos with metadata to prove when they were taken. And—this was critical—

she had to confide in at least one other person who could be counted on to testify as a corroborating witness.

Kelly did none of those things. She turned the shower on full blast as hot as it would go, and when the room was thick and swirling with steam, she stepped in and scrubbed her body and watched the evidence swirl down the drain. She unhooked the handheld shower and irrigated every orifice. She sprayed it into her mouth and spat and spat again. When she was done, her skin was flushed crimson. It tingled like a million tiny needles were pricking her. That was good. Her body was decontaminated.

But not her mind. *This is so much better than Rohypnol,* he'd chortled at one point. *With roofies, it's all a haze afterward. She can't be sure whether it happened or not. But with my little potion—you'll know it did.*

She grabbed a coat from a hook in the hall and wrapped it around her naked body. She buttoned it up to her neck and tied the belt tightly around her waist. Then she gathered up her clothes and shoes from the bathroom floor and went out into the garage and stuffed them deep, deep into the trash can.

Back inside she made her way through the dark to the front hall and crept silently up the stairs. She paused outside Lexie's door, where she listened until she heard the soft sounds of the child's breathing. She crossed the hall to Justin's room. Through his door came percussive sounds, blips and pings, the soundtrack of one of his video games, leaking out around the edges of his headphones.

The opposite had happened with the headphones Anton placed over her ears in the helicopter. With those, the outside noise leaked in. She could hear the high-pitched whine of the engine, and the rhythmic beating of the rotors. She could hear the pilot shouting at Anton: *Is she all right?* And Anton's reply: *Too much celebrate.* The pilot's laughter. *A real party girl, huh?*

Party girl. She'd remember that detail forever.

She hesitated outside Justin's room. It was a school night; she should rap on the door and tell him to turn off the game and go to sleep.

She didn't. She tiptoed away, down the hall into her own bedroom. This room was never completely dark, never completely quiet. The monitors sent out a steady beeping sound, like the sonar pings of a submarine. They shone a soft blue light into the room while the CCTV camera shone a steady green light toward the window alcove. She switched off the camera and went into the walk-in closet and exchanged the coat for her pajamas.

The monitor lights lit her path out of the closet, around the queen-size bed in the middle of the room, and into the alcove where the hospital bed stood. She unlatched the rail and lowered it and climbed up onto the bed.

Adam smelled of soap and shampoo. His hair was clean and combed back from his forehead. His ear hair and nose hair were neatly trimmed, too, and his face was freshly shaved. It felt baby soft against the palm of her hand as she smoothed it over his cheek and chin. Todd took such good care of him. She didn't know what they'd do without him. Through the window she could see the lights go off in Todd's apartment over the garage. The CCTV camera sent live video feed to a monitor in his apartment and to apps on her phone and his; switching it off signaled that Kelly was on duty now. He could go to sleep.

Adam's eyes were wide open in the dark, but that didn't necessarily mean he was awake, the doctors told her. Awake or asleep didn't actually have much meaning anymore, they told her, but she didn't believe it. He couldn't talk or move or eat or drink, but he could breathe, and his heart could still beat, and she knew he was still in there, locked inside his frozen body.

He was still in there, her strong, funny, whip-smart husband. The

man who turned heads in every room he ever entered. Who was de-
ferred to in every meeting he ever attended. Who founded his own
law firm and represented the biggest real estate developer in New
England and was almost single-handedly responsible for most of
the high-tech office parks in suburban Boston. He was still in there,
locked inside this useless body, subjected to the daily humiliation
of being turned this way and that, his catheters inserted, his anus
wiped, his mouth forced open to have his teeth brushed.

He was still in there, and almost every night before she got into
the big bed across the room, she slipped into this narrow bed beside
him and held him and kissed his cheek and told him about her day.

She wouldn't tell him anything tonight, though. She would never
tell him, or anyone else. Tonight she slipped into bed beside him and
held him and kissed him. She listened to the pings and beeps of his
monitors and the deep raspy breaths from his lungs. Tears streamed
down her face as she told him something else. "Oh, Adam, my love,
my sweet, sweet Adam, I know now. I finally know. I know exactly
how you feel."

5

LEXIE WAS BORN ON A snowy day in January, two weeks before Kelly was ready. She hadn't started her maternity leave yet; she had filings due the end of the week; she had a court appearance the next day. She hadn't even packed a bag, and she couldn't find her nursing bra or her favorite slippers. She went tearing through the room in a flurry.

But Adam was unflappable. He was an old pro at this, along with everything else in their lives. He sat her down and handed her his watch while he packed her bag. He called the doctor, the sitter, Kelly's assistant, then his own assistant. He called her mother and rebooked her flight. He got Justin out of bed and fed him his breakfast, and by the time the sitter arrived and it was time to go, everything was in order.

The snow was already inches deep on the unplowed streets, but Adam was undaunted. He was a native New Englander, and this was old hat for him. Kelly, on the other hand, was from southwestern Virginia, and she had to squeeze her eyes shut as he drove. They liked to joke that theirs was a mixed marriage. Everyone assumed they meant Jewish-Catholic, but there really wasn't much of a divide between secular Jew and lapsed Catholic. It was the culture clash of North and South they were joking about.

There were other divides, of course. He was almost twenty years older, but lean and fit, dark-haired and handsome, and she was as besotted with him as on the day they'd met. They practiced in different worlds—criminal prosecution and commercial real estate—and their paths never would have crossed if Kelly hadn't decided to join the ethics committee of the bar association. She was a newly minted lawyer who was newly disgusted by the tactics of so many of the other lawyers, on both sides of the courtroom. Flush with her own moral superiority, she stepped right up to volunteer for the grunt work of the ethics committee.

Most lawyers joined bar committees only to bolster their CVs and *Martindale* bios, but Adam took his responsibilities seriously and so did Kelly. He was the chair, and she soon became his principal assistant/scrivener. It was their job to respond to ethics questions or concerns raised by other lawyers. Once a week they met to review the queries, research the applicable rules, then issue either written opinions or confidential advice. Because their workdays were full, they met after hours. Sometimes they sent out for sandwiches. Sometimes they went out for dinner. Sometimes there were drinks.

It started innocently enough. Compliments on each other's committee work. Conversations that strayed to other subjects. Their caseloads, their schedules. When Kelly made her first solo court appearance that January, and won, she turned around with a relieved smile for her supervisor in the gallery, and there was Adam in the back, doing a stealthy little fist pump and grinning like a fool.

He was the cheerleader then. He followed her cases and watched her in court when his schedule allowed. He egged her on and bolstered her up. Whenever she expressed any doubt about her chances, he'd encourage her with a play on her name: *Of course you can do it. You're Kelly McCann, not Kelly McCan't.*

One night in his conference room, she tried to reciprocate with a pun of her own—*Adam Fineman, you are one fine man.* She laid it on thick with her best southern accent—*fahhn man*—but the joke was lame, and too revealing. He didn't laugh or even smile. He only stared at her for a long moment until he leaned over the table and kissed her.

It was unexpected but by no means unwelcome. Kelly was weary of dating men her own age. Men her own age were boys. Adam was a grown-up. He knew how to be serious without taking himself seriously. He knew what he wanted, and he didn't have to look over his shoulder to check what his buddies thought of his choice. He didn't boast. He didn't have to.

For his own part, the opposite factor was at work. He was drawn to her youth. She was a bright young thing, unsullied by experience, devoid of bitterness, smooth of skin, firm of body, adoring of gaze. Every middle-aged man's dream girl.

So their initial attraction was based on the wrong reasons, like many, and entirely superficial, like most. But over time their ages ceased to mean anything. He could be as goofy and carefree as a boy of twelve. She could be as practical and shrewd as a middle-aged farmwife. Their expectations were dashed, and the surprise of that was what they finally fell in love with.

Though the course of their love never did run smooth. There were obstacles, road bumps, brief ugly scenes, long teary recoveries. But by the time that snowy day in January arrived, everything had been overcome. They had a lovely home, rewarding careers, an adorable four-year-old son, and a little girl on the way. Their life was as perfect as Kelly ever could have hoped for.

Adam drove with one hand on the wheel and one hand on hers, one eye on the road and one eye on the clock to time her contractions. And between it all he still managed to handle some work calls. He spoke at length with his biggest client, Erik Kloss, about his pending purchase of a huge tract of land along the Route 128 corridor. It was a mega deal: hundreds of millions of dollars were at stake. It was all so different from Kelly's career. She loved what she did, and she'd achieved a good bit of success by then, but she'd never earn more than a five-figure income. Not that it mattered, not when Adam's was almost seven figures.

At the end of the call, Erik wished them luck and shouted to his assistant to send a box of cigars.

"A onesie would have been fine," Kelly grumbled when he rang off.

Adam laughed and placed his next call to his top associate, Kevin Trent, and told him to meet them in the hospital parking lot. By the time they arrived, Kevin was already there, idling in his snow-covered car. Adam pulled in alongside him, driver's window to driver's window, like two cops confabbing behind a highway billboard. He passed him the Kloss file along with some terse instructions for the day's tasks. "Understood," Kevin said, carefully keeping his eyes on his boss and away from the panting woman beside him. "Don't worry about a thing." Adam wasn't worried. He trusted Kevin so well that he planned to offer him a partnership in another year.

Neither of them was worried about the baby either, even when the obstetrician rose from between Kelly's legs with a furrowed brow. The baby wasn't positioned quite right for delivery—sunny-side up, they called it, a term Kelly found warm and cheerful. Yes, the position was causing the dreaded back labor, but Kelly had a famously high threshold for pain; she could manage, especially with Adam there by her side. He coached her through every contraction, massaging her back, telling her how brave she was and how much he loved her.

There was a risk the baby's head would get wedged against the pelvic bone, but there were tricks they could do to rotate her. They had Kelly get down on the floor and labor on all fours. Adam got down beside her and kept up a running patter of off-color jokes. *Doggy-style when it comes out, too*, he quipped, and Kelly's scandalized laughter helped her ride out the next contraction.

When the baby still hadn't turned, they helped her back into bed and the OB tried manual inversion. She inserted her arm up to what seemed like her shoulder, and Kelly's breathing technique abandoned her. The pain assaulted her from all directions, and when she let out her first whimper, Adam gripped her hands and told her she could do it, she could do anything, she was *Kelly McCann*, not *Kelly McCan't*. That reminder was all it took. She laughed and nodded and gritted her teeth and made it through the pain until the OB withdrew her arm and shook her head. The baby still wouldn't turn.

That was when they brought out the vacuum. And that was when Adam crumpled to the floor.

Kelly gasped, but the doctor and the nurse only laughed as they helped him up into a chair. "Not the first dad to faint dead away," they told her. "A bit too much excitement, eh, Dad?" they said and patted him on the back as he sat with his head in his hands.

"Adam?" Kelly called across the room.

"Give him a minute to get the blood flowing again," the nurse said. "He'll be fine."

Kelly had hoped for another drug-free delivery, but the vacuum extractor necessarily changed her birth plan. She received an epidural, panted through her contractions until it kicked in, then pushed when they told her to, and at last Lexie was delivered. Alexis, a name they'd chosen based on their shared love of the law, the same as they'd done with Justin.

"Adam!" Kelly called, laughing and crying as the infant was placed on her chest. "Come and see! She's beautiful!"

Later no one could reconstruct how long it was that he'd been slumped in that chair across the room. Later no one wanted to admit that they'd paid no attention to him during that time. Later it was discovered that while Kelly panted and pushed and delivered their child, Adam had suffered a massive intracerebral hemorrhagic stroke. A vessel burst and leaked blood into his cerebrum, a trickle at first, then a pool, then a flash flood that carved canyons through the landscape of his brain, killing thoughts and memories everywhere it flowed.

You're Kelly McCann, not Kelly McCan't. Those were the last words he ever spoke to her.

6

S HE MADE PANCAKES IN THE morning, and before the first ladle of batter hit the griddle, Lexie was at the kitchen table with knife and fork in hand. Justin came down only minutes later. Normally Kelly had to call him again and again before he would drag himself out of bed, but today he bounded into the kitchen and up to Kelly at the stove. "Up high!" he shouted, palm held high.

Her reflexes were slow, and her aim was off. She swung and missed.

Ordinarily he would roll his eyes at a blunder like that, but today he only laughed and gave her a hug. She winced a bit when he squeezed her, but he didn't notice. "You rock, Mom!"

"Do I?"

"You won your case!"

She turned back to the griddle. The little puddles of batter swam in her vision. "I win all my cases," she said.

"Yeah, but this time, justice was served, or whatever. You know?"

"Done talking to your girlfriend?" Lexie sneered.

"Shut up," he said and plopped into his chair beside her.

Lexie was ten and still tiny except for an abundant mane of dark curly hair, inherited from her father. Justin was fourteen and gangly, with a head of wild, carrot-colored curls that could have come from either side of the family. Whichever genes were to blame, they both hated their hair so much that Lexie wore hers in a tight bun every day and Justin wouldn't leave the house without a beanie clamped down on his head, even in summer heat. Perhaps that was why it didn't strike him as odd that Kelly was wearing a turtleneck under her bathrobe.

"I mean, we can't let Dr. Benedict be taken down, or canceled, or whatever," he said. "Not by some dumb bimbo."

Her reactions were as slow as her reflexes. It was a moment before she answered. "Dr. Patel is hardly a bimbo. She's a highly respected scientist."

"Yeah? Then why'd he fire her?"

She blinked in surprise. "You followed the trial?"

He shrugged his bony shoulders. "Sure."

She ladled another puddle of batter on the griddle. "You never followed my trials before."

"You never represented anybody this cool before. I mean, come on! The dude's a certified genius. MD, PhD, neurologist, virologist, biochemist, and I can't even remember what else. I mean, jeez, he cured Alzheimer's!"

"*Maybe* he cured Alzheimer's."

"What's Alz-heim-er's?" Lexie pronounced the word carefully.

He explained while Kelly stared dazedly at the pancakes. Last night she felt everything, but today she couldn't feel anything except a pounding in her temples and a dull throb between her legs. She was numb to everything else. When her children greeted her, she could only pull her lips back in an imitation of a smile. She received hugs and kisses that made her want to draw back in revulsion. It was appalling to feel this way. Or to not feel this way.

The numbness was a self-defense mechanism, she thought, her body's way of protecting herself from the trauma. The pain would fade, she knew it would. The horror would recede. She would forget. She would make herself forget. Life would go on. It had to.

She flipped the pancakes while Justin held forth about Alzheimer's.

He was at that stage of male adolescence where he either spoke in monosyllabic grunts or pontificated at great length, with nothing by way of ordinary civil conversation in between. He was obviously in pontificating mode this morning. He described the deposits of protein that built up in the brain—he even called it by its scientific name, amyloid beta—and how they destroyed memory, personality, the ability to perform simple tasks. "Remember old Mrs. Brannock down the street?" he asked, and Lexie's eyes and mouth went round. The poor woman once wandered nude through their backyard before her mortified daughter was able to coax her back home.

Kelly stared at the griddle as bubbles began to rise like tiny dimples in the batter.

"The only thing the other doctors could come up with were drugs that maybe slowed down the buildup of these proteins. Nobody but Dr. Benedict ever tried to figure out what was causing the buildup in the first place."

"So what was?" Lexie asked.

"A virus!" Justin pronounced the word with a histrionic flourish.

The back door swung open, and Todd breezed in wearing his turquoise scrubs. "Morning, fake children," he called.

"Morning, fake dad," the kids answered in unison.

"Welcome home, conquering hero," he sang out with a salaam bow at Kelly.

She pointed the spatula at him. "Pancakes?"

"No, thanks." He reached around her for the blender. "We ate already. Bruce has an early session today."

His husband worked as a fitness trainer at a gym downtown. He was built like a boxer while Todd had the body of a dancer. Barely taller than Kelly, he was lean and lithe and moved fluidly about the kitchen as he set to work assembling Adam's breakfast—a pirouette to the refrigerator, a deep plie to the bottom cabinet, a grand jeté to reach to the end of the counter for the protein powder.

"Is it a virus like the flu?" Lexie asked.

"Yeah, or like herpes simplex," Justin said. "That's the virus that causes cold sores—you know, those things people get on their lips?"

"Yuk!"

It wasn't clear whether Lexie's remark was prompted by the mention of cold sores or by the salmon, broccoli, and oatmeal Todd was pouring into the blender. The kids always gagged at what went into the feeding tube, and Kelly always had to remind them that it bypassed the taste buds. The nutrients were all that mattered.

"But it is kinda like the flu," Justin shouted over the whir of the blender. "You know how we get shots every fall so we don't get the flu? That vaccine? Well, Mom's client invented a vaccine for this Alzheimer's virus. Except it's only one shot and you'll never get Alzheimer's for the rest of your life." Todd shut off the blender, but Justin was still shouting when he said: "It's incredible!"

Kelly flipped the pancakes onto two plates and set them on the table. "There's no vaccine yet," she said.

"There is, too," Justin said. "It's still in clinical trials, but that's just FDA red tape."

"Morning!" Another voice joined the clamor as Gwen popped her head in from the hallway. A girlish woman in her thirties, she was their occasional sitter, though Kelly was careful not to call her that anymore. Now she was the *cook*, the one service she provided that Justin deigned to accept. She had a duffel strap looped over her shoulder and a rollaboard by her side. "Just wanted to say goodbye."

"Goodbye, Gwen!" Lexie cried and jumped up from the table to give her a fierce hug.

"Breakfast?" Kelly asked.

"Thanks, no. Gotta run."

"Bye, doll," Todd said, and the two of them swept out of the kitchen, Gwen headed for the front door, Todd for the stairs.

"I don't like to get shots," Lexie said, picking up the conversation.

Justin considered that. "You know, I bet he'll come up with some kind of alternative delivery system. Cuz that's the kind of guy Dr. Benedict is. Always thinking outside the box."

"Alternative, like how?" Lexie asked.

Justin shoveled a forkful of dripping pancakes into his mouth. "A cherry-flavored drink in a little cup, how's that?"

"Could it be grape?"

"He'll probably offer thirty-one flavors!"

Kelly watched her children talk and laugh over their breakfast. It was a rare sight. Justin didn't often speak to his sister at any length, and never with this much enthusiasm. Ordinarily Kelly would have been thrilled by this conversation. But not this time. She kissed the top of Lexie's bun and the back of Justin's curls and left the room.

7

THE OFFICES OF LEAHY & McCann occupied three floors in a high-rise on the edge of the Boston Common. Kelly parked in her reserved spot in the underground garage and rode the elevator to the twentieth floor. The sound struck her the moment the elevator doors opened. The reception desk was unmanned, and a slow rhythmic smacking sound was coming from the corridor to the left. She stopped, puzzled, then let out a little moan when she realized what it was.

Harry instituted the ritual the first time she returned from a high-profile, out-of-town trial. He had everyone line up and clap her into the main conference room for a celebratory gathering. Now it was a tradition, but not one she ever enjoyed, even under normal circumstances. There was nothing purifying about this acclamation. This was only about the money.

She adjusted the scarf at her neck, took a big breath, and turned the corner into the corridor. They were all there, partners, associates, paralegals, and staff, all the way down to this month's temp, all of them beaming at her as they brought their hands together in an exaggerated slow clap. Her own team was among them, Patti and Cazzadee, of course, but also Javier, who spent little time in the office and must have come in especially for the occasion. It was their victory, too, Kelly reminded herself, and she forced a smile and made her way through the gauntlet. She shook proffered hands as she went, shuddered under sudden hearty back slaps, and accepted a kiss from Javi that had all the women swooning.

Harry Leahy stood at the end of the corridor. He held his hand out as she approached. She held hers out, too, but only to hand him the check. His eyes lit up. He flipped it over to verify that she'd endorsed it over to the firm, then a big grin split his face. "The smartest thing I ever did," he shouted to the assemblage as he held the check aloft, "was persuade this lady to join me here." With his other hand he grabbed both of Kelly's and raised them up high. "Our star!" he cried, and the slow clap turned into riotous applause.

THERE WAS HOPE for Adam, at first. The doctors operated within hours, repaired the broken artery, and sucked the pools of blood out of his skull. He didn't wake after the surgery, but that was common. Yes, the lack of oxygen had killed certain brain cells and they'd never come back to life, they told her, but the brain had an amazing ability to heal itself. There was this phenomenon called neuroplasticity, in which healthy areas of the brain might eventually take over the functions damaged by stroke. He was only fifty-two, and he ran five miles three times a week. He was an excellent candidate for a good recovery, they told her.

Kelly's mother had been planning to come up from Roanoke to help out with the new baby. Instead she flew up and looked after four-year-old Justin while Kelly sat vigil in the ICU, nursing the baby and talking to Adam in an endless patter of platitudes and nonsense. Speaking to him might help him regain consciousness, they told her. At any rate it couldn't hurt.

After a week they said the ventilator could come out, and she dressed for the occasion like it was a first date. She dressed up the baby, too, in a fussy little pinafore and bonnet that she thought would make him laugh. She was there when they extracted the tube from his throat, hovering as close as they would allow, and she watched and waited with a welcoming smile on her lips. They turned off the machine, and his chest rose up and down as he breathed on his own. But still he didn't wake, and when the doctor peeled back his eyelids and moved his finger back and forth, Adam's eyes didn't move with it.

The doctor left the room. The nurses left the room. Eventually, Kelly sat down.

The next day Adam had surgery to insert a feeding tube into his stomach. Two weeks later he was transferred to what the doctors called a long-term-care facility but Kelly insisted on calling *rehab*.

Her routine changed after the transfer. Now she spent her evenings by his bedside and her days at his office with the baby strapped to her chest. She'd had access to his office email from the start, and she'd sent out replies over his name to anything requiring an immediate response, explaining that he was out of the office for a short time celebrating the joyous arrival of his new daughter. But the emails and phone calls grew more impatient, particularly from his most important client, Erik Kloss. She needed a different excuse. She sent out emails in Adam's name explaining that he had a bad case of laryngitis, so he'd be doing all his talking by text and email for the next few weeks. Please bear with him.

That brought a flood of well-wishes and deliveries of flowers and fruit baskets.

She remembered the stories about Woodrow Wilson and how his wife concealed his stroke and acted as shadow president. Kelly decided she could do the same for Adam. A real estate law practice ought to be easier to run than an entire country. Adam had anticipated almost every potential pothole in the road to closing the Kloss land purchase. By insisting on making written replies to every query and demand, Kelly bought herself time to dig through his files and figure out what his response would have been.

But this wasn't her field, and she was soon out of her depth. A pothole emerged that threatened to turn into a sinkhole, and she didn't know how to fix it. Adam's top associate, Kevin Trent, had been sticking his head in the office every day, asking after Adam's laryngitis, sending his best regards. He'd been copied on all the Erik Kloss emails and was more or less up to speed on the project. And she knew how much Adam trusted him. She decided to confide in him.

The color drained from his face, and tears stood in his eyes when she told him the truth of Adam's condition. "Kelly, I— I don't know what to say. I can't believe it. Adam—he's like the strongest man I've ever known. For sure the smartest. I can't even imagine him like . . . that." His wet eyes wandered the room. "I never got to tell him—"

She cut him off before he could deliver his eulogy. "He's going to recover, Kevin. He's going to come back as good as ever. But we need to keep this place afloat so he has something to come back to. Can I count on you?"

"Absolutely," he said and hugged her before he left with his list of assignments.

One night she was by Adam's side when his eyes suddenly flashed open. She nearly screamed with excitement. He was awake, he was back! But he didn't respond to her, or to anything. He'd simply moved from a coma to a vegetative state. That was good news, the doctors said. Some patients never emerged from their comas at all. The next step would be to a minimally conscious state. His eyes might regain movement first, then other voluntary responses would slowly follow.

She spent every evening after that gazing into his eyes, more intently now than when they were falling in love.

Adam didn't have long-term-care insurance. He didn't have disability insurance either. All he had was a $500,000 life insurance policy for the benefit of his daughter Courtney, a condition of his divorce settlement. His basic medical insurance was covering most of the rehab fees, but they also had a mortgage and Courtney's private-school tuition to pay, and the bills were piling up. Kelly's boss had agreed to extend her maternity leave, but it was no longer paid leave, and she was draining their savings to remain afloat. A second mortgage on the house would have helped, but since Adam couldn't sign the papers, she'd have to petition the court for guardianship, which meant going public with his condition. Instead, she borrowed money from her parents, enough to last until the closing of the Kloss deal when Adam's final bill would be paid. After that? She convinced herself that Adam would be back to work.

The bad news was fired out of two barrels on the same day, and both hit their mark. The director of the rehab facility asked to see her, and when she arrived at his office, six other men were in the room, too, on folding chairs dragged into a semicircle. There was a new face among them, and from the deferential manner the others showed him, Kelly assumed he was the chief doctor. But no . . . he was the insurance company rep.

There was no therapeutic benefit to Adam's current course of care, the doctors told her.

In the absence of therapeutic benefit, his insurance would no longer cover the costs of his care, the company rep told her.

In the absence of insurance, he could no longer remain at the facility, the rehab director told her.

Kelly patted the baby's back while they spoke, and when the room finally went silent, when the men cleared their throats and looked at the floor, she got up and left.

ADAM'S OFFICE WAS strangely quiet that afternoon. She sat behind his desk while Lexie slept in the stroller beside her. There were no emails or texts to respond to, and she did nothing but stare vacantly until the receptionist came in with a piece of certified mail. It was from Erik Kloss. Regrettably, he was switching all of his business to the newly formed law firm of Kevin Trent & Associates. Please send all files to Kevin's new office by courier today.

She walked out of Adam's office and down through the deadly quiet corridors. Most of the offices and workstations were dark. The best and the brightest of Adam's employees had gone with Kevin.

She returned to Adam's office and rocked the stroller back and forth and back and forth while she made a series of phone calls. First were all the arrangements to discharge Adam from rehab and move him home, buy a hospital bed and all the equipment, and hire a home health-care aide. Then all the arrangements to dissolve Adam's firm and liquidate what few assets remained.

Her final call was to Harry Leahy. "Harry," she said when his surprised voice came over the line, "let's talk."

THE CREDENZA IN the main conference room was set with platters of doughnuts, a bagel bar, pitchers of orange juice, and bottles of champagne. Everyone funneled in from the corridor and filled their plates and mixed their mimosas before taking seats around the long conference table. Harry sat himself at the head, with the firm's other lawyers clustered around him, while Kelly's own team gathered around her at the foot of the table. Harry's group was mostly male and white, while Kelly's was mostly female and included an African American, a Chinese American, even a Venezuelan American.

The buzz of voices swelled around the table, a mechanical buzz, like the sound of a generator. It was always awkward, pretending to have a party in a room designed for business meetings, and to do it at the start of the workday, when everyone had calls to make or papers to file. Their gaiety seemed forced. Certainly Kelly's was. The pounding was gone from her head and the throbbing from her groin, but the numbness hadn't left her yet.

Cazzadee leaned over. "You okay?" she whispered. She was hyper-competent and hyper-observant, too.

"Just a bit tired," Kelly said and nibbled at the edge of her doughnut.

Harry tapped a pen against his glass to call for silence. He was seventy, bald and squat, with a round, cherubic face that gave him a look more benevolent than he really was. That was his secret weapon back in his heyday—that he looked like a priest or somebody's harmless bachelor uncle. Adverse witnesses were caught off guard when his ruthless knives came out for cross-examination. But as the years passed, he started to seem more like a creepy bachelor uncle than a harmless one, particularly when cross-examining the female victims of his clients. He started losing most of his cases, notably those prosecuted by Kelly.

Now he raised his glass in a toast. "Here's to Kelly McCann," he crowed. "The lady who never loses!"

Technically that was true, but only because she refused to take any case to trial that she wasn't sure of winning. She got rid of the losers, either by settling them, pleading them out, or referring them to other counsel. She lost some fees in the process but kept her reputation intact.

"Kelly, regale us," Harry called down the length of the table. "We'd all love to hear how you did it. Especially how you destroyed that woman on cross."

She shook her head with a little self-deprecating wave of her hand.

"Oh, come on. At least give us the highlight reel."

"Yeah! Come on." The lawyers flanking him took up the call and pounded their fists on the table. These were the men who handled the firm's bread-and-butter cases, small-time matters in the local courts. Their work never made headlines, but it kept the lights on between Kelly's splashier paydays.

She shook her head again. "No, but let me call on Patti Han to recap it. She was the architect of my cross, and I couldn't have done it without her."

Patti flushed with pleasure at the praise and threw a quick glance at Javi to see how he'd reacted to it. Sadly, he didn't. He was busy trying to flirt with Cazz, who was busy ignoring him. Patti's face fell a little. She was plump and plain and painfully in love with Javier, who only had eyes for the beautiful Cazzadee. While Cazz kept her eyes firmly on her work.

"Well, I guess it all turned on Dr. Patel's corroborating witness," Patti began haltingly. Her command of written English was flawless, but she still showed some hesitancy in public speaking, which was why Kelly forced her to practice in moments like this. "That was her employment lawyer. As soon as he testified about what she told him, we were able to establish that the privilege was waived as to the entire subject matter. So Kelly was able to question Dr. Patel about all her efforts to get a monetary settlement from Dr. Benedict before she went to the police and claimed rape."

"A shakedown, in other words," Harry said.

"That's what the jury seemed to think."

The firm's receptionist slipped into the room and whispered into Harry's ear.

"I have a question." This came from Steven Schultz, one of the lawyers flanking Harry, and he addressed it not to Patti but to Kelly. "Evidence of settlement negotiations is inadmissible, so how'd you get around that?"

Kelly nodded at Patti to answer, but she'd barely begun before Harry interrupted. "Excellent," he said to the receptionist. "Patch the call in here and put it on speaker."

The receptionist scurried from the room, and everyone's eyes moved expectantly to the speakerphone in the middle of the table.

Schultz seemed peeved at being cut off from what he hoped was his gotcha question. "Well, who is it?" he demanded.

Harry silenced him with a sharp frown.

Kelly knew who it was. What she didn't know was how she'd react to it. She didn't know whether she'd tremble in fear or vomit in revulsion, or maybe she wouldn't react at all. She still felt numb.

The speakerphone was a black Bakelite oval supported by three flying buttresses. It looked like a miniature spacecraft, and everyone stared at it as if waiting for an alien life-form to emerge. What finally did emerge was a crackle of static.

"Hello!" Harry answered heartily. "You're on speaker."

The dry, flat voice of George Benedict entered the room. "Good. I wanted to speak to the whole firm. I know it took a team effort to win my case and clear my name, so let me take this opportunity to thank the whole team for all your support and hard work."

Harry grinned at the speaker. "But Kelly most of all, am I right?"

"Yes, but I already thanked Kelly privately. Last night."

Kelly's numbness was gone in an instant. Feeling returned in a whoosh like a match tossed on a trail of gasoline. It blazed into wildfire as Benedict droned on about her. How special she was. How he'd never forget her.

"Well, thank *you*, George," Harry effused. "For choosing us and for giving us this opportunity to see that justice was done." With that he brought his hands together, and the rest of the group picked up the cue and applauded along with him. By the time the applause died down, the light on the speakerphone had blinked off. The call had ended.

Kelly was trembling, but it wasn't with fear. It was with loathing. Rage rose up like gorge in her throat. Her breath came in fast, heavy pants.

Harry beamed down the length of the table. "Good to have a grateful client, isn't it?"

"Always is," she said, rising to her feet as anger boiled hot and furious inside her. "Thank you, everyone. If you'll excuse me, I have three weeks' worth of mail piled on my desk."

"Of course, of course, go." Harry waved her off as he reached for another doughnut.

She walked out of the conference room with her fists swinging like wrecking balls at her sides. Her fury felt volcanic, as if it could spew out in a river of hot lava down the long corridor to her corner office. She closed the door and pressed her knuckles to her skull and opened her mouth wide in a silent scream.

I already thanked Kelly privately. Last night.

She hated him with a force she'd never felt before. She wanted to kill him. She wanted to stomp on his corpse until there was nothing left but mush and slime.

She paced the perimeter of her office, from door to window, bookcase to credenza, back again to door, to window. Her office overlooked a lovely stretch of lawn and trees on the Common, but today she was seeing red, not green. Her arms were rigid, her fists clenched tight, and the steam of her hatred built up higher with every lap.

She stopped short when her phone rang in her bag. She knew who it was even before she saw his name on the screen. He had her cell number, of course; it was how they'd communicated for the last three weeks. But to call it now was a clear signal. Last night was only the beginning. He wasn't done with her.

"Well," he said to her silent answer. "You passed your first test. You obviously said nothing to your colleagues."

She'd convinced herself that she would get over this trauma. She was a survivor, and she would survive this, too. She'd made herself believe that the only aftereffects of his attack might be disease or pregnancy, both of which could be medically dispatched. But now it was clear: he meant to mindfuck her forever.

"Just a reminder, though. Say anything, to anyone, and you'll be ruined. Try to destroy me and you'll destroy yourself."

The rage filled her lungs and surged up thick in her throat. She couldn't speak.

"And here's another reminder. Check your camera roll. I left you a memento of our time together."

Her hatred roared like a thousand beasts inside her chest, and she stabbed her finger at the End Call button as furiously as if she were stabbing a fork into his face.

A memory stirred in the back of her mind. She stopped and stared at the phone as something flickered slowly into focus. Something that happened during those long minutes last night when she could only stare fixedly at the white ceiling. When he was out of her range of sight. Doing something outside her peripheral vision. She felt him pick up her hand. She felt him press her thumb to something she couldn't see, but she remembered now, the slick feeling of glass against her skin.

He'd used her thumb to unlock her phone. He'd used her camera to . . . what? She opened the camera roll. The last photo she'd taken was of Lexie getting on the bus for her first day of fifth grade. It was still there. But there were two new photos after it, and she gagged when she saw them. The first was a photo of her, naked and laid out on the desk. The second was a photo of him or, rather, a part of him.

She pounded the Delete button, missed it wildly, and pounded it again until both photos disappeared. The phone felt filthy in her hand, befouled, and she lobbed it hard across the room. It landed with a noisy clatter on her desk.

He'd been in her phone. In her photos. He'd seen the photo of her little girl, and she nearly gagged again.

She couldn't think of anything worse than that, but in the next instant, she did. By unlocking her phone, he'd gained access to all of her usernames and passwords. He could penetrate her social media accounts. He could raid her bank accounts.

But it was even worse than that. Not only was he in her phone, but he now had a way into all of the electronic devices at home. He could control the camera and microphone on her computer, on all the smart devices in the house. He could activate the CCTV camera and spy on Adam. He could control all of Adam's health monitors.

Heat spread through her body until it felt like flames could burst from her head. She grabbed the phone and took out the SIM card and struck it with a heavy lead paperweight until it shattered. Then she pounded the paperweight on the phone itself, again and again, until hailstones of glass and aluminum rained through the room.

8

JAVIER KNEW A GUY—HE knew lots of guys, a whole stable of men and women he could tap for assignments or consult on a host of topics, which was what made him such a good investigator. This particular guy was a cybersecurity expert, and he brought him to the house that afternoon.

His name was Paul, and he was a pale, soft-jowled young man with unkempt hair and eyes that couldn't quite make contact with Kelly's. He wanted to begin with her phone, of course, and she had to confess that she'd destroyed it after she discovered the hack.

"What made you think it was hacked?" Javi asked her.

"I don't know. It seemed off?"

Paul nodded at the ceiling. "Running slow, strange pop-ups?"

"Right," she said. "Exactly."

He needed an inventory of all the devices currently connected to the household Wi-Fi, and she led him on a tour to count them all. The security system. Virtual assistants in several rooms. Smart plugs and lightbulbs. A smart thermostat. Her laptop and Justin's, and both their cell phones. Lexie's tablet. Justin's gaming platforms. Two smart TVs and a smart refrigerator. Doorbell cameras. The wildlife camera Justin had installed in the backyard in hopes of capturing something, anything. The camera in the bedroom that livestreamed to her phone and Todd's. All the other monitoring equipment at Adam's bedside.

She remembered then that Todd and Bruce were also on the household Wi-Fi, and that Gwen and her boyfriend often logged onto it as well. By the end, the total count of Wi-Fi-connected devices: forty-two.

It was ironic, Kelly thought. So many smart devices and yet she'd been so stupid. To be alone with a man she knew was a rapist. To have a drink with him.

The router was on the floor of the coat closet in the front hall. Paul squatted beside it to run his diagnostics. "Here's the problem," he said almost at once. "You got remote access turned on. That means anybody who knew the IP address could have hacked in."

Kelly felt an auger tear through the pit of her stomach. She groped her way to a chair in the living room and sat down heavily.

Javi was hovering over him. "How'd that happen?"

"I don't know. The default is remote off."

"So somebody did it."

"Had to."

Paul confirmed that the only devices currently connected were the ones he'd already inventoried. As to whether they'd been hacked in the past? No way to be sure, but he'd check all their devices for malware or spyware or any other mischief.

Mischief, Kelly thought. Such an innocuous term. Harmless. Almost adorable.

Paul's recommendation: he'd replace the router, lock out remote administration, and change everyone's log-in credentials. For a further fee, he'd encrypt them and build a new firewall that would block any further intrusion.

"Do it," Kelly said.

Javi sat down across from her. He had beautiful dark eyes, a key element of his seductive charm, but now they were narrowed with suspicion. "What the hell, Kelly? Who did this to you?"

She lifted a shoulder in a weak shrug. "A lot of people hate me."

"Sure." The ease with which he agreed was no surprise. "But they fight you in court and in the media. Not in your home."

That was it. Right there. The violation, the intrusion, the *penetration*. As horrific as it was last night, it was even worse now that it was her home and her family he'd invaded. She cast her mind back over all that he might have seen and heard. Her tearful confession to Adam—how satisfying that must have been to him, to hear her describe how helpless she'd felt. He would've gotten off all over again on that admission. Today he might have seen Adam being fed and cleaned and changed, all those unavoidable humiliations she never wanted anyone but Todd to witness. And finally she imagined him spying on the kids this morning, on Lexie as she got dressed.

She wanted to destroy him. She had to do it. No matter the price.

Javi was watching her with his head cocked, wondering why she wasn't answering him. She pretended to think. "Maybe it was that LaSorta woman," she said finally. "She's a techie, right? She could've done it."

He looked skeptical. "Why would she want to spy on you? On Benedict maybe, but not you."

"Oh, you know"—she waved a dismissive hand through the air—"they always blame the lawyer."

"You made her a millionaire. She came away happy."

"It was a hard-fought negotiation. She probably came away feeling cheated." That was the hallmark of a successful settlement negotiation—when both sides were unhappy at the end.

He still wasn't buying it, and she wondered why she was trying so hard to conceal the truth. It would all come out soon enough. After she went to the police. After she spoke to the press. Everyone would know everything then. Even if Benedict couldn't be charged, the media would broadcast her story, and that should be enough to destroy him. If it wasn't, she'd reveal the names of all the other women he'd violated, the ones who'd been silenced by NDAs. Kelly would be disbarred if she did that, but so what? Her career would be over anyway.

Bruce arrived soon after, summoned by Todd to bring his phone and laptop home, and Cazzadee arrived soon after that, armed with a new phone for Kelly. Then Gwen arrived with her boyfriend, Josh, a bearded white boy with a penchant for African attire. The kitchen island, the coffee table in the living room, the dining room table— electronic devices were spread out on almost every surface as Paul the cyber guy went from one to the next, scanning for malware.

The school bus rumbled to a stop outside at the corner, and Lexie burst in the front door a minute later. As soon as she understood what was going on, she clamored to help and ran from room to room to be sure they hadn't missed any devices.

When Justin joined them twenty minutes later, he wasn't quite so cooperative. "No way," he said when Kelly told him to unlock his phone and laptop. She tried to explain the hack and the antidote, but still he was adamant that this would be a heinous invasion of his privacy. *Heinous* was a word often in his vocabulary these days.

Todd took him aside for a whispered huddle and after a few minutes beckoned to Paul to join them; somehow détente was reached and Justin surrendered his passwords.

IT STARTED TO feel like a carnival atmosphere. Ten people milling about, renewing acquaintances and making new ones. Gwen was sneaking looks at Javi while her boyfriend sneaked looks at Cazz, and Paul still couldn't look at anybody. Gwen went to the kitchen and put together a cheese and fruit tray, and Justin brought out soft drinks from the garage refrigerator. Bruce put on some music, and he and Todd did a brief pas de deux through the front hall, Bruce in a muscle shirt and Todd in his scrubs. Lexie followed Javi from room to room chattering about her favorite Marvel characters and quizzing him about all the movies she hadn't yet been allowed to see. She had a crush on him, like all the girls did.

Kelly sat stunned through it all. These were her people, and they'd all come together in the middle of a weekday afternoon to solve her problem, without a word of recrimination that she'd exposed them and all their private information to this intrusion. She was grateful to all of them.

But it occurred to her that they were all on her payroll or otherwise dependent on her. Todd and the kids, of course. Javi and Cazz, who were the highest-paid staff members of Leahy & McCann. Gwen, to whom she paid an hourly wage plus a regular retainer to ensure she'd always be available when Kelly needed her. Then there was Gwen's boyfriend, who lived largely off Gwen's income. Bruce, who lived rent-free over the garage. And even Paul for the length of this work session. She could throw in the weekly cleaning lady and the lawn man, too. They all relied on her. Her and her income. Her livelihood was their livelihood.

Cazz came over and squatted by Kelly's chair. "Want a real drink?" she whispered.

It wasn't yet four o'clock, but Kelly nodded, and Cazz went to the kitchen and soon returned with a G and T in a highball tumbler.

"Thanks." Kelly took a sip, and as soon as the bitter fizz hit her tongue, it ignited a blaze of memories. *It was already in the tonic.* She remembered snapping the plastic seal on the cap before she poured it. She definitely remembered that. Which meant he'd figured out how to reseal the bottle, which told her how long he must have planned his attack, how carefully he'd prepared for it.

She had to destroy him.

But she'd destroy herself in the process.

She didn't care about herself.

But she cared about these people, all these people chatting and laughing and meandering through the house. All these people who depended on her.

She got up and took her glass to the window and looked out over the front lawn. A sugar maple tree stood to one side of the front walk, its leaves still a rich green, but in weeks they would turn to brilliant shades of gold and crimson and flaming orange, the prettiest tree on the street. She remembered the day Adam planted it while she watched from a lawn chair with baby Justin in her arms. It was a ten-foot sapling then, and he dug the hole by hand, shirtless, the muscles bunching and straining across his sweating back. She worried he was working too hard, he might pull something, but he only shook his head. *I think you labored a lot harder than this,* he said with a nod and a smile at their son. He wrestled the root ball into place, eyeballed it and straightened its trunk, and then backfilled the hole with rich loamy soil and compost. He mulched it over and watered it in, then he took the baby from Kelly and carried him over to the sapling like he was introducing the two of them. *This is your tree*, he told him. *It's going to grow up big and tall just like you.* He was right. Today it was almost thirty feet tall.

They planned for Lexie's tree on the other side of the walk, but because she was going to be a winter baby, he dug that hole in the fall, before the ground could freeze, and stored that sugar maple behind the garage until it could be planted.

All that long winter Kelly watched the hole fill up with snow until she couldn't see where it was anymore. In the spring, after the melt, the lawn man filled it in and hauled away the withered sapling.

Abruptly Kelly turned and put down the glass. "I'm going up to see Adam," she announced to the room, and everyone slipped sad, knowing looks at one another as she headed up the stairs.

THERE WAS AN abiding hush in their bedroom, the kind that evoked whispers and soft sighs and the faint waft of air from a hand-held fan. *Like a funeral parlor*, his daughter Courtney once said, but Kelly preferred to think of it like a church before the service began or like a nursery after the baby dropped off to sleep.

She slipped off her shoes and turned off the camera and stretched out beside him in the narrow bed. His hair was pure white now, and in the dim light of the room it took on an otherworldly glow. Another memory surfaced, of a night she saw him frowning at himself in their bathroom mirror. His hair was thick and dark then, and she saw what he was looking at—a single silver filament. *Well, hey there, Grandpa*, she teased him. He pretended to swat at her, and she pretended to squeal, and he chased after her out of the bathroom and around their bed until she allowed herself to be captured and tossed onto the covers. He jumped in after her and they rolled and tussled until they were both breathless with laughter. Then the laughs turned to pants, and they were tugging off each other's clothes, and twisting and turning and flipping positions until they fitted together perfectly.

He always enjoyed a robust appetite for sex, and she always enjoyed it, too. So there were moments in those early days when she wondered if she should do that for him, give him that pleasure. She even wondered if it might bring him back. Once she gave him a few gentle, tentative strokes, but he didn't respond, and she quickly gave up. It felt wrong, touching him that way when he was incapable of giving consent.

Incapable. Incapacitated. As incapacitated as she'd been last night, but in her case it was deliberate. It was vile. It was beyond heinous.

"I don't know what to do," she whispered.

Adam's chest rose and fell and rose and fell again.

She gripped his hands. They were baby smooth, hands that hadn't dug a hole or hammered a nail or even picked up a pen for ten years. "What should I do?" she asked.

His only answer was a trickle of urine into his catheter bag.

"Something happened last night," she began, but she stopped and glanced over her shoulder. The green light was off on the camera, but she couldn't trust that anymore. Anyone could be listening, from downstairs or from a mansion outside Philadelphia.

She tried to speak to him through her mind, but that was too great a leap of faith even for her. She tried to lie still beside him, but she was too agitated, and soon she had to slide out of his bed. She paced the floor then, from his bed to hers, from window to door.

Her reputation was built on the premise that her clients were always innocent and that their accusers were always lying. If she went to the police or the press with the truth of what happened last night, that reputation would be demolished. If they believed her, it would mean every case she'd ever won was a fraud. If they didn't believe her, it would mean she was a crank, a nut job, a vindictive bitch with some ax to grind. No man accused of a sex crime would ever come to her again. Harry Leahy would jettison her from the firm. She'd be bankrupt within months. She'd have to let Javi go, and Cazz and Patti Han. Gwen, of course. The cleaning lady. And Todd. There was no way she'd be able to pay Todd. She'd have to stay home and take care of Adam on her own, which was fine, she could do it, but how then to pay his other medical bills and the mortgage and all the other expenses of living?

She couldn't. She pivoted and paced the other way.

She couldn't do it, but she had to do something. She couldn't live much longer with this corrosive rage inside her. It was a cancer, and it would metastasize and spread its poison through her body until she exploded.

That morning she'd told herself she could get through this. She could survive. She would put it behind her, forget it ever happened.

But she knew now that she never would. He wouldn't let her. He'd call the office, he'd call her cell phone, he'd spy on her house. He'd violate her in every way possible.

It wasn't enough to survive. She needed to win. Survival wasn't winning. Revenge was winning.

She wanted to kill him. She never would have guessed that murder lurked in her heart, but there it was, pumping its black blood through her veins. She wanted to stab him through his gimlet eyeballs and bore like a jackhammer into his genius brain.

But she couldn't kill him. That was too blunt, too risky, it would end his suffering too soon. There had to be other ways. There really were fates worse than death. She simply had to find the right one for Benedict.

She pivoted and paced.

It would be poetic justice if he were raped. Sodomized. Brutally. She didn't have a stable of guys like Javi did, but she knew people who knew people. A career spent in the criminal justice system introduced her to a lot of unsavory characters. She could hire one of them to do it.

But again, too risky. The trail would inevitably lead back to her.

She pivoted again.

What she needed was a more devious way to humiliate him. A way to destroy his reputation and his income without destroying her own in the process. Some financial crime, perhaps. Insider trading, market manipulation—but no, that wasn't vile enough. That kind of behavior was almost expected among the executive class, and even when caught and tried, those men always bounced back.

She pivoted and paced again.

A series of taps sounded on the door as she passed it on her next circuit. Three shaves and a haircut—Todd's signal. This room was his workplace, but it was also her marital bedroom, and he always respected that.

"Okay if I interrupt?" he asked as she opened the door. In his hands was the oversized syringe carrying Adam's blenderized meal.

"Is it already dinnertime?"

He nodded. "Everyone's gone now. And the cyber guy said to tell you everything's safe, and no harm done. All the dude did was take a look around. If that much."

Only because she'd caught him early. She hated to think what he would have done if she hadn't remembered her thumb against the screen.

Todd glided to the bed to check the monitors. "Courtney dropped by yesterday," he said, in an oh-so-casual tone.

"I heard. What did she want?"

"Same as always."

"What'd you tell her?"

"Same as always."

There was a sigh in his voice, and she turned away and went down the hall.

Lexie was in her room doing multiplication homework. "Quiz me, Mommy?"

Kelly came in and perched on the edge of the bottom bunk and ran the tables. Lexie rattled off the answers like a machine. She didn't need the drill. She just liked to shine. She was too much her mother's daughter: accomplishments didn't count unless there was someone there to applaud them.

"Book group tonight?" Lexie asked when Kelly stood to go. Last year she'd decided she was too big to be read to at bedtime, but Kelly was reluctant to give up those thirty minutes of snuggle time. Together, they'd come up with book group as a replacement. They'd each read the same book and discuss it at bedtime.

"You bet," Kelly said, but she couldn't remember what this week's book was. "What chapter are we on?" she asked instead.

"Four. Remember? Margaret didn't wear socks on the first day of school, and she got blisters?"

"Right." Now Kelly remembered: *Are You There, God? It's Me, Margaret.*

Downstairs the house was back in order, the dishes done and put away in the kitchen, the cheese rewrapped and back in the refrigerator. Gwen, probably, though it could have Todd or Bruce or even Cazz. All these people who looked after her household. All these people she paid to look after her household.

The TV was on in the family room. She glanced in and saw Justin's orange curls peeking up over the back of the couch. He was in his perpetual slouch, but unusually for him, he was watching a cable news network. She recognized the on-air reporter, Rick Olsson. He was saying something dramatic about something. He mentioned huge costs. Next to climate change, the darkest cloud hanging over our lives. Then he said *breaking news* or *breakthrough* or something equally portentous. The subject didn't register with Kelly. She was too surprised to see Justin staring so fixedly at anything other than a video game on the screen. It was a pleasant surprise, though, so she left him to it and went back to the kitchen to think about dinner.

There was nothing in the refrigerator, and everything in the freezer required a few hours of defrosting. She'd have to order in. She picked up the landline and pressed the third number on speed dial. "Vinnie's Pizza," a girl answered as a robotic voice in the family room pronounced: *The Phase II results were astounding. Ninety-two percent efficacy with no measurable side effects.*

Kelly dropped the phone like it was electrified. For a second she thought the voice was coming through the phone, but no, it was the TV. She stumbled to the family room doorway. George Benedict was there, on the screen, in the room, in her house. Beside him was Rick Olsson, looking rapt, his head bobbing in a sycophantic nod.

"Hey, Doomfist," she called to Justin. "Could you turn that off?" Her voice echoed in her ears, thin and strained.

Justin didn't answer, and he didn't move, and Benedict kept on talking. He spoke like a machine, with cogs and gears and metal plates that scraped against each other. It scraped against *her*.

"Justin," she said, sharper. "Turn it off."

"No. I'm interested in this."

Is it fair to say, Olsson was asking, *that your entire reputation, not to mention your personal fortune, depends upon the success of these Phase III trials?*

Benedict deflected the question, droning on in dry tones but grandiose words about the whole world depending on the vaccine, the very future of humankind. Kelly didn't hear him. She was still hearing the reporter's words before that. *Your reputation. Your fortune.*

Suddenly she knew. She knew exactly how to do it. And she knew that she could. She could almost hear Adam speaking by her side. *You're Kelly McCann.*

He didn't need to say the rest.

9

SHE COULD DO IT, BUT she couldn't do it alone. She didn't have the skills or knowledge to pull this off. Javi probably had some guys who could do it, but she couldn't involve him or anyone else on her team; she wouldn't make them complicit in her crime, and no matter how loyal they were, she couldn't count on their silence if they were caught. For the same reason, she couldn't risk hiring any outside help.

What she needed were people who had the ability to do it and hated Benedict as much as she did. Whose silence was as certain as her own.

She knew exactly who those people were.

She arrived early at the office the next morning, before Cazz or any other staff were there. She turned on the lights as she went, down the main corridor, past her own office, and into the file room. George Benedict's files occupied a full bank of lateral drawers, from ceiling to reinforced floor.

Reeza Patel was the only one of his victims whose case went to trial, but there were a dozen others. Kelly zeroed in on the three women who showed up at the courthouse. The only name she remembered was LaSorta, and only because Javi had reminded her. But the NDA files were all grouped together, and it didn't take her long to find the other two. She took them all to her office and closed the door.

LaSorta first. Ashley LaSorta, onetime chief information officer of UniViro. She was a woman who defied every expectation of what a techie looked like, not to mention what a woman over fifty should look like. She was unabashedly sexy, with brunette hair that fell in long voluminous waves past her shoulders, and she dressed in leather skirts and plunging necklines and always wore a bold red lip. She had a master's degree in computer science and had worked in Silicon Valley before landing in the executive suite at UniViro. She was divorced, and had a college-age son and a long string of lovers.

One of her lovers, for a brief time, was George Benedict. It was after his divorce from the brittle blonde and before his marriage to the sweet but dowdy Jane. According to LaSorta, she ended the affair after a few months, but Benedict refused to accept that it was over. He battered her with calls and texts until she changed her phone number, then he battered her by company email. He pleaded with her to take him back, he professed undying love, then he called her a cow and a whore and an idiot. She ignored him, and after a few weeks, the emails stopped. All was quiet for a few weeks more, and she thought it was finally over. Until one day she came home from work and found him inside her house. She claimed that he grabbed her, bound her, gagged her, and over the course of the next twelve hours, with the help of a pharmaceutical aid, raped her three times. At the end of it, he said *Now it's over*, and he untied her and left.

LaSorta preserved all the evidence, she confided in a friend—standard rape victim protocol—but she didn't call the police. Instead, she called a lawyer and demanded $10 million. Kelly suspected she'd settle for five, but she was able to get it down to half that amount, thanks to Javi's legwork.

He was a smooth operator. He met LaSorta at a bar one night, charmed her away from her then-date, and generally romanced his way into her life all the way up to, but not quite crossing her bedroom door. He wasn't aiming to get into her bed. He was aiming to get into her confidence and thereby into her past, and he did, far enough to discover the identities of some of her previous lovers. One of them was feeling vindictive, and he was the one with the sex tape.

When Kelly confronted her with the tape, LaSorta was shocked, she was furious, but mostly she was humiliated. What she'd thought was a thrilling, slow-burn seduction by Javi turned out to be nothing but a setup to shame her into silence. She railed against Kelly and her dirty tactics, she threatened to go to the police, the press, the world, but it was all a bluff. She didn't want her son to see her like that, and in the end she resigned her position at UniViro, signed an NDA, and walked away with $2.5 million. Now she worked for a tech start-up in New Jersey.

Kelly put the LaSorta file aside and picked up the next one. Emily Norland was the name of this woman. She was thirty-two, a PhD microbiologist married to a patent lawyer. She'd been a member of Benedict's vaccine research team at UniViro. Thin, with short brown hair and glasses, she far better fit the stereotype of a scientist than LaSorta did the tech geek. Norland was no siren or seductress. Nonetheless, on a business trip to Chicago, after they'd presented their results to an audience of other vaccine researchers, Benedict forced his way into her hotel room and raped her. It was over in minutes, and it was only a few minutes more before he left the room and called Kelly to do damage control. He'd learned a lesson from his previous incidents, just not the right one.

Kelly booked the next flight to Chicago and got on the phone to Emily's husband, who'd just booked his own flight. She talked to him all through their respective cab rides to their respective airports, through security, at the gate, and on board until the signal sounded for her to turn off her cell phone. She arrived first at O'Hare and was there to meet his flight with the NDA in hand. Only the amount was left blank. They shared a cab to the hotel while they negotiated the figure, and she waited in the corridor while he talked to his wife in her room. It took an hour, but he came out with a thumbs-up. She then knocked on the room next door and woke Benedict up from a sound sleep to get his signature on the NDA, too, along with a check for $500,000.

The third NDA woman was only a girl. Tiffy Jenkins, age twenty, who worked for the company that did the overnight cleaning of the UniViro offices. She was a high school dropout who grew up in foster care, a washed-out blonde, thin and pale and timid. On the night in question, as every night, she came into Benedict's office to empty his trash can. She was startled to find him stretched out on his leather couch with his pants open. Stammering apologies, she tried to back out of the room, but he was too fast for her. He grabbed her and bent her over his desk and finished what he'd been doing.

He didn't even bother to call Kelly about that one, it seemed so insignificant to him. It was only when she was prepping him for the Patel trial and quizzing him about other incidents that he thought to mention it. He didn't know the girl's name, so Javi had to do some digging to find out who she was and where she lived. Kelly recruited a small-time local lawyer to take it from there. Tiffy was bewildered when the man introduced himself as her lawyer and advised her to settle immediately. She overcame her hesitation when she heard the number. Twenty thousand dollars was a lot of money to her and her live-in boyfriend, and she agreed to everything on the spot.

Kelly closed the last of the files and leaned back in her chair to think. The office was waking up outside her door. Phones were ringing, voices were buzzing, the aroma of barista-made coffee was drifting by. She turned on her desktop monitors and stared blindly at the two screens while she tried to think how these women could fit into her plan.

Ashley LaSorta was obvious. She'd designed UniViro's information systems, and unless they'd done a complete overhaul since she

left, she'd know how to penetrate them. The project also required a
scientist, and Emily Norland ought to fit that bill. As for Tiffy Jenkins, Kelly didn't know what value she could bring to the job. But
something tickled her memory, and she went back to Javi's notes
and confirmed it. Unlikely as it might be, Tiffy still worked the same
shift at UniViro. Even with an extra $20,000, she couldn't walk
away from a steady paycheck. As for Benedict, he probably never
noticed her, before or after.

That meant Tiffy probably still had access to Benedict's office.
Ashley LaSorta would provide the virtual access into the company
systems. Emily Norland would provide the content. And if they
needed anything on-site, Tiffy could get them inside.

There was one more woman to consider for this project, and Kelly
didn't need to pull a file to refresh herself on this one. Reeza Patel. She'd been a high-ranking member of Benedict's virus research
team. She'd have to know where any of the scientific bodies were
buried. But she wasn't an NDA woman; she was the exact opposite
of an NDA woman. She'd gone public with her accusations and had
endured a very public trial. She might want revenge, but she'd want
public vindication, too. Her silence couldn't be counted on, and that
automatically disqualified her.

So: LaSorta, Norland, and Jenkins. Kelly's own version of the
Avengers. These women had the right abilities; they had every reason to hate Benedict and to want revenge; and they had even more
reason to keep quiet about it. Specifically, the money they'd forfeit
if they violated their NDAs.

The problem was that they also had every reason to hate Kelly.
She was the woman who'd enabled Benedict's behavior, who was
complicit in it, to use Courtney's words.

Of course, if any of them had blown the whistle on Benedict and
gone to the police, he might be in prison now. Instead, they took

his hush money and sealed their lips and left him free to rape other women. Kelly included. Viewed that way, she had as much cause to hate them as they did her.

They wouldn't view it that way, of course. They couldn't, since they could never know that he'd attacked her, too.

A knock sounded on her door. She slid the NDA files under some other papers. "Come in."

It was Cazzadee, pushing a file cart stacked with the morning mail. "The Wexford file arrived from LA."

"Oh. Right." A lawyer in Los Angeles had asked Kelly to partner with him in defending an actor who'd been sued for—not charged with—sexual assault. The actor was Tommy Wexford, a soulful-looking young man who was lately a darling in the indie-film world. He guarded his privacy ferociously—a ploy, many thought, designed to enhance his mysterious allure. Which it did.

His accuser was a woman named Margaret Staley, who claimed that he'd forced her to perform fellatio in the back room of an LA restaurant. Her evidence consisted of a shirt with semen on it and a detailed description of a birthmark on the actor's penis. The police declined to pursue charges, finding the circumstances to be *insufficiently coercive*. She then filed a civil lawsuit. For weeks now, the case had been the subject of lurid tabloid headlines.

Wexford denied the fellatio, denied the semen, and denied the birthmark, too. The woman was a stalker, he maintained, who'd been harassing him online and on set and at his various homes for months. Now she'd upped the stakes with this fabricated story. But despite his vehement denials, he was so far refusing the easiest route to exoneration: a DNA test and a certification by some neutral doctor that he possessed no such birthmark. *I'm not going to dignify that lie by refuting it,* was his steadfast response. The LA lawyer hoped Kelly could persuade him to submit to the examination.

"Does it ever bother you?" she said suddenly as Cazz wheeled the cart to the worktable by the window.

"What?" Cazz was busy sorting the mail by case, and within each stack, by urgency.

"What we do. Represent these clients."

Cazz turned and tilted her head to one side. She was a beautiful young woman, regally tall, with a self-assurance it had taken Kelly years to acquire. "Why are you asking that now?"

Kelly shrugged. "I don't know. Something Adam's daughter said."

Cazz snorted. "Let me guess. We're gender traitors. Hashtag BelieveWomen. Hashtag MeToo."

"More or less. But even apart from that— I mean, these men. They're so . . ." Kelly trailed off before the adjectives could spew out.

Cazz shook her head, and her corkscrew curls fanned out in a glossy shimmer that evoked Cleopatra's headdress. "These men?" she repeated. "They're no different from any other men."

"Other men aren't rapists."

"It's a question of degree, though, isn't it? To some degree, they all have that sense of entitlement. Like, every match-up on Tinder has to lead straight to a hookup or he feels cheated. Every two a.m. booty call, and you're supposed to get out of bed and unlock the door because he wants it right then. And God forbid he buys you dinner and you don't give him a blow job on the drive home."

Kelly sat back in astonishment. They'd never discussed her love life—Cazz was far too professional for that—but Kelly assumed she had a string of men dancing attendance on her, and that she was the one calling the shots. "Cazzie, is that what it's like for you out there? I thought a girl who looks like you—"

"Gets me nothing. You look like I do? You're reduced to it. You're a commodity. That's what prostitution and porn have taught men to believe. A woman's body is a commodity. It's something they can buy."

"Still. It's a quite a leap from there to rape."

"Is it? Anything they can buy, they can steal, too, if they feel like it."

Kelly didn't want to believe it, but her experience of men probably wasn't as extensive as Cazzadee's. Certainly it wasn't as current. It was ten years since she'd had sex.

The other night—that wasn't sex.

"So to answer your question," Cazz said as she went to the door. "Does it bother me to represent these men? Sure, but no more than all the other men out there bother me."

"I'm sorry if that's been your experience."

Cazz gave an indifferent shrug. "You know what I don't understand? Bisexual women. I mean, if you have an actual choice which way to go"—she flashed a brilliant smile—"why would you ever choose men?"

Patti Han came in as Cazz left. "I heard the Wexford papers arrived?" Patti said with a quick glance at the worktable. "I was wondering if I could dive in?"

"I don't think I'll need you on this one, Patti."

Her face fell. In so many ways, Patti was too good for this job, but in this one respect, she wasn't good enough. She didn't have a poker face. Every disappointment, every slight, every worry livestreamed across her features. The work Kelly did required only two real talents: an intricate knowledge of the rules of evidence and a certain flair in the courtroom. Patti had the evidence rules down pat, along with the penal codes of almost every state in the nation and a huge body of case law besides. But she was never going to master the art of courtroom theatrics.

Kelly tried to mollify her. "This case comes down to factual disputes. There aren't any thorny legal issues for you to sink your teeth into."

Patti cast another longing glance at the file. "We won't know until we look, though, right?"

She needed to cut her loose, Kelly thought for the hundredth time. Patti was ten times smarter than Kelly. She should be teaching constitutional law at an Ivy League law school. She should be prosecuting complex antitrust suits for the Justice Department. Or defending them at a big Wall Street law firm. Anywhere but here.

"Okay," Kelly said. "Have at it."

Patti's face lit up, and she grabbed the file and hurried out before Kelly could change her mind.

Kelly turned back to the NDA files. Her challenge was how to approach these women. Their first instinct would be to refuse to have anything to do with her. If she called, they'd hang up. If she sent an email, they'd delete it. She could pretend to be an old friend of each of them and dummy up an email account to contact them. But LaSorta would see right through the dummy email. Maybe Norland would, too.

She could just show up on their doorsteps and make her pitch. But those doors would probably be slammed in her face.

Her best bet was to make her pitch to all three of them together. They needed to know that Benedict had other victims besides themselves. And they needed to know that this scheme could actually work. Meeting the other women and understanding the roles each could play might convince them.

So how then to draw the three of them together?

Her mind hit a wall, and she was still sliding down it when her intercom buzzed. "Kelly, it's Rick Olsson, on line two," Cazz said. "He says it's urgent."

The name rang a bell, then a louder bell. He was the TV news anchor who'd interviewed Benedict on air yesterday.

"Same answer. No interviews," she said to Cazz.

"He says he's not asking for one. That this is some private matter."

"He's lying," Kelly said.

"Got it," Cazz said and rang off.

Kelly turned her mind back to the threshold problem. How to get these women together long enough for her to make her pitch. They didn't know one another. The only time they'd ever been in the same place at the same time was in front of the courthouse steps on verdict day. She remembered how their faces jumped out at her in the crowd. She'd been near frantic at the sight of the three of them together, but now she was wishing she could replicate that scene and bring them all together again. Though she could hardly do a replay of verdict day.

Her email in-box blipped, and she glanced at the screen, and away, then glanced back again. The email was from Rick Olsson. *Please call me. I have no interest in interviewing you. This is an urgent personal matter.*

Of course he wanted to interview her. He would've included her in his segment last night if he could have. He would have quizzed her about the trial and Patel's accusations. He would have asked her to opine on how Benedict's ordeal might have slowed down his research, or how his exoneration now cleared the way for his vaccine. A joint interview with the savior-doctor and the lawyer who saved him? It would have been a ratings coup for Olsson. If there'd been a live studio audience, it would have been packed. The NDA women would have lined up to join it.

Kelly went suddenly still as the solution surfaced. She realized that she *could* do a replay of verdict day. A modified replay that the NDA women wouldn't be able to resist.

10

ON A BRIGHT TUESDAY MORNING in October, a charter bus pulled up to the main entrance of a bucolic college campus. The gray stone buildings shone in the early autumn light, and the first small bursts of crimson and gold appeared in the trees all around, like the pointillistic brushstrokes of a neo-Impressionist painter.

Two dozen men and women filed off the bus. The men and women were old and young, but mostly young. Most were clutching a single-page printout in their hands. They streamed through the Gothic-style stone archway and into the quad. Students on their way to or from class were flowing in crosscurrents over the green. Some of them cast curious glances at the new arrivals. They looked like they were on a campus tour but minus their campus tour guide.

A little titter of excitement rippled through the new arrivals when they spotted a famous face. TV news personality Rick Olsson stood beside the towering bronze statue at the center of the quad. Beside him was a cameraman with full gear. The campus wasn't far from the courthouse where George Benedict was acquitted last month; it made them wonder if there might be some new development in the case. A few students were clustered around Olsson, peppering him with questions while he was busy punching out an email on his phone.

The new arrivals were tempted to stop and cluster around him, too, but they walked on, following the cardboard arrows staked in the ground until they reached the hall that would be the venue for to-day's event.

They climbed the marble steps to the portico and followed more cardboard arrows inside to the double doors at the rear of a small auditorium. They looked around uneasily as they filed in. The house-lights were up, but the stage was in darkness, and there was no one there to greet or direct them. They mumbled to one another, con-sulted their printouts, and took the seats they'd been assigned. Three seats remained empty after they were settled, in separate spots in the middle rows, none on the aisle.

The audience members watched the darkened stage for some minutes, but nothing happened. They looked at their watches, took out their phones, introduced themselves to their seatmates, and ex-changed résumés in whispered conversations.

When the rear doors opened again, a young woman entered, alone. Everyone turned and stared, and she froze there, blinking behind her glasses until the audience members turned back to the stage. She scanned the rows, spotted one of the empty seats, and hurried to take it. She was clutching a single-page printout, too. One of her seat-mates craned his head to read it. It was different from the one he had.

The doors opened once more, another woman entered, and again the heads whipped around. This one wasn't rattled by their stares. She gave a cool stare back as she sauntered to her seat. She wasn't clutching a printout; hers was inside her Fendi bag.

A third woman entered on her heels, slipping in so unobtrusively that almost no one noticed her.

A loud click sounded, and all eyes turned front as the stage lights came on. Now the audience could see a panelists' table at center stage with two chairs behind it and a microphone set up at each chair. Off to stage right stood a lectern with its own microphone.

A louder click sounded, this one more like a pop and a clang, and the footlights came on to illuminate the nameplate on the lectern. It read RICK OLSSON, and the audience members buzzed with excitement as they realized that he was here for the same event. The camera might pan the audience, they whispered to one another; they might be on TV!

Another set of footlights switched on, and the panelists' nameplates were revealed: GEORGE BENEDICT at one chair and microphone; KELLY MCCANN at the other. The audience buzz grew louder. Their speculation was correct. This did have something to do with that trial that happened down the street, and it would probably be broadcast on the news tonight.

Abruptly the houselights went down, and a loud groan of disappointment rumbled through the auditorium. Because that was their exit cue. Their promised walk-ons had turned out to be nothing more than walk-in and walk-out. Frustrated, they rose from their seats and shuffled into the aisle and followed the dim ankle-level auxiliary lights to the exit. One by one they left the auditorium.

Kelly watched from backstage until the last one passed through the doors. Then she pushed a button on the control panel, and the stage lights shut off, plunging the whole auditorium into darkness. She pressed another button, and the houselights came up again.

Only the three late arrivals remained in the audience. They blinked at the sudden blaze of light and looked around in confusion at the empty seats all around them. Kelly picked them out, one after another: Ashley LaSorta. Emily Norland. Tiffy Jenkins. Her little ruse had worked. She'd drawn them out. The only no-show was Reeza Patel. At the last minute Kelly had decided to take a chance and add Reeza to the list. But it was a risky play. It was just as well that she hadn't taken the bait.

Kelly adjusted the scarf at her neck and the microphone on the lapel of her suit jacket, then took a breath and walked out onstage. She removed Olsson's nameplate from the lectern as she passed it. "He needs to be somewhere else," she said, her voice echoing loudly through the empty auditorium. She walked to the panelists' table and turned Benedict's nameplate over and dropped it with a loud clunk on the table. "And he needs to be destroyed." She pointed to each of the women in turn. "And I need the three of you to help me do it."

Ashley LaSorta surged out of her seat. "What the fuck is this?" she shouted. She stalked out to the aisle. She was dressed casually, probably in hopes of blending into the audience. Though in her skintight leggings and a one-shouldered sweater, she never would.

"Sit down," Kelly said. "Hear me out."

Now Emily Norland was on her feet. She, too, was dressed casually, in a cardigan and jeans. "This isn't a real program? I mean, I saw Rick Olsson out there . . ."

Tiffy Jenkins looked bewilderedly from one woman to the other. She was wearing a pink nylon smock with a company name embroidered in purple over her right breast: *Whistle-Kleen*. She must have planned to go straight to work after this.

"No, it's not real," Kelly said. "It was only a way to get the three of you together."

Ashley directed a suspicious glare at the other two women. "Who are they? What's going on?"

"They're his victims, too. Just like you. Just like God knows how many other women he's brutalized."

They looked at one another again. The question seemed to pass between them. *You, too?* A nod. *Me, too.*

"NDAs?" Ashley said, out loud, and when Emily and Tiffy nodded, she jabbed a finger up at Kelly. "You're not allowed to broadcast this!"

"You're right," Kelly said, and as she spoke, all three women made their way down the aisle until they stood below her. "I could be disbarred for this." Her voice was too loud now that they were so close. She unhooked the microphone from her lapel. "But he's a monster," she said. "And we need to bring him down."

"We?" Ashley repeated with a sneer.

"The four of us together," Kelly said. "Maybe we can't expose him as a rapist, but we can destroy his reputation and his fortune. He'll be a ruined man by the time we're through."

"Us, work with you?" Emily Norland said in a choked voice. "It's because of you that he got away with it. Because of the way you pressured and cajoled and took advantage—" She turned away with her hand over her mouth.

Kelly frowned. This particular accusation seemed unfair. She'd only pressured and cajoled Emily's husband. "You were all represented by counsel," she said. That was only technically true in Emily's case and barely at all for Tiffy, but neither one spoke up to contradict her. "You made your own decisions. We all did. Which is why it falls to us to do something about it."

"But what could we do?" Tiffy asked in a small voice.

Kelly gave her an approving nod. This was the right question. "We can destroy his reputation," she said. "By destroying his science."

Emily scoffed.

"Hear me out. He's world famous for curing Alzheimer's, right? But what if he doctored his results? What if he manipulated the data and none of it's real?"

"But it is real," Emily said.

"Because the records say so. Right?"

Ashley saw where she was going. "Records can be altered."

"Exactly," Kelly said. "If we had someone familiar with the information systems at UniViro"—she nodded at Ashley—"and someone who knows the science"—she nodded at Emily—"and someone who could get into his office to alter anything that's not in the company system"—her final nod went to Tiffy—"and then we leak the information to a well-placed journalist, Benedict will be totally disgraced. It'll be just like Elizabeth Holmes and Theranos. The SEC will go after him. He'll be indicted for fraud. The FDA won't approve the vaccine. His stock in UniViro will tank. He'll go bankrupt. He'll be utterly ruined."

They were silent, and Kelly fell silent, too, waiting for them to respond or question or even chip in with their own suggestions. She thought Ashley looked intrigued. Emily looked doubtful, as if she was searching for the flaw in the plan. Tiffy simply looked bewildered. "But— but isn't that hacking?" she said. "Isn't it against the law?"

"Yes!" Emily said. "We could go to prison for this!"

"Only if we're caught," Kelly said.

"What's this *we*?" Ashley said. "You're not the one doing the hacking. Your neck's not on the line."

"Not true," Kelly said. "If we're caught—we won't be, but if we were—I'd be named the ringleader. The instigator of the whole conspiracy. Add in the fact that I'm an officer of the court who used to represent Benedict, and I'd get a stiffer penalty than any of you."

They still looked skeptical, and Kelly realized she was too removed, too distant from them up on the stage. It was a four-foot drop from the edge of the stage to the floor below, but she hitched up her skirt and jumped and landed in an awkward crouch in the middle of their little circle.

Instantly, they fell away from her, like the crowd in a stadium wave. Ashley continued stepping away, backing up, her heels beating the sound of retreat on the auditorium floor. She stared at Kelly and her eyes narrowed. "This is a trick," she said. "A ploy. You're trying to get us to breach our NDAs so Benedict can claw back all the money he paid us."

"No. Trust me, it's nothing like—"

"Why should we trust you?" she said. "You're his fucking lawyer!" She raked her eyes over the other two. "You do what you wanna do. I'm outa here."

She strode up the aisle to the exit doors, and after only a second's hesitation, Emily and Tiffy turned to follow.

"Wait, please!" Kelly called after them. "You've got it all wrong. I'm not his lawyer anymore. I'll never represent him again!"

None of them stopped or looked back. The doors slammed shut behind them, and the sound echoed throughout the empty auditorium.

KELLY TALLIED THE cost at the airport while she waited for her flight to be called. Round-trip airfare and last night's hotel. The rental car. The auditorium rental. The booking fee to the talent agency, and the walk-on fees for the twenty-five would-be actors. The charter bus that delivered them to campus. The print shop invoice for the nameplates, the directional arrows, the mockup of event tickets for the three women. The internet service that emailed the manufactured press release to those women along with their tickets. A ridiculous expense for a ridiculous stunt, and all for nothing.

She shouldn't have been surprised. Those women had achieved their revenge already, in the form of cash. Or, if not revenge, then at least satisfaction. That was her mistake: imagining they had as much reason to hate him as she did. Kelly was the only one who still had this caustic swill in her belly. Now she was left with a choice. Either learn to live with it or figure out a way to do this on her own.

She couldn't do it on her own.

She would have to learn to live with it. She would have to figure out how to get over this. How to go on.

The airport loudspeaker crackled with an announcement from the gate agent. There would be a ten-minute delay in the departure of Flight 906 with service to Boston.

Kelly heaved a sigh and opened her laptop. There were a half-dozen emails from Rick Olsson, wanting to know why she didn't meet him on the campus as she'd agreed. His tone went from slightly worried to impatient to indignant at the end. She sent a brief reply. "I don't do interviews."

His reply zipped back, and she could almost hear his outrage: *I didn't even ask for an interview. You offered it!*

She didn't respond.

Five minutes later her laptop pinged with another email. *Look,* he wrote, *the reason I've been trying to reach you is that I came into some information that made me concerned for you. I wanted to make sure you were all right. I'm attaching a video file. Please watch it and call me.* The email ended with his cell number.

She rolled her eyes. She knew exactly what the video would be. A highlight reel of his proudest moment in interviewing. Snippets to show how respectful he always was, what rapport he developed with his subjects. She started to type: *Not interested—*

But she stopped and opened the file anyway. The video started to play, and instantly she saw that the setting was wrong. This wasn't a well-lit TV studio. It was outdoors, at night. On a tarmac? The sound was off on her laptop, so she didn't hear it coming, and she wasn't sure until the moment the skids touched down.

Her hand flew to her mouth. It was a helicopter, Benedict's company helicopter, landing at the heliport in Boston. She held her breath as the door swung open and Anton emerged. He reached back in, and Kelly threw a glance over both shoulders, terrified that someone else might be watching. No one was near, but she lowered her face until it was mere inches from the screen. Out came her body, her dress riding up high on her thighs, her limbs flopping wildly, her hair undone and tangled, her glasses askew and her head lolling back like a loose cannonball. The camera tracked Anton across the helipad to the waiting taxi. He opened the door and heaved her inside like a sack of cement.

The video ended there.

She slammed the lid shut on her laptop. *Oh my God, oh my God, oh my God*, she whispered to herself. Hot tears scorched her throat. It was worse than reliving the horror of that moment. It was reliving it and knowing that someone else had seen it, too. Someone else had recorded it. It felt like she'd been raped a second time. *Oh my God, oh my God, oh my God.*

She sat trembling for long minutes. Her fists were clenched and pressing hard on either side of the laptop, as if she could squeeze that video out of the processor. Out of existence.

Olsson was a journalist. He was a broadcast journalist. This video could be *broadcast*. In minutes it could be all over the airwaves. In hours it could go viral on the internet.

What to do, what to do.

She could deny it. She would deny it. That wasn't her in the video. She was somewhere else that night. No, it was her, but it wasn't what it looked like. She'd fallen ill. Food poisoning. It was nothing. People were carried off helicopters all the time.

The loudspeaker crackled again. *Attention, passengers. Shortly we'll begin boarding Flight 906 with service to Boston.*

Kelly looked up in a daze as the people around her rose from their seats and towed their rollaboards behind them to line up at the gate.

What to do, what to do?

She took out her phone.

Rick Olsson answered on the first ring.

"Where can we meet?" she said.

11

IT WASN'T YET FOUR WHEN Kelly arrived at the hotel bar, and most of the tables were still empty, so it was easy to spot Rick Olsson in the corner even before he stood. He was a pleasant-looking man with salt-and-sandy hair and crinkly eyes behind steel-rimmed glasses. He looked older in person than on TV. Closer to fifty than forty. He wore a button-down blue shirt with khakis, more like a suburban dad than a TV celebrity. She walked stiffly toward him.

"Rick Olsson."

He held out his right hand and pulled out a chair with his left. She ignored the hand and took the chair. He was a foot taller than she was; she needed to bring him down to her level from the start.

After a beat he sat down, too, and twisted around with his arm raised, but the server was already there, hovering behind him with a nervous smile on her face.

"What'll you have?" he asked Kelly.

"Gin and tonic." She didn't say *light on the gin* like she usually did. She needed a real drink.

The server nodded, though she was looking only at Olsson. "Another one for you, sir?" she asked.

He shook his head. His pilsner was still more than half-full. The girl backed away with a nervous giggle.

"Where did you get it?" Kelly said. No niceties. No preamble.

Olsson studied her for a moment before he answered. "There's a cameraman up at WBZ in Boston. Buddy of mine. He knows I follow Benedict, so when the UniViro chopper flew into the station's heliport, he filmed the landing and sent it to me. I was concerned after I recognized you."

But not before, she noted wryly. If he wasn't concerned for some anonymous woman, then he probably wasn't concerned for Kelly either. He was merely intrigued that there might be a story.

"I am so embarrassed." She placed her hand on her heart for dramatic effect. This was the script she'd prepared in the cab, and she had it down pat. "I've never been passed-out drunk in my life, and the first time had to be in front of a camera?"

A crease appeared above the rims of his glasses. "That's what it was? You were drunk?"

"Oh God," she groaned. "Was I ever. I don't know what came over me. Exhaustion, I guess. Relief that the trial was finally over. I had a couple drinks to celebrate right after the verdict. Then I polished off a split of champagne in the Uber. And *then* I helped myself to the minibar back in the hotel. By the time I got on the helicopter, I was totally smashed." She shook her head ruefully. "I am absolutely mortified that you saw that. I'd die if anyone else did. I mean, I have young children. Imagine them, seeing their mother like that."

"Huh." His eyes narrowed a bit. "I was afraid something else was going on."

She let out a tinny laugh. "As if that weren't bad enough!"

The server returned to their table with a highball glass festooned with an artfully spiraled lime zest. Kelly put her hands in her lap. After the tale she'd just spun, suddenly it didn't seem like a good idea to pick up her glass. The server took a step back and stood watching Olsson with an expectant smile until he said, "Thanks. That'll do it." He was used to fawning fans, Kelly imagined, and knew how to get rid of them nicely.

"How old?" he asked. "Your children."

"Fourteen and ten."

"Boys? Girls?"

"One of each."

"I have two boys," he said with a grin. "Fourteen and sixteen."

Somehow their discussion had veered off into family chitchat. She needed to bring it back on track. "I have to ask," she said. "Who else has seen that video?"

"Besides the cameraman? Only me and my producer."

"Can I ask you to keep it that way? You must understand. My children—"

He picked up his beer and eyed her over the edge of the glass. "You're sure nothing else was going on? When you didn't show up for dinner that night—"

"Wait." She sat back, blinking. "Where?"

"At the Benedicts' house."

"What makes you think I was there?"

"Because I was there, too, with the other guests. Mrs. Benedict told us that you and the doctor would join us shortly for cocktails, but we were already sitting down to dinner by the time he showed up. Without you."

"Oh. Well . . . I realized I'd had too much. I asked him to make my apologies to his wife."

"Maybe he did, but nobody said anything to the rest of us. And then when I saw that video—"

"You jumped to an outrageous conclusion." Kelly made her face stern. "May I remind you that Dr. Benedict was acquitted? He's been completely exonerated of all these libelous accusations."

Olsson raised both hands in an "I surrender" gesture. "Sorry. I've been hearing some rumors that made me wonder."

"I would have thought a journalist of your standing wouldn't pay attention to rumors."

"To the contrary." He smiled. "That's where leads come from. All you have to do is separate the wheat from the chaff."

"I can assure you—all those rumors are nothing but chaff."

He paused. "You've heard them, too, then."

"I was defending him from the worst of them. Successfully."

"Yes, I know." His smile deepened, carving marionette lines at the corners of his mouth. "Congratulations, by the way."

She inclined her head in an acknowledgment. "You're a friend of the Benedicts?"

"No."

"But you were at their party."

"Along with other people they're hoping to cultivate."

"Ah. So are you?"

"What?"

"Cultivated."

He gave a short laugh. "I'm a journalist. I have to remain objective."

"Even now that the story's over?"

He shook his head. "It's hardly over."

She gave him a pained look. "The jury said otherwise."

"I'm not reporting on the trial. I'm reporting on the science. The virus, the vaccine, the cure to Alzheimer's in our lifetime. If it's true, it's the story of the decade."

She watched him closely as she asked her next question. "And if it's not true?"

"If it's not?" He pulled a sad face. "There goes my book deal."

"Oh. You're writing a book." Now she did allow herself to reach for her glass.

He nodded. "Like I said, the story of the decade. Maybe the century. And one that I'm personally pretty invested in. See, I lost my father to Alzheimer's."

"Oh. I'm sorry."

It was after four by then, and the bar was starting to fill up with men and women in business suits. Some of them elbowed one another when they spotted Olsson from across the room.

He seemed oblivious to the interest he was stirring. "It's what we all fear, right?" he said. "Losing our memories, our personalities, everything that makes us who we are. Our dignity. Not to mention the huge societal costs of caring for people who can no longer care for themselves. Economic and emotional and every other kind of cost. Next to climate change, it's probably the darkest cloud hanging over the future of the human race. And nobody in medicine or science could offer us any real hope. Nobody until George Benedict."

"A real live hero," she said and took a second sip of her drink.

He frowned a little at the sarcasm in her voice. "You know the worst for me, personally? I lost *my* memory, too, of who my father was. He was a brilliant man, a physicist, but the image that's topmost in my memory? Him sitting in a circle at the nursing home batting around a yellow balloon. Once he could have graphed the aerodynamic properties of that balloon, but by then all he could do was swat at it while drool ran out of his mouth." His face folded as if he were seeing that tragic scene all over again.

"I'm so sorry," she said. "That must be an awful thing to live with."

He nodded, and with a blink, his eyes cleared again. "But maybe future generations won't have to. Thanks to George Benedict."

She felt a sudden twinge—almost a kick—as an unexpected thought surfaced. If her plan had worked, if she'd actually succeeded in mobilizing the NDA women to destroy Benedict, she would have destroyed the cure for Alzheimer's in the process. It was a sobering thought. It was one thing to stop watching movies or reading books created by a sexual predator, but it was something else entirely to destroy the hopes of the whole world.

A man in a suit and a half-loosened tie approached Olsson with his phone out. "Hey, sorry to interrupt," he said. "Huge fan here. Can I get a selfie?"

Olsson gave an amiable shrug. The man squatted beside his chair and clicked his camera. He scrutinized the photo and asked for a retake, and Olsson indulged him. When the fan finally got a shot he liked, he backed away, looking at Kelly now and apparently recognizing her. He returned to his table and went into a quick huddle with his colleagues as he pointed her out. She looked away. The idea was still gnawing at her, that by canceling Benedict, she would have doomed people to dementia. Maybe it was just as well that she'd failed.

Olsson was still holding forth. "Think of all the so-called treatments the medical establishment came up with before this. Use your left hand instead of your right. Walk backward. Learn a foreign language. That's all they had to offer. Even that new drug, Aduhelm, only promises to reduce the amyloids that are already there, and who knows? By then the damage might be irreversible. George Benedict was the only one who decided to look at what was causing that buildup in the first place. Prevention is better than cure, after all."

"Erasmus," Kelly murmured.

He gave a smiling nod of acknowledgment. "That's how he found the virus, and how he developed the vaccine. The results of Phase II were amazing. The preliminary results of Phase III look just as promising. When this vaccine goes into production, it'll be like the polio vaccine back in the sixties. People will line up around the block to get it. Can you imagine?"

"Wow." Kelly was also imagining Benedict pocketing his license fee from every one of those doses. "And UniViro will have the monopoly on all that."

Olsson shrugged. "On its own patented vaccine, sure. But the rest of Big Pharma will soon follow."

Her gaze sharpened. "They're working on vaccines, too?"

"They all feed off one another's work. Though of course UniViro has a huge head start."

A woman was hovering nearby with her phone out, waiting for an opening to approach Olsson. He didn't notice until Kelly pointed her chin that way. "Oh. Sorry," he said and waved the woman over for another selfie. He was a genuinely nice man, Kelly realized. It wasn't what she expected from a TV talking head.

She pretended to glance at her watch as the fan departed. "Look at the time," she declared. "I have a flight to catch." She pulled some bills from her wallet and laid them on the table.

"No, I got this."

"No, I insist." She got to her feet. He stood, too, rising far above her. She stepped close enough to whisper up to him. "May I ask you to destroy that video file and not mention it to anyone?"

"If I can ask you something first."

She lifted an eyebrow and waited.

"Why'd you stand me up at the college today?"

"Excuse me?"

"We were supposed to meet. In the quad at ten."

She shook her head as if baffled. "I'm afraid someone's been playing a prank."

He looked askance. "You didn't reply to my email and set up a meeting?"

"I did," she said. "To set up this meeting. Here. But nothing else."

"Hmm." He still looked doubtful. "Yes, I'll kill the video file."

He held out his hand, and this time she shook it.

THAT NIGHT THE Mom-and-Lexie book group started a new book. *The Phantom Tollbooth*. "It's like the wardrobe, isn't it?" Lexie said with a yawn. "You go through it, and there's a different world on the other side."

They talked a bit about Narnia versus the Island of Conclusions until Lexie's eyelids drooped, then Kelly kissed her goodnight and went for a run.

Her customary late-night route took her through nearby Regis College, where she could count on well-lit trails and campus police. But tonight when she reached the quad it reminded her too much of a different college campus and her abject failure this morning. Her elaborate setup had crumbled in an instant. The trip was a total bust.

She picked up her pace and ran faster out of the campus and up and down the residential streets. She recited a mantra while she ran. Not the usual one of *Keep on going, keep on going.* A new one: *Get through this, get through this. Go through the wardrobe, the toll-booth, get to the other side.*

She had to get past this. Her bruises had faded to yellow, her aches were mostly gone, and she knew now that she wasn't pregnant. She assumed that a medical doctor/bacteriologist/virologist wouldn't carry any STDs, and at any rate she had no symptoms so far. So that took care of all the possible physical consequences of Benedict's attack.

As for psychological consequences? She could control her mind. She could control her emotions, as much as she needed to, if she were to survive this. She'd done it before, after all, in the wake of another horrible tragedy. Well-meaning people told her it was the worst thing they could imagine happening to a young wife and mother, and later they told her she was the bravest girl they ever knew. She was still that brave girl—even braver, she hoped, now that she was older and wiser.

She finished her run with a final sprint to the house and in the back door and up the stairs. Lexie's room was dark, but the lights of Justin's video game flashed and strobed from beneath his door. She gave him the two-knock signal that she was back and would soon be ready to play *Overwatch.*

She continued down the hall to her room, where Adam seemed to be asleep. She turned off the CCTV camera, her go-off-duty signal to Todd, then peeled off her sweat-sopped clothes and headed for the shower. She returned to the bedroom in her robe and gave a quick glance to the camera. It was off, just as it should be, but something made her freeze where she stood. A memory was surfacing, another detail that she'd blocked from her recall, and the hot lava that had been roiling in her stomach suddenly calcified into bone-sharp claws. A green light, a camera on and recording, up high on the shelf beside the cat Jonas Salk.

A scream ripped from her body before she could jam her fist into her mouth to stifle it. He'd recorded her. He'd recorded his whole savage attack. He could watch it and relive it whenever he liked. He could be watching it this very minute.

"Mom?" Justin called from the hallway. "Everything okay?"

She took her fist from her mouth and sucked in enough breath to answer him. "I— I only stubbed my toe."

"Need some ice?"

"No— no, thanks, sweetie. I— I'm fine."

She had to press both hands over her mouth to keep from screaming again. She'd thought that Rick Olsson's video file was horrible, but this—*this*—was a thousand times worse. She knew she would never get past this. Not in a hundred years.

Let someone else develop the Alzheimer's vaccine. George Benedict had to be destroyed.

12

ALTHOUGH JAVIER SPENT LITTLE TIME in the office, he had a cubicle and a desk and a dedicated file bank in a remote corner on one of the lower floors. Kelly found her way there early the next morning. She knew he kept his own files on all their cases and submitted only selected materials to the official files. With Javi, everything was *Need to Know* or *Eyes Only*. He said he wanted to give her plausible deniability, but he didn't understand how the law of agency worked. She was responsible for everything he did in her name.

She sat down at his desk and opened the first file drawer. She needed to know what other guys might be in his stable. People who, for a fee, would do what she asked of them. If the NDA women wouldn't help her, she'd have to rely on hired help. Specifically, a hacker, a scientist, and a burglar.

She found a file labeled *Cyber*. Inside were photocopies of business cards. She recognized the name of Paul, the tech guy who came to the house the other day, which told her she was in the right place. She took out her phone and snapped photos of all the cyber-guy pages.

She opened the next drawer. Would Javi actually label a file *Burglary*? And would he even have a scientist among his guys?

"Help you find something?"

She looked up with a start. The seldom-seen-in-the-office Javier was standing over her. He wore a slight smirk on his handsome face.

"Oh! Hi. Yes, I'm looking for that file, you know"—she ad-libbed—"the movie star?"

"Tommy Wexford. Right. Patti has it, I think."

"Oh. Okay." She stood up and sidestepped out of his cubicle. "What brings you in today?"

"Same case." He slung his bag over the back of his chair and leaned over to power up his computer. He looked back at her. "We have that video call at ten?"

"Right." If she ever knew about that, she'd forgotten.

He straddled his chair and peered at the screen as it came to life. "Funny thing," he said.

"What?"

"Margaret Staley—Wexford's accuser?"

Kelly had trained every member of her team to refer to the complainant this way. Not victim. Accuser. "What about her?"

"Big-time lesbian."

"You're kidding."

"Nope." He continued scrolling through his email. "Has a long-time partner, and they're both LGBTQ activists."

"Jesus. Doesn't sound likely for her to be a Wexford groupie. Or—what did he call it? A stan."

"Well, I don't know if she was a fan, but she was definitely a stalker. Cyber, anyway. She's all over his social media. *Tell the truth. You're a fraud.* Like that."

"Huh."

"Anyway," he said. "My usual playbook probably won't work this time."

"No. Probably not." Javi's powers of seduction were considerable, but they had their limit.

BACK IN HER own office she opened her phone and studied the pages she'd photographed. There were five business cards of five different men, each listing some variant of cyber services. Paul of the no eye contact was one of them, and an obvious reject for her purposes. But another card got her attention. A card for Edward P. Russo, with an address in nearby Lowell. Slashed across it was a big red X, and she recognized Javi's handwriting beside it: *too shady*.

That was her man. She called him at once. It wasn't until the line was ringing that she thought to use a pseudonym. Her eyes fell on the ten a.m. slot on her desk calendar. "Hello, Mr. Russo," she said when a man answered. "This is Tammy Wexford. Can we meet?"

"What about." His voice was so rough it sounded like it scraped his vocal cords on the way out.

"Retaining your services."

"What's the target?"

"A research database."

"What kind?"

She hesitated. "Big Pharma."

"Hmm. Which one?"

She wasn't expecting such directness. "Let's talk first."

"Yeah. Okay. When and where?"

Noon, she said, and named a coffee shop with outdoor tables on a quiet side street nearby.

TOMMY WEXFORD WAS in Spain shooting a movie—a *motion picture* as he called it. Kelly gathered her team in the conference room, and Cazz worked her magic until the call connected and Tommy's face loomed large on the wall-mounted video screen. He was twenty-eight, but he looked like a teenager with his thin, almost ascetic face. He had pale skin and a thick flop of black hair tumbling over his brow that he kept out of his eyes with periodic tosses of his head. He wore a scarf triple-wrapped around his neck, despite the fact that he was sitting on a sun-bleached cliffside terrace overlooking the azure waters of the Alboran Sea. It must have been ninety degrees there.

The LA lawyer was on the call, too, but Cazz shrunk him into a little box at the bottom of the screen, and no one noticed him again.

Kelly began as she always did, with the worst-case scenario, a litany of all the evidence against the actor, viewed as unfavorably as possible. According to Margaret Staley, she was waiting tables at an LA café when Wexford left his table, followed her to a storeroom at the back, cornered her there, unzipped his pants, and demanded oral sex. She didn't know how to escape without physical violence, and she was too intimidated by his fame to hit him, so she submitted. He left her with lasting trauma, a searing image of his penis, and a semen stain on her shirt.

His pale face was flushed by the time Kelly finished. "It's a lie," he said. "She made the whole thing up."

"Any idea why?"

"How should I know?" His soulful eyes could look dead when he wanted.

Javi passed a note to Kelly. She nodded. "There's a witness who overheard the two of you having words at your table before the alleged incident," she said.

"She was stalking me! I told her to stay away from me!" Now Wexford's eyes sparked with anger. It was amazing, Kelly thought, how quickly he could change expressions. But then, she remembered, he was an actor.

"The witness heard you say, *Please, I'm begging you.*"

Back to dead eyes. "So?"

Kelly shrugged. "Seems a rather plaintive tone to use with a stalker."

He shrugged, too, as if mirroring her. He was wearing a muscle shirt that showed off well-rounded deltoids and a nice bulge of biceps on his arms. That must be the benefit of having a personal trainer, Kelly guessed—the ability to be slender and muscular at the same time. "What can I say?" he said finally. "I'm a polite guy."

"All right." She thought a moment. "Can you think of any way she could have obtained your semen? An ex, maybe? Who might have preserved a sample?"

He looked mortified at the very idea. "No!"

"Well, is there any way Staley could have seen photos of your nude body? Full frontal, I'm talking about. Sexting selfies, early modeling pics, anything like that."

"No," he said with equal firmness. "I've never done anything like that. I won't do nude scenes in my motion pictures either. You can check with my agent. It's in every one of my contracts."

Patti made a note of that. So did Javi.

"Then she's lying, both about your DNA and the birthmark."

"Yes! That's what I've been telling you. Or him. Whoever." He waved limply at the lawyer at the bottom of the screen.

"Good," Kelly said. "Then all we have to do is have a doctor examine you and take a DNA sample and this whole thing goes away."

His lips pulled tight. "This is such a fucking outrage," he said. "She lies, and I have to jerk off into a cup to prove it? No way. No fucking way."

"It doesn't have to be a semen sample," Kelly said. "A mouth swab will suffice."

"Oh." This clearly caught him by surprise. He looked off into the distance, out over the sea, she imagined. "I could do that, I guess."

"Good," Kelly said. Down in his box at the bottom of the screen, her LA counterpart did a little fist pump. "Then a doctor does the exam—"

Wexford's gaze shot back to the webcam. "No. No, I won't do it. Anybody can come along and make a false accusation, and I'm supposed to strip down and bare myself—*my soul!*—to disprove it?" A single tear wobbled on the edge of the lower lid of his right eye. "It's not right, and I won't do it. I just won't." As if on cue, the teardrop spilled out over his lashes and rolled down his cheek.

Kelly was not impressed, though she could see that a jury might be. "All right," she said. "No exam. We'll make arrangements for somebody over there to do the swab." She glanced at Cazz, who nodded; she'd figure out the logistics. "If the DNA doesn't match, that should end it."

"It won't match, I swear to God." Wexford looked off into the distance again, and the call ended there, with his tortured profile frozen on the screen until it finally went dark.

The team turned to face Kelly. This was what she called the gut-check moment. "First impressions?" she asked them.

"He's so gentle," Patti said. "I can't see him forcing anybody."

"Yeah, he doesn't have the cojones," Javi said, and Patti flashed him a smile, happy that he was on her side even if his route there was a bit different.

Cazz rolled her eyes.

"Go," Kelly said, pointing at her.

"I think he did it."

"Because—?"

"The pretty boys are the worst. That little trick he did with the teardrop? It's right out of their playbook. They sigh and make you pity them, then guilt you if you don't give them what they want. He totally did it."

Javi was watching her with a smile tugging at the corner of his mouth. "Cazzie's right," he said. "I'm changing my vote."

Patti looked stung. She turned to Kelly. "What do you think?"

"He's lying," Kelly said, and when Patti's face fell a little, she added: "I just don't know about what." She pushed back from the table. "Let's get the DNA swab and figure it out from there."

13

EDWARD P. RUSSO WAS TWENTY years older than she expected. Hackers were supposed to be high school kids, but he was older than she was. He had a jutting jaw and a gray brush cut. Add a headset and a windbreaker and he could have been a pro-football coach.

He was the only one seated at the coffee shop's sidewalk tables. He looked her over as she approached, a quick scan from head to foot, then a lingering look at her feet. He was studying her shoes, she guessed, which was the only way to assess her wealth in the absence of jewelry or a car. Could she afford him, he was wondering. She didn't know, but she was wearing good shoes today, and he gave a satisfied nod before he rose to shake her hand.

She was barely six feet away when she knew she'd made a mistake. She kept walking straight toward the door of the coffee shop. "Miss Wexford?" he called, and she shook her head no and joined the line at the *Order Here* counter.

What had she been thinking, to hire someone even Javi considered too shady to work with? She couldn't count on this man's silence. Even if she paid him handsomely, he'd be back with a demand for more, and she'd have to pay him again and again, on and on forever, every time he resurfaced with another threat to expose her.

There was a mirror behind the baristas at the counter, and in it, she could see Russo still on his feet, watching her as she shuffled forward in line. He took out his phone and pressed a single button, and she knew he must be calling the number she'd called him from. She bit her lip, bracing for the telltale ringtone from the handbag she clutched to her ribs. But her cell didn't ring, and with a wave of relief she remembered that she'd called him from the office phone. His return call would go to the main switchboard, with no way to trace it to her line. She watched his lips move in the mirror. He'd be asking the firm operator for Tammy Wexford, and she'd be answering that he had the wrong number.

She ordered plain coffee, black. That wasn't how she took it, but it would be the fastest route out of the shop. In short order, she paid, tipped, collected her cup, and walked out. Russo was back at his table by then, watching her through narrowed eyes. She kept walking down the block and didn't risk a look back until she was around the corner. There was no sign of him.

She tossed the cup into a trash receptacle and walked on, thoroughly disgusted with herself. Even apart from the money and the risk of exposure, it was a lamebrained plan, because she didn't know enough to execute it. She couldn't have told him what servers to breach at UniViro or what databases to target, or what content to add or delete. Without Ashley LaSorta and Emily Norland, it was never going to work. It was a fool's errand from start to finish, and she was clearly the fool.

From a block away, she spotted a crowd gathered in front of her office building. An unruly crowd from the looks of it, jostling and shoving one another in an effort to push through the revolving doors to the lobby. They had cameras and microphones, she saw as she came closer. She wondered what could have drawn the press here today. A member of the Federal Reserve kept an office in this building. Perhaps there was some breaking economic news. As she neared the entrance, she saw that the security guards were blocking the doors. She was fishing in her bag for her building pass when someone shouted: "There she is!"

Shouts and cries erupted from the crowd. They pivoted from the doors and closed in around her, shouting *Kelly* and *Ms. McCann* and thrusting their microphones in her face. She rocked back on her heels, but they were behind her, too, pressing in from all sides.

It had to be about Tommy Wexford. The news that she was representing him must have been leaked. Not by anyone on her own team, but maybe by her LA cocounsel. "No comment," she said and tried to push through the throng.

"Did you see this coming?" one reporter shouted.

"Do you hold yourself responsible?" called another.

"For what?" She knew better than to respond, but she was astonished by the question. She was responsible for a lot, but surely not for whatever Tommy Wexford did to Margaret Staley.

"Will this tragedy make you reevaluate the kind of work you do?"

"Tragedy?" She was baffled.

A security guard was beckoning her to come through, and she tried again to weave a path to the door, but suddenly she was blocked by a solid wall of bodies. People were pressing too close to her, and she couldn't see what was happening. Suddenly, an arm was around her shoulders.

"Back off!" a voice shouted close to her ear. "You know better than this. Show some scruples, people!"

She looked up into the face of Rick Olsson. "Get out of her way," he said, shielding her as he pushed past the reporters. "She's got no comment."

"Hey, Olsson! No hogging the story!" somebody shouted, but the crowd fell back as he hurried her past them and into the building.

The din died down the moment they cleared the door, but the faces were still there on the other side of the glass. Kelly turned to him in bewilderment. "What's going on? What are they talking about?"

Before Olsson could answer, Javier was there. "I got this," he said. He pushed Olsson aside and hurried Kelly to the elevator.

"What?" she said when they were inside and the doors were shut. "What's going on?"

Javi looked straight ahead when he answered. "Reeza Patel," he said. "She was found dead in her apartment this morning. Apparent opioid overdose."

Her breath stopped. "Suicide?"

"I'll find out," he said. But he also nodded.

A MONTAGE OF her cross-examination of Patel played through her mind that afternoon. She sat unmoving at her desk as the highlights unspooled. *You wanted to sue Dr. Benedict for wrongful termination, didn't you? You went to a lawyer, you asked for damages. But he told you you didn't have a case, didn't he? He told you Dr. Benedict had every right to fire you. And it was only after that conversation that you told your lawyer Dr. Benedict raped you? Isn't that right? It was only after you realized you weren't going to get any money the legal way.*

Kelly had conducted her entire cross from the lectern twenty feet away, but in her memory Reeza appeared in close-up, her lip trembling, the angry tears spilling from her eyes as Kelly pressed her point home again and again. It was no more brutal than any other cross she'd done of any other accuser, but it was still brutal. They were all brutal.

Her phone kept ringing throughout the afternoon, both office line and cell, from friends and foes alike, but mostly foes. She watched the names scroll by on her caller ID screen. The media, of course, with their endless requests for comment. Her stepdaughter Courtney, probably calling to accuse her of gender treachery again. Then an unexpected text from Justin: Not your fault, Mom. Her heart warmed at his sudden sensitivity, until she read the rest of his text. She was obv a nut job.

Patti appeared in her doorway, red-eyed and struggling to hold herself together as she offered some platitudes. "W-we couldn't have known," she stammered. "There was n-no way—" But her sob broke free, and she bolted away with her hand over her mouth.

Cazz came in soon after with a cut-glass tumbler holding two fingers of Scotch—she must have raided Harry's liquor cabinet. Kelly gulped it down, but she was too numb even to feel it burn down her throat.

Emails were pouring in, and she watched the senders' names scroll down the monitor with the same dazed detachment as she watched the caller ID screen on the phone. More reporters; more lawyers; Courtney again. She didn't open any of them until Rick Olsson's name popped up. *You okay? Call me.* He'd given her his number before, and now he gave it again. She called it.

"Kelly, are you okay?" he answered.

She didn't register his use of her first name beyond the fact that it sounded kind in his voice. "Thank you for saving me from that ambush," she said.

"Is there anything I can do to help? I'm in town for at least another day."

"Why are you? Here."

"Working on a story. A different story. When I heard the news, I thought you might need a friendly face. I didn't realize you'd be surrounded by a mob with pitchforks and torches."

"Your fellow journalists," she murmured.

"Different strokes," he said. "Listen, Kelly . . ." This time she did notice the use of her first name, but it sounded natural now. Normal. "This wasn't your fault."

"You don't know that."

"You don't know either. That's my point. You don't know what else was going on in her life. She could have had other problems. Maybe her boyfriend left her or somebody died or who knows what."

This was only a variant on what Justin tried to say in his text, but it sounded more politic in Olsson's kind voice. And something rang a bell. Other problems. She vaguely recalled a medical issue of some kind in Reeza's file.

"Maybe," she said.

"Look, if it was anyone's fault," he said, "it was Benedict's."

Obviously, but she couldn't let him believe it. "He was acquitted," she said.

"Because he was innocent? Or because he had a great lawyer?"

"Mr. Olsson—"

"Rick. And I withdraw the question. Can I do that, Counselor?"

She could hear his smile over the line, and it almost made her smile, too.

"Anyway, as I said, I'm in town. If you'd like to talk, or have dinner or something."

"Thank you, but I think I'll just lie low."

"Smart move," he said. "But call me if you change your mind. Or even if you don't. Call me."

LATE IN THE afternoon Javi came in and closed the door. He had a guy who knew a guy in the coroner's office in Bucks County, Pennsylvania, who gave him a quick lowdown. Reeza Patel was found in her Doylestown apartment that morning, dead of an apparent drug overdose. On the floor beside her was a prescription bottle for Oxycontin.

"She had back pain," Kelly said as the memory hit. "From a car accident?"

"Right," Javi said.

"Any chance it was an accidental overdose?"

"Always a chance," he said, but she could tell he didn't believe it either.

TODD CALLED AT four to let her know that a reporter rang the bell at the house. "But his bad luck—Bruce the Bruiser answered the door," he said with evident glee. The reporter beat a hasty retreat, and the coast had been clear since then. All was quiet.

Kelly glanced at the time. The kids would soon be home from school. She packed up her briefcase and was halfway out the door when her landline rang again.

Something made her go back to her desk and look at the caller ID. She picked up the phone so fast she nearly bobbled it in her hand. "Yes?" she blurted.

"Yes," Ashley LaSorta said. "Let's get this fucker."

14

ANYONE WATCHING WOULD HAVE GUESSED it was a girl-friends' weekend away when four women in four different cars arrived at the beachfront property. It was a four-unit condominium built on stilts fifty feet back from the dunes. The Porsche would have attracted the most notice as it pulled into the open parking beneath the units. The brunette driving it unloaded a Louis Vuitton suitcase along with a metal-clad case on wheels that looked like it must have contained state secrets or nuclear waste.

Soon after, two other cars pulled in and parked on either side of the Porsche, while the fourth car, a cab, pulled in without parking. A young woman got out of the cab with a battered backpack, while one of the older women, the blonde, came up to the driver's window to pay the fare.

But anyone watching would have wondered at the coolness with which these women greeted one another. Or didn't greet, really. Three of them lugged their bags into the elevator and turned in silence to face the doors as they closed. The fourth, again the blonde, had a trunkful of groceries that she was left alone to unload. Anyone watching would have thought this strange behavior for a girls' weekend away.

But no one was watching. Kelly felt certain of that. The season was over at the Jersey Shore, which was how she was able to snag this last-minute rental. That plus the fact that she asked to take the whole building. It had four units, two up, two down, each with a deck facing the dunes and, beyond them, the ocean. Each woman would have her own two-bedroom apartment. They'd agreed to work together, but it was too much to expect them to room together, too.

She'd first thought to do this at an isolated cabin in the woods, but internet service would be spotty there, and a good connection was the threshold prerequisite for their project. According to the online reviews for this beachfront building, the internet speeds were *primo*, a comment that came from a foreign currency trader who'd spent most of August there. The other selling point? The fact that the buildings on either side had recently been demolished to make way for even bigger and more lavish structures. They'd be nearly as isolated here as they would have been in that mythical cabin in the woods.

One of the units would have to serve as hub central, so that was the one Kelly took for herself—the top-floor apartment on the north side. The layout was the same in all units: an open living room and kitchen off the front deck, with two bedrooms and a bath off to the side. The decor was all the same, too: rattan furniture, cushions in blues and greens, and seashells everywhere.

While the others settled into their apartments, she unpacked the groceries in her kitchen. She'd assigned herself the role of cook, since she had little else to do this weekend. Hers was merely a supporting role in this play. She didn't even have any lines until Act Three. For now she could serve only as a facilitator. She would act like the moderator at a seminar: introduce the panelists and sit back to let them work.

She opened the sliders to the deck and went out to fire up the grill. The mid-October sun was warm enough to be welcome. She leaned over the railing, smelling the sea and feeling the salt breeze on her face, watching the wind ripple the dune grass. Then she turned her face to the sun while she checked in with Cazz at the office and Todd and Gwen at home. *Don't worry about a thing*, they all told her. *You deserve a vacation. Unwind. Relax.*

Tiffy Jenkins wandered into the living room, dressed in tiny denim cutoffs and an Eagles sweatshirt. "This place is so nice." She drifted to the bookcase and stood a moment, staring at the shelves. She didn't turn her head to read the spines, so Kelly knew that she was only attempting to look occupied. Tiffy had even less to do this weekend than Kelly did. She didn't know computers, and she didn't know science. She barely even knew what UniViro did. But she knew what George Benedict did, and her call to Kelly had come right on the heels of Ashley's and Emily's calls. *I'm in.*

"Anything I can do to help?" she asked, so Kelly set her to work chopping vegetables for the salad while she seasoned the steaks. She made zucchini boats, too, stuffed with quinoa and mushrooms in case anyone was a vegan, then took everything outside to grill. Tiffy set the table, and Kelly summoned the other two women and opened a bottle of red and a bottle of white and a bottle of sparkling water in case anyone didn't drink.

No one was vegan, and everyone drank. And drank.

They ate and passed dishes and refilled glasses in awkward silence. It was impossible to find enough shared interests to support an actual conversation. They were four women from four different walks of life. A lawyer, a microbiologist, an IT specialist, and a cleaner. They had absolutely nothing in common apart from their attacks and their payoffs, and the ground rules for the weekend declared those two subjects taboo. The details of their attacks were off-limits because this wasn't group therapy or a competition to see whose trauma was the worst. Their payoffs were taboo because the discrepancy in amounts was too great. Whatever solidarity they felt now would quickly vaporize if Emily and Tiffy learned that Ashley walked away a multimillionaire. There were enough differences among them without slapping price tags on their foreheads.

Every attempt at dinner conversation was a nonstarter:

Ashley: Internet speed's pretty good.

Emily: Lovely wine.

Tiffy: This place is so nice.

The meal was finally nearing its end when a ringtone broke the silence. They all lunged for their phones, both their own and the prepaid disposables they were using with one another. It was Tiffy's phone that was shuddering in her pocket. "Oh. Sorry," she said, checking the screen as she rose. She went out on the deck to answer, but before she closed the sliders, they could hear her say, "Hey, babe."

They should have looked away. They should have talked among themselves, about anything. But they had nothing to talk about, so they watched Tiffy instead. They watched how she twirled a finger in her hair, then how she suddenly tugged it a bit too hard. How she doubled over and hugged her ribs. How she rolled her head back and squeezed her eyes shut. And how she stood staring at the sea long after the call had ended.

She returned to the table with her eyes downcast. "Sorry about that."

"Trouble at home?" Ashley asked, getting right to the point each one was speculating about.

"Sean, my boyfriend." Tiffy picked at the remains of her salad. "I never been away from him before. I told him I was visiting my cousin. He gets jealous sometimes, and now he thinks I'm lying." She barked a little laugh. "Well, I guess I am. I made up a whole family I don't even got."

Kelly looked around the table. "Anybody else have trouble with their alibis?"

"Not me." Ashley tossed her head. "I answer to nobody."

"Emily? What did you tell your husband?"

"Nothing." Emily picked up her wineglass and stared at the dregs. "Since he's soon to be my ex-husband."

"Oh." Kelly flushed. She'd spent a few hours with the husband while they negotiated the NDA. He seemed a nice enough man. "I'm sorry," she said. "I didn't realize."

Emily glared at her. "Your investigator didn't update my file?"

"The dreamy Alejandro?" Ashley was glaring now, too. "That treacherous son of a bitch."

Kelly flushed hotter. Alejandro was the pseudonym Javi used on what he called his special assignments. Ashley had obviously figured out that the man who briefly romanced her was the one who'd unearthed her sex tape. Emily and Tiffy exchanged a puzzled look. They'd never met Alejandro; Kelly hadn't needed to use that particular dirty trick with either of them.

She hurried to change the subject. "What did you tell Sean about this cousin of yours?" she asked.

Tiffy lifted a skinny shoulder. "Not much. I said her name was Nancy and she was from Georgia like my mom was—my birth mom— and that she lived in New Jersey now with her husband and a bunch of kids, and that she wanted to meet me, you know, after all these years, to kind of make up for—I don't know." She shrugged again.

"That's it?"

"Yeah, I think so."

"Okay then. I got this. Call him back."

"Huh?"

"Tell him Nancy wants to say hello."

"Oh. I don't know—"

Tiffy looked frightened, but Ashley was grinning. "Come on. Let's see this."

Reluctantly, Tiffy pressed a button and passed the phone to Kelly. A man answered, spitting with anger. "I ain't fucking talking to you, you little bitch."

"Well, hey there, Sean," Kelly said in her most sugary drawl. "This here's Nancy. Tiffy's mama's cousin? I jest wanted to thank y'all for partin' with her this weekend. Means the world to my hubby and me to have her here and to get to know her a tad better. She really is a sweetheart, iddn't she? You're a lucky guy there, Sean, to have a honey like her. Maybe next time the both of y'all might could come for a little visit? Now you take care, Sean. You be good, ya hear?"

"Yeah, okay," he said, along with some other incoherent grunts of acknowledgment before she disconnected.

Ashley hooted when the call was over, and Emily applauded.

Tiffy still looked scared. "You think he fell for it?"

"Of course he did." Ashley stabbed her fork in Kelly's direction. "This is the woman who made twelve good people believe George Benedict was innocent."

Kelly could feel the hot stares of all three women, but this was nothing new to her. She stacked their plates and pushed them aside and spread out her notes. "Let's review," she said, and grudgingly the others pulled their chairs close and gave her their attention as she sketched out their work plan for the next day.

Ashley would set up her equipment and hack into the company's servers. She'd already tested the waters and confirmed that her successor at UniViro hadn't installed any new firewalls since she left. "Incompetent asshole," she muttered, but it meant she could easily penetrate the company's systems.

Emily would then access the files containing the raw data from the Phase I vaccine trials and decide where to manipulate the results.

Where the published reports claimed the vaccine had 95 percent efficacy, the raw data would now support only 62 percent. Where the published reports touted a percentage of experienced side effects at less than 1 percent, the altered raw data would show that 31 percent of the test subjects had experienced side effects. And where the published reports showed the worst of the side effects to be itching and a rash at the injection site, the raw data would now report eleven instances of severe anaphylactic shock.

If results like these had been published, the vaccine never could have gone to Phase II. It would have been declared a failure, and the project scrapped. But because it did go on to the next phase, Emily would target that raw data, too, and manipulate it the same way. Ashley would write the code to accomplish all of these changes, with a trigger that she would later pull to make them go live in the UniViro system.

They'd print out a few examples of the reconstituted test results—enough of a teaser to spark an enterprising journalist into searching for the fire that created such smoke. That was when Kelly would finally play her assigned role, a lawyer bound by the duty of confidentiality but suddenly racked by conscience. She'd search out a likely journalist, extract a promise of anonymity, and leak the documents.

As soon as the journalist ran with the story, as soon as it was fact-checked with an audit of UniViro's databases, George Benedict would be exposed as the biggest fraudster in the history of the pharmaceutical industry. He'd be the Bernie Madoff of bioscience, a man who duped investors out of millions of dollars and shamelessly exploited the hopes of the whole world.

Around the table, the women looked at one another and slowly nodded their agreement.

KELLY EXPECTED EVERYONE to retreat to their separate apartments after that, but Tiffy insisted on helping with the dishes, and

Ashley and Emily settled into chairs in the living room with another bottle of wine. Ashley switched on the TV and started flipping rapidly through the channels. "What the hell are the stations here?" she kept muttering until she finally landed on whatever channel she was searching for. "What time is it?" she called to the room.

"Almost nine," Emily answered.

"Perfect." Ashley turned up the volume.

Kelly listened to the audio while she put away the leftovers. It sounded like a TV newsmagazine or a special segment on one of the cable networks. The opening story was about the California wildfires. She glanced into the living room and saw clouds of smoke on the screen and Ashley watching intently with her elbows on her knees. She remembered then that Ashley used to work in Silicon Valley. "You have friends in harm's way?" she called.

Ashley ignored her and kept her eyes fixed on the TV.

It was futile, Kelly thought, turning back to the sink, to expect any kind of pleasantries from these women, or even civil discourse. Just because they had a common enemy didn't mean they were ever going to be friends. Her only role here was to cook and pay the bills.

She was loading the dishwasher, sliding plate into slot, when a voice from the TV made gooseflesh rise on the back of her hand. ". . . will revolutionize the aging process." A flat, unmodulated voice like a robot. Instantly acid lit fire in her belly.

"Ha!" Ashley cried and turned the volume up again.

"Oh my God," Emily said.

Tiffy turned from the sink, and finally, slowly, Kelly turned, too. On the screen was George Benedict, seated on a sofa with his wife, Jane, beside him.

"How'd you know he'd be on?" Emily asked.

"I set up a Google Alert," Ashley said, then, "Ssshh!"

Tiffy scurried across the room and sat cross-legged on the floor in front of the TV.

Kelly shuffled slowly closer. Video clips played while a voice-over talked about the discovery of the virus that was linked to Alzheimer's. Here was Benedict wearing a lab coat and looking through a microscope. Here he was lecturing to an overflow class of medical students. And here he was with Jane touring an Alzheimer's nursing home, bending to murmur to the glassy-eyed residents, laying hands on their shoulders. The broadcast cut to a series of still photos: Benedict as a boy with a chem lab set, as a teenager at Harvard, as an intern at Mount Sinai. His wife was given the same memory-lane treatment: a photo of her as a child bandaging a beagle's paw; another of her as a young woman smiling proudly during the pinning ceremony at nursing school; and finally, their wedding photo, Jane in an ecru lace dress, George in a gray suit.

The next video played, and Kelly felt a jolt when she saw herself on the courthouse steps, utterly jubilant, her face glowing with triumph as she swept an arm back to present Benedict to the crowd. She watched it now with her stomach heaving. She was afraid she might vomit.

The next image on the screen was of Reeza Patel, a serious young woman with big dark eyes looking quizzically at the camera. The image held for a full thirty seconds before the broadcast cut back to the Benedicts on the couch.

I do regret it, Benedict was saying. *She was a gifted young scientist with so much to offer in her field.*

Yet you fired her, the interviewer said.

For personality reasons only. She couldn't accept constructive criticism. It made it difficult for her team to work with her.

The poor girl, Jane Benedict put in. *We all knew she had . . . issues . . . but I don't think any of us thought she was this troubled. I mean, HR would have referred her to a psychiatrist, wouldn't they, dear?*

She laid a hand on Benedict's knee, which he seemed to ignore.

I blame the government prosecutors, he said. *They encouraged her in this fantasy. Then when the reality of the jury verdict struck, she couldn't accept it.*

The poor girl, Jane said again with a sigh.

The segment ended, and the broadcast cut to a commercial. Ashley switched off the TV, and the four of them stared at the blank screen for a long time.

Ashley was the first to speak. "That motherfucking son of a bitch."

"He's a monster," Emily said. "He's an absolute monster."

Tiffy's gaze darted between the two of them as she waited her turn to speak. "He gets away with it. He always gets away with it."

Ashley looked at the ceiling and hissed out a long breath through her teeth. "He always will. He's got more money than God, and the whole world bowing at his feet."

Emily's mouth twisted. "While he treats women like toilet paper."

"Guys like that, who . . . who . . . ," Tiffy struggled to find the words for a minute before she gave up with a sigh. "They always win. They always will."

"No," Kelly said, then louder, fiercely, as she circled around to face them. "No!" Now she knew what her true role was this weekend. More than cook, more than moderator, she would be their cheerleader, their motivator-in-chief. "This time we win," she said. "We're going to stop him. We're going to stop him by destroying him and everything he values."

Ashley's eyes narrowed to slits. "You had your chance," she said. "But you defended him. You enabled him. You set him free to do it again. This"—she swept her arm in a gesture that took in the other two women as well as the darkened TV screen—"this is all on you."

Kelly bit her lip. "You're right," she said. "And you have no idea how much I regret it. That's why I'm doing this—"

"You must have known Reeza was telling the truth," Emily said. "After dealing with the three of us. You knew what he was capable of."

"I know—"

"But it's really on all of us, isn't it?" Tiffy said. She looked from Ashley to Emily and back to Kelly. "I mean, on me, anyway. If I'da went to the police . . ."

She didn't finish her thought.

Ashley refilled her glass and Emily's, and after Tiffy fetched fresh glasses for herself and Kelly, Ashley tipped the bottle into their glasses, too. They drank in an uneasy silence.

"I have nightmares," Emily blurted. She threw a defiant look at Kelly. "I know we're not supposed to talk about what happened to us, but we can talk about the aftermath, can't we? I have nightmares."

"Me, too," Tiffy said. "Sometimes."

"I have them all the time. I'm in a hotel room—well, never mind the details. But I can't go on business trips anymore. If we'd held this weekend in a hotel? I wouldn't have come. And my marriage, the reason it fell apart—our sex life ended. Every time he touched me, I fell apart."

"That's classic PTSD," Ashley said. "My therapist gave me some techniques to deal with it."

Emily made a face. "Mine did, too. We . . . I have a spa on the back deck, and I soak in it every night after work. It helps with my muscle aches, I suppose, but not with the nightmares."

"My therapist gave me a visualization exercise."

"Like what?" Emily scoffed. "Waterfalls and puppies?"

Ashley shook her head with a coy smile. "I visualize myself putting on my favorite, thigh-high boots. The ones with the six-inch stilettos."

The other women nodded. Tall boots were a familiar symbol of power—they could see that.

"And then I stomp all over his face," she finished.

Their jaws dropped before they all sputtered out astonished laughs.

Kelly enjoyed the image as much as the rest of them, but she couldn't add to this discussion of PTSD. She couldn't say *me, too*, because she hadn't felt any of those symptoms, at least not since she embarked on this quest for revenge. That was the secret, she felt certain.

Don't get mad, and for God's sake, don't get weepy. Get even.

15

KELLY WOKE IN THE NIGHT to a thunderous pounding on her apartment door. She bolted upright in bed. The pounding sounded again but muted this time, as if it were farther away. Then it sounded again, close by. She ran through the darkened living room and put her eye to the peephole. Emily was outside, in her pajamas. She looked wild-eyed. She must have had one of her nightmares, Kelly thought, and she threw the door open. "What is it? Are you okay?"

"Get up! Get up!" Emily cried as she ran across the landing to pound on Ashley's door again.

"What the fuck?" Ashley came out in a black satin nightgown with her hair in pink foam rollers.

Emily swiveled back and forth on the landing between them. "We got it wrong!" she sputtered. "We got it all backward!" The words seem to burst out of her. "Because the vaccine *does* work! It *is* effective against the virus, and all he'll have to do is repeat the trials to prove it. It'll slow him down, but it won't ruin him."

"But it'll look like he falsified the earlier test results," Kelly said. "He'll be disgraced—"

"No," Ashley said. "He'll be exonerated. He'll say he was hacked, and eventually he'll be proven right."

Kelly felt the air leave her lungs, and, with it, everything that had kept her going these last few days. It was true. Emily was right. She sank against the stair railing, her body heavy with defeat. She was stupid to have made herself the architect of this scheme. Her genius for trial strategy didn't translate into even moderate competence for anything else. She didn't know science—computer or biology or whatever else this plan required. All of this work, all of this striving, all for nothing.

Emily was still pacing across the landing. "But here's the thing," she said. "There's a better way!"

With a start, Kelly realized that Emily wasn't wild-eyed with fear. This was excitement.

Ashley realized it, too. "Get in here," she said and waved them into her apartment. Kelly belted her robe and followed Emily in, and after a minute Tiffy came up, too, wearing only a T-shirt and panties. They sat down in Ashley's beach-themed living room, but Emily stayed on her feet, pacing as she spoke, from the front deck to the rear kitchen and back again.

"He's a hero because he cured Alzheimer's, right? Well, who says?"

"You," Ashley pointed out, pained. "You just said the vaccine works. It kills the virus that causes Alzheimer's."

"Ha! But there's the fallacy. It's effective against the virus, all right, but who says that's what causes Alzheimer's? Let's back up and examine his first great breakthrough. Aha! he says. Here's the virus that causes the buildup of amyloid proteins in the brain. But think—how did he know that?"

Kelly searched her memory. "Wasn't it—didn't he test people with Alzheimer's and find the virus in their systems?"

"Sure, but guess what? There are over 380 *trillion* viruses in the average person. It's the human virome. We all carry the common cold virus, too. Who's to say *that's* not the one that causes Alzheimer's?"

"Wait," Ashley said. "I remember this. He did studies. He injected the virus into rats whose brain scans were normal, then did scans six months later and they had plaque buildup."

"But—" Emily said, "what if they were going to develop plaque anyway? It's the causation versus correlation trap."

"There must have been a control group," Kelly said.

"Sure. And most of those rats didn't develop any plaque. But here's the thing: one of them did!"

"What does that mean? That there's more than one cause?"

"Maybe. Or maybe the virus doesn't cause the protein buildup at all. Its presence is merely correlated with whatever does cause it."

"Okay," Ashley said slowly. "So we leak the info about that one rat? And throw his whole hypothesis into doubt?"

Emily shook her head rapidly from side to side. She was too jacked up to answer in words, so Kelly did it for her.

"Why stop at one?" she said.

WORK BEGAN IN the morning. Ashley sauntered in at eight wearing a tropical-print bikini and a side-knotted sarong that rode low on her hips. She rolled her steel-sided case behind her like a well-trained dog. Inside was her equipment, which she painstakingly set up on the dining room table. She established a connection through an anonymous proxy server in Ukraine, while the others watched in wide-eyed wonder, as if she were a shaman performing some mysterious ritual. In minutes, she was inside the UniViro system.

She accessed Benedict's calendar first, and somehow it was a comfort to all of them to know where he would be at any point in time. Then she reached the heart of the matter: the rat studies. Emily sat beside her at a separate monitor and studied the data. She hadn't been involved in this research—"This was all Reeza," she said—and much of it was new to her. She'd need some time.

Kelly made a pot of coffee, assembled a bagel and lox platter, and stayed busy refilling cups and replenishing plates. Ashley peeled off her sarong, smoothed on some sunscreen, and went out onto the deck to bask. Tiffy tried and failed to make herself useful and finally went for a long walk on the beach.

Hours passed. Kelly switched from bagels and coffee to sandwiches and iced tea. Tiffy came back then went out again.

At last Emily declared she was ready. Ashley rewrapped her sarong and returned to the table. Emily identified the data to be altered, and Ashley set to work. But barely fifteen minutes later, she stopped and threw up her hands. "It won't fucking work!" she shouted. "I should have remembered! This can never work!"

Kelly froze where she stood, halfway across the room with a pitcher in her hands. "Why not?"

"He keeps a backup. Off-line. His fail-safe." Ashley raked her hair back from her face. "He'll have all the original data there, with metadata showing when it was entered."

Emily looked up from her screen. "You mean . . . he'll be able to prove he was hacked?"

"Exactly."

Emily slumped in her chair as Ashley pushed to her feet and began pacing through the room.

Kelly didn't move as the cold condensation from the pitcher seeped through her fingers and left them tingling. That meant that Benedict wouldn't be exposed as the villain in this drama. He'd be the victim. It would be the Reeza Patel trial all over again.

She couldn't let that happen. She set the pitcher down and wiped her hands dry. "Where does he keep this backup computer?"

"Computers," Ashley said, emphasizing the plural. "Belt and suspenders. A laptop at the office and another one at home."

Kelly thought a moment. "Security cameras?"

"In his office? No. I don't know about his home study. But what difference—?"

"Can you write a program to make the same changes on his laptops that we're making to the company database?"

Ashley rolled her eyes. "Don't you get what *off-line* means? I can't access his laptops remotely."

"Then let's not do it remotely."

Ashley stopped her pacing and glared at Kelly. "You don't get it. Someone would have to physically go to his home and office and overwrite those files to sync with the company database."

"I get it," Kelly said. "Now, can you write the code to do that?"

SHE WENT LOOKING for Tiffy while Ashley set to work.

She knocked on her apartment door first, and then, when there was no answer, set out across the dunes. This stretch of beach was nearly deserted, and she spotted Tiffy fifty yards down the coastline. The young woman was on her knees, vigorously ruffling the fur of a big black dog on a leash. On the other end of the leash was a middle-aged man in a windbreaker. Kelly jogged over the path through the dunes and around the tide pools and down the beach. By the time she arrived, the man and dog were gone. Tiffy was sitting on her Eagles sweatshirt with her chin on her knees, gazing out to sea.

She smiled up at Kelly. "It's so nice here," she said.

"Who was that?" Kelly looked at the man now fading into the distance along the coastline.

"Just a guy with a sweet dog. Don't worry, I didn't tell him anything."

Tiffy wore a tank top that left her arms exposed. Bruises in the shapes of fingers appeared on both upper arms. Kelly started to say something, but time was short. "We need you," she said instead, and Tiffy clambered to her feet and snatched up her sweatshirt to follow Kelly back to the house.

THEY HAD A new plan. Ashley wrote the code to make Emily's changes, but she didn't go live with any of them. Instead, she wrote code that would sync those changes with Benedict's local storage, and all of it would go live at the same time. Wednesday at five o'clock, they decided. Benedict's calendar showed he'd be in a meeting in Atlanta then, so Tiffy could access his office.

The tutorial took the rest of the afternoon and a few hours into the evening, too. First Ashley had to teach Tiffy how to use the password-cracking program to get into Benedict's office laptop, then how to execute the data-overwrite program. Tiffy wasn't a regular computer user, and she was slow to learn and easily confused. She kept at it, though, even when Ashley threw up her hands and walked away. "She's our weakest link," Ashley railed, while Tiffy bit her lip and tried again.

By ten o'clock that night, Tiffy seemed to have it down. Kelly uncorked a bottle of champagne, and they raised their glasses to one another. "Here's to the destruction of George Benedict," Kelly cried.

They all chugged back a swallow.

"Here's to Reeza," Emily said in a quieter voice, and they drank more slowly to that.

It was done. In the morning they'd have a leisurely breakfast, pack up, and set out for their respective homes.

AT TWO A.M., Kelly bolted upright in bed. Something Emily had said—four words were looping through her mind—*This was all Reeza*, and she thought, *Why not make it so?*

She turned on all the lights in her apartment and ran barefoot across the landing to pound on Ashley's door. "Get up! We did it wrong! There's a better way!"

She ran downstairs and pounded on Emily's and Tiffy's doors shouting the same message. "We did it wrong! There's a better way."

They all gathered outside Ashley's apartment, since she was the last to emerge. "What the fuck now?" she groaned.

"What's he famous for?" Kelly said. "Besides rape."

"Curing Alzheimer's?" Tiffy said.

"Go back," Kelly said. "Earlier."

"Identifying the virus that maybe causes Alzheimer's," Emily said.

"Yes! So what if he didn't?"

"If he never ID'ed it? Then I guess we never develop the vaccine, we never cure Alzheimer's—"

Kelly shook her head wildly. "No, no, no. I mean—what if *somebody else* discovered it?"

Ashley cocked her head. "You mean, like he stole somebody's research?"

Tiffy got there first. "Reeza!" she said.

Kelly nodded. "Let's go back to the early virus research and dummy up some documents to make it look like Reeza was the one who actually discovered the virus."

"Strip away all his glory," Ashley said.

"But without sacrificing the science," Emily said. "It's perfect. Besides," she added. "Who can say Reeza wouldn't have discovered something equally momentous? If she hadn't died."

"If he hadn't raped her," Tiffy said.

Ashley crossed the landing to fetch her equipment.

BREAKFAST SUNDAY MORNING wasn't as leisurely as they'd planned. Ashley had to hack into UniViro again, into a different database, and Emily had to sift through the files to identify the key lab notes and reports from the early virus research. Then Ashley wrote the code to change the initials on every note from GB to RP, and the author name on every memo from George Benedict to Reeza Patel. Ashley hummed as she worked, and Kelly hovered behind her, practically glowing with how perfectly it was coming together.

Until Ashley sat back suddenly. She shook her head. "Nah, this won't work. If he actually did this? Stole her work? He wouldn't let her ID stand on all these notes. That would be a dead giveaway. He would have overwritten his own."

She was right, of course, and Kelly almost screamed with frustration. She walked away with her hands raking her hair. Every idea she'd come up with had ended in a roadblock.

"Cool your jets," Ashley said. "I have a solution." She'd leave the documents as they were, she explained, but manipulate the metadata behind each one to show Reeza as the original author with Benedict coming in later and editing the files to make himself author.

"You can do that?" Kelly asked.

Ashley rolled her eyes. "Of course I can."

"Yes! That's even better," Emily said. "A digital trail to make it look like he stole her work and falsified the records to cover it up."

"You pass the so-called originals to your reporter," Ashley said to Kelly. "He confronts George, who says *how dare you* and *these documents are a fraud* and *here, take a look at the company's records*. That's when the metadata comes out. Making him look like a thief *and* a liar."

Kelly exhaled. "Okay," she said.

HER OWN CONTRIBUTION came next. She'd spent the last few months studying everything written and spoken by both George Benedict and Reeza Patel. She knew their voices as well as anyone— what tones they'd use, what words they'd choose. Reeza was tentative, self-deprecating, but always earnest. Benedict was by turns critical and praising, and always condescending. She captured those voices in a series of fictitious emails: from Reeza to Benedict discussing her identification of the virus; from Benedict to Reeza alternately questioning and complimenting her work; and finally, inevitably, from Benedict to Reeza attaching a draft of the announcement of *his* discovery of the virus *for all the reasons we discussed.*

Emily edited the emails for scientific accuracy, and Ashley wrote the code that, when triggered, would embed those emails in the Uni-Viro system. Again, though, Benedict wouldn't have allowed them to remain where anyone could find them, so she created a file accessible only by him and moved the fictitious emails there, but with footprints left behind to show that emails to and from Benedict and Reeza on those dates had been deleted from the system. More evidence to paint him as having covered up his theft.

It was almost noon by the time it was all done. They toasted one another again, with orange juice this time. "Justice for Reeza," they said.

Kelly raised her glass, too, but she didn't join in the refrain. She was remembering a line from Adam's favorite movie: *That is not justice,* the Godfather told the undertaker. *Your daughter is still alive.* This wasn't justice for Reeza, Kelly thought. She was still dead.

This was justice for George Benedict.

AT FOUR THAT afternoon they congregated in the garage. Their luggage was packed, the units were locked, the road beckoned. They stood in a circle and marked the date and time on their calendars. Wednesday at five p.m.

"Go Time," Ashley said.

"D-Day?" Emily suggested.

"V-Day," Kelly said. "V for Victory. The day we win."

Ashley handed over the thumb drives to Kelly and Tiffy. "Don't lose them," she said with a hard look at Tiffy. "And remember—you text Emily the minute you're done."

"I got it. I promise," Tiffy said.

They lingered another moment in their circle, but there was nothing more they could do. Nothing more they could say. They peeled off to their cars. Emily paused at her open door, one leg already inside. "This is goodbye, I guess. We'll probably never see each other again."

"Nope." Ashley settled behind the wheel of the Porsche and started the engine with a roar. "No reason to."

Tiffy slid into Kelly's car for the ride to the bus station. "Thank you for inviting me," she said. "I had a really nice time."

16

Tiffy Jenkins

BY WEDNESDAY AFTERNOON THE SWELLING had gone down mostly, but the red mark around my eye socket was turning purple and Sean still weren't home. He stormed out at two in the morning, which was when the bars was closed, so I didn't know where he coulda gone. Cooling off/sleeping it off in his truck was what I was hoping for, but crashing with that girl Kylie was what I was afraid of.

I leaned in close to the bathroom mirror. I could hide the bruise with sunglasses on the bus, but I couldn't keep them on at work. People might notice. I never much liked people to notice me, ever, but especially tonight. I needed to be invisible tonight.

I patted on some foundation around my eye until the bruise looked more grayish than purple. Like I had a smudge of soot on my face. That oughta work. Nobody would take much notice of a cleaner with a smudge of dirt on her face.

I recited the steps again. Ashley made me go over them so many times that I knew them by heart now. *Close the door partway. Put on the gloves. Find the laptop. Turn it on. Stick in the first little thumb drive thingy. Type in the first command.* That part was too long to remember, so I had it wrote down on a slip of paper in my jeans pocket. *Wait for the password to unlock it. Take out the first drive and put in the second. Type in the second command. Wait for the word*

Complete. *Take out the second drive. Turn off the computer and put it back on the bookshelf. Take off the gloves. Get back to work.*

Tonight I could skip the first step because last night I already scouted out where Dr. Benedict kept his laptop. He was there in his office when I went in for the trash, talking on the phone with somebody—somebody important, I could tell, because he sounded a lot nicer than he usually did. I pretended I was having trouble opening a fresh plastic liner, and that gave me time to sneak a look around. He didn't seem to notice me looking. He never ever noticed me except that one time. I spotted his suitcase first, by the door, and that was good, it meant he was still going out of town like we was counting on. Then I spotted the laptop up high on a bookshelf. I memorized where it was. I felt pretty proud of myself for that part. Saving a step meant I was gonna save some time. *In and out*, Ashley kept telling me. *You need to be in and out.*

You got this, I told my face in the mirror, and for half a second I believed it. But then I thought about Sean again and knew I couldn't do nothing right.

It was so stupid, leaving the mail laying on the kitchen table like that. But I was running late yesterday, and Sean was already out in the truck leaning on the horn for me to get a move on, so I ran out without looking through it. Without slipping that one piece of mail in my pocket like I usually did.

It weren't like it was a love letter or nothing. It just looked like a bill with my name and address showing through the little window. Sean never opened the bills. There was no reason for him to rip open this envelope. But last night he did. Then probably stood there with his jaw hanging open when he seen what it was. A bank statement showing a balance of twenty thousand dollars plus a few dollars more in the interest they added on over the year.

He didn't pick me up at the bus stop after my shift. I shoulda guessed right then there was trouble. But I was stupid about that, too. I walked home in the midnight dark and into the trailer and right into his fist.

He totally bought the Cousin Nancy story when Kelly called him, but not no more. Now he was sure I was cheating on him. That I'd spent the weekend fucking another guy. That the money was from my new boyfriend.

Like I'd ever get the kind of boyfriend who'd give me $20,000 just like that.

I shoulda told him everything back when it happened. But I knew he'd turn it around and make it out to be my fault that Dr. Benedict did what he did. That I came on to him or something. That I got what was coming to me. I was afraid he'd call me a whore. He did that anyway, sometimes.

And sometimes I was afraid it really was my fault. Like my jeans were too tight or I looked at him the wrong way.

So I never told Sean or nobody else neither. It was only gonna come back on me. I learned that lesson back when I was fourteen and living with the Robersons. They were good people, and they were nice to me, mostly. Until I told them what Larry was doing to me after lights out. They called in the social worker who made me sit with her for an hour and think about what was real and what was made up and why I might be having trouble telling things apart. She wanted me to take it back, and when I wouldn't, all the adults put their heads together and decided that since Larry had been a *difficult placement* and seemed like he was doing better with the Robersons, he should be the one to stay and I should be the one to go. So I had to up and move again, dragging a garbage bag of all my stuff behind me.

I knew the same thing would happen if I told anybody at work what Dr. Benedict done. And I couldn't afford to lose my job, not since Sean's unemployment ran out. And it never even crossed my mind to tell the cops. What would be the point? Cops never believed girls like me.

Then out of nowhere, a stranger showed up on my doorstep. He was Mexican or Puerto Rican or something, and so handsome I was scared of him. He asked me all kinds of questions, and I was afraid not to answer. Then the next day another man came by and said he was my lawyer and Dr. Benedict wanted to make amends and how did twenty thousand dollars sound?

It sounded like he was bullshitting me. But the more he talked, the more it started to sound like it was real. I said of course I'd keep quiet and sign the paper. I'd been keeping my mouth shut all along, for free. Taking twenty thousand dollars to keep on doing it was a total no-brainer.

That check seemed like some kind of miracle. Like something that happened in the movies. I went straight to the bank and opened a savings account, and when I handed the check over, they looked at me funny and made a phone call. But the check was good, and I walked out feeling like I was a different person. I was a girl who never had much to call my own, but now I did.

That shoulda been the end of it. I could put the whole thing right out of my mind, and I mostly did. Until the Reeza thing happened.

If he did it to somebody else, somebody smart and almost as important as him, then it couldn'ta been my fault. I wouldn't have nothing to be ashamed of. I gobbled up the news stories about the case, and on the day they said the jury was coming back, I couldn't resist it. I hopped on a bus going the wrong way and stood there with the crowd to hear the good news. And even though the news turned out bad, I still couldn't resist. When I got that ticket in my mailbox, I just had to take the wrong bus again. I weren't even sure what a *panel discussion* was, but I needed to hear it anyway.

That was probably the day Sean first started getting suspicious, when I made up a lame excuse for where I'd been. But I couldn't tell him about the Reeza case without telling him why I was so interested.

It was stupid of me. Now that he knew about the money, and that

I was keeping secrets from him, of course he was gonna believe the worst. Of course he was gonna get mad. The only way I could see around it was to tell him everything, beg his forgiveness, and give him the money.

If he ever came back. If he didn't decide to stay with that Kylie girl instead.

I finished my face and looked at the clock. Without Sean to drive me, I had to walk to the bus stop, so I knew I'd better get going. I couldn't be late today. I had to be at Benedict's office at exactly five minutes to five.

I went into the bedroom to wriggle into my jeans, lace up my sneakers, and pull on my smock. *Whistle-Kleen.* The company name always bugged me. What was so clean about a whistle? Or were we supposed to whistle while we cleaned? And why was *clean* spelled wrong?

Then I went back to the bathroom mirror for one last look. There was still a shadow there under my eye, but it would have to do.

I was reciting it one more time—*Put on the gloves. Turn on the laptop*—when I heard the knob rattle on the front door.

Sean was home! That meant he weren't with Kylie. He might not be drunk. He might even be sorry.

I gave the mirror a grin and hurried to open the door for him.

17

ON WEDNESDAY, A FEW MINUTES before five, George Benedict would be rising to the podium at a seminar in Atlanta. Ashley LaSorta would be at home, unusually early for a weekday, booting up her home computer and establishing a connection through a proxy server. Emily Norland would be at work watching the screen on her burner phone. Tiffy Jenkins would be in her pink smock wheeling a trash hopper through the executive suite at UniViro. And Kelly McCann would be where she was, in Gladwyne, Pennsylvania, driving a rental car down a long lane that curved around a lily pond and past a formal knot garden into a cobblestone entry court.

She parked behind a dark sedan as two men climbed out of it, one Black, one white, both about forty, both wearing dark suits. A third man, dressed casually, got out of the back of the sedan and hoisted a video camera to his shoulder. He panned to the right to capture Kelly as she got out of her car and followed the first two men up the wide front steps. Then he turned the camera on the entrance to the mansion as one of the men rang the bell and the other knocked with the side of his fist—*thump, thump, thump*—on the massive wooden door.

A uniformed maid opened the door but quickly backed away when Jane Benedict arrived breathless beside her. Jane looked to be fresh from her bath. Her cap of curls was wet, and she wore a terry-cloth robe and a pair of fuzzy slippers on her feet. She stared at the men through glasses still fogged with steam. "Yes? May I help you?"

"FBI," the two men shouted, and they pulled out their flip wallets to flash their picture IDs and gold shields. "Special Agent Mackey," the white man said. "Special Agent Carter," the Black man said.

"What's this about?" She peered at their badges.

"Mrs. Benedict?" Kelly called from the steps behind them.

Jane looked up and out. "Kelly McCann? Is that you?"

"Ma'am." Mackey stepped up close, wingtips to slippers. "We have a warrant to search the computer of George Benedict."

Jane gasped. "You have *what*? Why?"

Kelly skirted around them. "The FBI alerted me an hour ago, Mrs. Benedict. I tried to reach your husband, but I was told he's giving a speech in Atlanta—"

"At the CDC, yes." She blinked at the cameraman who brought up the rear. "Are you filming this?"

"That's for your protection, Mrs. Benedict," Kelly said. "To ensure that they follow all the proper procedures."

"I don't understand. What's this all about?"

"Move aside, please, ma'am," Agent Carter said.

She didn't, but the double door left plenty of room for the two men to step around her into the rotunda. Kelly came in, too, and drew Jane aside. She spoke in a confidential whisper. "The FBI received a tip that Dr. Benedict's home computer contains certain . . . images . . . of certain children . . ."

The woman's fleshy face went florid. "Wh-why that's outrageous!" she cried. "He would never! They can't come barging in here—"

"I'm afraid they can. The judge issued a search warrant. I was alerted, and I insisted on coming along to protect Dr. Benedict's interests. Especially since he can't be reached."

Jane looked up, and Kelly followed her gaze to an oversized

clock high on the wall. Their own little Big Ben. "No," she said forlornly. "He's only beginning his presentation." She had a sudden inspiration. "If they could just wait an hour. If I could just speak to George first—"

Agent Carter stepped up on cue. "No, ma'am. This can't wait." He pulled a folded document from his breast pocket and presented it to her with a flourish.

"Ma'am." Mackey closed in on her other flank. "If you'd step outside with me, please."

Jane threw a desperate look to Kelly.

"I'm afraid you have to do as he says," Kelly said. "But I'll go with Agent Carter and make sure everything's done right."

Jane chewed her lower lip before she gave a reluctant nod. "All right," she said. "If you say so." She threw a helpless look over her shoulder as Mackey steered her outside.

"This way," Kelly said to Carter and the videographer, and she led the way down the hall to the left.

Her stomach clenched hard as she opened the door to Benedict's study. Here was that awful room, the office that looked like a laboratory that she now knew was a torture chamber. Her eyes swept over the white cabinetry, the mortuary slab of a desk, Jonas Salk perched on a shelf with his chin on his paws. But she couldn't bring herself to look up any higher than that, at that blindingly white ceiling she'd been forced to stare at during her ordeal. She couldn't see the camera mounted on the top shelf of the bookcase. But she knew it must be there.

She went to the desk with the videographer following close behind. "As agreed," she announced loudly for the benefit of every recording device that might be in the room, "I will first examine Dr. Benedict's laptop computer for any documents protected by attorney-client privilege."

"We're only interested in images," Agent Carter said.

"Nonetheless." She sat down at the keyboard. "The warrant prohibits you from accessing privileged files. So please stand over there." She pointed across the room. "Until I'm through."

Carter put his hands in his pockets and strolled to a bookcase. The cameraman panned that way, then back to Kelly as she touched a key on Benedict's laptop. The monitor glowed to life. "Please stand here and aim the camera here," she instructed him, and she waited for him to move into position. His camera was aimed at the screen, but his body was blocking it from any other electronic eyes in the room. She inserted a thumb drive in the USB port and typed in a series of commands. The program launched, and she hovered over the keyboard, watching until the password was found and the laptop unlocked. She removed that drive and inserted a second one. She typed Ashley's next series of commands and watched the lines of code scroll down the screen until a pop-up message declared *Complete.*

But she wasn't done yet. She did a search for every video file saved to this laptop. There was only one, and her flesh crawled when she found it: a file he'd named *Insurance.* He'd saved it, to watch again no doubt, but also as something he could use against her, his insurance that she'd maintain silence. She inserted a blank thumb drive into the port and copied the video file to it. When she ejected it, she put it not in her bag, but in her pocket. Then she deleted the file from Benedict's laptop. He'd never watch that video again. She'd just insured *that.*

"All yours," she told Agent Carter, and he squared his shoulders and sat down at the desk with his hands poised above the keyboard like a concert pianist.

Ten minutes later it was done. Agent Carter stood up and shook out his arms like it was the first break he'd had in hours. "Keep rolling," she told the videographer, and both men followed her out of the office and down the hallway and out the front door to where Jane Benedict stood wringing her hands.

"Anything?" Agent Mackey asked his partner.

"Nothing," Kelly said before Carter could answer. "Your tip was false. I told you it was a malicious lie."

"They didn't find anything?" Jane said.

"Of course not," Kelly assured her. "Nothing but business documents, which are far outside the scope of their warrant. Confidential and proprietary business documents, I might add," she said with a flash of angry warning toward Carter and Mackey.

"Our apologies, ma'am," the agents mumbled.

Jane turned to Kelly and grasped both of her hands. "Thank you, Kelly. Thank you so much. You've rescued us yet again."

"I'm only glad I could help."

"Please come in and have some refreshments. We can speak together to George when he's finished his speech."

"Thank you, but I'll have to speak to him later. I have a plane to catch."

"Oh, of course." Jane seemed suddenly to notice the state of her undress, and she clutched her terry-cloth lapels together. "Well, thank goodness you were here when this happened. How lucky for us that you were in town."

"Yes," Kelly said. "We were lucky."

She said her goodbyes and followed the three men down the steps to their car. "And scene," she whispered.

She slid behind the wheel of her rental and followed their car to the end of the lane. They stopped there, and she got out and went to the driver's window. The three men had their hands out, and she placed a few crisp twenties into each one. Tips on top of their day rates.

"That lady was good," the actor playing Mackey said. "She stayed in character the whole time we were outside."

"She was," Kelly agreed. "I'll take that memory card," she said to the cameraman in the back seat.

"I still need to edit—"

"No need. I've decided to go a different way on this training video."

"But we can still put it on our résumés, right?" the other actor asked.

"Absolutely." Kelly kept her hand out until the videographer ejected the card and handed it over.

Back in the rental car, she took the burner phone out of her bag and sent a group text to Ashley and Emily and Tiffy. A single word: Done.

18

THERE WASN'T TIME TO RETURN the rental car to the airport
and still make her nine o'clock meeting in New York, so she left
it at the Amtrak station in Philadelphia. She'd worry about how to get
it back to Hertz when all of this was really done, at the end of Act
Three. There were five scenes in that act: leak to the press, investigation, breaking news, public disgrace, financial ruin. The first scene
would be played out tonight.

Her train was already boarding when she entered the concourse,
and she had to sprint to the gate with her heels clattering wildly
across the marble floor. She made it through only a second before
the ticket agent roped off the escalator. Down on the platform she
ran for the car, hoisted her bag into the overhead rack, and collapsed
panting into an open seat.

She checked her watch. So far, on schedule. Yesterday when
she'd called Rick Olsson to tell him she'd be in New York tonight,
he'd suggested dinner. She'd countered with drinks at her hotel at
nine. If the train kept on schedule, if she could get a cab on the
other end, if there wasn't a delay in checking in at the hotel . . . if all
those things happened, she'd be fine.

She checked her phone next and found a dozen missed calls and
texts from the office. She'd been AWOL for most of the day.

She took a moment to catch her breath before she called the

office. It was after six, but Cazz was still at her desk. "Hey, I was worried," she said. "The way you disappeared—"

"Yeah, sorry. I had an emergency."

"Is Mr. Fineman okay?"

It was sad the way Cazzie's mind went there first. But years of working for Kelly had taught her to go there first.

"Dental emergency," Kelly said. "Any emergencies on your end?"

"No, but Patti wants a word. Javi, too. Oh, and your stepdaughter called again."

It was the *again* that reminded her: she never opened Courtney's email from last week. "Hey, could you go into my in-box and dig out Courtney's last email?"

There was a long pause. Cazz was a quick reader, but lately there were too many unread emails in Kelly's in-box to scroll through.

"Okay, found it."

"Read it, would you?"

"Dear Kelly, I wanted you to know that I passed the Bar—"

"Oh!" Kelly interrupted. "That's great news!" She'd been paying Courtney's tuition—prep school, college, law school—for ten long years. Now Courtney could get a job, and Kelly could start putting that money into Justin's and Lexie's college funds. "Send her some flowers—a big arrangement—plus, I guess, a bottle of champagne, and, I don't know, a box of chocolates? You decide."

"What's on the card?"

"Congratulations. We're all so proud. Love, Dad, Kelly, Justin, and Lexie."

"Got it."

"Thanks. Put me through to Patti?"

Cazz transferred the call, and Patti answered only seconds later. "Hi, Kelly. Everything okay?"

"Fine. What's up?"

"Margaret Staley."

Kelly's mind went blank. "Remind me?"

"Lesbian. Movie star. Blow job?"

"Oh. Right."

"I had a call from the *medico* in Madrid," Patti said. "He was supposed to do the DNA swab this morning. Tommy arranged a set pass and everything. But when the doctor got there—"

"Let me guess. Our young hero refused."

"Eventually, yes. But get this—first he wanted a science lesson in exactly what the test would show."

Kelly laughed. "He thought he could fool a DNA test? Like the old Breathalyzer trick. Hyperventilate and reduce your blood alcohol by ten percent."

"Beats me. But listen, I took a look at his film contracts. It's just like he said. No nudity, plus he provides his own hair and makeup people, his own wardrobe lady, the works. He's a guy who really, really guards his privacy. Which is why I can't see him dropping trou in the back of a restaurant."

"And yet he won't take a simple DNA test to clear his name?" Kelly scoffed. "Nobody's that private."

Patti's sigh sounded over the line. "I know. He just seems so innocent."

"He's an actor," Kelly said. And a far better one than the two part-timers she'd hired today. "Okay. Call opposing counsel. Get a settlement demand from this Margaret Staley. We need to make this one go away fast."

"Got it."

"Listen, could you connect me to Javi?"

Patti's tone brightened immediately. "Hold on, I'll conference him in."

"No, wait—" Kelly began, but the hold tone was already buzzing in her ear. Patti's time was too valuable for her to waste joining in on a call with Javier. *She* was too valuable to waste on Javier.

Patti came back on the line. "I've got Javi."

"Hey, Kell," he said. "Let me call you back."

Javi was a stickler for *need to know* and *eyes only*. *Share with the group* wasn't in his vocabulary. He hung up, and Patti rang off, too, with a stung-sounding "Oh. Well, bye."

Javi's call came through. "I heard back from my guy in Bucks County."

Kelly had no idea what he was talking about. "And?"

"They're gonna rule it an accidental overdose."

She realized then. Reeza Patel. "Really?" she exclaimed. Relief bloomed inside her. It wasn't suicide! She wasn't to blame! But her lawyer's brain demanded that she pause to examine the evidence. "Based on what?"

"Her Oxy prescription was for ten milligrams every twelve hours. Based on the date she last refilled it, she should have had twenty pills left. And she did. That's exactly how many pills were in the bottle the cops found beside her."

"Okay," Kelly said, waiting.

"When the pathologist examined her stomach contents, there was only one ghost pill in there."

"Ghost pill?"

"Time-release Oxy leaves a wax shell in the stomach after the drug dissolves. So based on the single ghost pill in her stomach, and the number of pills left in the bottle, it looks like she was taking the Oxy as prescribed. She did not deliberately overdose."

"I don't get it. It wasn't Oxy that killed her?"

"Oh, it was Oxy, all right. Tox results show ten times the pre-scribed dosage in her blood."

"You mean—" Her eyes opened wide. "It was an accident! A packaging accident. One of the tablets must have been for a hundred milligrams!" Reeza's family would have a whopper of a lawsuit against whatever pharmacist or drug manufacturer had made such a terrible error. But the only thing that mattered at the moment was that Reeza didn't commit suicide.

"It'll be another week or two before the official ruling, but I thought you'd wanna know now."

"Yes. Yes! Thanks, Javi."

She ended the call and sank back into her seat as the weight of guilt seemed to lift from her shoulders. She'd carried that weight for a week. So had the NDA women, and she started to send them a text so they could share in her relief.

She caught herself. Guilt was the only thing that brought them together. If Reeza's death had looked accidental from the start, the NDA women never would have been spurred into joining Kelly's operation. So until they reached the end, until the curtain fell on Act Three, it was best to keep her silence.

19

IT WAS RAINING WHEN SHE arrived in New York. The taxi line at Penn Station was a mile long, and it was nearly nine by the time she got to the hotel. She'd made a bad choice there: there was a convention underway, and the lobby was mobbed. After she finally checked in, she hurried to her room to drop off her bag. Her hair was wet and straggly, and, with no time to dry it, she slicked it back into a bun even more severe than her usual style. She frowned at herself in the mirror. She wasn't out to seduce Rick Olsson, but she couldn't risk scaring him off by looking like a schoolmarm either. She swiped on some lipstick and left her glasses by the sink.

The lobby buzzed with the hoots and squeals of partying conventioneers. She followed the loudest hubbub to the hotel bar, tucked away in a dim, low-ceilinged space at the far side of the lobby, a room of mirrored surfaces and turquoise velvet, with a long bar to the right, booths to the left, and a string of high-top tables down the middle. Dozens of people were on their feet in that space in the middle, elbows on the tables, drinks in hand.

She spotted Rick Olsson toward the back, standing beside a corner booth while he talked to a couple other men. It looked like they'd buttonholed him on his way to his table, but he was acting his usual genial self. He wore a dark suit and an open-necked shirt in a shade of blue that looked good on him. He didn't see her yet, and she hung back by the host stand to let him finish his conversation.

Her phone pinged in her bag. She pulled it out and was puzzled when the screen was blank. Then she realized: it was the *other* phone. The one she forgot about the second she texted Done to Emily. She rooted for it now in the bottom of her bag.

A dozen texts had landed since she left Benedict's mansion. First from Emily at five thirty: Haven't heard from Tiffy yet. Another at five forty: She's not answering. Either phone. Then a text from Ashley: She got cold feet. I told you she was our weakest link! Emily: Kelly, what now? Ten minutes later: Kelly? Ashley: Fuck! She got cold feet, too? Emily now: Still no answer from Tiffy.

Kelly felt suddenly dizzy. Today at five o'clock. Go Time. Ashley, Kelly, and Tiffy would simultaneously execute the code to alter the UniViro files. That was what they'd planned. That was the only way this would work. If Tiffy hadn't come through, that meant that Benedict's office computer still had all the original lab notes and none of the new emails. Kelly had ten pages of documents in her bag, carefully selected to whet the journalistic appetite of Rick Olsson. They were worthless if Benedict could refute them with the unaltered documents on his office laptop. And he could. Everything they'd done last weekend, everything she'd done this week—booking the actors and the videographer, manufacturing a search warrant, flying to Philadelphia, renting a car, returning to that temple of torture in Benedict's mansion—it was all for nothing.

She heard her name and looked up in a daze. Rick was grinning and waving his arm over the heads of the people around him. She pasted a smile on her face and waved back.

It couldn't be for nothing. She couldn't let Benedict win. She had to fix this. She tapped in a quick reply to Ashley and Emily. I'll do it myself tomorrow.

When she looked up again, Rick was threading his way through the crowd. She couldn't escape now, and she couldn't stand him up again and expect him to meet her another time. She'd have to pivot. Tonight couldn't be the handover she'd planned on, but she could still have a friendly drink and lay the groundwork for a later meeting. She dropped the burner in her bag and weaved her way toward him with her hand out and a smile on her face. "Rick!"

"Kelly!" He took her hand but kissed her cheek instead, and she made that pivot, too, and kissed the air between them.

"I've got a table over here." He pulled her by the hand around the high-tops until they reached a semicircular booth in the back. On the table was a sign reading RESERVED, and a coat was spread out over the seat on one side. He waved her in on the other side, and she slid in across the turquoise upholstery. "G and T?" he asked her.

"Only a T tonight, thanks. I've got an early morning."

His eyebrows went up, but he flashed an okay and headed off to the bar.

She peeked at the burner under the table. HOW? Ashley had texted. HE'S IN THE OFFICE ALL DAY TOMORROW. Then, We never should have trusted that girl.

I never should have involved her, is what Kelly was thinking. Poor Tiffy. She didn't know how to say no, but she couldn't go through with it. Kelly pictured her in her pink smock, wheeling her cart through the halls of UniViro earlier tonight, stopping at Benedict's office door with every intention of doing as she'd been told. Trying her best to do as she'd been told. Then hanging her head in shame as she pushed the cart past without going in.

I'll figure something out, Kelly texted back.

Rick was back with her drink and one of his own. He sat down and slid over until he was only inches away from Kelly. "Philadelphia, Boston, and now New York," he said, clinking his glass against hers. "We're meeting at all the whistle stops along the Northeast Corridor."

"Next time Trenton," she joked.

"Name the date and time," he said, not joking.

"Well," she said in her all-business voice. "Thank you for meeting me here."

He heard her tone and acknowledged it by leaning back as he took a sip of his drink. "What brings you to New York?"

"The usual. Meeting a new client."

"Ah yes. The city that never sleeps never stops committing sexual assault."

"Those two things *are* related."

With a grim nod, he segued to his next topic. "I hope the fallout from Patel's suicide wasn't too bad."

"Oh!" She brightened. "It wasn't. Suicide, that is. It looks like it was an accidental overdose due to a manufacturing or packaging error."

"Really?" He sat back even farther. "That's good news for Benedict, I guess. Unless the pills came from UniViro?"

"They don't do opioids. As you know."

He smiled and nodded.

"But speaking of that"—her segue was no more graceful than his—"the reason I wanted to see you . . . I've been hearing some rumors."

"You, too?" He leaned in close again. "What do you think? Any basis in fact?"

"I think so." She didn't stop to wonder what he could be talking about. She had a script to follow. "I mean, I'm hearing it from someone inside, who would know."

"Me, too." He caught himself with a chuckle. "I guess I shouldn't appropriate those words. Let me say instead, same here."

"Excuse me?" she said, her brow creased. Now she did wonder.

"It's such a fraught issue, isn't it? Separating the work from the man. Do we still go see Woody Allen movies? Can we watch reruns of *The Cosby Show* in good conscience? But here the stakes are so much higher than in entertainment. I mean, the man's a genius. He's in the middle of curing what's arguably the worst scourge known to humankind. Do we pursue justice and risk losing that cure? Or do we give him a pass no matter how heinous his crimes?"

Her face froze as realization dawned. "We're talking about two different things," she said, her lips tight. "I haven't heard any rumors about any crimes. Apart from the one he was just acquitted of."

He squinted at her. "Then what are you talking about?"

"Rumors about his discovery of the virus. About data being falsified."

"You're kidding."

"I wish I were."

He shook his head. He wasn't buying it.

"I hear there's a paper trail," she said, doubling down. "Emails."

He stared at his glass, swirled it a moment, then took a hasty gulp. "If this is true," he said finally, "it would be absolutely devastating."

"I know," she said sadly. "As soon as I heard, I thought about you and your book deal."

"Fuck my book deal," he said. "I'm talking about the cure for Alzheimer's. If it's not real? This would be the worst news I could imagine."

Kelly felt a little swell of self-satisfaction. Thanks to her last-minute idea to change the focus of their hack, she'd avoided this calamity. "Oh no, you misunderstand me," she said. "There's nothing wrong with the research. Only with who should get the credit for it."

Rick noticeably relaxed a second before his gaze sharpened. "He stole it?"

"So I've heard."

"And there's evidence?"

She nodded. "When I heard these rumors, of course I thought of you, Rick." She made a point of speaking his name. "I thought that, as a journalist, you'd want to know."

"Absolutely." He gave a sheepish smile. "Sorry. About jumping to the wrong conclusion. And about my language there. It's just—" He stopped and swirled his drink again. "If you've ever watched someone's mind disintegrate—"

She remembered his father. "Oh. Yes."

"I'm already looking over my shoulder like it's coming for me. Every time I misplace my car keys, a little voice starts whispering, *Is this it? Am I starting?*"

"Oh, Rick." Without thinking, she put her hand on his arm, and he smiled and laid his hand over hers. It was cold from holding his glass, but somehow warm, too. She thought she could feel his pulse quickening, though maybe it was only hers.

"Anyway. Thank you for thinking of me. I'll keep my ears open, and if you should happen to hear anything more—"

"You'll be my first call." She pulled her hand free. She'd succeeded. The groundwork was laid for a second meeting, and that was when she'd leak the documents. She pretended to look at her watch. "I'd better call it a night. I have an early morning."

He slid out of the booth and stood aside for her to climb out, too. "Let me walk you to your room."

"Oh, that won't be necessary."

He gave an eye roll that took in the bar crowd. "Lots of drunken conventioneers around tonight. I'll get you to your door."

There was a finality to the way he said it, punctuated by his hand on her elbow, gently steering her out of the bar and across the lobby to the elevator.

He was going to make a pass at her. She knew this. She'd suspected it from the moment he slid too close in the booth, and now she was certain. But she wasn't alarmed. She'd fended off countless such overtures through the years, occasionally from colleagues, but mostly from clients, who were, after all, sexual aggressors. *Allegedly.* She had a technique that always worked well. She'd smile indulgently at the innuendo, she'd allow the hand on her waist, she'd even allow the lean-in prelude to a kiss. But then she'd back away with one hand pressed to his chest, the other hand clapped to her heart to show how much this was costing her, how sorry she was that her scruples wouldn't allow her to act on her undeniable attraction to him. He'd get away with his ego intact, and, in most cases, she'd get away. And when some of her more aggressive clients wouldn't back down, she'd lay down her trump card. *You wouldn't want to have to get a new lawyer, would you?* Their self-preservation instinct would always triumph over their lust.

Rick Olsson wasn't a client, so she didn't have that trump card in her deck. But she wouldn't need it. He was a gentleman. He'd step back as soon as she reminded him she was married. Hopefully he'd remember that he was, too. He'd look regretful, she'd look regretful, and they'd part as friends.

She'd actually be regretful in this case. She might live like a nun, but she wasn't one, and she still felt those urges. Rick was an attractive man, and she genuinely liked him. If she were a different person, living a different life? If she didn't need him to play his part in Act Three? But she wasn't and she did, so this would have to end the same way these encounters always did.

A group of men crowded onto the elevator with them, some rowdy conventioneers among them, so they didn't speak as the elevator rose. Rick's fingers tightened on her waist, but she'd already stopped thinking about him. She knew what he was going to do, and she knew how she had to react. What she didn't know was how to gain access to Benedict's office laptop in the morning, and that was where her thoughts were circling when the chime sounded and the elevator doors opened on her floor.

"Here I am," she said, and Rick stepped off with her and remained at her side as she turned down the long, carpeted corridor.

She figured she could get into Benedict's office easily enough, but how to get him out of it would be the bigger challenge.

"Here I am," she said again when she reached her room. She pulled her key card out of her bag. "Thank you for meeting me tonight."

"Thank *you*," he said, and he turned her toward him and bent his head.

This was the moment. One hand to his chest, one hand to her heart. He was a foot taller than she was, and when she looked up, the ceiling seemed to light up over his head. It was blindingly white, as if the sky itself had opened up, and suddenly she was catapulted back into that room, that laboratory of an office, frozen in place, staring up at that white, white ceiling while George Benedict ravaged her.

Rick leaned in to kiss her, and his face as it descended was like the roof falling in. Her knees buckled, and she threw her arms over her head as if beams were crashing down on her. A strangled cry ripped out of her throat.

Rick lurched backward with both hands in the air. "Kelly, what the—"

She was shaking. "I— I—don't—know. I'm—sor—" she panted.

"No. No. I'm sorry. I should've—" Her bag had dropped to the floor, and he stooped to retrieve it. The key card had landed a few feet away, and when he moved to get it, she turned to hide her face from him. She couldn't breathe. She couldn't even stand up straight. She was doubled over and clutching her belly as if she'd been kicked. Something was rising up inside her. It was gagging her.

He unlocked the door and pushed it in as far as it would go without his feet crossing the threshold. He handed her the bag. "I'm sorry, Kelly. I should have known."

She didn't look up at him. She didn't dare. She squeezed past him into the room and pressed her back against the door to seal it shut. The rising thing was in her throat now. It was a sob, and it tore out of her like an organ being ripped from her body. Her legs crumpled, and she dropped to the floor, crying in great heaving gulps.

It was a long time before she could pull herself to her feet. She went into the bathroom and groped for the light switch. Her face in the mirror was red and blotchy, her eyes black-rimmed and swollen. Her lipstick was smeared, and her nose was running. This was what they called ugly crying, and it was hideous. No wonder Rick turned heel and ran. Anyone would. It was humiliating, and she felt like a failure on every level.

The failure that stung the most was this: by driving Rick away she'd lost her best avenue for leaking the story about Benedict. Now she'd have to cultivate some other journalist, but it seemed unlikely she'd find anyone with the platform and reputation he enjoyed.

She squeezed her eyes shut and threw her head back with a moan. Their whole plan was falling apart. She'd lost Rick Olsson. Tiffy had lost her nerve. And since Benedict would be back in his office tomorrow, they'd lost any chance of access to his laptop.

She opened her eyes. She was staring up at the bathroom ceiling, and the bright white surface made her start to cry again.

But only for a second. She stared back at the mirror, at her ravaged face and her body still trembling with the aftershocks of her crying jag. She didn't have PTSD—she wasn't like those other women— but the white ceiling had triggered this reaction. It had brought back that endless hour when she'd been forced to stare unblinking at the great expanse of white ceiling in Benedict's study. She looked again at her ugly face in the mirror, and an idea struck her.

She knew exactly how to get Benedict out of his office.

20

THE RENTAL CAR WAS STILL parked at the station when she arrived in Philadelphia the next morning. It was almost as if she'd known she'd be back, and perhaps she had. Perhaps she'd always known that she'd have to come face-to-face with Benedict one more time before this could be over.

It was easy enough to get a slot on his calendar when she called. She'd been his lawyer for more than two years, and his assistant, a young man named Grady, had no reason to think anything had changed. "Of course, Ms. McCann. Can you do eleven o'clock?"

"Hmm. Could we make it eleven thirty?"

"Afraid he has a board meeting at noon."

She'd seen that on his calendar when Ashley hacked into the company server. Grady's confirmation was all she was waiting for. "No problem," she said. "This won't take fifteen minutes."

The UniViro campus was a complex of five buildings on twenty acres on the north side of the 202 corridor. The buildings were low-rise, granite and glass, arrayed around courtyards and open-air plazas landscaped with generic office-park trees and shrubs. A fountain spurted in a man-made pond, and trees stood along both sides of the lane with their branch tips meeting overhead, like a saber arch at a military wedding.

The executive suite occupied the top floor of the tallest, center-most of the buildings. Kelly found an open parking space in front of it and stepped out of the car.

For a moment her feet wouldn't move. She stood rooted next to the car, gazing up at the windows she knew were Benedict's. Pictur-ing him at his desk. Then picturing him as he loomed over her with his teeth bared in a horrible grimace of a smile.

She tried to remind herself. This wasn't where it happened. Yesterday—that was when she'd been forced to enter the house of horrors. Today it was only an ordinary office building, full of ordinary people going about their business. And as soon as she finished her business here, she never had to see him again, except on the news. In his disgrace. After today, she could put him out of her mind forever.

Still, she didn't move until she felt someone watching her. On the far side of the parking lot, a man was walking a dog along the edge of the grass. He seemed to be glancing her way. Wondering why she was lingering. What her problem was.

She hitched her bag up on her shoulder and set out across the lot to the building's entrance. The baby-blue Bentley was parked in the prime space closest to the door, in front of a sign that read DR. BEN-EDICT. She felt a ripple of dread as she passed it. This was the car that had delivered her to her torment. It was Hades's chariot. Driven by Anton.

For the first time, she stopped to think about Anton and the role he'd played. Driving her to Benedict's mansion could have been innocent enough. But carrying her in and out of the helicopter? Did he honestly believe she was drunk that night? Or did he know exactly what was going on? Was he one more person complicit in Benedict's crimes?

UNIVIRO HAD ELABORATE security systems and protocols that had become even stricter since Benedict had started drawing protesters. Kelly had to sign in and show identification and go through a metal detector and, even then, wasn't permitted to go farther without an escort.

She was relieved when her escort stepped off the elevator. It wasn't Benedict, and it wasn't Anton either. It was Benedict's assistant, Grady, a slender young man in a blue turtleneck and coordinating plaid trousers. His face wasn't as well coordinated: he had bleached blond hair with heavy black eyebrows.

"Ms. McCann!" he sang out, pumping her hand. "I hope it's not too late to offer my congratulations. What a great victory! I wish I could have been there to see it!"

"Yes, it was a good result."

"You're a real hero around this place, I don't mind telling you!" With a theatrical arm wave, he ushered her to the elevators and used his access key to push the button for the penthouse floor. The car whooshed upward.

"Dr. Benedict still has a board meeting today?"

"Yes, at noon." He looked at his watch, suddenly stricken. "I'm afraid it's already eleven-forty."

"Don't worry. I'll be in and out."

The elevator chimed, and Grady waved her through the opening doors with the same elaborate gesture, then led the way from the elevator bank through a glass atrium to the corner office that was Benedict's domain. The door was closed. He tapped once, waited to hear "Come," then swung the door in and stepped back to admit Kelly.

Benedict was at his desk, in shirtsleeves, glasses low on his nose. He didn't rise or extend his hand. He leaned back in his chair and steepled his fingers together, tips to his mouth. "Close the door, Grady," he said.

His voice chilled her in its lack of inflection. She heard the door click behind her. He didn't invite her to sit, and she didn't move any closer.

She'd never been in this office before. She'd met him twice in a conference room around the corner; all their other meetings had been off-site. There was a wall of glass behind him, but the other walls were dark wood and lined with book-crammed shelves. Two chairs stood opposite his desk, and a sofa was positioned against the interior wall. On the shelves were framed photographs of Benedict with the president, the governor, four US senators. A desktop computer sat at his right elbow, with a network cable running from the back of it through a rubber-capped hole in the desk to a hidden connection below. A stack of papers stood at his left elbow. Trophies and statuettes in glass and gleaming metals adorned the credenza. This decor was nothing like his all-white laboratory/study in his home, but something was the same.

He was staring at her over the clasp of his hands. "I suppose you're here to tell me what that raid was all about yesterday."

It was something in the air, the air he was breathing that she was now forced to breathe, too. It was the same in this office as it had been in that other office. Not an odor so much as a lack of odor. "No," she said.

An eyebrow lifted over the rim of his glasses.

"That was nothing," she said. "An anonymous tip and a couple overzealous FBI agents. I shut it down. They won't bother you again."

Rubbing alcohol. That was what she smelled or didn't smell. Antiseptic. Against poison.

"Ah. So you're here expecting me to thank you."

"No." She drew a ragged breath. "I'm here to apologize to you."

Now both his eyebrows lifted.

"I thought about what you said to me that . . . that night. About how I muzzled you. How humiliated you felt." She gulped and forced herself to go on. "I realized you were right. I did do that."

The tears wouldn't come. She wasn't an actress—no matter what her courtroom opponents might say—and she couldn't cry on demand. All she could do was stammer and gulp. She looked away, to the sofa against the wall. The one he must have been reclining on when Tiffy stumbled in on him. It was upholstered in sleek black leather. Easy to clean.

"And I— I realize now that I shouldn't have," she said. "I was so focused on my own talents, on reaching my own victory, that I simply disregarded you and all your own talents."

The words tasted foul in her mouth, but still, she couldn't cry. She remembered Rick Olsson and the hotel corridor, and wondered if it was true, that she had a trigger. She sucked in a breath and tilted her head back and opened her eyes wide. The ceiling was white. In contrast to the dark wood walls, it was blindingly white, and suddenly she began to tremble. Her throat burned and the tears flooded her eyes and spilled down her cheeks.

"I— I realize now that you were your own best witness. It was"— she choked and swallowed again before she could go on—"a mistake for me not to put you on the stand."

She pulled her gaze from the ceiling, blinking hard, and that was when she spotted the laptop on an upper shelf of the bookcase. The lid was closed. It was hardly more than a file's thickness lying flat, and she might have overlooked it, but she saw it now and knew that it must be his off-line computer.

"It was a mistake for me to muzzle you. I should have— I should have let you speak to the press. I mean, it wasn't even my right to grant you permission. As if *I* were in charge of *you*. I— I understand that now. I only wanted to win. For me. But it was your case to win. Not mine." She stopped to catch her breath. "And I'm sorry. I'm so sorry."

She was blubbering by then, just as she'd hoped to be. Tears flowed down her face, and mucus streamed from her nose in two slimy strings. She swiped the back of her hand over her nose and mouth, then clapped both hands over her eyes. Her shoulders heaved as she watched him through the lattice of her fingers. She could see his eyes gleaming behind the lenses of his glasses.

The intercom buzzed, and Grady's voice entered the room. "Five minutes, Doctor."

Benedict stood and came around his desk. He reached out an arm, and Kelly recoiled with a gasp, but he was only reaching for his suit coat hanging on the back of the office door. He pushed his arms into the sleeves. "I accept your apology," he said.

"Thank you," she whispered.

He slid the knot of his tie up to his throat and reached for the doorknob. "After you."

"Oh!" She wiped at her sopping face. "May I have a few minutes? To pull myself together? I don't want to go out there looking like . . . this."

His chin came up, and he looked down at her through hooded eyes. A noise of disgust buzzed through his thin lips. "No," he agreed. "You look revolting." He turned the knob. "Make yourself decent and close the door when you leave."

"I will. Th-thank you."

He pulled the door shut behind him.

It was a moment before she could move. Her body didn't seem to know that she'd been fake-crying. Maybe she wasn't. Even after he was gone, her breath still hitched and the tears still trickled. It was a few minutes more before she could mop her face dry and push the button lock on the doorknob.

She checked for security cameras, but Ashley was right: there weren't any. And of course he wouldn't have them here, not considering the uses to which he put that black leather sofa. She opened her bag and pulled on a pair of latex gloves before she lifted the laptop down from the shelf and powered it up on his desk. She tried entering the same log-in that opened his home computer the day before, and the gamble paid off. Benedict might be an original thinker when it came to science but not when it came to usernames and passwords. She slid in Ashley's thumb drive and ran the overwrite program, and in minutes she was done.

She shut down the laptop, and when the screen went dark, she used it as a mirror to try to repair her face. Then she closed the lid, replaced it on the bookshelf, peeled off her latex gloves, and stuffed them back in her bag.

Grady looked up from his desk when she stepped out of the office. "Everything all right, Ms. McCann?"

"Allergies," she said, breezing past him. "These suburban office parks get me every time."

She didn't need an escort to exit the building. Outside she hurried to the rental car and ducked behind the wheel. The tears may have been fake, but the degradation was real. Groveling before that monster, begging his forgiveness, even in pretense, left her feeling soiled. The way he swelled with pleasure at her humiliation—her hatred of him burned so hot it blistered.

Nothing could cure this feeling. Nothing until the moment of his own humiliation and degradation. That was when *she* would swell with pleasure.

She sent a quick group text to burners. Done. Ashley and Emily zipped back their acknowledgments before she'd even turned the key in the ignition.

But it was Tiffy who was in her thoughts as she left the parking lot. The girl must have felt stricken with guilt that she'd let them all down. She didn't respond to the text, and she hadn't answered any of Kelly's earlier calls. She could picture Tiffy clutching her phone, biting her lip when it rang, afraid to answer, ashamed not to.

Kelly was the guilty one. She never should have involved Tiffy

in this scheme. She owed her an apology. She glanced at the dash-
board clock. It was only a little past noon, and her flight wasn't until
three. And Tiffy, she recalled, lived not far from here.

She pulled over in another suburban office park and scrolled
through the files on her phone until she found Tiffy's address. She
entered it in the car's navigation system and followed the directions
onto the highway. After a few miles, the system directed her off again,
onto a long stretch of a local artery studded with strip malls and
chain restaurants. She was prompted to turn just as she spotted the
faded blue sign: HAPPY DAYS MOBILE HOME PARK. It swung from
two chains beside the entrance to a bowling alley. The trailers were
tucked almost out of sight on the downslope behind it.

The asphalt that once paved the driveway lay mostly in chunks
and rubble strewn over a rutted road. Kelly's car bumped and lurched
along the way, past an unmanned guard shack surrounded by tufts
of weeds, a row of green dumpsters, and an array of mailboxes in
columns and rows with little glass windows that made it look like a
miniature apartment house. The pretense of a paved road ended at
that point. From here, branches of dirt-and-gravel road meandered
past trailer after trailer, some still on their wheels, some on concrete
blocks, some with decks and porches added on.

Kelly started down one branch until she noticed that the house
numbers—when they were present—were wrong. She turned around
and tried another branch. A brindle pit bull crawled out from under
a trailer and charged at her tires. He ran after her, snarling furiously,
until she finally crossed his territory border, then he turned around
and trotted back to his under-trailer lair.

She grew more and dejected as she drove on, thinking of Tiffy
and her life full of hardships and setbacks. Removed from her drug-
addicted mother, shuttled from foster home to foster home, finally
emancipated at eighteen but only to end up living here and cleaning
offices and getting raped. Only to be silenced by Kelly, who took one

look at the girl's profile and thought, *$20,000 should do it. She'll be thrilled.* When what really thrilled her was getting to spend a week-end at the shore with a group of women who never would have given her the time of day under different circumstances.

Her guilt stabbed deeper with every dilapidated mobile home she passed.

The house numbers finally started going in the right direction: 92, 94, 96. An old pickup truck missing its right front fender was parked in front of Number 98. Kelly parked and got out. She walked around the truck and stopped short at the cinder-block steps. Forming a giant X across the dented aluminum door were two strips of yellow tape. They read: POLICE LINE DO NOT CROSS.

She stood and stared.

"You can't go in there," someone called from behind her.

She turned. A young woman was standing on the stoop of another trailer across the way. She held a toddler on her hip, and in her free hand a cigarette drooped. "Oh, hi," Kelly called to her. "I must have the wrong address. I'm looking for Tiffy Jenkins?"

The woman hitched the baby higher on her hip. "You a friend of hers?"

"A work friend," Kelly said. "I thought it was Number Ninety-Eight."

"It was."

Kelly glanced back nervously at the trailer. "Did something happen?" Had Tiffy been arrested? It couldn't be for cybercrimes. She hadn't even done anything. Conspiracy to commit cybercrimes? They were all guilty of that. By now there could be yellow crime-scene tape across Kelly's own front door.

"It's been happenin'," the woman said. Her baby was reaching for the cigarette, and she gave him a shake. "I had to call the cops on him a couple times myself."

"Oh?" Kelly remembered the bruises on Tiffy's arms, and suddenly she knew that she hadn't been arrested; she'd been assaulted.

"But I didn't hear nothin' this time." The woman tapped her cigarette, and an inch of ash fell to the stoop. "Sean called it in hisself. He was drunk off his ass, but he called it in."

"Is Tiffy all right?"

"Not hardly," the woman snorted. "He cut her throat. She's dead."

21

I T WAS DARK WHEN KELLY got home, and as she pulled into the drive, her headlights shone on a strange car. A sporty little black BMW. She cut around it and pulled into the garage. As she got out, the interior light came on in the BMW to show a well-dressed woman climbing out.

"Can I help you?" Kelly called from the garage. Then, "Oh, my goodness, Courtney! I didn't recognize you." She'd seldom seen Adam's daughter dressed in anything but leggings and Ugg boots, but today she wore heels and a pencil skirt. And somehow suddenly drove a BMW.

Courtney took a few hesitant steps toward the garage, but Kelly didn't wait. She rushed at her and wrapped her in a hug that made Courtney let out an *oomph* of surprise. Kelly couldn't blame her—their relationship had always been more cordial than affectionate—but still she held the hug for a long moment.

Displacement, a psychiatrist might call it. She was thinking of that other fatherless girl, the one who probably never got enough hugs in her life. The guilt that Kelly felt driving to Tiffy's trailer was nothing compared to the guilt she felt driving away from it. She'd seen the bruises on the girl's upper arms. She'd heard the boyfriend's surly tone over the phone. And she'd done nothing. Said nothing.

She leaned back, still gripping Courtney by the shoulders. The girl wore a silk blouse that felt luxurious and expensive, and her hair, usually a snarl of black curls, was styled in a sleek blowout. "It's so good to see you!" she said, beaming. "And congratulations again! We're all so proud!"

"Yes, so you said," Courtney murmured. "Thank you for the flowers, and . . . all the rest. I wondered, do you have a minute?"

"Of course! Come on inside." Kelly's voice was pitched too high. She could hear it herself.

"No, really, this won't take—"

"Come in! See the rest of the family."

Kelly's bag was still in the trunk of her car, but she left it there and, with one arm around Courtney's waist, steered her up the walk and through the front door. "Hello, everyone!" she shouted and kicked off her shoes. She could hear the mania in her voice. She was just excited to be home, she told herself. Excited to have her mission behind her.

"Mommy!" Lexie screeched and came vaulting down the stairs.

"Hi, sweetie!" Kelly stooped to give her daughter a hug even tighter than the one she'd given Courtney. "How was school today?"

"Boring. Why are you so late? You said you'd be home early."

"Something came up. Sorry. Say hello to Courtney."

"Hullo," the child mumbled, looking nowhere near Courtney. "Mom's home!" she shouted to the house.

"Hey, Kelly." Gwen poked her head out from the kitchen at the end of the hall. "We waited on dinner for you."

"You didn't need to do that."

"Oh, you know Lexie. And I invited the boys to join us, if that's all right."

"Of course."

"Mom, come see—you got a delivery!" Lexie tugged her by the hand into the living room where a cellophane-wrapped fruit basket stood on the coffee table. "Open it. See who it's from," she clamored.

Kelly tore open the envelope and read the card. *Hope you're feeling better. See you soon? Rick.* "Oh!" she said.

"Who? Who's it from?"

"A work friend." She was surprised, not only that he'd sent it but that it was exactly right. Flowers would have suggested that something happened last night that didn't, but a fruit basket held no sexual connotation. It was merely a kind gesture, and this fruit basket in particular—nothing over-the-top, just apples and pears and a bag of cashews—hit the right balance. The note was just right, too—*hope you're feeling better*—as if she'd had indigestion last night and not a total meltdown. But the best part was *See you soon?* The question mark at the end putting the ball in her court, but the words before it promising that her volley would be returned. She was touched, but more important, relieved. She wouldn't have to go looking for another journalist to leak to. Rick Olsson was still her man.

She looked up with a broad smile. She felt almost giddy. "Courtney!" she cried when she saw the girl still standing uncertainly in the front hall. "Come in. Sit down."

"I really just need a minute, Kelly."

Gwen came out of the kitchen with a stack of dinner plates. "Hey, Courtney. There's plenty," she said with a raised eyebrow at Kelly before she turned into the dining room.

"Yes, please," Kelly said. "Join us for dinner!"

"No, I can't stay—"

The rest of Courtney's sentence was drowned out by a clamor in the kitchen as Todd and Bruce came in. "Something sure smells good," Bruce yelled.

"Oh, that's me," Todd said.

"Huh. You wish you smelled that good."

Sounds of tussling followed. Kelly went back to the front hall to sort through the mail on the hall table, and when the doorbell rang, she was right there to admit Gwen's boyfriend, Josh. He stopped short when he saw Gwen setting the table. "Am I too early? Gwen said to pick her up at seven thirty."

"No, it's my fault," Kelly said. "I'm late. But please, Josh, stay for dinner."

He cut a look to Gwen, who nodded. "Sure, thanks," he said.

"Earn your keep," Gwen said. "Go get two more plates."

"I'll do the silverware," Lexie said and scampered ahead of him to the kitchen as Todd and Bruce were coming out. The three men exchanged fist bumps as they passed. "Hey, sweetie," Todd said when he saw Courtney. "I didn't know you'd be here." He air-kissed her cheeks before he pulled back dramatically. "And look at you! So chic! Let me see." He tried to turn her in a twirl, but she refused to budge.

"I really just need a quick word with Kelly—"

Kelly put down the stack of mail. "Justin!" she hollered up the stairs. "I'm home and dinner's ready. Two good reasons to emerge from your cave!"

"Shall I open some wine?" Gwen asked as she headed back to the kitchen.

"Sure," Kelly said, then, "No, make it champagne! We're celebrating Courtney tonight."

"No, really—" Courtney said.

Todd planted his hands on his hips. "Okay, girl, what'd you do now?"

"She passed the Massachusetts Bar, that's what," Kelly declared and patted Courtney on the back as she skirted around her to the dining room. "She's a full-fledged lawyer now, just like her dad."

"And you," Lexie said amid an indignant clatter of cutlery on the table.

Gwen and Josh emerged from the kitchen carrying steaming

bowls of vegetables and creamy potatoes. "Dinner's ready," Gwen called, heading back to the kitchen.

"Sit anywhere you like," Kelly said to the room at large, and took a side chair for herself. Lexie plopped down beside her as Gwen returned with a platter of roast chicken. Everyone else did a circuit of musical chairs around the table until they decided on their seats. Courtney sat down last, reluctantly.

"Hey, who's driving the Bimmer?" Justin shouted as he finally came clattering down the stairs.

"Your sister!" Kelly turned to Courtney at the end of the table. "What a nice car!"

"No way!" Justin said as he grabbed a chair.

Courtney shook her head. "It's not mine. It's a . . . company car."

"What company?" he asked at the same moment that Kelly said, "Courtney! Did you get a job?"

"Yes." She met Kelly's eyes across the table. "Like I told you in my email. I'm with Kevin Trent and Associates."

The hubbub continued around the table as congratulations were offered, dishes were passed, the champagne cork popped. But for Kelly the soundtrack went silent. All she could hear was a rush of air through her head, like the rhythmic whoosh of a ventilator. She stared at Courtney, but what she saw was a mountain of bills on Adam's desk and herself wading through them with an infant in the stroller beside her when she came upon a certified letter from Erik Kloss.

She pushed back her chair with a screech. "I'd like a word." Her voice reverberated inside the echo chamber of her mind. She walked out of the dining room and through the living room to the study. Courtney rose to follow her, and silence fell over the table as everyone else exchanged nervous glances.

"What?" Lexie asked, but no one answered.

Kelly stood waiting at the study door until Courtney went through, then she closed the door and turned to look up at her. She was barefoot, and Courtney was six inches taller plus three inches of heels. But Kelly was undaunted in her fury. "Kevin Trent," she said. The name hissed through her teeth. "The man who stole your father's firm. How could you possibly go to work for him?"

"He didn't steal anything." Courtney's diffidence was gone. Now her eyes blazed with defiance.

"He stole his biggest client."

"Dad was never going to practice again. Erik wanted Kevin to take over the account. Dad would have wanted it, too."

"Erik?" Kelly nearly shrieked. "You're on a first-name basis with Erik Kloss?"

Courtney lifted her chin. "It was Erik's idea that I join the firm. As a way of honoring Dad."

"*Honoring* him?" Kelly threw her hands up and spun away across the room, past the desk where Adam had toiled on Erik Kloss's deals night after night. "He would have honored him a hell of a lot more by not bankrupting him."

Courtney folded her arms and jutted out her chin. "I'm not here to talk about that. I'm here to talk about my petition."

"Petition? For what?"

"Guardianship. I haven't filed it yet. I'm giving you a week to consent."

Kelly's forehead creased. "Guardianship? Of whom, by whom?"

"Of Dad. By me."

Kelly scoffed. "Really? You want to take over his care and feeding?"

"No," Courtney said. "I want to stop it."

Kelly stared at her. The rush of air howled inside her head, so loud she had to shout over it to hear herself. "You want your father to starve to death?"

"For God's sake, Kelly. He's already dead. He's been dead for ten years."

"Don't say that! He's still in there! I know he is!"

"There's nothing but an empty shell up there. And you need to let me bury it."

"*It!*" Kelly screamed. She lunged at Courtney and grabbed her by the hand. "Come with me."

She flung the door open and pulled the girl after her through the living room to the front hall. Everyone else was still at the table in the dining room, and they stared in horror as Kelly tried to drag Courtney up the stairs. "Come say that to your father. Tell him to his face!"

Courtney planted her feet and yanked her hand free. "You and your fucking Catholic guilt!" she shouted. "You're keeping him up there like . . . like some kind of Frankenstein's monster! For the sake of his memory, for the sake of his children"—Courtney jabbed a finger at Justin and Lexie—"you need to let me bury him!"

Lexie burst into tears and slid under the table.

"I know what this is about!" Kelly cried. "You're after his life insurance. You've been waiting for that money for ten years!"

Courtney's eyes went cold. "Read the fucking papers," she bit out, and she jerked the front door open and stomped out of the house.

Kelly ran up the stairs and down the hall and into the bedroom. Adam's eyes were wide open, as if he'd heard every word of that ugly exchange. He didn't stir when she spoke his name, but he had before, a few times over the years. Once he lifted his hand and unmistakably said *water* before he slipped away again. Many times she saw his eyes move in what looked like REM sleep, which had to mean he was dreaming. His last EEG definitely showed some brain activity. So he was breathing on his own, his heart was beating, and the synapses were firing in his brain . . . How could anyone call him dead? *Wasn't likely to improve*, the doctors said, but *wasn't likely* didn't mean *wouldn't*. No one had ever said *wouldn't*.

"Don't worry," she said, her chest still heaving. "It's not going to happen. We'll fight this. We'll win."

She searched his eyes for a reaction. "Adam. Sweetheart," she murmured, and she stroked his hair and kissed his lips. "Don't worry. You'll be fine. Everything will be fine."

22

THE DINING ROOM WAS EMPTY by the time she came downstairs in her running gear. From the kitchen came the clatter of dishes, and from the family room the blare of the TV. Everyone was occupied. No one would miss her. All she needed was a long hard run to get this rage out of her system.

The neighbor was in his driveway across the street, and he had a dog on a leash who must have been a new addition to his household. Any other time she would have stopped to admire him, but tonight she gave only a quick wave as she pulled on her reflective vest. He waved back, and she broke into a sprint down the block.

She took her usual route across town to the college, but she ran faster than her usual pace. Her feet pounded on the pavement, and with every percussive beat she seethed a little more. At Courtney. At Kevin Trent and Erik Kloss.

She took the turn onto the campus, and her thoughts looped back; for the next half mile she seethed about Tiffy's boyfriend instead. She remembered his grunt over the phone. How he had spat out the word *bitch*. She remembered Tiffy chewing her nails. *Do you think he bought it?* Then she remembered how Tiffy stood up to the domineering Ashley. *It's really on all of us, isn't it?* She wondered if Tiffy had finally stood up to Sean, if that was the trigger. Some men couldn't abide being challenged.

Or silenced. Her thoughts threatened to veer to a place she didn't want them to go. Not yet. When all this was over, when he was ruined, then she'd be healed, then she could think about him. Or not. He'd be of no consequence to her. She'd never have to think of him again.

She forced her thoughts back to Courtney. Anger was a wasted emotion unless she could channel it into something constructive. Unless she could weaponize it. That was what she'd done throughout her career. Every time opposing counsel insulted her or did something outrageous, she doubled down on her offense and went for the win. That was what she would do with Courtney. Don't get mad. Win.

She had a partner at the firm, a lawyer named Lyle Firth, who specialized in probate and family court matters. She'd get him to defend against Courtney's petition. Nobody in Kevin Trent's shop did that kind of work, so Lyle would have an automatic advantage. Then there was Kelly's built-in advantage as the wife and the person who'd been caring for Adam every day for the past ten years. As opposed to the daughter who merely visited now and then. Kelly's win was practically assured.

She ran on, around the athletic fields and across a quad that was strangely empty. On most mild autumn evenings like this one, she'd pass by knots of students walking from library to dorm and groups sprawled on the lawn with cans of beer and apple cider doughnuts. But no one was about tonight. There must have been an event underway, a concert or a mixer on the other side of campus. That would explain the absence of foot traffic. The car traffic was light, too. Only one car had passed her since she'd entered the campus, and one more was behind her now.

She glanced over her shoulder. The posted speed limit on campus was twenty mph, though few drivers obeyed it. This car, though, the dark coupe behind her, was driving even more slowly than that.

Almost as if it were keeping pace with her run. The road took a curve, and she followed it, and when she glanced back again, the car's high beams flashed in her face.

For a second she froze where she stood. But only a second. Her legs bunched up under her, and she took off in a burst of speed. She veered off the pavement and sprang out across the grass, running even faster now at the end of her run than she'd sprinted at the start of it. She tore at the Velcro straps on her reflective vest and peeled it off and pitched it into some shrubbery and ran on.

Her heart pounded hard against the wall of her chest. It had to be the man with the dog in the driveway across the street. She didn't recognize the dog, and now she realized that she didn't recognize the man either. She'd simply assumed he was the neighbor. Suddenly she remembered the man with the dog watching her that morning in the UniViro parking lot. Then the man with the dog talking to Tiffy on the beach. It could have been the same dog. It must have been the same man.

The car sped up and overtook her around the curve of the road. She ran even faster as she heard it brake hard with a screech of rubber against asphalt. The car door popped open with a sound like a gunshot, and she swerved the other way and ran faster still.

"Kelly! Whoa, it's me!"

She knew that voice. She lurched to a stop. "Javi?" she called, wheeling around.

"Sorry," he said as he emerged from the shadows. He held her vest in one hand. "Didn't mean to scare you."

She waved a nonchalant hand to say she was fine. She was blowing too hard to answer in words.

"I heard something from one of my guys down in Philly. I thought you should know." He was dressed in tight silver pants and a deep purple shirt, and Kelly knew he must have been out for the evening.

He'd interrupted a date or, more likely, a conquest, to track her down tonight. "Remember Tiffy Jenkins?" he asked. "She was one of Benedict's? The office cleaner? She was murdered yesterday."

Kelly nodded. "I know," she said, still panting. "It's awful."

His head tilted to one side. "How'd you hear?"

She caught herself too late. There was no reason for her to know about a noncelebrity crime three states away. She blew her breath out and sucked it in again while she conjured up an explanation. "That local lawyer we hired for her?" she said finally. "He called me when he heard. The poor girl. Bad enough to be attacked by Benedict, but by her own boyfriend?" She shook her head sadly.

Javi studied her. "You think that's what happened?"

"Sure. They've already arrested him." The neighbor woman had been happy to give Kelly a blow-by-blow account of how the cops hauled him out of the trailer in handcuffs. He struggled in their grip all the way to the patrol car, and once inside, he'd tried to kick out the window with both feet. Yet the whole time he was sobbing about how much he'd loved her.

Javi shook his head. "It's too much of a coincidence."

"What is?"

"Jenkins *and* Patel."

"You think— God!" She sputtered a laugh. "You think Benedict killed them?"

"Maybe." He shifted his weight. He seemed a little embarrassed by her dismissive laugh. "I mean, what are the odds?"

"Well, first off, Patel was an accident. You told me that yourself."

"I told you it wasn't suicide. Somebody could have given her that hyper-concentrated Oxy. Somebody like maybe a Big Pharma guy?"

She laughed again. "Why? What's his motive? He was already acquitted. And he already paid off Tiffy and got her NDA. If he were going to kill either of them, he would have done it before, not after."

"Death's a guaranteed silencer."

"Come on." She remembered something else. "Benedict was in Atlanta yesterday. While Tiffy was getting her throat slit."

That gave Javi only a moment's pause. "He doesn't have to do his own dirty work," he said. "He has that goon. Anton."

She dismissed that idea, too. "He had to be in Atlanta, too. Benedict never goes anywhere without him." But even as she said it, the memory surfaced, of Anton picking her up and carrying her from car to helicopter to cab. From Philadelphia to Boston and back again, alone. Still—"He's a rapist," she said. "Not a murderer. It's only a coincidence that Reeza and Tiffy happened to die so close in time."

Javi set his jaw. "I don't believe in coincidences."

She rolled her eyes. It was such a hackneyed thing to say. Besides, she *did* believe in coincidences. Almost every major event in her life was the result of a coincidence. Signing up for the ethics committee the same week Adam became chair. Running into Todd at the hospital right after his last long-term patient died. It was even a coincidence that she came to represent George Benedict, who happened to read a news article about her shortly after his first victim made a claim.

"If it makes you feel any better," she said, "we're done with Benedict."

Javi's eyebrows shot up. "You fired him?"

"It was a mutual parting of the ways."

"Fine. But if he's behind these deaths—"

"Javi, stop. You're not making any sense."

Now she'd really offended him. He looked away, and his jaw was clenched tight when he turned back. "Want a lift home?" he offered, grudgingly.

Despite his tone, she was tempted. Her heart rate was still too high, and she still felt a wrinkle of unease about the man with the dog. But like so many other things in her life, this was something she had to tough out. "Thanks, no," she told him and turned to go. "I need to finish my run."

"Hey!" he called after her. He was holding out her vest, and she looped back and grabbed it from him and ran on.

IT WAS PAST Lexie's bedtime when Kelly got home, but her night-light was on, and she was lying on the rug next to it with her head drooping over a book.

Kelly came in and squatted beside her. "Hey, sweetie. Let's get you into bed."

Lexie looked up drowsily. "You hate her now, too, don't you?"

"Courtney? No. No. We had a disagreement, that's all. I lost my temper."

"She said the F-word."

"I guess she lost her temper, too."

"She wants to kill Daddy."

"I shouldn't have said that. We're only having a disagreement about his medical care. That's all. Come on. Up you go."

Lexie rose to her elbows and army-crawled across the room to haul herself up into bed. "She's not our friend."

"Maybe not today." Kelly bent to kiss her forehead. "But she's always your sister. Remember, Daddy loves her just as much as he loves you."

"Does he, though?" Suddenly Lexie's eyes were wide open. "Love me? He doesn't even know me."

Kelly wasn't sure how to answer. *He loved you before you were born? He'd love you if he knew you?* "If he knew you," she said finally, "he'd love you even more than he already does."

The answer seemed to satisfy Lexie. She closed her eyes.

Kelly went down the hall and tapped on Justin's door.

"What?" he hollered.

"Want to talk?"

"Um, I'm busy right now. Maybe tomorrow."

That suited Kelly fine. She went into her bedroom and up to Adam's side. The monitors were beeping steadily. The CCTV camera was on. Everything was fine.

She opened her phone and found Courtney's email. She talked about passing the bar exam, glossed over her job with the traitorous Kevin Trent, then landed the killer punch: I've drafted a petition for my appointment as Dad's guardian so that I can have his feeding tube removed. I'm hoping you'll consent. I'll wait ten days to file.

Kelly forwarded the email to her partner Lyle Firth. She wrote: See me first thing tomorrow.

"There." She bent to kiss Adam's forehead. "It's all taken care of. You don't need to worry about a thing."

Somebody had brought her luggage in from the car. She switched off the camera and wheeled the bag into the dressing room before she went through to the shower.

Afterward, toweling off, she heard the ping of a text landing. She checked her phone, but there was nothing there. Then she remembered the other phone in the bottom of her suitcase. She opened the bag, rummaged through it, and pulled out the burner. A text glowed on the screen: I see you.

She dropped the phone like it scorched her. The text was from Tiffy. From the burner phone she bought for Tiffy.

I see you.

It couldn't be. It couldn't be from Tiffy, and it couldn't be meant for Kelly either. Nobody knew this phone was hers. All the burners were unregistered. She'd purchased them from a kiosk in the Philadelphia airport. She'd paid cash.

There was a simple explanation. Tiffy must have tossed the phone out, and some random person picked it up and sent that text as a joke. A prank. That was all it could possibly be.

Still. She turned the phone off and took out the battery. Tomorrow she'd figure out some other way to communicate with Ashley and Emily.

She put on her nightgown and walked out into the bedroom to say goodnight to Adam. His eyes were closed, and she kissed him on each eyelid and then his lips.

When she turned around, a green light was glowing like a cat's eye in the dark. Somebody had turned the camera back on.

I see you.

23

JAVI'S CYBER GUY PAUL WAS on another job when Kelly reached him. It was three in the morning before he could get to her house, and he worked through what was left of the night to add another layer of encryption to the firewall.

Kelly spent most of the night in the backyard creating her own firewall: she tossed the burner phone into the Weber grill, doused it with lighter fluid, and set it aflame. Then stood and watched until it melted into nothing.

She wanted to rip out the modem and every connected device in the house. The kids would kick and scream, and maybe some of the adults, too, but they could learn to live without streaming TV and virtual assistants to turn on the lights. They could spend their evenings together reading books in silent communion. Occasionally they might even have conversations. It could actually be good for them.

But then she thought of Adam. He depended on his internet-connected monitors. Which meant that Kelly would have to live with this gnawing fear of constant, anonymous surveillance. That feeling of being watched that made the hair rise on the back of her neck.

I see you.

Even after the burner was a puddle of sludge, that text was imprinted on her brain.

She told herself it wasn't true. He couldn't see her, whoever he was. It was only a coincidence that whoever found Tiffy's burner happened to send that text at the same time that Benedict switched on the CCTV. She believed in coincidences and this was clearly one. There was no way Benedict could have gotten his hands on Tiffy's burner. He didn't know where she lived and had no reason ever to try to find out. He forgot about her the minute he zipped up his pants. The day Kelly directed him to write Tiffy's settlement check, he'd actually asked, "Who's this again?"

She tried to convince herself that it wasn't even Benedict who'd hacked the household internet. It could simply be another coincidence. Some other hacker went after her, or anyone else in the household. Bruce had an ex-boyfriend who worked in IT; he could be the culprit. Or it could have been a completely random incursion.

But she knew it was Benedict. The first cyberattack came the night after he physically attacked her. This second hack came the night after she visited his office. That was more than a coincidence.

BY DAYBREAK THE firewall was reconstructed. She woke the kids and buzzed Todd and Bruce, and called in Gwen and Josh, and they all gathered at the dining room table and listened groggily as Paul walked them through the steps to change their log-in credentials yet again.

He was baffled as to how this latest intrusion could have happened. His earlier work should have insulated the system. "Unless somebody gave the Wi-Fi password to somebody?" But they all swore they hadn't.

"Well, that should do it," he said to Kelly at the door as he left. But she could hear the doubt in his tone. Since he couldn't identify the cause, it was hard to be sure of the cure.

* * *

DESPITE HER SLEEPLESS night, she was in the office by nine. Stacks of mail and unread pleadings were teetering on her desk, and Cazz's reminders of everything that required her attention were beginning to take on an urgent tone. But before she tackled any of that backlog, she had to plan her approach to Rick Olsson. The fruit basket gave her the perfect excuse to make contact, but she wasn't sure whether to call him or text him or email him, and she wasn't sure how long she should wait. Too soon and he might wonder about her motives.

Patti Han tapped her knuckles on the door. "Bad news," she said. "I talked to Margaret Staley's lawyer."

Kelly gave a distracted nod as she opened her email to search for Rick's contact information.

"You remember," Patti prompted her. "Lesbian. Movie star—"

"Yes," Kelly snapped. "I remember."

"Oh, okay. Well, she won't give us a number. She refuses even to discuss settlement until after Tommy responds to discovery. Specifically, until after he provides a DNA sample and submits to a physical." Patti showed a sad little pout. "I mean, I suppose she doesn't want to bid against herself—"

That was something Kelly always drilled into her associates: never go first in a negotiation if you can help it. Especially in suits for emotional injury where the monetary damages were not objectively measurable. A defendant making an opening offer might name a figure that was double what the plaintiff's opening demand was going to be. Then be stuck with that as the floor.

"—but I'm afraid it blows my theory out of the water," Patti said.

"That he's innocent, you mean."

"No. Well, yes. But what I've been thinking is that this whole case is a publicity stunt. Margaret's an LGBTQ activist, right? What if she's trying to out him?"

"You think he's gay?"

"Maybe? He's so sweet and gentle."

"So our defense would be he doesn't like girls?" Kelly wrinkled her nose. "Gay men have been known to assault women, too. It's not a get-out-of-rape-jail-free card. If he even is gay."

Patti sat down with a sigh. "I know. And since she's insisting on the discovery, it's obvious that she's got his DNA. Which is the only explanation for why he's refusing."

"Still?"

"He's adamant." Patti hooked her fingers to make air quotes. "*It's an outrageous invasion of privacy designed only to embarrass him.*"

"Hmm." Kelly suddenly sat up straight. "You know—you might be right. He might be the rare Leahy & McCann client who's actually innocent."

Patti looked flummoxed. "What? How?"

"Let me stew on it awhile."

"Should I schedule a video call later today?"

Cazz walked in at that moment with the morning's mail. "For Tommy Wexford? His assistant said voice only from now on. No video."

"What's that about?" Patti was perplexed. "A movie star who's camera shy?"

"The pretty boys are the worst," Cazz said as she sorted the mail on the worktable. "Ever try taking a selfie with a good-looking guy? He deletes a dozen before he finds one that he likes. Vanity, thy name is—"

"Tommy Wexford?" Patti guessed.

Cazz turned with a smirk. "I was going to say Javier Torres."

Patti flushed pink.

"Never mind. I'll call him later," Kelly said. "Meanwhile . . . Cazzie, could you get me DVDs of all his movies?"

"You got it."

"No, I got it," Patti said, rising to her feet. "I have all of them. In my office."

"Great. Thanks."

Kelly dismissed her with a nod, and as soon as Cazz left, she turned back to the computer to search for Olsson's number. And was interrupted again by another knock on the door.

This time it was Lyle Firth, the firm's family and probate lawyer. He was forty, prematurely white-haired, with glasses and a smooth pink-cheeked face. It gave him a sexless look that probably endeared him to his many widowed clients. He held a sheaf of papers in his hand. "I've looked over this petition." He seemed solemn but nervous, as if he were a pallbearer trying to show the requisite respect while also worrying about the weight of the casket. "May I start by offering my sympathies? I didn't realize your husband's situation was quite so dire."

"It's not," Kelly said. "Sit down."

He sat, gingerly, and crossed one pin-striped leg over the other. "These allegations—" He slid his glasses to the end of his nose and paged through the document, touching his finger to his tongue and daintily flicking the corner of each page. "*Persistent vegetative state, no cognitive response to stimuli, no awareness of surroundings, no volitional activity, no hope of reversal.* That's not true?"

"Not entirely."

"What do the doctors say?"

"People have come out of comas after as long as nineteen years. That's documented medical science."

He looked up over the rim of his glasses. "But what do *his* doctors say?"

"Nothing recent," Kelly said.

"You'll need a fresh examination then, and a medical consensus of some kind."

"Okay." She'd shop around, find somebody younger who kept current with all the latest research. A doctor who hadn't yet lost his optimism. "But here's the thing. I'm his wife. Isn't it my decision?"

Lyle shook his head. "It's his."

"But he can't—"

"The standard is substituted judgment. The judge has to determine what decision he'd make if he could."

That struck her as ridiculous. "How could the judge possibly know?"

"If your husband ever expressed any thoughts on the subject. If you ever had any conversations—?"

"Oh. Well." She pulled herself upright. "We talked about watching our children grow up. We talked about our someday grandchildren. We talked about growing old together. So obviously he'd want to live for all that."

"Ah," Lyle said. "But would he want to live if he couldn't be present for any of that?"

She answered through a clenched jaw. "He'd want to live if there was any chance of it."

"Then you'll have to prove that chance."

AFTER LYLE LEFT, she swiveled her chair to the window and sat motionless for a long time. The stack of papers on her desk was forgotten. Tommy Wexford was forgotten. Rick Olsson was nearly forgotten. Of course Adam never spoke about what he'd want to happen in this situation. Why would he? He was a healthy, vigorous man with a young family and every expectation of a long and bright future. All their conversations had been about life. Not death.

The words Lyle quoted kept echoing in her mind. *Persistent vegetative state.* But persistent didn't mean permanent. *No cognitive response to stimuli.* But cognitive meant inside his brain, and who knew what responses might be going on in there? *No awareness of surroundings.* Again, who could say? *No hope of reversal.* That part was flat-out false. Because there *was* hope. Kelly hoped for it every day.

Her desk phone rang, and when she saw Javi's name on the display, she picked up.

"Hey, listen," he said. "Turns out you were right about Benedict. He *was* in Atlanta at the time of the girl's murder."

"Yes, I know." Her tone was peevish. She didn't want to think about Tiffy right now.

"But that doesn't mean Anton was with him."

"Javi." She said his name wearily. "We've been over this. There's no conceivable motive—"

"Let me run it down, okay? For peace of mind, if nothing else."

"And bill your time to whom? Benedict? Imagine explaining that charge to him. *Oh, that's what it cost to convince ourselves that you're not a killer and neither is your hired man.*"

Javi didn't like being ridiculed, and his tone was sullen when he spoke again. "Then I'll eat my time. *And* my expenses."

She was too exhausted to argue further. "Do what you like," she said.

Cazzadee came in a few minutes later with a stack of message slips. "You got a couple weird calls today. That TV newsman, Olsson? I told him you don't do interviews, and he said you were old friends." She lifted one perfectly groomed eyebrow.

"He's lying," Kelly said. She had to hide her relief as she took the message slip from Cazz. The fact that Rick called first resolved all her uncertainty about how and when to reach out to him. She could call him back today.

"Then there was a woman who wouldn't give her name. *Tell her it's the gal with the thigh-high boots and I have a new number.*"

Ashley LaSorta. Kelly looked up, puzzled. They weren't supposed to talk ever again. Then she realized: that phantom message from Tiffy's burner was a group text. It went to all of them. Ashley and Emily must have experienced the same panic Kelly did last night when the words *I see you* lit up the screens of their burners. "Some kook," she said and reached for the message slip.

24

KELLY LEFT THE OFFICE SOON after that. She walked two blocks to an ATM, then two more to a generic phone store, where she purchased a new burner for cash. Then she took one of the city's pathways deep into Boston Common.

The elms in the park glowed a bright golden yellow in the sunlight. A yoga class was in progress, and the students' multicolored mats formed a pattern like a barn quilt spread out over a bed of fallen leaves. Autumn had arrived while she wasn't looking. Most of the summer was lost to the case of *Commonwealth versus Benedict*, and now much of the fall to the case of McCann versus Benedict. But she wouldn't lose much more. She promised that to herself.

She found an unoccupied bench in the sun and dialed Ashley's new number from her new burner.

Ashley answered at once, cautiously. "Kelly?"

"Yes. It's me."

"What the fuck is Tiffy up to? First she bails on us, then she texts out this teaser? *I see you*? Christ. I told you we shouldn't—"

"Ashley. Tiffy's dead."

There was a long silence before Ashley breathed, "What?"

A stream of pedestrians was passing by Kelly's bench. Joggers, moms pushing strollers, people walking their dogs. Kelly twisted sideways on the bench and lowered her voice. "She was murdered by her boyfriend. On Wednesday afternoon."

"Oh my God!"

"That's why she didn't show up at Benedict's office."

"Oh God, I feel like a shit. But wait a minute. Then who the hell sent that text last night?"

"I don't know."

"Jesus."

"Whoever it is, he can't trace us, but just in case, destroy that phone."

"Already did. Have you talked to Emily?"

"Not yet."

"I'll do it. I can call her office without anyone getting suspicious."

"Good."

"Where do you stand on the rest of it?"

"On track," Kelly said. "It'll be done in a day or two."

"Then we sit back and wait for the shit to hit the fan."

"Yes."

Ashley was silent a moment. "But Jesus . . . Reeza and now Tiffy? It's like Benedict's spunk is the kiss of death."

"Pure coincidence," Kelly said. But as she ended the call, she thought that was exactly what he felt like when he was inside her. Death.

She remembered that smell in his office. In both offices. It wasn't rubbing alcohol it reminded her of. It was embalming fluid.

SHE CHANGED PHONES for her next call, and she changed tones, too.

"Thank you for the beautiful fruit basket," she cooed after Rick's exuberant *Kelly!* "That was so thoughtful of you."

"Feeling any better?"

"Completely. I think it was some twenty-four-hour bug. I feel fine now. Better than fine. It's a beautiful day in Boston."

"I hope it'll be a beautiful weekend, too." His tone was strangely mischievous.

"Why?" Then she guessed it. "Are you coming up?"

"I am," he said. "Please tell me you're free for dinner tomorrow night."

This was perfect. She could make her pitch in person and slip him the documents under the table. "I am," she replied in an echo of his playful tone.

He named a restaurant in Somerville, and she knew it, though she was surprised that he did. It was a local favorite and off the tourist track. He wanted to pick her up at home, but she invented an earlier appointment. "So I'll meet you there at seven, okay?"

"It's a date," he said.

She'd let him think so, for now. "See you then," she said and rang off.

"Hope you don't stand him up," said a voice behind her. "Like you did me."

"Excuse me?" She twisted around. Someone had taken a seat on the other end of her bench. A man with a gray brush cut and a big yellow Lab sitting politely at his side.

"You don't remember me," he said with a sneer of a smile.

A second later, she did. He was Edward Russo, the cyber guy who was *too shady* for Javi, the hacker she blew off at the coffee shop. She looked at the dog beside him and in the next instant she knew that he was also the man in her neighbor's driveway last night.

"I'm sorry," she said. "I think you're mistaking me for someone else."

"Tammy Wexford. Or should I say—Kelly McCann?"

"Have we met?"

"Not quite." He gave a pat to the dog, whose tail thumped contentedly on the grass. "You walked right past me at the coffee shop the other day."

She dropped her phone in her bag and rose to her feet. "As I do to strangers every day."

"You called me."

"I don't think so."

"And whaddya know, I traced the call back to the offices of Leahy & McCann."

She should have realized that a hacker hoping for a big score would take the trouble to track her down. "I didn't call you," she said. "It must have been one of the sixty-plus people we employ in our firm."

"You wanna hack into Big Pharma, you tell me, then I find out, whaddya know, you represent UniViro. You got some kinda grievance against them, is that it? They stiff you on your bills?"

He knew who she was, where she worked, and where she lived. He knew about UniViro, and suddenly she remembered a man with a dog in the UniViro parking lot yesterday morning. Then a worse memory struck her: there was a man with a dog talking to Tiffy on the beach last weekend. Russo might know everything.

A curious calm came over her. It was the same kind of calm she mustered in the courtroom when her opponent sprung a surprise witness or the judge made an unexpected ruling. A moment of Zen in which she accepted that she was in peril and that the only way to escape it was to maintain control, of herself and the situation.

"I'm afraid you're mistaken," she said. "I've never represented UniViro. My relationship is with one of their executives. And he's current on all his bills."

"Something's got you steamed, though. I could tell from the way you ran out of your house last night. Like a bat outa hell."

"Sir, you realize you just admitted to stalking me."

He chuckled. "Somehow I don't think you're gonna report me."

She looped her bag over her shoulder. "You're mistaken," she said. "About my ever contacting you. And also about my reporting you to the police. Which is exactly what I'll do if you don't leave me alone."

He grinned up at her. "Or maybe I report *you* to the police. Or the FBI. Or corporate security at UniViro."

She scoffed. "Report me for what? I haven't done anything."

"You're planning something, though. You decided you don't need me. You think you can cut me out. But I'll be watching. I'll know when it happens."

Her face didn't move but her brain turned somersaults as she realized the import of those words. He'd be watching? That had to mean more than walking-the-dog surveillance. That had to mean cyber-surveillance. The hacks into her household Wi-Fi—they could have been the work of this man. He could be the one watching, and the realization brought a gush of relief. It was a thousand times better to imagine this small-time grifter spying on her than to picture George Benedict doing it.

She turned heel and walked away. This man didn't scare her. He was only after money, and she knew how to defend against claims like that. It was what she did every day for her clients. Deny, obfuscate, block him at every turn, and, if all else failed, settle cheap.

25

Emily Norland

OUR COUPLES THERAPIST HAD A three-cushion couch instead of chairs in her office. She explained why during our first session. It was a couch instead of a love seat so that the clients could face each other as they spoke, rather than sit rigidly side by side. And it was a couch instead of chairs so that they could move closer, or not, depending on how they were feeling.

She always referred to the couples as her clients, never patients, and I wondered about that. Weren't they here to be treated? And cured of whatever ailed them?

Not in our case, of course. Greg and I were here only to placate our mothers. Mom and Diane bonded during the wedding planning, and presented a united front on running our lives ever since. They knew that we both had important jobs and little time for domestic concerns, and they were happy to relieve us of the burden. Together, they shopped for our first house, then our second. They furnished and decorated them for us. They sat down with their calendars at the start of every year and decided where Greg and I would spend each of the holidays, dividing them up equitably between the two sets of parents. They suggested what we should get each other for birthdays and anniversaries and sometimes even shopped for and wrapped the gifts. And, most recently, they decided that this marriage could be saved. *Would* be saved, if they had anything to say about it.

They had a lot to say about it. *We just don't understand what happened. Everything was so perfect. And then out of nowhere, it's not?* Mom took me aside, and Diane took Greg. *You can tell me. What happened?*

But of course we couldn't. Greg was a signatory to the NDA, too, so he was also bound to silence. With a penalty of half a million dollars if either of us should breach it. Half a million that we'd already spent on the second house and decor.

Mom and Diane decided we should see a marriage counselor, and they interviewed a half dozen before settling on Dr. Louise, a tidy little woman with a tidy little office on a tidy suburban street. We'd been seeing her once a week for the last two months. I sat on one end of the three-cushion couch and Greg on the other, both of us facing straight ahead, while Dr. Louise tried and failed to get us to open up about our problems.

The problem was our sex life, or lack thereof. But Dr. Louise's attempts to diagnose the cause hit a brick wall every time.

"It's because she blames me," Greg would say. "That's why she pulls away."

"Blames you for what?" Dr. Louise would ask.

Silence.

"It's not that I blame him," I would say finally. "It's that he feels guilty."

"Guilty about what?"

Silence.

Not really silence, though, since Dr. Louise kept music streaming softly from a smart speaker on her credenza. Her selections usually ran to spa and New Age music. *Think of it as white noise*, she said once; *it helps you relax.* But I was a classically trained violinist, and music could never be white noise to me. I listened closely to every note.

"Anything you tell me is in confidence. You understand that, right?" the doctor would say.

Greg was a lawyer, though, and he felt certain that the NDA prohibited disclosures even to people bound by a duty of confidentiality. We couldn't tell our doctors, our lawyers, even our priest if we had one, not without risking forfeiture of the settlement money. *How would they ever find out that we told her?* I asked him once early in our therapy. If Dr. Louise couldn't talk about it, then Dr. Benedict would never know and would never try to claw back the money. But Greg only set his jaw and said we couldn't take that chance.

The money meant a lot to him, that was obvious. It was obvious that night in the hotel when I was still shaking and crying and barely able to speak. *He did a terrible thing to you*, Greg said, and I nodded my quivering agreement. *He needs to pay for it*, he said, and I nodded again, picturing Benedict in prison stripes with chains around his ankles. *This is an incredible opportunity for us*, he said, and I stared at him through swollen eyes. *We could work hard every day of our lives and we'd never see a million dollars in one lump sum.* A million was Greg's opening demand, but the same thing was true of the half million we ultimately settled for.

I did blame him. He pressured me to make a decision that very night, only hours after Benedict attacked me. *It's now or never,* he said. *They'll revoke the offer if we don't lock this down now.* He didn't know that, not for certain. All he knew was that Kelly McCann was waiting in the hall right outside the door. He kept saying it—*She's right outside. She's ready to do the deal now*—in such a sinister tone that I pictured her as a female version of George Benedict—gray-suited, gray-skinned, with wispy hair and sneering lips. By the time Greg convinced me to sign, that image was so fixed in my mind that I bolted up in shock when a petite blonde entered the room with a warm smile and a sugary *Hello, Emily. My name's Kelly.* Then she placed the document on the hotel desk, and Greg guided my hand to initial each page and sign at the end.

My greatest mistake was calling Greg that night instead of the police. Though what could I have told the police anyway? I could barely find the words to tell Greg what Benedict had done to me. My own husband. A man with whom I'd been intimate. How could I ever have described it to strangers?

"I don't blame him," I told Dr. Louise. I did, but that wasn't the source of our marital problems. It had nothing to do with why I burst into tears and pushed him away every time he tried to touch me.

"That's not why," I said now to Dr. Louise. "I've just . . . lost interest, I guess."

"When did this start?" she asked.

Silence.

Dr. Louse waited a full minute, through two key changes in the soundtrack, before heaving a sigh. "You understand that most couples come here to talk," she said. "To tell their side or to get things off their chest. Most couples feel that's the principal benefit of therapy."

I always marveled at how professionals in the soft sciences would throw out such loosey-goosey statements. *Most couples?* In my field, I'd have to say the exact percentage and back it up with three double-blind studies. I needed that kind of precision in my work. I relished the objectivity.

As a child, all the way through high school, I studied violin. Devotedly. Obsessively. I once thought it would be my career. But the standards in music were maddeningly subjective. One instructor would praise my bowing technique; another would ridicule it. One audience would rise to their feet at the end of my solo; the next would offer tepid applause. I loved music, I always would, but I couldn't work in such a woolly world. Science suited me so much better.

WHEN OUR SESSION was over, we took out our phones and dutifully calendared next week's slot and said goodbye to Dr. Louise.

"Apartment okay?" I asked Greg as we headed for our cars in the parking lot.

He shrugged. "It is what it is."

He'd wanted the new house more than I did, but he volunteered to be the one to leave. *Wouldn't be fair for me to keep it,* he said. *You earned the money that bought it.*

Earned was the actual word he used. As if I were a prostitute.

I'D MISSED SOME calls while I was in Dr. Louise's office, and I listened to my voicemail now as I drove home. One of my lab techs called about the results of our latest trials, and my division VP called to compliment me on the results of our latest trials. There was a missed call from Ashley LaSorta, too. I decided not to return it. I knew what she was calling about. We all received Tiffy's weird text last night. Ashley had been griping about Tiffy all along, especially after she bailed on her part of the job. Now she obviously wanted to gripe some more. I was baffled by that weird text, too, but if I had to choose sides between Ashley and Tiffy, I'd choose Tiffy. She was a true victim, like me, whereas Ashley—well, everyone at UniViro knew she'd slept her way up the ladder. Her affair with Benedict was what landed her that corner office and flashy title. I didn't know what her specific grievance against him was—I couldn't know, thanks to *her* NDA—but assuming she was crying rape—well, it rankled. An affair that ended badly was nothing like what happened to me. Not even close.

The hours I spent in that hotel room waiting for Greg to arrive felt like days. Weeks. I'd never been so terrified in my life. Benedict was in the very next room, and even though I threw the deadbolt and hooked the chain, I was sick with fear. I imagined him tunneling through the wall, crawling through the ductwork. I pictured his leering face lunging through the bathroom mirror with a cry of *I'm baaack!*

* * *

AT HOME, I went upstairs and changed into a swimsuit and robe, poured myself a glass of white wine in the kitchen, then went outside to the pool deck.

It was like a concert stage, raised above the lawn and illuminated with uplights and surrounded by an amphitheater of woods. The pool was already winterized and sealed up with an aqua-blue cover, but the spa at the far end was still open, and swirling wisps of steam rose in the cool night air. I set my glass down beside the spa and went to the pump house for the turntable. Twilight was sinking through the sky, and the woods were turning black as I stretched the extension cord to reach. I selected a vinyl recording—Hilary Hahn's *Retrospective*—and placed it on the turntable. Then I shed the robe and lowered myself into the water.

This was the one good takeaway from my sessions with Dr. Louise. Her lessons in self-care. *Allow yourself to relax*, she said. *Indulge in what pleases you.* So this was how I ended every day now—listening to beautiful music while my body steeped in water heated to the ideal 37.7778 degrees Celsius.

I took off my glasses and laid them on the deck beside my wine. The warm water, the warm vinyl sounds of Hilary's violin, the dark woods around me, and the stars lighting up overhead—I could almost imagine that I was the one onstage, that I was the one playing the shimmering tones of *The Lark Ascending*.

I closed my eyes and sank into the water.

26

THE KIDS HAD BIG PLANS that weekend. Justin was compet-
ing in a science fair in New Haven, and Lexie was going to a
birthday party extravaganza—a whale-watching cruise followed by
a clambake followed by a beach bonfire and ending with a slumber
party in the host family's seaside cottage.

Saturday morning was a frenzy of packing, going over checklists,
and loading the car. First stop was Justin's school, where the activity bus and chaperones and his fellow science nerds were waiting.
The next stop was the birthday girl's house, where a caravan of cars
packed with overexcited children was waiting. Lexie bounced out of
the car to join them, leaving Kelly with the rest of the day to herself.

Tonight at dinner she would leak the documents to Rick Olsson
and pound the final nail in George Benedict's coffin. That meant that
she could relax today and do her actual job. She turned her attention
to the Tommy Wexford case. Cazzadee had packed her briefcase
with DVDs comprising the complete Tommy Wexford oeuvre. Kelly
settled in on the family room sectional with the remote control in
hand to watch

The first disc she loaded was a biopic with Wexford starring as
a brooding Percy Shelley. He made a credible Romantic poet, she
thought, though the costuming certainly helped: he wore a loose-
sleeved poet's shirt and neckcloth throughout.

The next DVD was a heist movie with a big ensemble cast. Wexford played the reluctant getaway driver. He was brooding in this one, too, and spent most of his screen time slouched low behind the wheel of the car with a camo neck gaiter pulled up over his mouth and nose.

The heist movie included a subplot about an embittered ex-Treasury agent who hacks into the Federal Reserve, and that got Kelly brooding, too, about her encounter with Edward Russo yesterday. He'd obviously put some effort into his pursuit of her. He'd traced her phone call, hacked her Wi-Fi, and staked out her house and office. Even if he wasn't the same man she saw on the beach and at UniViro—she seemed to recall now that those were different dogs—he'd still dedicated a lot of time to this venture. He had to believe there was a big payday at the end of it.

So far, he didn't have anything beyond speculation and wishful thinking, but all the pieces would fall into place after her plan was complete and the news hit the street. Benedict would vociferously deny that he'd stolen Reeza's research. He'd protest that the incriminating documents were forgeries and that the company server must have been hacked. That was the moment when Russo would know exactly what she'd done. That was when he'd come at her with his demand: pay him off or he'd report her.

She needed to know more about him. She hit Pause on the DVD and called Javier.

The line rang four times, six. It was early on a Saturday. He was probably still in bed. Probably with his latest conquest. She was ready to hang up when he finally answered. "Kelly?"

"Javi, hi, sorry to bother you, but a name came up I was hoping you could run down for me."

"Shoot."

She could hear a loud buzz of background noise. He wasn't in bed. He was out in public somewhere. Probably buying breakfast for his latest conquest. "Edward P. Russo," she said.

"Huh. Well, if he's looking to hire you, just say no."

"It's nothing like that." Now she could hear the crackle of a loud-speaker on Javier's end of the call. "You know him?"

"Yeah. He's a total sleaze. A hacker. Feds nabbed him a while back. He did some time."

"For hacking?"

"That plus extortion. Get this: instead of going into rich guys' networks to steal their files, he'd go in and plant files. Then threaten to expose them if they didn't pay up."

"What kind of files?"

"Kiddie porn."

"Ahh." Kelly started to relax again. Russo was an ex-con, which meant he couldn't report her to the police or the FBI, not without admitting that he was still working as a hacker. His threat was empty.

"What else you need on the guy?" Javi asked. "Want me to run his credit?"

"No, but if you could check on his parole status?"

"Sure. First thing Monday."

The loudspeaker crackled again, and this time she could make out a few of the words. *Attention passengers for American Airlines Flight 849* . . . "Javi," she said, bewildered, "are you boarding a plane?"

"My time, my dime," he snapped.

After the call ended, abruptly, she gave in to the impulse and googled the flight number. Sure enough, it was a flight to Philadelphia. She sighed. Javi was wasting his time, but he couldn't see it. He was on a mission to get Benedict, and she could hardly fault him for that.

She returned to her Tommy Wexford retrospective. The next DVD was a family drama in which he portrayed the son with a drug addiction. That was followed by two different love stories. One was gay, one was straight, and both were tragic. Despite some explicit sex scenes with abundant female nudity, Wexford never took his clothes off in any of them. Just as he'd told her.

After lunch she went into the study and scrolled through TMZ and E!Online and other celebrity gossip sites in search of ambush photos of Wexford. He'd been captured going in and coming out of his house and assorted LA restaurants, usually with his waifish girlfriend. There were no cavorting-on-the-beach shots, or photos of him drunkenly stumbling out of a club. He was always buttoned up tight.

She had a pretty good idea by then that her hunch was right. She sent him an email. Need to talk. Urgent. Video call Monday. Time and link to follow. She copied Cazz to set it up, but she didn't copy the rest of her team. This would be a closed meeting.

She looked up when she heard Todd on the stairs. The house was so quiet with the children away that his footsteps were audible even in his soft-soled shoes. Instead of heading down the hall to the kitchen, he turned and padded through the living room. He tapped on the study door. "Got a minute, Kell?"

His expression was so solemn that she half surged from her chair. "Adam—?"

"No, no." He hurried to wave her back to her seat. "He's fine. Well, he's stable."

"Okay," she said, waiting.

"It's Justin. He asked me to tell you something."

"He called?" Her eyes shot to her phone. She wondered how she'd missed his call.

"He asked me earlier. He wanted me to wait until he was gone."

She sat back. That sounded ominous. Could he be failing a class? He was an excellent student, though he did have a bad habit of blowing off any subjects that weren't math or science. But she couldn't imagine why he went to Todd instead of her. She hoped she hadn't put too much pressure on him to work harder in English class.

Todd perched on the arm of a chair. "He's worried you'll get mad. And I'm worried that you'll worry more than you need to. It's not that big a deal. Well, it's serious, but it's not the end of the world."

"For God's sake, Todd!" Now she was alarmed. "What is it?"

His face screwed up in a wince. "He knows who hacked into the Wi-Fi."

Her eyes opened wide. "How?" If Edward Russo dared to contact her child, she'd report *him* to the FBI.

"Because he gave her the password."

"Her?" She blinked. "Who?"

"His girlfriend. Or I should say the girl he'd like to be his girlfriend. They only meet online."

She remembered then . . . Lexie ribbing him about a girlfriend. She also remembered how quickly she'd discounted it, so content to think that he was the kind of boy who wouldn't have an actual girlfriend yet. Virtual ones never crossed her mind.

"Why did he give her our password?"

Todd shifted in his chair. "Okay, here's where you might get upset. She sent him photos of herself." He hesitated. "Nude photos."

Kelly's mouth fell open before her hand flew to cover it. "Oh God!"

"No, now don't overreact. It's just something straight boys like to look at. It doesn't make him a pervert or a criminal or anything. He's just a normal, hormonal teenager."

She blew out a huff of breath. "That's why he didn't want to hand over his phone and laptop after that first hack. Because we'd find the photos. But you talked him into it." She looked up sharply. "You promised him you wouldn't tell me."

Todd gave a sheepish little shrug.

"Was there porn, too?"

"A bit," he admitted.

"And sexting?"

Todd looked at the floor.

Her son. Soliciting nude photos. Sexting with a young girl. Watching porn. She had another horrible thought. "Did he send her photos of himself?"

Todd nodded. "But no dick pics. No nudes."

She bit her lip. "Did he send her photos to anyone else?" That was something else boys did, and it *would* make him a criminal.

"He swears he didn't. And that's why she wanted the password. So she could check that he wasn't sharing them. He never thought she'd use it to hack into the rest of the household. He was really upset when he found out that she was spying on his dad. He feels sick about it."

Kelly felt sick, too, that her son was feeling sick about the wrong thing. His internet girlfriend wasn't their hacker. She wouldn't have any interest in spying on an invalid. It was Edward Russo who'd switched on the CCTV. Justin should definitely feel guilty, but not about that.

"I need to see those pictures," she said.

"I figured you might." Todd stood up and reached in his pocket. "I copied them, then I watched him delete them all from his phone and laptop."

He held out a thumb drive, and she took it with numb fingers.

"He's learned his lesson, Kelly. He won't have anything more to do with this girl. So try not to worry." He added in a softer voice: "He's a good kid. And you're a good mom."

She looked away as tears welled in her eyes. A good mom would have been on the bus to New Haven with him this weekend. A good mom would have been someone he could talk to about his online girl-friend. A good mom wouldn't need an employee to serve as a liaison to her own son.

It was a long time after Todd left before she could make herself open the files on the thumb drive. What she found were a dozen pho-tos of a teenage girl. Her face was barely visible behind a swooping curtain of glossy dark hair. But her body was on full display. Some of the photos showed her in a state of undress that seemed designed to tantalize—a nipple escaping here, an up-skirt shot there. But most of the photos were complete, full-frontal nudes. She had a firm young body, with small round breasts and pink-tipped nipples, and it made Kelly sick to her stomach to think of her son salivating over these photos. Masturbating over them. Violating this girl by objectifying her, even if she wanted to be objectified.

Todd said Justin had learned his lesson, but it was the wrong lesson. The only reason he confessed was because he thought the girl switched on the CCTV. He saw her as the wrongdoer in this drama. Not himself.

Tears streamed down her face. Her own son—her sweet little boy—was preying on a young girl. Even if the photos were entirely the girl's idea, Justin was still using them for his own gratification. Exploiting them. Exploiting her.

Where were the mothers? everyone cried whenever boys were caught abusing girls. For most mothers the answer was *Right there, doing their best.* Or maybe *Flailing helplessly.* But for Kelly it was *At work, defending men who did the exact same thing.*

Of course Justin thought it was okay to prey on girls. It was the only lesson he could have learned from a mother who did what she did for a living.

27

OST OF JAVI'S GUYS WERE in fact girls, or rather—he reminded himself to say—women. True, the ones he had to hire, the ones who presented invoices for their services, were usually men. But the ones who happily exchanged information for a little bit of sweet talk, a smile, a schmooze—they were always women. The secretaries, the records clerks, the ER nurses. It wasn't a case of loose lips—these women weren't irresponsible about what they disclosed, and he seldom asked them to be. Their willingness always came after a careful consideration of *Where's the harm?* Their tight-ass male bosses would say *None of your fucking business* or *It's need to know and you don't*, even if the information was trivial or would become public the next day. It was a power thing with men to withhold information. It was a friendly thing with the women to share it.

And the women knew everything. They didn't just file those reports, they read them, and they discussed them with the clerk at the next desk who'd seen a related report, and together they connected all the dots. It wasn't gossip. There was nothing mean-spirited about it. It was a community of shared knowledge, and everyone was the wiser for it.

Javi started building up his network during his years on the force. Life as a cop didn't much suit him, though—too much empty posturing and bullying for its own sake. He'd had enough of that machismo bullshit growing up. So after a few years he swung over to work as an investigator in the DA's office. It turned out most of the lawyers there were dicks, too, and always measuring theirs against the next guy's. Kelly McCann was the notable exception, and when she left for private practice, Javi went with her.

He worked with an all-female crew now, and other guys liked to give him shit about it. Putdowns like was his cycle synched to theirs, or jokes about him being the only stud in a stable of mares. But every sling missed its mark. Javi enjoyed working with Kelly and her crew. He was a man who appreciated women, and they appreciated him right back.

That was how he knew it wasn't a gender thing that left him seething at Kelly this weekend. This wasn't about wounded male pride. It was simpler and more honest than that: he was the investigator on their team. He was the one who had hunches and followed leads and gathered facts. In all their years together, she'd never second-guessed him before. She'd never tried to rein him in.

But she hadn't been herself lately. Ever since the Benedict trial, there'd been something off about her. Cazzadee had hinted that there might be trouble at home—so, okay, he resolved to cut Kelly some slack. Give her some space. He'd do this on his own and not report back to her until he had it tied up with a bow. And then he'd put in for expenses.

HE PICKED UP a car at the Philly airport and drove out of the city to Tiffy Jenkins's address. He'd been there once before, during trial prep, when Benedict suddenly remembered there'd been some incident with an office cleaner. It took some digging for Javi to figure out which cleaner she was. Based on the shift schedules, he'd narrowed it down to two employees: Tiffy and a fifty-year-old woman named Marisol Fuentes. He knew enough by then not to assume the victim was the young skinny blonde. None of these creeps ever chose their victims based on their attractiveness. That whole excuse of *she was asking for it, her skirt was too short, her neckline was too low*—that was all total bullshit. So he called on Mrs. Fuentes first, spoke to her for twenty minutes in her native tongue, and came away convinced that she had no idea what he was talking about. Then he drove to this trailer park.

Tiffy's reaction said everything when he told her who he worked for. Her face went white, and though she was too timid to slam the door on him, she did back away with her hands out in front of her— what his police training called the "classic defensive" posture. He had to raise his own hands in the classic "no harm intended" posture to make her calm down. Even then she was reluctant to admit that she was the one Benedict had attacked. He knew that meant she'd settle quickly. A look around her shabby home told him she'd settle cheap. He reported back to Kelly, and the deal was done.

Today he planned to trawl the neighbors for gossip, starting with the trailer across from Tiffy's place. He parked on the shoulder of the rutted lane, and when he got out of the car, a dog started barking hysterically in a high-pitched frenzied yip. Javi looked around and found the dog two doors down, straining so hard on the end of his chain that his pitch went higher and thinner still, until he gave one final strangled squeal and fell limp in a cloud of dust.

In the sudden silence Javi could hear the music blaring. His head swiveled. The music was coming from Tiffy's place. She didn't have any roommates that he knew of, or family, and her boyfriend, Sean, was in jail. That meant it was probably a squatter. He crossed the lane to check it out.

The music was death metal, turned up loud. The vocals growled something guttural and unintelligible. He knocked on the door, and when no one answered, he pounded hard a few times, and when no one answered that, he hollered as he pounded. The holler seemed to do it. The flimsy aluminum door was flung open, but whoever opened it immediately retreated into the murk. The inside of the trailer looked like a cave. No lights were on, and the curtains were drawn.

"Hey," Javi said into the darkness. He stepped inside, and as his eyes slowly adjusted to the dim light, he could make out a man slumped on the couch. He had a bottle in his fist. A fifth of something.

"You a friend of Ms. Jenkins?" Javi asked.

A loud sniff sounded, full of snot and tears. "You a cop?" the man slurred.

"Revenue Bureau," Javi said. "Refund department."

No such thing existed by that name, but it was usually enough to get him a sit-down with a certain demographic. He waited, but the next sound to come from the couch was the ratcheting inhalation of a snore.

"Sir?" he said, louder, but when the bottle hit the floor, he knew it was a lost cause. He looked around for a minute, flipped through some junk mail on the counter, and went back outside.

A young woman was standing by his rental car. She was skinny and blond like Tiffy, though Tiffy was a natural blonde and this woman had two inches of black roots showing along the crooked part on the top of her head. She grinned. "He's been on a bender ever since they sprung him," she said.

Javi looked back at the trailer. "That's Sean in there?"

She nodded and took a drag on a cigarette.

"He made bail?"

"Nope. They let him go."

"Why?"

She shrugged. "The cops been back out here askin' everybody up and down the park what they seen that day." She tapped the ash into the gravel at her feet as a child's wail came from inside the trailer behind her. "I hear somebody told them they seen a fancy car at

Tiffy's that day. I didn't see nothin', though. And I live right here."
With a sly smile, she pointed at the door behind her. "If you wanna
come in a minute—"

Javi was already running to his car. "Thanks. Gotta go." He dove
behind the wheel and sped out so fast the gravel kicked up from the tires.

HE SPENT THE rest of the afternoon at the township police department. It was a small department in a jurisdiction where the only
regular crimes were retail theft and DUIs. They didn't have a com-
munications officer, and the chief wasn't on duty and wasn't to be
disturbed at home, at least according to the sergeant at the desk. Nobody was at liberty to speak to Javi, and everybody wanted to know
what his interest in the case was. It was his bad luck that everybody
on duty today was male. He left empty-handed.

MOST OF HIS guys were Boston-based, but his guys had their own
guys, and those guys had guys, too, and the result was an inter-
state network of guys—girls—he could tap into. His best contact in
Pennsylvania was Suzanne Browning, a longtime admin manager in
the AG's office who seemed to have a finger in every law enforce-
ment pot in the commonwealth. After he checked into his motel, he
called her to confirm their date tonight. "And by the way—" he said
and rattled off his wish list of intel.

She let out a put-upon groan, but she didn't say no.

SUZANNE WORKED OUT of the Norristown office and lived in the
nearby sprawl of King of Prussia. She'd named her favorite neighborhood bar for their meeting place, and he parked the car and found

her inside, keeping a table warm for him. She was in her forties, divorced and pleasingly plump. She waved him over and leaned back in her chair as he bent to give her a quick peck on the lips.

"What're you drinking?" he asked.

"Dirty martini," she said and waggled her penciled-in eyebrows.

He laughed and went to the bar and came back with a beer for himself and another martini for Suzanne. She planted her elbows on the table. "Okay, here's what I got," she said. She wanted to get their business out of the way, and he was grateful he didn't have to wait for it. "The boyfriend's got an alibi. A bar up in Pottstown's got him on video for like three hours around the time of the murder."

Not the boyfriend, then, Javi thought. He knew it.

"And here's something else," Suzanne said. "Her throat was cut, right? In your typical rage murder, that's a slash across the neck, left to right or right to left, depending on handedness. But this victim wasn't slashed. The knife was plunged straight into her carotid. The pathologist says it's almost surgical."

"Somebody knew what he was doing." Benedict was an MD, Javi recalled, before he amassed all his other degrees.

"Or got lucky."

"Anything else?"

"Jesus, Javi—it took me most of the afternoon to get this much."

"Right. Sorry."

"Okay, next. Bucks County." She was friends with somebody who knew somebody in the coroner's office, and word was that Reeza Patel's death would shortly be ruled accidental. The lab couldn't identify the source of the megadose of oxycodone that killed her, but in the absence of any evidence that her meds were deliberately manipulated, accidental was the default.

"Right," Javi said. The absent evidence, he knew, was the connection between Patel's death and the murder of Tiffy Jenkins. But the coroner didn't know about that connection, and neither did anyone else outside of Kelly and her team. Except, of course, for George Benedict.

All the pieces were lining up and pointing straight at Benedict. Someone driving a fancy car who knew where the carotid artery was. Someone who knew how to deliver a super-concentrated dose of Oxy. Someone who knew both women. Someone who'd already violently assaulted both women.

The only problem—Benedict was in Atlanta at the time of Tiffy's murder.

But that still left Anton. He was the actual driver of that fancy car, and Benedict easily could have instructed him how to pierce the carotid artery. Assuming he didn't already know.

Javi went to the bar for another martini for Suzanne and a soda water for himself, and they sat for another hour and talked of other things. But his mind was on Anton and all he knew about him. Which wasn't much. He was built like a slab of rock and with even less emotion. Javi had spent a few hours in his company on various occasions and never once saw the man crack a smile.

He'd tried to run a background check on him when Kelly first started representing Benedict, but all he could find out was his full name, Anton Sebastian Balkus, and that he was born in Lithuania. Anything about his life for the next forty years was lost in the opaque tangle of foreign records. The US records began in 2008, when he immigrated to the States. He got one of those genius visas under the corporate sponsorship of UniViro. That kind of visa was supposed to require a showing of extraordinary ability in some field or other, but Javi had never been able to ascertain exactly what Anton's abilities were. On paper his only job was driver. Though clearly he did more than that.

One day, while waiting for Kelly in the UniViro parking lot, Javi had watched Anton open the trunk of the Bentley and pull out a three-foot pole with a disk at one end. Javi recognized it as an

under-vehicle inspection mirror, the kind they used at border cross-
ings, and he watched Anton do a full circuit of the car with the mirror angled under the frame. Apparently satisfied that there was no
incendiary device, he'd stopped to polish a spot on the fender before
folding himself behind the wheel to wait for his master.

He'd obviously made the jump from driver to bodyguard, but it
was a bigger jump from bodyguard to assassin. Javi needed more
intel before he could make that leap of logic himself. After Suzanne
decided against finishing her third martini, he paid their tab, saved
the receipt, and walked her to her car. "Coming back?" she asked on
the pavement outside.

Once that was the natural way the evening would have ended,
but he wasn't doing that anymore. "Sorry," he said. "I have to work
tonight."

"Your loss," Suzanne said, and he clutched his heart and reeled.
She laughed out loud, and they parted with kisses on the cheeks.
Still friends. Still part of the network.

BACK IN HIS motel room, he spent some time studying an aerial
photograph of the Benedict property that he'd downloaded from a
real estate website. Anton lived somewhere on the grounds, Javi
knew, probably in one of the many outbuildings that fanned out
behind the mansion. According to the website listing, there was a
guesthouse with two bedrooms and a bath. There was a six-car garage with a second story that could easily accommodate an apartment. A conservatory and potting shed. A kennel. And finally a
cabana by the pool that was the size of a small house. The photo
and listing details dated back to before Benedict bought the place,
so they might not be accurate anymore. Still, Javi memorized the
layout before he changed clothes and headed out.

* * *

THERE WERE NO gates barring the entrance to the mansion, but the lampposts were mounted with conspicuous security cameras. Instead, Javi navigated a maze of back roads that led him finally, circuitously, to the far side of the estate. He pulled off the road and parked behind the screen of an old hedgerow, then set out through the woods with the narrow beam of his phone light leading the way.

The mansion came into view as he neared the edge of the woods. He stopped at the treeline and pocketed his phone. Lights shone in a few downstairs windows and one upstairs, but the windows that wrapped around the dome of the rotunda glowed from lights that could have come from a dozen different rooms. He couldn't guess which room the Benedicts might be occupying at the moment. If they even occupied the same room. He couldn't picture them doing anything together on a Saturday night. Or ever. It was safest to assume that all of the rooms were occupied and stay well away from the mansion.

He skirted to the rear of the property and scanned for security cameras. He couldn't see any. Still, he pulled the ski mask over his head before he stepped out from the cover of the woods. He was dressed all in black, head to foot, and he did a ninja-creep out onto the lawn.

The garage and cabana were dark, while a patch of amber light glowed through a single window in the guesthouse. He stole past the pool and cabana. He was wary of the kennel, and he stopped and sniffed the air before going any farther. He could smell grass and chlorine and, carried high on the wind, some woodsmoke from a distant fire. But he didn't pick up any scent of fur or feces. If the Benedicts kept any animals, they must have had them sanitized and deodorized around the clock.

He stole around the kennel without setting off any barks or

growls. Next up was the conservatory. It was the size of a basketball court, built on a half wall of brick with glass panels rising up and meeting in an arched roof overhead. Multiple lights were on inside. He dropped to a squat and raised his head a few inches above the bricks to peer in. The lights were grow lights hanging over tables and racks and shelves of potted plants. He scanned the length of the room. There was plenty of plant life inside but no animals, human or otherwise.

He cut behind the potting shed. Ahead of him was a stretch of open lawn to the guesthouse. He did another scan for cameras, then dropped to his belly and army-crawled through the damp grass until he reached the back of the house. Slowly, he rose to his feet and flattened his body against the wall. He sidestepped in small, silent movements to the window and leaned over far enough for one eye to get a glimpse inside. The room was a kitchen, and Anton was in it.

Javi pulled back and held his breath, listening hard. He picked up the sound of running water, then the clattering of something metallic. He leaned in again. Anton stood in profile at the kitchen sink, facing the window on the adjacent wall. He was dressed all in black, like Javi, with his sleeves pushed up to his elbows. His hands were scrubbing something in the sink. Dinner dishes, Javi thought, until Anton shifted his weight and held up something that glinted like silver in the overhead light. It was a knife, stainless steel, blade and handle both, and looked more like a surgical instrument than a kitchen tool. He snapped it onto a magnetic rack on the wall where a whole array of similar knives was hanging.

Suddenly Anton's spine stiffened. He spun on his heel.

Javi jerked back. Footsteps sounded inside, and he pressed his belly tight against the wall, trying to bleed into it in the dark. He heard Anton's feet thud across the room. He heard him stop at the window, inches away. Javi held his breath. He imagined Anton peering into the night as he reached for one of those knives. He listened hard for the sound of metal detaching from the magnetic strip.

Anton's footsteps sounded again, going the other way.

Javi breathed again, and after a few minutes he retreated, slowly, back the way he'd come, and when he reached the woods, he broke into a run all the way to his car.

28

THAT NIGHT KELLY WORE A black silk dress, sleeveless, with strappy heels and a white cashmere wrap to guard against the evening chill. It was the kind of outfit that called for a small clutch. Instead, she carried a black leather document pouch. It didn't complement her ensemble in the least, but it was big enough to hold her wallet, her phone, and the folder of doctored documents she intended to pass to Rick.

She felt as nervous as a girl on her first date as she parked and made her way to the restaurant door. This was the final act in their drama. The next hour would decide everything—if Rick would take the bait, if Benedict would be destroyed, if Kelly could finally purge herself of his poison.

She pushed through the door. Rick was waiting by the bar, and he called to her—"Kelly!"—with a warm smile and his arm in the air.

Instantly she relaxed. For a second she almost wished this was a date, as if an evening with this kind, congenial man was all the antidote she needed. But only for a second. "Rick!" she replied with the same cheer and extended her hand.

He didn't try for the European kiss as he had the other night. Instead, he took her hand in both of his and held it there. "So good to see you," he said. "You look great."

He'd booked a secluded table in the back, and the hostess led them there through a gauntlet of other tables. A few diners raised their eyebrows and whispered to their companions as Rick passed by, but most didn't seem to notice him. Kelly took a seat and tucked the document bag under her chair. A young man arrived immediately for their beverage orders. "G and T for you, Kelly?" Rick asked. "With just a splash?"

She nodded at the server. "And that's just a splash of gin, not tonic."

Rick laughed and ordered a Dewar's highball for himself.

The server departed, and Kelly shook out her napkin and opened with the classic icebreaker. "So, what brings you to Boston?"

"The usual. Chasing a story."

"Same story as your last trip?"

"Same one."

"Must be a big one," she mused, "for you to give up your weekend."

"I imagine you sacrifice a lot of weekends for your work, too."

"When I'm in trial, yes."

They lapsed into silence as they each studied the menu and made their selections. Their server delivered their drinks and left with their dinner orders. Rick raised his glass. "Here's to making time for a little bit of pleasure in a working weekend."

She lifted her own glass in a brief salute and took a sip.

"Must be hard," he said, "being away from your children when you're in trial."

She nodded, but it rankled a little, how often such a comment was directed at mothers and not fathers, so she parried: "Same for you, I imagine, when you're chasing a story."

A shadow flitted over his face. "Same for me all the time, I'm afraid. My boys live with their mother in New Jersey."

"Oh." So he was divorced. She wondered if the ex–Mrs. Olsson was any better at raising fatherless boys than she was. "Actually," she said, "my kids are the ones who are away this weekend. Sleepover at the Cape and science fair in New Haven."

"Hey, I love science fairs! What's his project?"

"It's way over my head, I'm afraid. Something to do with staining bacteria?"

"Oh, right, I think I know that one. It's the Gram test for identifying classes of bacteria. Well, here, let me show you."

He pulled his phone from his breast pocket and tapped in a few letters to pull up a website. Then he came around the table to squat beside her chair. He pushed Play on a video and held it up for her to watch. It showed a hand with an eyedropper squeezing indigo dye into two different petri dishes. As she watched, the substance in one dish turned purple, and in the other, pink.

"See? The purple one is Gram-positive, and the pink is Gram-negative."

"Yes. But what's the point?"

"It helps you identify the bacteria." He circled back to his seat and laid his phone on the table. "If it's Gram-positive, that includes things like MRSA. Gram-negative includes most of the food contaminants. Like salmonella."

He delivered that last line at the exact moment that two servers arrived and simultaneously laid down their salad plates. Kelly and Rick looked down at the lettuce leaves, then up at each other, and burst out laughing.

"How do you know this stuff?" she asked after the servers backed away.

"Apart from being a big nerd in high school?" He chuckled. "That was my first beat as a journalist. Science and medicine. Until the network honchos noticed that I knew how to conduct an interview and started steering me into other assignments. You'd be amazed how many big names in broadcasting don't know the ABCs of interviewing. Their producers give them a script, and they stick to it no matter what. And miss some big stories along the way."

She nodded. "A lot of lawyers are guilty of the same thing when they're examining witnesses. They have their prepared questions, and they don't pivot when they get an unexpected answer. They don't even hear the unexpected answer. They're so focused on their next question that they break the first rule of examination. You have to listen to what the witness is saying."

"And sometimes what she isn't saying."

That last remark struck her as too pointed. The gender choice was telling, too. She shifted in her chair, and her foot brushed against the document case. She needed to get to the point of this meeting, and this seemed the moment. "When we met in New York the other night," she began, "you remember we discussed some of the rumors about Benedict's discovery of the virus. About falsified records."

"Hmm." He looked around for their server and raised his arm to beckon him. "I'd like some olive oil for this bread. How about you?"

"Some of the published reports seem to differ from the internal notes."

"Excuse me," Rick said as the waiter arrived. "Could we get a little plate of olive oil?"

"Certainly, sir."

"I've seen that happen," he went on when the waiter left. "I'm doing a story on PTSD right now, and I've been watching video interviews of these trauma victims, and you'd be amazed how the therapists' write-ups of the interviews deviate from what these women actually said on camera. I mean, paraphrasing is one thing, but actually changing the symptoms they experienced—"

"Yes, but these reports weren't based on anything subjective. This looks like a straightforward case of"—she hesitated; it was too soon to use words like *theft*—"misattribution."

"Kelly." Rick put down his salad fork. "I have a confession to make."

"What?" She tried to tamp down her impatience at the way he kept hijacking their conversation. It was something men often did, and she usually called them on it. But this time she couldn't. She needed to keep Rick on her side.

"The other night," he said, "when I tried to kiss you? It wasn't because I was making a move—although, obviously, I'd like to, at some point." He winced a smile. "But that night? That was a test."

She huffed a laugh. "Of what? To see how easy I might be?"

"No." He was suddenly solemn. "To see how easily triggered you might be."

She stared at him. She could feel the blood ebb from her face. "What?"

"Kelly, I know he attacked you that night. I'm guessing he raped you. That's why you had that meltdown when I tried to kiss you."

Her head started to spin. "No— I told you—I had a bug."

"That video . . . of the helicopter landing. It couldn't be any plainer."

"No." When she shook her head, she felt even dizzier. "I was drunk. I told you."

"I had a neurologist look at it. He said you showed signs of neuromuscular paralysis. For God's sake, Kelly, he drugged you."

"You showed it to someone else?" she gasped. "You said you'd destroy it. You promised!"

"I'm sorry. I couldn't. It's evidence."

"It's not! It's nothing! Nothing happened!" Her voice roared inside her head, but she didn't realize that she'd actually shouted until she saw the curious glances of the diners around them.

"Why else would you be waging this vendetta against your own client? Even if you knew he was guilty of raping Patel, you wouldn't go this far. You certainly wouldn't be trying to leak documents to me."

Her head felt like it was floating off her shoulders. "I thought you'd want to know! Your book— You'd want the truth of who discovered the virus! If he's taking credit for something he didn't do—"

"Kelly . . ." he said sadly, softly.

His phone started to rattle on the table, and he hurried to turn it over. But he wasn't fast enough. She could read the caller's name on the screen before he flipped it facedown. *Dad.*

Her eyes shot to his face. He bit his lip and looked down. His phone continued to vibrate.

"You told me your father was dead," she said. "You said you lost him to Alzheimer's."

"It was my uncle actually. I'm sorry. I embellished—"

"You lied!"

"I did. I'm sorry. But you lied, too. You lured me to that campus—"

"Your book deal— You're not writing a book about Alzheimer's. It was never about that." She pushed back hard from the table, and her chair screeched across the floor. "You're writing a book about— what? Me?" Her voice screeched, too.

"No! It's about them. Benedict and the other big names in medicine and science who are serial abusers." He half rose from his chair to lean closer. "Kelly, he has to be exposed. He has to be stopped. This book is critical, critical work."

"Oh, I'm sure," she said bitterly. "It'll be a bestseller. I mean, the man who cured Alzheimer's? That's way bigger than a Hollywood producer or a TV comic. You'll win a Pulitzer. Every talk show will want to interview *you*."

"He's a predator. He doesn't get a pass for genius. We need to take him down."

She stood, and when the room started to spin, she grabbed the chair back to hold herself steady.

"You want revenge," he said. "Believe me, I get it. But revenge isn't justice. Let me expose him for what he really is. Tell the truth about what he did."

She squeezed the chair so hard her knuckles bled white. "You write anything about me, and I'll sue you for every royalty you receive. Because it's a lie. It's all a lie."

He straightened to his full height. "I know it's not."

She grabbed her wrap and cut around him, stumbling for the door.

"Kelly, wait!" he called.

She kept on walking.

"You forgot this."

She looked back. He was striding toward her with her case in his hand.

"Are the documents in here?" he asked. "I'll take them if you really want me to."

She snatched the case away from him. She didn't want him to see the documents. She couldn't trust him anymore. She couldn't trust him not to see through her lies. She turned and hurried out of the restaurant.

THE HOUSE WAS dark when she got home. The only lights were in the upstairs alcove window. She parked in the garage, went into the kitchen, and mixed herself a gin and tonic with just a splash of tonic.

The living room was dark, and she left it that way as she sank into the sofa and took a gulp of her drink. Her light-headedness was gone, and in its place was the heavy burden of defeat. She'd been played. The whole time she thought she was working Rick Olsson, he was working her. He'd been chasing her story from the moment he watched the helicopter video. That was what prompted his first call to her. That was why he agreed to meet her on the college campus, and why he agreed to meet her at the bar even after she stood him up on campus. That was the only reason he was in Boston on the day he rescued her from the press mob. That was the only reason he rescued her. And it was the only reason he tried to kiss her.

Her only consolation: he failed. Despite the great lengths he'd gone to, he'd failed to get her story.

But that was small consolation in the face of the fact that she'd failed, too. Her revenge scheme was a bust. Even if she could find some other journalist to leak the documents to, she couldn't go through with it now. Not when Rick could tie her to the manufactured documents. She'd be ruined. Disbarred for sure and maybe also prosecuted and convicted and even sentenced to prison. While Benedict would sail on unscathed. He wouldn't suffer any professional disgrace. He'd win the Nobel Prize.

She needed to call Ashley and tell her to go back into the Uni-Viro database and restore all the original entries. Then back out and leave no footprints. Undo everything they'd done, because it was all for nothing.

She drained her glass and went to the kitchen for a refill. The remnants of Rick's fruit basket sat on the counter, and she was reaching for the gin bottle beside it when something suddenly occurred to her. Rick sent the basket here, to her home. He knew where she lived. She never told him, but he knew. Of course he did. He was an investigative journalist, and she was a story. No lengths were too far to go.to God, for all she knew, he was the one who'd hacked into the home network.

She started to pour the gin into her glass when she thought better of it. She put the glass in the sink and went back to the living room with the bottle.

Revenge isn't justice, he'd said. As if such a thing even existed in this world.

She put the bottle to her lips and drank.

29

SUNDAY MORNING JAVI CHECKED OUT of the motel and drove back to Gladwyne. This time he turned into the Benedicts' lane and drove between the lampposts, in full view of the security cameras. He followed the road around the lily pond and past the knot garden to the entry court in front of the mansion, then he looped around behind it to the service court at the back. A flagstone walkway led from the terrace to the cluster of outbuildings at the rear of the property. He parked and followed it.

Last night's recon had accomplished nothing beyond learning that Anton lived in the guesthouse and owned a fancy set of knives. Javi's plan today was to knock on his door and reintroduce himself, then tell him some issues had come up in connection with post-trial motions and he needed to ask him a few questions. It wasn't much of a strategy, but it would get him through the door. From there, his only plan was to look around. Try to find out if he'd accompanied the doctor to Atlanta. Ask some bland questions about Reeza Patel and Tiffy Jenkins and gauge his reaction.

He reached the guesthouse and rang the bell.

"Yoo-hoo? Mr. Torres?" a contralto voice called. "Is that you?"

He turned with a hand visored over his brow. A squarish figure stood in silhouette against the glare of the morning sun—a woman wearing a wide-brimmed straw hat and a loose-flowing white dress. "Mrs. Benedict?" he said.

"I thought I recognized you!" she declared as she picked her way across the lawn. Over one arm was a basket of yellow flowers. She looked like something out of an old-fashioned pastoral painting. "What brings you here this lovely Sunday morning?"

"I was hoping to see Anton."

"Oh?"

"Yeah, I, uh, borrowed some cash from him during the trial. I was in the neighborhood, so I thought I'd swing by and pay him back." A second later he wondered if anyone still borrowed cash, in these days of phone apps that paid for everything.

But Mrs. Benedict was old enough not to question the concept. She reminded him of his *abuela*, gray-haired and thickset and always beaming fondly. "Oh, what a shame!" she said. "You just missed him."

"Okay. I can come back later."

"No, I'm afraid he'll be gone until late Thursday. If you'd like to leave the money with me? Oh, wait! What am I saying?" She tapped a knuckle against her forehead. "He's driving up to Boston today! You can probably track him down up there!"

"Oh? What's he doing in Boston?"

"George is running a symposium at Harvard Medical School this week. He doesn't like to fly, you know. All those closed-air systems. Bacteria and viruses circulating about everywhere."

"Huh. I never thought about that."

"Oh yes. George avoids flying whenever he can."

"So I guess he drove to Atlanta last week?"

"Oh no." She shook her head, and her jowls shook with her. "That's too long a trip with his busy schedule. No, he flew that time. With his respirator mask, of course."

Javi hesitated. One question too many and she might get suspicious. But he needed to tie this up. "And Anton, he wore a mask, too?"

"No, no, Anton sat out that trip."

"Ah."

"Won't you come up for a glass of tea?" She waved a flabby arm toward the rear terrace of the mansion.

"Thank you, ma'am, but I better hit the road to Boston myself."

She glanced down at the basket over her arm. "I've just been harvesting some of my arnica. Could I make you a bundle to take home?"

"No, thanks."

"Are you sure? It does wonders for muscle pain."

"I'm okay, thanks."

"Oh, you young people!" She laughed. "Never a care in the world, or an ache either."

JAVI FELT PRETTY well satisfied as he drove away. It was a lucky break, running into Mrs. Benedict. It would have been a lot dicier to get that same information out of Anton. But now he had it. Anton was in town at the time of Tiffy's murder. He drove a fancy car. He owned a set of surgical-looking knives.

He thought about those knives. He remembered Anton dressed all in black last night, scrubbing one of those knives clean, and suddenly he stomped on the brakes and pulled off to the side of the road. For a second he let the thought sink in: something must have happened last night.

He called Ashley LaSorta first and got her voicemail. He called Emily Norland next and got her voicemail, too. He called the airline last and pushed back his flight.

* * *

THE LAST TIME he visited Ashley, she lived in a stone Colonial in the Philadelphia suburbs. It was a nice place but nothing like the Italianate villa she now owned in Princeton.

Cameras were mounted on the decorative gateposts, on the front corners of the facade, and at the front door beside the intercom. It looked like a good system. He hoped it kept her safe last night.

He rang the bell and felt a wave of relief when her husky voice blared through the speaker. "Jesus fucking Christ. You got some nerve, Alejandro, or whatever the fuck your name is."

"It's Javier," he shouted into the box, "and I'm sorry to bother you, but I need to tell you something. It's important. Can I come in?"

"And let you screw me twice? You think I'm a fucking idiot?"

He'd never even screwed her once, but he understood she wouldn't quite see it that way. "Look, I'm sorry for how all that played out. If it makes any difference, I don't do that anymore."

"Oh, right." The static in the speaker didn't obscure the sarcasm in her voice. "You found God."

He smiled. "Sort of. I got married."

"Ha. Now I know you're lying."

"Ashley, please. Let me in. I have to tell you something. It's about Reeza Patel's death."

"I already know. It wasn't suicide."

"Yeah. And it wasn't accidental either."

A slow hiss of static sounded from the speaker. He looked up at the camera and gave a nod. A minute later an electronic buzz sounded, and Ashley opened the door. She immediately turned her back on him and stalked away.

He followed her inside. The foyer was a large octagonal space with four doors opening off it like compass points into the rooms beyond. She turned to face him from ten paces away. She was wearing an elaborately embroidered kimono, and her face was hidden under the dried white veneer of some kind of facial mask. She looked like one of those kabuki actors. Still hot, though. He always thought so.

"You're saying Reeza was murdered?" she said.

He nodded. "Somebody tampered with her meds."

She let out her breath in one long syllable. "Fuucck."

"I know."

"It's gotta be George." She had dark eyes, and when they opened wide within the facial mask, they looked like the empty sockets of a skull. "It was him punishing her. He raped her for embarrassing him at work, and he killed her for taking him to trial. Just like he raped me for breaking up with him."

"Maybe. There's another one, though. A girl—"

"But that was the boyfriend."

He cocked his head. "You know about Tiffy Jenkins?"

She flapped a hand as if to bat the question away. "That was an ordinary domestic."

"Nope. The boyfriend alibied out. Her killer's still at large."

Her eyes went even darker inside her skull. "He's killing all of his rape victims?"

"Seriously," he asked. "How do you know about Tiffy?" Compliance with the NDAs was hardly an issue anymore, but he couldn't help wondering how the information had traveled.

Ashley ignored the question again. She pivoted in a swirl of purple silk and paced off the angles of the foyer. "He's coming after me. That's what you're telling me?"

He turned to follow her circuit around the room. "It's a possibility. I thought you should know."

"What am I supposed to do? What the fuck am I supposed to do? Call the cops? Leave the country?"

"You could go and stay with your son for a while. Give the cops time to figure things out and put a case together."

"Yeah. Maybe." She stopped and wheeled on him. "What about Emily Norland? I left her a voicemail on Friday, but she hasn't called me back."

She shouldn't have known about Emily either, but this time Javi didn't bother asking. "She's my next stop," he said.

Ashley bit her lip as she walked him to the door. It turned her mouth momentarily red, and now she really did look like a kabuki performer. "I guess I should thank you, but I'm still fucking pissed at you."

He nodded, accepting the reproach. "Like I said, I'm not doing that anymore."

She narrowed her eyes. "You didn't really get married."

"Sure I did."

"Then tell me where you're registered. I'll send you a gift."

He pointed at the security panel by the door. "Keep this on," he said as he left.

JAVI NEVER MET Emily Norland—Kelly had the deal done and signed before he even knew her name. But he did a full workup on her afterward and had been keeping tabs ever since to ensure compliance, as he did with all the NDA women. He had her new address and followed the GPS to a suburban subdivision full of so-called executive-style homes. It occurred to him that this weekend had been a tour of the whole gamut of residential real estate, from Tiffy's trailer to Benedict's museum piece of a mansion, with Ashley's Italian villa and these faux farmhouses falling somewhere in between.

He followed the GPS through the maze of suburban streets. It was Sunday afternoon on a warm autumn day, and people were outside raking leaves and hanging Halloween decorations. Witches flew on broomsticks and skeletons fluttered weightless in the breeze.

Emily's house stood on a wooded lot at the end of a cul-de-sac. Her car was in the driveway, and he pulled in beside it and got out. He scanned for cameras or motion detectors but found none. There were no Halloween decorations either. No kids lived here, and no husband, if his latest intelligence was still good.

The paved path to the front door was lined with tiny boxwoods. He rang the bell and heard the chimes echo inside the house. When no one answered after a minute, he rang again. Still no answer.

He came down off the porch and looked up from the front lawn. The lights were on in an upstairs room. It was a sunny day, and the windows faced the street, not the woods. There was no reason for those lights to be on, and he felt his worry deepen.

He looped around the house. In the back was a pool, tucked in for the winter under a blue vinyl cover, and at the far end, a hot tub leaking chlorinated steam into the air. He climbed the stairs to the deck and peered in the windows and French doors all along the rear of the house. There was no sign of anyone inside, but no sign of a struggle either. Everything was tidy. He pressed the buzzer by the back door and heard the same echoing chimes inside. He put his ear to the glass and listened for footsteps. Nothing.

There was an innocent explanation. Someone came by early this morning to pick Emily up for the day's outing. She ran out without turning off her bedroom lights. She forgot her phone. It was a beautiful day; she could be out bike riding. He headed around the other side of the house to check the garage for a bike rack.

Something long and black curved across his path, and he shied for half a second, thinking it was a snake. Then laughed at himself when he saw it was only an extension cord running from the pump house. Still dangerous, though, this close to the water, especially since a section of the cord looked frayed. The insulation there had been stripped off, exposing an inch of bare wire inside. Even more dangerous, the other end of the cord was submerged in the hot tub.

He went to the pump house and pulled the plug, then tugged on the cord to pull it out. It gave a surprising amount of resistance, and he went to the water's edge to see what it was hung up on. It was connected to some kind of box. An old-fashioned record player, he saw as he hauled it up. There was something else in the water, too, submerged at the bottom of the hot tub. He squatted and peered through the murk until there was no doubt.

It was a body.

30

BIRTHDAY PARTY PICKUP WAS AT four on Sunday, and Kelly arrived to find a game of tag in progress around the hosts' house. Her head was pounding, and it grew worse as she hauled herself out of the car and the high-pitched squeals of a dozen little girls pierced her ears. She drank more gin last night than she typically consumed in a month, and she was paying a steep price today.

She spotted Lexie caroming from one corner of the yard to the other, in sharp, hyper-strung diagonals, like she was bouncing off the paddles on a giant pinball machine.

"Afraid nobody got much sleep last night," the host mother admitted. The dark circles under her eyes told the story, too.

Kelly kept her sunglasses on over her own bleary eyes. "You'd never know it from all this energy," she said.

A guilty laugh escaped the hostess. "They had chocolate chip pancakes for brunch, with whipped cream and syrup."

Kelly managed to corner her own child and extract her from the game. Lexie hopped in the back seat of the car and for ten minutes chattered happily about her friends and the boat and the beach and whether it would be too cold to do the same thing for her own party in January. Kelly's head was splitting as she tried to smile and nod.

Abruptly Lexie went silent, and when Kelly glanced in the mirror, she found the child out cold, her face lolling from side to side like a broken bobblehead. When they got home, Lexie staggered to her room and pitched face-first into her bed, where Kelly suspected she'd spend the rest of the day.

JUSTIN'S PICKUP WAS at six, and Kelly's headache was finally beginning to abate. Now it was her stomach that plagued her, churning with anxiety as she drove to the high school and parked in a line with the other parents waiting for the bus to arrive.

She was ashamed of how nervous she felt. A mother ought to be able to talk to her own child about sex without this crawling sense of inadequacy. She'd spent the afternoon mulling over different approaches to take. Sympathetic and supportive: she could assure him that his curiosity was perfectly normal and healthy. Stern and judgmental: she could tell him that the objectification of women's bodies was a gateway to misogyny and abuse and he should be ashamed of himself. Benignly cautionary: she'd warn him that sexting could be a crime, and he should be more careful in the future. None of the above? All of the above? Even if she could settle on an approach, she knew she'd get it wrong. She also knew he'd burrow into himself, no matter what she said.

The other parents were out of their cars, mingling and hobnobbing and watching their phones for updates on the arrival time. Kelly didn't feel up to socializing today. She slouched behind the wheel and returned a few waves, but whenever anyone beckoned her to join them, she held up her own phone like a shield to fend them off.

But one woman caught her eye. She was farther down in the lineup of cars, leaning on the hood of her BMW. She wore leggings and Ugg boots, and her dark curly hair was loose and wild.

"Courtney?" Kelly called as she jumped out of her car and strode toward her. "What are you doing here?"

"Oh. Kelly. Hi." The girl straightened as Kelly drew near. "I'm waiting for my boyfriend."

"Your . . . boyfriend?" Kelly's voice dropped to a suspicious whisper. "You're dating a high school student?"

"God! No!" Courtney rolled her eyes. "The science teacher. Marcus Sealy. Didn't Justin tell you?"

"Oh." Kelly flushed. "No, but then he doesn't tell me much."

"Well, he's pretty absorbed in his studies."

"Or something," Kelly mumbled.

"Great news about his prize."

"Prize?"

"Didn't he tell you that either? He won first prize at the science fair!"

"Oh. Right." She wondered if Justin was afraid to call her with the news, or whether it simply never occurred to him. She wondered which was worse. "Sure," she said. "He called me. Yes. Great news."

"Marcus was thrilled for him."

"Uh-huh."

The silence went on too long. Courtney's Ugg boots shuffled on the pavement as she shifted her body away. "Was there something else, Kelly?"

"As a matter of fact, yes." Kelly pulled her shoulders back and looked up at her. "I wanted to tell you that Lyle Firth in my office will be handling your petition. You can correspond with him about it from now on."

Courtney's expression was suddenly so forlorn that Kelly had a flash of memory—it was the same look the girl had at fifteen when she first saw her father after his stroke. "You're opposing it?" she said, her voice thin.

"Of course I am. And by the way—not because I'm Catholic and pro-life, or whatever you think. Because it's the right thing to do."

Courtney blinked. "I didn't mean—" she began, and her face

changed again, from desolate teenager back to the brisk and confident twenty-six-year-old lawyer she now was. "What I meant was your Catholic guilt."

Kelly barked a laugh. "What should I be guilty about?"

"You shouldn't. That's my point. You think you deserve this"— she struggled to find the word—"this *torment*. Like it's your punishment for stealing Dad away from us."

"I—" Kelly gaped at her. "I what?"

"But you didn't steal him. He left us. He chose to leave. If this is anyone's punishment, it's his." Courtney looked at the ground and shook her head. "And for God's sake, he's had enough."

Kelly stood stunned. She didn't feel guilty. She *wasn't* guilty, and neither was Adam. They fell in love. It was the best thing that ever happened to her. To him, too, she hoped. Yes, he was still married at the time, in name at least, and yes, she often felt bad for his ex and their child. But that had nothing to do with Adam's care.

She took out her phone and tapped furiously on the screen.

"What are you doing?" Courtney said with a rasping laugh. "Calling the cops on me?"

Kelly looked up, glowering. "I'm sending you a link to an app that accesses the camera on your dad. I want you to watch him. I want you to think about what you want to do to him. Think about him starving. Dehydrated. Dying."

"How dare you?" Courtney blinked back tears. "I loved him."

"Well, there's the difference," Kelly said, walking away. Over her shoulder, she added: "I still do."

The bus rumbled into the parking lot, and she joined the throng of parents moving toward it as the kids clambered off. They called to their sons and daughters, gave hugs and hearty backslaps, grabbed backpacks, and lined up to grab their bags and boxes out of the luggage compartment. Mr. Sealy, the science teacher, stood at the curb with a clipboard, checking off names and high-fiving his students as they came off the bus. A frown flickered briefly across his face when he saw Kelly, and she recalled how cool he'd been with her lately. Now she knew why. She could only imagine the things he'd heard about her from Courtney.

Justin was one of the last students off the bus. He wore a green beanie squashed down over his orange curls, and his body listed to one side under the weight of the backpack looped over his shoulder. He held his trophy down by his other side, as if it were an embarrassing article of clothing his mother made him wear. His eyes moved anxiously through the other students and their parents. When they landed on Kelly, he stopped where he stood and looked down at his feet.

She threaded her way through the crowd and threw her arms around him. "Congratulations, Justin!" she cried.

He stiffened for a second before the relief coursed through his gangly body. Kelly could tell that he'd been as nervous about seeing her as she was about him. Yet despite that dark cloud hanging over him all weekend, despite knowing trouble awaited him at home, he'd still managed to capture first place in the competition.

"Congratulations!" she said again. She lifted his arm with the trophy in it, up high over their heads. "You won!"

He ducked his head with an embarrassed smile and loped alongside her to the parking lot. Courtney passed them on the way. "Congrats," she called to Justin a moment before Mr. Sealy caught her up in a twirling hug.

Kelly waited until they were on the road to speak again. "Todd told me what you did," she said.

Justin's cheeks flamed. He looked at his knees. "I'm really sorry," he mumbled.

"We need to talk about this," she said.

He squeezed his eyes shut, and her heart pinched to see him bracing himself like that. She hated to lecture him now, on the heels of his big win. It wasn't fair to deprive him of the chance to bask in his victory for a while. Tomorrow they could talk about respect and responsibility. Maybe by then she'd know what to say.

"Later," she said. "For now, though, you need to know one thing: it wasn't that girl who hacked into our Wi-Fi. It was someone else who spied on your dad."

His head snapped up. "Really?"

"Really."

His relief was visible this time. Tears welled in his eyes. Kelly reached over and gave a reassuring pat to his knee. "I'm so proud of you," she said.

She was proud. He was a model of triumph over trouble. Despite being worried all weekend, despite feeling ashamed and, she hoped, racked with guilt—despite all that, he knuckled down and won the competition. Victory under that kind of pressure was even more of a triumph.

She thought about that as they rode the rest of the way home.

Last night she thought her plan was a bust, but it didn't have to be. Most of the work was already done. It would be foolish to turn back now. All she had to do was cultivate some other reporter to leak the documents to. And if either Rick Olsson or Edward Russo reared their ugly heads, she'd find some way to shoot them down.

She could still pull this off.

31

Ashley LaSorta

THIRTY MINUTES AFTER HE WAS gone, I was still seething at Alejandro—or Javier, or whatever the hell he was calling himself now. I scrubbed furiously at my face until the collagen infusion mask dissolved and disappeared in milky eddies down the drain. I'd seen that sneer as he looked around at my house. Even if it didn't quite curl his luscious lips, the sneer was there in his eyes. I knew exactly what he was thinking—that I'd fucked my way into these riches.

The balls on that son of a bitch! Like he wasn't a total man whore himself. A litigation gigolo, seducing women with promises of sensual delights only to worm his way into their lives and suss out all their secrets and bludgeon them into settling cheap. My original claim against George had been $5 million. I had to cut it in half after they confronted me with that ridiculous sex tape supplied by that traitorous Roger or Rodney or whatever the hell his name had been.

Which meant my so-called romance with Alejandro had cost me $2.5 million. So who was the bigger whore now, *Javier*?

I looked up at the bathroom mirror. I'd rubbed too hard, and now my skin was an angry red. I was still furious at that man, that gorgeous man with the velvety-brown, judgmental eyes. Who was he to judge me?

It wasn't fair. I earned every penny of my settlement, and not by sleeping with the boss, no matter what the gossips said. My claim against George was based on the damage to my career, not the assault on my body. Not that the assault wasn't awful—it was: twelve hours tied to a bed and fearing for my life as my onetime lover revealed himself to be an utter psychopath.

But it was the loss of my career that hit me the hardest when he finally untied me and left. Tech officers seldom made it to the C-suite of multinational corporations. They didn't get a senior VP title to go with CTO. They didn't get corner offices or options or a parachute. But I'd achieved all of those things, and I did it all through sheer talent and hard work. I fucking earned it.

There was no way I could stay on at UniViro, though, not after what he did to me. One of us would have to leave, and not in a million years would it be George. He headed up research and development. He was the company's biggest noninstitutional shareholder. He was the headliner, the distinguished fellow, the shoo-in for the Nobel. He was their star. The board wasn't going to oust him on my say-so. It took more than a hundred complaints and a looming indictment before the Weinstein Company finally got rid of Harvey. I knew that my voice alone would never suffice to get rid of George.

I also knew that I'd never get a comparable position, in Pharma or anywhere else. Look at where I finally landed: at an undercapitalized start-up that developed apps for teenagers to play on their phones. The other officers and employees were twenty years younger and talked to me like I was their grandma. I no longer had options or a parachute, and my office was merely a desk in a big open space with a skateboard track looping the perimeter.

I knew this would happen. So that day after George finally left, I photographed my injuries and preserved the DNA, then sat down with a whiskey and ran the numbers. I calculated my worth before the attack versus my worth after and reached a delta of $5 million.

Then I reached my lawyer, who agreed with my numbers. His strategy: go in at ten; settle for five.

It would have worked, too, if the dashing Alejandro hadn't entered the scene. I'd always kept my private life private. My social media posts were never for public consumption. No one who wasn't already close to me could ever find out anything about my sexual history. So Alejandro got close to me. It was the longest, slowest seduction of my life, an old-style courtship of candlelit dinners and slow dances and tête-à-têtes that left me panting with desire. My Latin would-be lover. It had been decades since I last went on a date that didn't end in bed, yet there I was, three weeks into the headiest romance I'd ever experienced and still full of anticipation.

Then abruptly, nothing. No more calls or texts or evenings under the stars. He disappeared so completely that I imagined he must be a spy, or a hit man. I almost imagined that I'd imagined him. Until Kelly McCann pushed a button at our negotiating session and there I was on the screen, undulating atop Rodney or Roger. I hadn't imagined anything. Alejandro was both a spy and a hit man.

He was the single biggest mistake of my life.

No, second biggest, I thought as I chucked the towel to the floor and went into the bedroom. The first was getting involved with George Benedict. I was a woman of the world, and still I was stupid enough to sleep with a man who outranked me at the company. A man with a hundred times my clout. He wasn't even my type. He was a nerdy scientist with cockeyed glasses and poor posture and barely any human emotion. It was only his big brain that attracted me. He was the first true genius I'd ever known, and I'd met both Jobs and Musk. I was fascinated by the way George's mind worked, and for a time, that was thrill enough.

The trouble was that his brain didn't come with a personality or much in the way of a bedroom technique, and after a few months,

I was over it. As gently as I could, I told him so. That was when I discovered that he was capable of expressing an emotion after all. Rage. The white-hot, strangle-with-his-bare-hands kind of rage.

But did he have the slice-somebody's-throat-open kind of rage? No way. Javier was batshit crazy to think that George could have killed either Reeza or Tiffy. Anyway, the timing was all wrong. The time to kill Reeza was before she dragged him through the international scandal of a rape trial. The time to kill Tiffy was before he paid her the hush money. Why now? It made no sense.

Anyway, George was at the CDC in Atlanta on the day Tiffy was murdered, so that ruled him out. I did wonder about Anton, though. He had Russian mob written all over him, even if he wasn't Russian and belonged to nothing and nobody but George. He was Sancho Panza, Little John, and Renfield all rolled into one. It used to creep me out, the way he shadowed George everywhere he went, especially all the times he sat in the Bentley in my driveway and waited to drive his master home. I used to wonder what he did out there alone in the car, and that creeped me out even more.

Still, I didn't believe it. Not of George and not even of Anton. It had to be a coincidence. Reeza's death was an accident, and Tiffy could have been killed by anybody. She was that kind of girl living that kind of life.

I tossed my robe on the bed and walked naked into the closet to survey my wardrobe. I had a drinks date at five with my latest dating-site match. If it went well, it would extend into dinner, and if it went very well, it would end back here, so I needed to dress for all contingencies.

I decided on the black leather pants, an off-the-shoulder red sweater, and ballet flats in case the guy wasn't as tall as he claimed in his profile.

My luggage was lined up under the shelves of sweaters, and it made me recall Javier's suggestion that I go stay with my son for a while. Which was a ridiculous idea. First, I wasn't going to blow off work just on his say-so. Second, I couldn't stay with Jeremy even if I wanted to. After he finished college, he turned down grad school and went to work on an organic rutabaga farm on an Appalachian mountainside. He was living in a yurt. He'd gone full Luddite—no smartphone, no laptop, no car. It was obviously a fuck-you to me. When I told him so, he pressed his hands together namaste-style, bowed, and said he hoped I'd someday find peace in my life. That kid. I loved him, but I didn't know where he came from.

I finished dressing and went looking for my phone to check the driving time to the bar where I was meeting Josh or Jason or whoever tonight's date was. When I found it in the bathroom, I saw that I'd missed a call. There was also a new text from an unknown number, but all it said was Call me. I deleted it, then saw that there was also a voicemail from the same unknown number. I pushed Play.

It's Javier, the message began, and I rolled my eyes at the ramped-up panic in his voice.

It's Emily Norland. She's dead.

I sat down hard on the edge of the Jacuzzi. *Electrocuted last night in her hot tub*, he said, and I shot to my feet again. *It was Anton. I'm sure of it.*

A surge of blood went whooshing through my body and ringing in my ears. Suddenly I understood the timing. It made perfect sense. George wasn't going after his victims. He was going after his avengers.

I put my hand to my throat and felt my pulse pound against it. We never should have embarked on our harebrained scheme. George had figured it out. He was coming after us, one by one. Tiffy, then Emily.

I would be next.

Get out of there, Javier was saying in his voicemail. *Find someplace safe. Turn off your location trackers.*

I flew into the closet and grabbed a suitcase. I had no idea how people dressed in the mountains, in a yurt, but I flung in a haphazard assortment of clothes and cosmetics and slammed the lid shut.

One more thing to do before I hit the road. I ran to my office downstairs and logged into a proxy server, this time in Belarus.

Twenty minutes later I was in the Porsche, heading south.

32

TOMMY WEXFORD'S SCOWLING FACE FLICKERED into view on Kelly's desktop monitor. Today he wore a blue batik scarf wrapped around his neck and sunglasses wrapped around his head. "I told you no more video calls," he griped. "I don't know why you insisted on this."

"I think you do," Kelly said. "Would you please take off your scarf?"

His hollow cheeks turned a furious pink. He didn't answer, nor did he make any move to unwind the scarf from his neck. She gazed steadily at the screen and waited. He was seated on an outdoor terrace under a pergola. The slats overhead cast a gridwork of shadows over his face.

"A lot of men don't have visible Adam's apples," he said finally.

"That's true," Kelly said. "But every cis man has a Y chromosome. Which would show up in a DNA test, of course."

"All right." His mouth trembled. "Big fucking deal. So you sussed out my secret."

"And so did Margaret Staley, I'm guessing."

Tears leaked out from behind his sunglasses, and he swiped at them furiously. "What business is it of hers anyway?"

Kelly shrugged. "She's on a crusade. That justifies anything in her mind."

"Look. I'm a man! I've felt like a man since I was eighteen, and before that I felt like a boy. My parents were cool with it. My doctors were cool with it. My girlfriend is super cool with it. So why is it anybody's business but mine?"

"It's not. But here's the important thing: she lied. She lied to the police, and she lied in her court filings. We can't let her get away with it. So give the DNA sample. Submit to the exam. She'll be exposed as a liar. The judge will slap her with sanctions, and she'll be publicly humiliated."

This time he let the tears flow. "She'll be exposed. But so will I."

Kelly sighed. "You can win the case, or you can keep your secret. You can't do both."

"I don't care if I win the case," he said. "I want to win my life!" He pronounced the last bit with a histrionic shout that any film director would have told him to tone down. Then he lapsed into silence as the shadow stripes shifted over his face.

Kelly decided to wait him out. She turned to her second monitor and resumed her Google search for reputable journalists specializing in the life sciences. She'd decided to go with a print reporter this time. Broadcast journalists like Rick Olsson were interested only in sexy sound bites. The superficial, lapel-grabbing kinds of stories that could be summed up in a crawler at the bottom of the TV screen. She needed a reporter willing to dig deep into a complex subject. She hit on a science reporter named Aidan Dunwoodie, whose byline appeared often in the *New York Times*. He'd already reported extensively on Benedict's identification of the virus. His curiosity would have to be aroused by the possibility that it was actually Reeza who'd first identified it.

Another Google search yielded a mailing address for Dunwoodie. She handwrote it on a big manila envelope and slipped in copies of the doctored documents. She'd stop at the post office on the way home and send them off.

Kelly looked back to the other monitor when Wexford spoke at last. "What happens if I refuse to play her little game?" he said. "I don't give the sample. I don't even respond to her lawsuit."

"Well—" This was a question Kelly hadn't anticipated. Rolling over wasn't a strategy she'd ever employed. "The judge will enter a default on liability. That means you're deemed to have admitted that you did what she said you did."

"That I forced her to give me a blow job." He smirked. "Okay. Then what happens at trial?"

"It'll be limited to damages. The only issue will be how much money she's entitled to."

"Hmm." He pursed his lips. "What would that amount to?"

"She doesn't have any medical expenses, and probably no lost wages—so it would only be compensation for pain and suffering. Which is always nebulous. Maybe punitive damages, too, which is absolutely arbitrary."

"Give me a ballpark."

"Worst case: maybe a million?"

He thought about that. Slowly, he nodded. "I can do a million."

She threw up her hands, incredulous. "You'd rather pay this extortionist a million dollars than go public?"

"My career is worth a hell of a lot more than that. I'm up for a role in the DC Universe. You think that's gonna happen if they think I'm a girl?"

"I don't know."

"Well, I do. And it won't."

This made no sense to her. "In what world is it better to be outed as a sexual predator than as a woman?"

He didn't even hesitate. "In my world." He leaned back and clasped his hands at his chest. "So that's our game plan."

"Do nothing."

"Exactly."

She gave a resigned sigh. "In that case, I'm going to send the file back to your LA lawyer. He can do nothing as well as I can."

Wexford aimed a thumbs-up at the camera. "But don't tell him why," he said as the screen went dark.

SHE PUSHED TO her feet when the call ended and went out into the corridor. "I'll be with Lyle Firth," she told Cazzadee as she headed for the elevators.

"Javier really needs to talk to you," Cazz said. "He left you some voicemails?"

"I'll call him as soon as I'm back."

"He says it's urgent."

"Right after Lyle," she said and kept walking.

Patti Han was getting off the elevator as Kelly stepped on. "Ship the Wexford file back to LA, would you?" Kelly asked, holding the doors open with her arm. "Tell what's-his-name the client wants to default on liability, and he can handle the damages case without us."

Patti looked stricken. "You mean he did it?"

"Looks like."

"Wow." She shook her head sadly. "So Staley was actually telling the truth."

"It does happen," Kelly said.

Patti laughed as she walked away.

LYLE FIRTH'S OFFICE was two floors down on the other side of the building, the side without a view of the Common. His door stood ajar, and Kelly knocked once and came in. Firth's pink cheeks turned red, and he immediately pressed a key to blank his computer screen.

Kelly rolled her eyes. Even eunuch-like Lyle Firth couldn't get through the workday without watching porn. Men, she thought. She didn't know why Tommy Wexford even wanted to be one.

Firth cleared his throat. "Kelly. How may I help?"

"Courtney's going ahead with her petition. I gave her your name, so you'll be hearing from her."

"Any progress on finding a doctor to testify?"

"Some," she said and made a mental note to start her search. "Meanwhile, I want to counterclaim or add an affirmative defense or whatever you civil guys call it."

He picked up his pen. "Seeking what relief?"

Relief? She hadn't felt any relief for ten years and wasn't likely ever to get any from Courtney. "Let's table that for the moment. The grounds will be self-interest. Courtney's doing this out of greed and concealing her motives. It's a fraud on the court."

"Please explain."

"When Adam and his first wife divorced, one of the provisions was a term life insurance policy naming Courtney as sole beneficiary. As soon as she has the death certificate, she'll get a check for half a million dollars!" She ended the sentence with the same trademarked flourish she used in her jury closings. Now she realized it sounded a lot like Tommy Wexford's overacting moments ago.

"Kelly." Firth folded his hands and spoke carefully. "Did you read the draft petition?"

"Of course," she said. She'd skimmed it anyway.

"Your stepdaughter discloses the insurance policy in her petition. And she attaches as exhibits the disclaimer and trust instrument that she's already executed."

"She . . . what?"

"Kelly," he said again. He spoke her name in a strangely wary tone, as if she were a dog that might bite. "She's already assigned her interest in the insurance proceeds to an educational trust she's set up for your two children. An irrevocable trust."

Kelly didn't answer. She couldn't answer. She stared at him a moment before she turned and walked away. Harry Leahy was in the corridor, and she passed him with barely a nod in response to his hearty greeting. "I love to see you deep in thought," he called after her. "It means a big payday is around the corner!"

Cazzadee looked up sharply when Kelly returned to her office. "I'll put Javi through now."

"No. Give me five minutes," Kelly said and shut the door. She opened her email and scrolled through the old messages until she found Courtney's. This time she opened the documents attached as exhibits to the draft petition. It was exactly as Lyle said. The girl had already assigned her interest in the insurance proceeds to Justin and Lexie, in trust, with Kelly serving as trustee. She read the papers carefully, searching for some booby trap, some fail-safe that would allow Courtney to back out. But it wasn't there.

She clapped her hands to her face with a ragged breath. She remembered how she'd accused Courtney of going after the money—in front of the children and everyone else gathered around the dinner table that night. And now she remembered Courtney's response: *Read the fucking papers.*

Kelly felt like a thousand hot needles were piercing her skin, but she didn't feel pain. It wasn't fear or grief either. What she felt was a burning sensation, and she knew it was the scorching fire of defeat. Courtney had won, and Kelly had lost. She'd lost the biggest case of her life.

And suddenly she knew that this was all it had ever been about. Winning, or at least not losing. That day ten years ago in the rehab director's office, when all the doctors drew their chairs around her and told her there was nothing more they could do—the reaction she felt steaming inside her wasn't pain or fear or grief. It was *Oh, yeah? Well, I'll show you!* It was as if battle lines had been drawn, and she was pitched into a competition with the entire medical establishment.

Courtney was wrong: it wasn't guilt that kept her fighting all these years. But Kelly was wrong, too: it wasn't some noble, self-sacrificing love either. It was her everlasting need to prevail. Her bottomless hunger for victory.

A knock sounded on her office door, a single hard rap like a mortar blast. Before she could call *Go away!* the door swung open and Javier stormed in.

"Not now—" she began.

"Now," he snapped back and shut the door behind him.

"Javi, you can't just barge in here—"

He didn't sit down. He stayed on his feet at the edge of her desk, forcing her to look up at him. "Emily Norland was killed Saturday night," he said.

Javi had only the slightest accent, but Kelly stared at him as if he were speaking a foreign language. It took her brain a few spins to realize what he was saying. "Killed?" she repeated.

"Electrocuted in the hot tub on her back deck. Somebody stripped the insulation off an extension cord. Gave her third-degree burns over her hands and arms, but it was the drowning that killed her."

Both hands flew to her mouth. "Oh my God!"

"And by the way, Tiffy Jenkins wasn't murdered by her boyfriend. He has a solid alibi. And he wouldn't be capable of delivering a surgical strike into the carotid artery anyway."

"Surgical?" She was repeating everything he said, stupidly, as if the words would make more sense coming out of her own mouth.

"The cops are calling Emily's death accidental. Just like they did with Reeza. And Tiffy will be filed under 'unknown assailant.' Because the cops don't know there's any connection between the three of them. But we do."

"But we don't. He was in—"

"Anton did it. And he did Emily, too. I saw him scrubbing up afterward."

"What?"

"But Reeza, now. I think Benedict did that one himself."

"No, that can't be." The faces of the three women swam in and out of focus in her mind. Now all three were dead. Reeza, by poison. Tiffy, by knife. Emily, by a fire that water couldn't extinguish. *Poison. Cut. Burn.* There was something familiar about that combination of words.

"C'mon, Kelly." Javi leaned forward, and his hands gripped the edge of her desk. "Even you couldn't believe in this many coincidences. We have to tell the police what we know. What links all of these victims. They'll never figure it out on their own. Not with all those secret gag orders."

The NDAs, she thought. They already guaranteed the women's silence. There was no reason for Benedict to kill them, too. "We can't. It's privileged—"

"Fuck attorney-client privilege. If it even applies."

"Of course it applies. We only know about these women because our client told us in the course of seeking legal advice."

"There's an exception, though, right? For future crimes."

Kelly started to shake her head—that wasn't how the rule was formulated—but he cut her off. "Ashley LaSorta," he said. "She's gotta be next on his list."

"I can't believe—"

"Well, she believes it! She's taking it seriously even if you won't."

"What do you mean?"

"She's gone into hiding. Far from here."

"From Philadelphia, you mean."

"No, from here. Benedict's here in town this week. Him and Anton both. Some conference."

"Here? In Boston?" Her flesh crawled at the thought of Benedict here in her city. At how close he might be.

"I'm going to the cops," Javi said. "They have to know what connects these women."

"Javi, no. Wait—" She needed more time. She had to think this through.

"Fuck privilege," he said. "And fuck you, too, if you don't do the right thing here."

She raised her palms, half placating, half surrendering. "Let me think it over. Please. Ashley's safe, right? Give me time to figure out the best way to handle this."

He set his jaw. "Twenty-four hours," he said, breathing hard. "Then I go to the cops."

SHE SAT VERY still after he left. She needed to think, and she was trying to, but the faces of the three dead women kept spinning through her thoughts. Reeza Patel, who sat rigid in the witness box for three days of Kelly's merciless cross-examination. Emily Norland, whose marriage was destroyed by Kelly and her strong-arm negotiation tactics. Tiffy Jenkins, who had the nicest time of her life holed up with three bitter women bent on revenge.

Poison. Cut. Burn. Or was it *Cut Poison Burn*? She couldn't remember where she'd heard that combination of words before.

No, stop, she needed to think about Benedict. Javi had to be wrong. It didn't make any sense. Why go after them now? They didn't pose any threat to him. There had to be a motive, and there simply wasn't one.

Yet all three women were dead. Could that be a coincidence? She believed in coincidence, but only when it was the combination of two incidents. Three strained the limits of her credulity.

Still, she couldn't think of any reason for Benedict to want these women dead. A year ago, maybe. But not now.

Her cell rang. She reached for it, but stopped when she saw the screen was dark. It had to be her other cell, the latest burner, and she reached into her bag and fished it out. The call was from an unknown number, but she recognized the first three digits: 484. That was an area code in eastern Pennsylvania.

A chill spread through her body so fast it was as if she'd been flash frozen. She stared at the screen while the phone rang and rang. It couldn't be Benedict. He didn't have this number.

After the ringing finally stopped, the phone pinged with an incoming text. Call me. From the same unknown number with a 484 area code.

Another text pinged from the same unknown number. We're next.

That chilled her even more. Ashley was the only one who had this number, but she wouldn't say *we*. She didn't know Kelly was among his victims. No one did.

No one but Benedict.

He was baiting her, luring her in, using this phone to track her, and she was fumbling to pull out the SIM card when a third text lit up the screen.

For fuck's sake, pull up your thigh-high boots and call me.

Kelly's breath came out in a sound that was almost a laugh. It *was* Ashley; she was simply using the royal *We*. Kelly pushed the Call button.

"He knows," Ashley yelled as she answered. "He knows!" A rumbling noise hummed in the background. Highway traffic. She was on the road.

"Knows what?"

"He knows what we did! The hack! The doctored documents! He knows!"

Kelly clutched the phone so tightly she could feel the pulse pound from her hand up to her shoulder. "How? How would he even know to go looking?"

"Who knows? Maybe I fucked up. Maybe you did. Whatever, he knows! It's the only explanation. Why else would he go after us *now*?"

Kelly sat stunned. There it was: the motive that had eluded her. He wasn't killing his victims. He was killing his victims who dared to retaliate.

"I went back in," Ashley was saying. "I put everything back the way it was."

Kelly felt a stab of pain deep in her belly. All their work, all their planning and scheming—it was all for nothing.

"But I was too late. He already figured it out. And now he's coming after us!"

No, it was worse than all for nothing. Her pathetic attempt at revenge had awakened the dragon, and now he was slaying them.

"And I'm next!" Ashley cried.

She didn't know that Benedict was here in Boston. She wasn't next. Kelly was.

33

SHE FLEW OUT OF HER office in a swirl of coat, bag, briefcase; rushed past a startled Cazzadee to the elevator bank; stopped and wheeled around to the stairwell instead; and clattered down twenty-two flights of stairs to the garage. She drove out of the city with the burner in one hand and made the calls while she drove. First she called the schools to explain the family emergency and schedule a lunchtime pickup for both children. Next she called the Four Seasons downtown and booked a suite. Name: Adam Fineman, and she used his never-canceled credit card to reserve it. Check-in: today. Check-out? Open-ended. She waited for confirmation that the card was accepted, then took the exit at Newton, parked on the road-side, and scrambled down the riverbank to hurl the phone far out into the Charles.

SHE PARKED TWO blocks from home and crept through a string of backyards to her own back door. The security system was armed—*good; thank you, Todd*—and she disarmed it only long enough to get inside and arm it again. She galloped up the stairs with a shout to let him know who it was, then she tore through Lexie's room, then Justin's, packing everything she could think of that they'd need or want. Clothes, a favorite toy, games, books.

She left their suitcases in the hall and went into her own bedroom to pack. Adam's upper body was elevated, his stomach tube exposed, while Todd stood beside him with his thumb applying gentle pressure to the syringe plunger. "Hey, Kelly," he said, eyes fixed on the tube. "What brings you home?"

She answered from inside the closet. "I'm taking the kids away for a while. I'm afraid we'll draw some protesters over the next few days. Definitely press."

"Oh?"

"Yes, sorry." She pulled out a suitcase and started stuffing it with her own clothes and toiletries. "Be sure to keep the security system armed. And don't answer the door."

"You got it," he said.

No questions asked. He was so trusting, and here she was, leaving him alone and unaware while a murderer was on the loose. But she didn't know what else to do. Adam couldn't be moved, and she needed Todd here to care for him. At least the murderer wasn't indiscriminate. He was after her specifically.

She went to the front window and looked out through the crimson leaves of Justin's tree. There were no strange cars parked on the street, no one slunk low behind the wheel or pretending to read the paper. Definitely no blue Bentley. She wondered if she was overreacting. It still didn't make any sense to her. If Ashley was right, if he was killing them because he found out about their little conspiracy, why kill Reeza? She was never part of it. And how could he have found out anyway? Unless he'd placed bugs in their homes and location trackers on their cars.

Which maybe he'd done.

She grabbed her suitcase and wheeled it to the bedroom door. "Call me if you need me," she said.

Todd nodded. "Take care."

THE HOTEL SUITE was on a lower floor with windows facing the street as she'd requested. It had a tiny kitchenette, a living room with a desk and a pull-out couch, and a bedroom with two queens. Justin immediately stomped into the bedroom and slammed the door.

He'd been furious ever since she picked him up at school. It was bad enough she wouldn't let him retrieve his phone from his locker, but when she told him they couldn't go home, he exploded into a fit of anger that she hadn't witnessed since his toddler tantrums. This was all total bullshit, he shouted. He wasn't afraid of some stupid reporters, he wanted to go home, he *needed* to be home. He ranted like that for a solid five minutes and hadn't spoken a word since.

Lexie, on the other hand, thought this was a grand adventure. She was fascinated by the miniature soaps and shampoo bottles, and for five minutes amused herself by opening and closing the double layers of curtains. She found the Cartoon Network on the living room TV and settled in happily on the couch.

Maybe this was all bullshit, Kelly thought. She might be wildly overreacting. She hoped she was. But she turned the deadbolt on the lock and hooked the chain on the door and stood at the window and watched the cars come and go on the street below. Alternately she stared at her phone as it trembled with incoming calls and texts. She skimmed through the texts as they popped up—Cazzadee asking Where are you? Are you OK? and Javi reporting eyes on B & A at the med school. But she let all the calls go to voicemail. She had an irrational fear of answering, as if the caller's voice could reach through the signal and broadcast her location to the world. Or, rather, to Benedict.

She didn't know whether he had the ability to geo-locate her phone, but he was a certified genius—he could figure out anything. Even onstage at a symposium, even under Javier's watchful eye, he might somehow track her phone. She wished she could turn it off, but she couldn't cut off contact with Todd. What she did instead was turn off the location services on every app on her phone, and when that didn't completely reassure her, she went back and deleted every app that might have ever used location services.

She didn't know what more she could do, short of going to the police as Javier was urging. But even that wouldn't keep her safe. The Pennsylvania authorities might open an investigation, but they couldn't arrest him while he was in Massachusetts. And she knew they wouldn't arrest him. There wasn't enough evidence yet.

That is, there wasn't enough evidence of *murder*. There was incontrovertible evidence against him of another crime. The crime against *her*, captured on video and copied from his laptop, and now stored on a thumb drive residing in a sealed envelope at the bottom of her bag. It was evidence that would lead to his immediate arrest—but only if she were willing to out herself as his victim. Only if she were willing to sacrifice her reputation, her standing, her entire career.

He'd already done enough harm to her. She refused to let him do more.

Lexie was watching a *My Little Pony* marathon on the living room TV, and Justin was waging some kind of fierce video game battle in the bedroom. Kelly sat down at the miniature hotel desk and tried to work amid the warring TV volumes. She opened her laptop but didn't connect to the hotel Wi-Fi, just in case. She opened her briefcase, too. Inside was the manila envelope hand-addressed to the science reporter, Aidan Dunwoodie. The one she'd planned to drop off at the post office on her way home. She stared at it dismally. She could never send it now, not now that Ashley had undone their hack. The envelope was full of documents that would no longer be found on the UniViro system. That were obvious fakes.

Her mind somersaulted back to her last getaway, the girls' weekend at the four-unit condo at the Jersey Shore. Two of those women were now dead and two were in hiding and all for nothing.

This was what her hunger for revenge had wrought. Certainly not victory, and not even only defeat. No, she had brought death. She might not be responsible for Reeza's death, but she was responsible for Tiffy's and Emily's, as surely as if she'd done the cutting and burning herself. She'd dragged them into her half-baked scheme, and now they were dead.

THE AFTERNOON CRAWLED by. Justin shuffled out of the bedroom toward dinnertime, mumbling an apology for his earlier behavior and wondering what there was to eat. Kelly found the room service menu and promised them anything they wanted. He and Lexie squabbled over their selections, and, unable to broker a compromise, Kelly placed a lengthy and exorbitantly priced order.

The food arrived on two carts, a bizarre buffet of kids' comfort food: mac-and-cheese and French fries and mozzarella sticks and cheeseburgers and chocolate cake and ice cream sundaes that, of course, they ate first. After they bulldozed their way through it all, Justin lapsed into a food coma on one end of the couch, while Lexie's sugar consumption had the opposite effect: she started bouncing trampoline-style on the other end of the couch.

Kelly sat at the desk and tried again to work, one eye on her laptop and the other on her phone as the missed calls piled up: Cazzie and Javi again. Harry Leahy. She was surprised and annoyed to see a call from Rick Olsson; they were supposed to be done with each other.

At five o'clock, Javi texted again: Conference over for today. Following B & A to their hotel downtown.

She did a hard blink at those words—hotel downtown. Of course

Benedict would stay in a hotel downtown. He might be staying right here in the Four Seasons. He might be in the room next door.

She raked both hands through her hair. What an idiot she was. Staying in a business-class hotel in the same city where Benedict was currently on business. She should have taken the kids to the Cape instead, or to a cabin in Vermont.

Javier's surveillance was of no value now. He couldn't watch every exit of whatever hotel Benedict was in. And if Benedict and Anton split up, he couldn't follow them both. Anton might be out searching for her this very minute. He'd go to the house first, and when he didn't find her there, he'd go to every hotel in Boston. He'd ask for Kelly McCann at first, but it wouldn't take long for him to ask for Kelly Fineman instead. Adam Fineman was such a flimsy excuse for an alias. They'd blow through that in no time.

A gentle tap sounded on the door, and Kelly spasmed as violently as if she'd been electrocuted.

"Housekeeping," called a heavily accented voice.

She crossed the room to the peephole. A uniformed maid stood waiting in the corridor beside a cart stacked with towels. "No, thank you," Kelly said. "We don't need anything."

The maid shrugged and pushed her cart away, and Kelly kept her eye pressed to the peephole until she was long out of sight.

She went back to the window again. The street was clogged with rush-hour traffic, and guests were streaming into the hotel entrance. She wished she could pack up the kids and flee the city, but she couldn't risk it. Benedict could be coming in the very doors they'd need to exit through.

The room seemed suddenly too quiet. She turned from the window. Lexie was no longer bouncing on the couch. Her sugar high had led to the inevitable crash, and now she was curled up next to Justin, both of them sound asleep.

Her phone rattled on the desk with another incoming call. She froze when she saw the name on the screen: George Benedict. She hurried, fumbling, to push Decline before it could ring again. But then it did. He was calling again.

He was hunting for her now.

He could be in this very building, walking up and down the hotel corridors, calling her phone and listening for a responsive ring through the room doors.

Her phone's ringer was muted, but now she disabled the vibration signal, too, in case he could hear that.

She crept to the peephole and looked out into the corridor again. It was empty. She crossed the room to the windows again. Night was beginning to fall, and the headlights of a half-dozen cars shone bumper to bumper in a lineup at the hotel entrance below.

He called a third time.

Her mouth was dry, and she swallowed a hard gulp. There was only one way to keep herself and her children safe, and that was for him to be arrested, immediately, on evidence that couldn't be denied. But if she couldn't look at that evidence herself, there was no way she could let anyone else watch it.

She sat down at the desk and reached for the sealed envelope at the bottom of her bag. When she slit it open, the thumb drive slid out with a tinny clink. Her hand shook as she picked it up and inserted it into the USB port on her laptop. She opened the file labeled *Insurance* and muted the volume and dug her nails into her palms as the video started to play.

Her eyes fell shut. Already she could picture the scene that would unfold. The all-white horror chamber of his home office. That mortuary slab of a glass desk. All viewed from that eye in the sky, the hidden camera mounted on a high shelf beside the all-seeing Jonas Salk.

She had to force her eyelids open to look at the screen. Then she blinked. Once. Twice. The camera angle was all wrong. This camera wasn't looking down on the scene; it was at eye level. And the room wasn't white. These walls were dark wood. And Benedict wasn't bent over his desk. He was seated behind it, fully clothed. And the woman in the video—it wasn't Kelly. It was Reeza Patel.

Kelly didn't understand. This wasn't a recording of her rape. It wasn't a recording of anyone's rape. She'd been so sure there was a camera up on the shelf beside the cat, but this was the only video file she'd found on Benedict's home laptop. Maybe he'd hidden her video somewhere else? Maybe he hadn't filmed her at all?

Insurance, he'd named the file, and she'd assumed he meant that her silence was guaranteed. What did that title have to do with an ordinary work meeting in his office? And why film it?

Kelly threw a look back at the kids. They were still asleep. She turned on the volume to whisper level and backed up to the start of the video. She leaned in close to watch.

34

SCENE: Early evening in the executive offices of UniViro. The corner office of Dr. George Benedict. He sits behind his desk and leans forward with his fingers laced. Across from him sits Dr. Reeza Patel. She's wearing a white lab coat and has her hands in her pockets.

George Benedict: I assume you understand the concept of work for hire.

Reeza Patel, nodding: Of course. And even apart from that, my employment contract specifies that everything I invent or discover belongs to the company.

GB: Exactly.

RP: I'm not looking to profit from this. Financially.

GB, smiling: I don't have to tell you what a monumental discovery this is.

RP, also smiling: Thank you.

GB: You miss my point. The identification of this virus is far too important to risk having the world overlook it.

RP, confused: I agree.

GB: It's vital that everyone immediately sit up and take notice and believe in it. That's the only way there can ever be any impetus to develop a vaccine. Any momentum. Any funding.

RP, slowly: Okay.

GB: This can't be dismissed as the pipe dream of some junior researcher. It's absolutely essential that someone with indubitable prestige and prominence be the one who discovered it. Someone with an international reputation.

RP: You mean . . . you.

GB: We're talking about the possibility of a cure for Alzheimer's! Think how consequential this is. It's far too important to let ego get in the way.

RP: I see.

GB, sliding a document across the desk: Which is why you need to sign this.

RP: What is it?

GB: A simple acknowledgment that I'm the one who designed the project. That you were a member of the team, but I'm the one who identified this virus as the cause of amyloid deposits.

RP, reading the document: It's a nondisclosure agreement, too.

GB: That's right.

RP: So I can never tell anyone about my work.

GB: No. Because, you see, it's *my* work.

RP, looking directly at the camera: You're filming this?

GB: Of course. So that you can never claim you didn't sign this of your own free will.

RP, after a long pause: I'll sign this on one condition.

GB, frowning: This isn't a negotiation.

RP: That you give your full support to my proposal to the funding committee.

GB: You mean—the causation-versus-correlation study.

RP: That the virus doesn't merely coexist with the amyloid buildup. That it actually causes it. Because any vaccine is worthless without that causation. I want your word that the study will be fully funded.

GB, sighing: Yes, all right. You have it. Now sign.

RP: You'll give me a copy of the video?

GB: You'll have one, and I'll have one, and this will stay between the two of us. Agreed?

RP, signing the document: [Silence]

35

KELLY STARED AT THE SCREEN for minutes after the video ended. Her brilliant brainstorm that last night at the Shore house—*Let's make it look like Reeza found the virus!*—turned out actually to be true. Their fiction turned out to be fact. They didn't falsify the records. Benedict did.

Save Our Savior, the courthouse picketers chanted, but they were rooting for the wrong party. The woman they were heckling was the one who actually cured Alzheimer's. The woman who fled the courthouse in defeat and disgrace. DON'T CANCEL DR. GEORGE, the placards read, when the whole time it was Dr. Reeza who'd been canceled.

Reeza, who cared only about the science. Who gave up glory in exchange for his assurance that the necessary research would be done.

Kelly pushed back from the desk and stalked the length of the suite. Her breath came out in sharp pants as her outrage built a head of steam inside her chest. He was a rapist and a murderer, and here was one more monstrous crime to add to the list. He'd erased Reeza and all her accomplishments. He'd stood on her shoulders and squashed her into the ground. He'd buried her.

Literally. Kelly finally understood the motive for Reeza's murder. He killed her because she could have destroyed him with this video. After the jury acquitted him, after she'd lost all hope of justice, he must have been terrified that she would go public with the truth about the virus study. He had access to UniViro's employee health records; he would have been privy to her medical condition and her prescriptions; he easily could have produced a super-concentrated dose of oxycodone to kill her with.

And now Kelly finally knew the answer to *Why now*. It was her own screwup that triggered him. She'd departed from their plan when she searched for and then deleted the video file from his home laptop. When he discovered it missing, right on the heels of her visit with the fake FBI agents, he realized what she'd done. And somehow he sussed out the involvement of the other three women and assumed they knew about the video, too. He wasn't killing them to retaliate. He was killing them before they could release that video or otherwise disclose the truth about who actually discovered the virus. He was killing them to silence them.

Lights began to swirl and flash in Kelly's peripheral vision. She'd been staring too long at the frozen video screen, she thought, until she blinked and realized the lights were coming from outside. She went to the window. Three police cars were parked haphazardly at the hotel entrance with their light bars swirling. Two uniformed officers were positioned by the door. Another was standing by his cruiser, talking into a radio. A bomb threat? she wondered. She looked back at her children, still fast asleep on the couch, then she looked back out the window to the street. No one seemed to be panicking, no one was evacuating, no one was even stopping arriving guests from entering the hotel. It must only be some minor fracas that brought the police, she decided. But having them on the premises gave her some small comfort. Benedict wouldn't strike, not while the police were there.

THE EVENING PASSED. They ordered room service again, something with vegetables this time, and found a movie that Justin and

Lexie could agree on. Kelly sat across the room and watched them watching the TV and remembered all the times she raised the back of Adam's bed so the four of them could watch TV together. So she could pretend they were watching TV together. Even when Adam's eyes remained closed and his hand lay lifeless in her grasp.

All for the win. Everything for the win.

Lexie crawled into bed before nine. Justin loped off to his own bed at ten, and Kelly closed their door and made up the bed in the living room. She was getting undressed when her phone rang.

She froze for a second, but it wasn't Benedict's name on the screen. The caller wasn't anyone in her contact list, but she recognized that 484 area code. It was Ashley, checking in, Kelly hoped, after having safely arrived at her own hiding place. "Hello?" she answered.

A choked sob sounded over the line.

"What is it?" she said. "Are you all right?"

"Oh, Ms. McCann . . . Kelly. I— I'm so sorry to bother you at this hour."

Kelly looked at the number again. "Who is this?"

"It's Jane." The woman's voice caught on another sob. "Jane Benedict."

"Mrs. Benedict?"

"There's been an incident. Up there in Boston. It's— It's Dr. Benedict. He's been arrested!"

"What?"

"Some woman—a hotel maid, I think?—she's claiming something happened, I don't know what exactly. He tried to reach you, but I guess you were in court? Anyway, she called the police, and they arrested him!"

Kelly sat down hard on the pull-out bed. He'd done it again. Here, in this very hotel. The police she saw earlier—they must have been here to arrest him. He'd raped a housekeeper in this hotel. It could have been the same housekeeper she'd watched through the peephole that afternoon.

Those three calls he made earlier to her phone. He hadn't been hunting her. He'd been calling her to fix the situation as she'd done so many times before. He thought that he could drug her, paralyze her, brutalize her body and soul, and that she'd still be at his beck and call, happy to swoop in and save the day with another NDA. This went beyond entitlement, beyond arrogance, beyond hubris and all the other male attributes she'd learned to deal with in her practice.

"I know it's late, and I'm so sorry." Jane wept softly. "But if you could possibly go to the station and do what you can for him?"

Kelly picked up a pen and the hotel notepad. It was like muscle memory, going through the motions of what she'd done a hundred times on the receiving end of calls like this. "What station?" she asked.

SHE TRIED TO reach Gwen to come and stay with the children, but when Gwen didn't call back within the next ten minutes, Kelly did something she'd always tried to avoid. She called Cazzadee at home.

A man answered. "Kelly—jeez, I've been trying to reach you."

"Javier?" She double-checked the screen, but she hadn't misdialed. "I was calling Cazz—?"

"Yeah, she's in the shower right now."

"You're at her apartment?" She was too slow to understand. Cazzadee Johnson, the consummate professional/fervid feminist who never showed anything but disdain for Javier and his roguish charms. "Oh," she said when it hit her.

"Listen," Javi said. "George Benedict's been arrested. He raped a maid at the Four Seasons. They've got him down at District A-1. Anton, too, for accessory after the fact. He tried to smuggle him out of the hotel. Anyway, they're both in custody. I called Ashley and told her she's safe, at least until they make bail."

If Kelly pulled her usual strings, she could have them out in six hours.

"Javi," she said. "I need a favor."

36

SHE DRESSED IN A BLACK suit, white blouse, and high-heeled pumps. She pulled her hair back in a tight bun and sprayed it with an armor coating of hairspray. She looked in the mirror and heard Adam's voice in her head. *Yes, I can*, she told herself.

Javier and Cazzadee were waiting for her in the lobby. Cazz couldn't quite meet her eyes, but she accepted the key card and nodded at Kelly's instructions and took the elevator up to the room.

"I don't get it," Javi said. "Why'd you bring your kids along to meet your client?" He spat out the word *client* like it was an obscenity. He was furious that she was answering Benedict's summons yet again.

"It's a long story," she said.

"My car's out front," he said, scowling, and turned heel.

He drove her past the Public Garden and around the Common and as far down Sudbury as he could get before the TV news vans blocked his way. The crowds had already gathered behind the barricades. Reporters. Protesters. Curiosity seekers and the cops trying to corral them.

"I'll get out here." She reached for the door handle.

Javi stopped her with a hand on her arm. "Kell, you don't have to do this."

"Yes," she said. "I do."

His fingers tightened. "You and your stupid rules!"

She shook him off and stepped out of the car.

Someone spotted her, and a cry went up through the crowd. People surged around her as she threaded her way around the barricades. The entrance to the police station was below grade, and a flight of wide granite stairs led from the street down to the glass doors. She stopped at the top of the stairs and turned to face the crowd. In all her courthouse victory speeches, the stairs were always in front of her. Now they were behind her, and she felt the drop, like she was teetering on the edge of a cliff.

Her gaze swept through the crowd. She registered the logos on the news vans and recognized Rick Olsson's network a second before she spotted him behind the barricades. He was staring at her with a frown on his face.

"Kelly! Kelly!" the reporters cried, as if they were old friends at a crowded party.

"Are you representing Dr. Benedict in this case?" another reporter called out.

"Did he do it?" somebody shouted.

"Are you seeking bail?"

"Reeza Patel!" a woman screamed.

Kelly looked for the shouter and found her at the back of the crowd, among a group of protesters waving their picket signs. #MeToo. Believe Women. She spotted a new slogan among them. Stop the Silence.

She didn't know if she could do this. Adam's voice was in her head, *You're Kelly McCann, not Kelly McCan't*, but still she didn't know. Her eyes moved through the crowd, and another phrase popped into her head, words she'd spoken herself that very morning. *You can win the case, or you can keep your secret. You can't do both.*

She took a deep breath. One last time, she'd go for the win.

AND THERE IT was again: the surge of adrenaline through her veins as she gazed out over a burst of camera flashes, a sea of up-turned faces, a bouquet of microphones pointed her way.

Her voice rang out through the street and echoed across the plaza and ricocheted through the complex of government buildings. "Last month George Benedict stood trial for the rape of Dr. Reeza Patel," she said. "He was acquitted of all charges." She waited a full beat before speaking the next word. "Wrongly."

A hush fell over the crowd, followed by confused whispers.

"I know this," she said. "I know he was guilty of raping Dr. Patel. I know he was guilty of raping other women as well. Women who couldn't come forward with the truth of what he did to them, because I persuaded them to sign nondisclosure agreements. Yet I knew they were telling the truth, just as I knew Dr. Patel was telling the truth."

A low hum rose up from the crowd as the spectators began to whisper and buzz. A single counterprotester, a man, raised his sign higher. DON'T CANCEL DR. GEORGE! Kelly lifted her chin an inch and raised her voice.

"I don't merely suspect he's guilty. I know he is. I know this be-cause after our triumph over Reeza Patel, George Benedict invited me to a celebratory dinner at his home. He made an excuse to get me alone in his office. And there he drugged me. He paralyzed me. And he raped me."

The reaction from the crowd was like a spark catching on tinder and bursting into flame. Their gasps exploded the air.

Javier came into her view then. He was standing by the farthest barricade, but not so far that she couldn't see his face. His eyes and mouth formed three perfect circles.

"So I became his victim, the same as Dr. Patel and all those other women. But I was his accomplice, too. I enabled his crimes by defending him to the utmost in court and by keeping all the other women from ever getting to court. I am complicit in his rapes. I'm even complicit in my own rape, because I chose not to report it. I kept silent to protect my reputation as a lawyer. I cared more about my career than I did about justice. And I cannot express how sorry I am. How guilty I am."

At the back of the crowd, the protesters lowered their placards and stared in silence at Kelly. The entire street was quiet now, so quiet that the traffic noise swelled out on Bowdoin until it sounded like the roar of engines on a racetrack. Everyone stood motionless. It was like a freeze-frame in a video, except for one person cutting his way around the others, making his way to the front of the crowd. Rick Olsson.

"Tonight George Benedict stands accused of yet another rape," Kelly said. "This time, of a hotel housekeeper, a woman working in one of the most vulnerable jobs in the world. I don't know the facts. I can't be sure he's guilty of this particular rape. But I do know this much: he's a rapist, and he belongs in prison.

"I'll never again appear in court for George Benedict. Or for anyone else. After tonight, my career is over. No one will hire me, and even if they would, I'm sure to be disbarred. But if George Benedict goes to prison, if justice is finally done, it will all be worth it."

She paused to gaze across the scores of men and women who stood before her, then looked directly into the cameras. "I appreciate your listening to me here tonight. But I know that I have your attention only because of who I am. Or was. Because I was the lawyer who represented George Benedict. But please, let me ask this one thing of you: Listen to all the other women, too.

"And finally, let me ask this of those women—Benedict's victims, but also the victims of every other rich and powerful man: Please, come forward. Speak up. Tell the truth about what he did to you."

She let out her breath. That was it. She had nothing left to say. She turned to go, and that was the moment she lost her balance. She teetered on her four-inch heels, one foot skidded out from under her, and she was pitching backward down the stairs into the hard granite pit below—until someone grabbed her and pulled her back from the edge. She looked down with a shudder, then up at Rick Olsson beside her.

"It's all right," he said, holding her steady. "I've got you."

She pulled his hand from her waist. "Rick, call your law department and tell them to send me a release. Tonight. Right now."

"What for?"

"When you run this story, I want you to use that video. From the heliport."

He nodded, but there was no triumph in his eyes, or even satisfaction. She didn't understand his reaction. Yes, her very public statement had deprived him of his exclusive, but the helicopter video would be his alone.

"Wait," she said and dug into her bag for the thumb drive. She pressed it into his palm. "Take this, too. It's the biggest story of all." If that didn't satisfy him, this certainly would. The exclusive on Reeza's story was worth far more than her own.

But again he barely reacted. He tucked the drive in his breast pocket with one hand and took her by the elbow with the other. "Let me drive you home."

By then Javi was at her other elbow. "I have a ride," she said and peeled herself free.

37

SHE SANK INTO THE SEAT of Javi's car and let her head sag back. She felt drained, more depleted than she'd felt even after a three-week trial. All her adrenaline had ebbed away. Her fire had burned out.

"Take me home?" she asked Javi. She didn't want to wake Cazz or the kids at the hotel, and she really needed to see Adam.

Javi nodded. His teeth were clenched hard. He was still seething as he drove out of the city. "That son of a bitch," he muttered, again and again. Some of his anger was directed at Kelly, too. "I can't believe you didn't tell me!"

"I know. I'm sorry. I should have." She said that again and again, too.

"All this time," he said to himself, then, as the rest dawned on him. "This is why you were at the hotel. You weren't meeting him there. You were hiding from him."

So she'd thought. She still shuddered to think that Benedict was staying at the same hotel she'd brought her kids to.

"I'm going to the cops," Javi said. He raised his chin defiantly. "With all of it. You can't stop me now."

"I wouldn't try," she said.

"First thing tomorrow. I'll head back to Pennsylvania. I'll buttonhole every cop in every Podunk department down there until somebody wakes up and listens."

Everybody was listening now. Her phone was chiming with alerts as every news outlet broke the story. Her own image appeared in pixilated miniature on the screen. She looked pale and drawn and a decade older.

"You'll have to go down and give a statement, too," he said.

"I will," she said, though she knew it was pointless. They'd never charge Benedict for her rape. She hadn't preserved any of the evidence. She didn't have a corroborating witness. She hadn't done anything right. There wasn't even the video evidence she'd been so sure of. She wondered if the recording could still be in that camera high on the shelf, or if he'd hidden it away somewhere else in his mansion. She wondered if there was ever a camera at all. What other details could she have gotten wrong? Even if they did charge him, any decent defense lawyer would tear her apart on the stand.

Competent, she amended in her mind. Not *decent*.

"So!" She forced a smile as she tried to lighten the mood. "You and Cazzie are dating!"

Javi stared straight ahead through the windshield. "Nope."

"Oh," she said as she realized it was only a casual hookup. It was none of her business, but she couldn't help feeling a little disappointed.

"Because we're married," he said as a smile broke out on his face.

"What? Oh my God—you and Cazz, married? When?"

"Last June." He lifted his left hand from the wheel to show the band around his ring finger.

She gaped at it. "How did I never notice that!"

"We don't wear our rings at work."

"I don't understand. Why the secrecy?"

"Cazzie's idea. She didn't want to ruin her rep."

"What rep?"

"You know. Big-time feminist. All-business. No time for men in general and my type in particular."

"Your type." She tried not to laugh. "You mean . . . womanizer?"

He made a face. "I prefer *ladies' man.*"

She did laugh then. "But somehow you changed her mind."

"Nope," he said again. He grinned. "I changed me."

THE PORCH LIGHTS were off when he turned into her driveway, but the windows were glowing upstairs in her bedroom. Todd was still on duty.

Javi stayed in the driveway with his headlights marking the way to the front door until she was safely inside. She disarmed the security system, then armed it again, though it hardly felt necessary anymore. Benedict and Anton were in custody, and she knew they wouldn't make bail until morning. If then.

She dropped her bag in the front hall and called out as she climbed the stairs. "Todd? It's only me. Home early."

She went down the hall and into the bedroom. The room smelled different. Todd always kept it clean and sterile, but tonight the antiseptic smell was almost overwhelming. Adam was lying flat, eyes closed, all his machines beeping in perfect rhythm. But Todd wasn't there, and the CCTV camera was off.

There was no reason for him to still be at work—it was one in the morning, after all—but he always left the camera on when she wasn't there. That allowed him to do a visual check on the monitor in his apartment if any of Adam's alarms went off. She looked out through the alcove window. The lights were off over the garage. She frowned. It wasn't like Todd to go to bed with the camera off when Kelly wasn't there.

She jumped when she heard the toilet flush, then let out a little laugh. Todd had simply taken a bathroom break. The faucet sounded next, and through the cracked door she caught a glimpse of his lavender hospital scrubs.

"Hello, I'm back early," she called again.

"Oh, good," he answered.

Kelly cocked her head. There was something wrong with his voice. "Todd? Are you okay?"

"Oh, he's fine," said the woman who bustled out of the bathroom. "He went to bed as soon as I turned off the camera. They're fast asleep now, the two of them."

Kelly gaped at her. This made no sense. Todd never booked a relief nurse without clearing it with Kelly first. And there was no scenario in which he would book this particular nurse. "Mrs. Benedict?" she gasped.

"Jane. Please." The woman wore a lavender tweed suit and low-heeled pumps, and a string of pearls around her jowly neck. She held up a urinal bottle. "I was just emptying your husband's collection bag," she said. "I hope you don't mind. I noticed it was full."

Kelly stared. "I don't— What are you doing here?"

"Here in Boston? I came up to take care of George, of course." Jane placed the bottle on the table beside Adam's bed. "But I was too late, so I came here to take care of your husband instead. Poor soul." She reached out and gently patted his shoulder.

"But . . . how did you get in? The security system—"

"Oh, that was no trouble. I have the passcode."

Kelly felt the room start to spin. "You— You're the one who hacked into our Wi-Fi?"

"Oh, goodness, no!" Jane trilled a laugh as she picked up a latex glove from the table. "As if I were capable of such a thing!"

Kelly squinted in confusion. "Then how—"

"Why, Justin gave it to me, of course. After you assured him that someone else was peeping into your electronics, he was happy to give me access again." She wiggled her fingers into the glove. "We'd arranged tonight to be our first in-person date. I was going to tiptoe in after you were in bed. Except that you weren't here, were you? You were downtown, making a speech." She stretched the glove into place and released it with a crisp snap.

Now Kelly's stomach was churning along with her head. She groped for the bedpost to hold herself steady. "You mean, you're the one he was texting with?"

"Sexting, I think they call it. Yes."

"Those photos—"

"Hmm. Disgusting what you can find on the internet."

Nausea swamped her. She nearly retched. "But—why?"

Jane snapped the second glove onto her other hand. "Well, I had to know, didn't I? All those hours you spent alone with George preparing for trial? I had to be sure you weren't a threat to him. And obviously you weren't. You behaved properly at all times. Until tonight, of course." She shook her head sadly. "You disappointed me badly tonight."

The threat was unspoken, but it landed like a punch to Kelly's stomach. She looked around wildly for her phone until she remembered that it was in her bag downstairs. She bolted for the door.

"Leave this room and he'll be dead before you get back."

Jane's voice sounded an octave lower and sharp as a knife. Kelly stopped dead. The realization hit her like a punch, too. When Jane said she was here to take care of Adam, she didn't mean to nurse him.

She sneaked a glance at the CCTV camera. The power switch was a button on the side. If she could turn it on, if Todd were awake, if he happened to glance at the monitor or his phone . . . She took a few shuffling steps toward the tripod.

"Over here," Jane said and pointed her chin at the floor beside Adam's bed.

A sob died in Kelly's throat as she veered away from the camera and came up to the bedside.

"That's better," Jane said in her usual melodic warble. "Violent deaths are so much worse, don't you think?" She picked up a small glass bottle. "Pharmaceutical deaths are so peaceful."

Kelly stared at the bottle. It had a black-and-white label, and in her vision it blurred and swirled until the words mutated into a skull and crossbones. "Poison," she whispered, then the full scale of the horror hit her. Those words: *Cut. Poison. Burn.* That was how medical science treated cancer—surgery, chemotherapy, radiation—and it was how Jane Benedict, the cancer nurse, chose to treat her husband's victims. Starting with . . . "Reeza Patel," she breathed.

"Why, yes, now that you mention it," Jane said. "Hers was a blessing, really—what with her back pain and her asthma. Her body was like a pincushion from all her Epi injections." She plunged the needle of the syringe into the bottle and watched closely as a clear liquid chased up the tube.

If any of Adam's alarms went off, Todd would wake up. He'd turn on the camera and see what was happening. He'd call the police. Kelly's eyes traced one of the power cords from Adam's monitor to the electrical outlet in the wall. If she could extend her leg under the bed and kick the cord loose—

"Stop right there," Jane said without turning her head. "Unless you want me to smash this bottle and pierce his carotid artery with it."

Kelly froze.

Todd's apartment was dark, but even so, he might be awake. If he saw that the bedroom lights were on and that the camera was off, he might realize that something was wrong. He might already have called the police. He might be hiding in the dark while he waited for them to arrive. They might be on their way already.

But she couldn't guess how long it would take them, because she couldn't guess when Todd might have placed the call. Jane could have been here an hour already, but she also could have just arrived. Time was the great unknown. But it was also Kelly's only weapon. She'd have to stall. Playing for time was her only play.

"That's why they couldn't tell that you'd injected her," she said. "She had so many injection sites already."

Jane didn't answer. She was concentrating on the fill line on the syringe.

Kelly tried to think of something, anything, to stall her. She took a step closer to Jane, close enough to smell something behind the odor of disinfectant in the room. It was something sweet. Too sweet. It was cloying. It was Jane's perfume, she realized, and the clash of odors made her stomach churn even more. She gagged, and the gorge rose in her throat. She doubled over and spewed out a puddle of vomit onto the hardwood floor.

"Oh, good heavens!" Jane jerked back, and the bottle and syringe clattered to the table. "Look what you've done!"

Kelly kept her head down as her stomach bucked and heaved.

"And after I had this room absolutely sterilized!"

"Sorry. Sorry," Kelly panted.

"Clean it up. I left paper towels and disinfectant in the bathroom. Go on now."

Kelly felt a surge of relief that had nothing to do with her stomach. Here was her best hope for killing time until the police arrived. She dragged herself to the bathroom, slowly, staggering as if she were about to faint. The disinfectant and paper towels were on the vanity, and when she caught a glimpse of herself in the mirror, she saw that her skin was ashen and beads of sweat dotted her forehead.

She returned to the bedroom. Slowly, laboriously, she dropped to her knees to mop up the vomit. Above her, Jane made a frustrated noise, and Kelly peeked up through her lashes to find her scowling at the syringe, then emptying it back into the bottle and starting over to fill it.

Kelly kept working on the floor, ripping off sheet after sheet of paper toweling and mopping and scrubbing until the floorboards glistened.

"That'll do," Jane said.

That bought her two minutes, maybe three, Kelly thought. No more.

She climbed to her feet and carried the sodden paper towels to the bathroom trash can. The window here also looked out at Todd's apartment, and she could see that it was still dark. He and Bruce were hiding, she hoped and prayed, but she knew they might simply be asleep. She washed her hands at the sink and looked at the light switch. If she could turn the lights on and off a few times, the flash might wake them. She started to close the bathroom door.

"What are you doing? Get back here. Now."

Her face crumpled in the mirror. Jane was alert to every move she made, and now she was out of ideas. She'd soon be out of time, and she couldn't stop the tears from falling.

But something was different when she returned to the bedroom. Her eyes swept through the room in search of what might have changed until they landed on the camera behind Jane. The green light was glowing, the camera was on, and Kelly nearly swooned with relief. Todd was awake. He'd activated the camera. It could have been on the whole time she was scrubbing the floor, maybe even before she vomited. Rescue was on the way. Adam would be saved in time.

But only if she could keep Jane from noticing the green light. She sidled around to the far side of Adam's bed.

Jane angled her body to keep her in sight as she reached for a second syringe. "I hope you realize that this isn't at all what I wanted," she said. "I truly hoped it wouldn't come to this. What you did for George—I was so grateful to you. And after watching you these past few months, I really admired how devoted you are to your husband."

Watching her. Adam. The children. The idea made Kelly's stomach churn again. She took a deep breath. "Just as you're devoted to Dr. Benedict," she said.

"Yes," Jane said with a satisfied sigh. "He's a great man. A very great man. I saw it the moment I met him. But I also saw that he needed protection."

"*He* needed . . . ? From what?"

"All great men have their Achilles' heel, don't they? Their little foibles. Winston Churchill was a drunk. Reverend King was a philanderer. Alan Turing was a homosexual. On and on and on."

"And Dr. Benedict's foible?"

"He's too susceptible to manipulative women."

Kelly wasn't fast enough to hide her reaction to that statement, because Jane hastened to add, "Oh, not you, dear. I've watched the video. I know you didn't throw yourself at him. Not like those others did." She inserted the second syringe into the bottle. "They were like a cancer eating away at him."

"Poison," Kelly said. "Cut. Burn. Reeza. Tiffy. Emily."

Jane smirked at her as she capped the bottle. "Yes, aren't you clever. And now we circle back to poison." She held up the two syringes. "Oxy in liquid form. In an even more potent dosage than I used on Dr. Patel." She looked down at Adam. "He's full of injection sites, too, just like her. But you"—she tilted her head up as she considered Kelly—"you probably don't have a needle habit of any kind."

Kelly's heart thudded. She cut a quick glance at the camera. The green light was still glowing.

"Not that it matters, though. This will be a murder-suicide. And so understandable, under the circumstances. No one will question it for a moment."

"But why? You just said it wasn't my fault!"

"No, *that* wasn't your fault. But you were up to something, weren't you? I knew it when I saw the text chain on that girl's phone. Then you showed up at my house with those phony FBI agents." She clucked her tongue as she pulled back the covers to expose Adam's arm. "But even after all that, I still gave you a chance to redeem yourself. If you'd done what I asked tonight, none of this would be necessary. But instead, you put on that performance at the police station." She pursed her lips at Kelly. "I'm afraid you crossed a line, dear."

She took out the alcohol wipe and carefully swabbed the tender white skin on the inside of Adam's elbow, then dropped the wipe into the hazardous waste receptacle below the bed. She reached for a length of rubber tubing.

Kelly inhaled sharply. She had to make one more play for time. "Tiffy Jenkins," she blurted. "How did— How did she throw herself at Dr. Benedict?"

Jane paused to consider. "I don't know the details. I only know her name from those papers I discovered in his office. But I did some digging. I found out who she was. How she lived. I know her type only too well." She turned back to Adam and tied the rubber strap around his arm, then tapped two fingers hard against his skin until a vein rose up.

"Emily Norland," Kelly said next. "How did she throw herself at him?"

"Traveling to another city with him? Staying in a hotel room right next door? She obviously meant to seduce him." Jane picked up one of the syringes.

"No, wait!" Kelly said. "You cut, poison, and burn to save lives. Not to destroy them."

"Ah. There she is." Jane pointed at her with the syringe. "The lawyer in you. She's come out. Playing word games to try to win points.

But it's too late, my dear. You've already lost." She tapped Adam's arm again and aimed the needle at his vein.

"No!" Kelly shouted, and she must have shrieked it. It was a shrill, piercing scream that reverberated inside her head and went on and on even after she closed her mouth. Then she realized: the scream wasn't coming from her. It was the security alarm going off.

Jane's hand froze above Adam's arm. "What is that?" For a second her eyes flared wide behind her glasses. But then they went small and hard. She turned and aimed the needle again.

"No!" Kelly lunged over the bed and grabbed the woman by the wrist and wrenched her hand away from Adam.

"All right, then! You first!" Jane screamed, and she stabbed the syringe deep into Kelly's neck.

The prick instantly flamed into a white-hot burn. Kelly's knees buckled, and she sank to the floor. She heard footsteps thunder on the stairs and down the hall, but they were ebbing away, fainter and fainter as she melted into the floorboards. "Freeze!" someone roared from a mile away. A black-and-white kaleidoscope opened behind her eyes, the angles folding in and opening out, forming a different pattern every time, until the white shapes got smaller and smaller and the voices faded away and it was all black.

38

Kelly McCann

ADAM DREW HIS LAST BREATH on December 8. He didn't die on December 8; I finally understood that now that I'd been briefly dead myself.

I didn't see a bright light, I didn't walk through a tunnel, and none of my grandparents were there to beckon me on. For me there was only a void. No sound, no light, no movement. No dimension or duration. It was an endless nothingness.

Until all at once something like a geyser erupted beneath me. It was like jet propulsion. It lifted me up and up, higher and higher, launching me out of nothingness and flinging me up into the world again. It was a power greater than anything that I'd ever experienced, that I'd ever been aware of, but somehow I knew that it came from inside me and that it had been there all along. It was my life force, and I finally understood that Adam didn't have it anymore.

The doctor came to the house the day after Thanksgiving to remove his feeding tube. He explained what he was doing in a low, soothing voice, then explained what we could expect to happen next. Adam wouldn't feel thirsty or hungry, he told us. He wouldn't experience pain. Even if he weren't in a vegetative state, he wouldn't feel any pain. The removal of the feeding tube guaranteed that. Dehydration was the dying man's friend, he said. It caused a release of endorphins that would give Adam a sense of well-being until the end.

But he warned that the physical changes could be alarming. Adam would begin to look thinner as his body tissues lost fluid. His eyes and lips would look dry. His muscles would contract. His breathing would become irregular, with periods of rapid shallow pants and other periods of slow deep breathing. Toxins would build up, leading to organ failure and eventually death, typically within two weeks.

I didn't want our children to see any of that, so I called them in for their final farewells soon after the doctor left. Then Todd disconnected all of the equipment and packed it up to return to the vendors.

After everyone was gone, I lowered Adam's bed and pulled up a chair beside him.

For the next ten days, I sat in that chair and held his hand and told him the story of his life. It was a narrative I cobbled together from tales he'd told me of his childhood and youth, my own first-person accounts of our life together, and various anecdotes I'd collected from his colleagues and friends over the years. Courtney came over every evening after work, and she added scenes from the years she knew her father best, along with stories her mother and grandparents had told her. We stitched it together like a patchwork quilt, pieced out of scraps from here and there, full of vivid colors and small details. Some of our stitches were uneven, some of our edges were raw, and sometimes the weight of it was almost too much as we worked. But it all came together at the end. It was a warm and cozy comfort to us both.

Todd came in for an hour or so every night. He'd already started a new job at a rehab facility in Wellesley, but he insisted on helping me with Adam's care, and he wouldn't accept any payment for it. He blamed himself for sleeping through Jane's attack, no matter how many times I told him it wasn't his fault. No one could be on duty twenty-four hours a day, though Todd had certainly come close.

Gwen moved into the guest room and took over the care and feeding of the children. Abundant feeding. She laid out smorgasbords of food around the clock so that there was always something to offer the streams of callers who dropped by. I didn't receive any of them; I emerged from my room only for a couple hours every evening at bedtime, only long enough to do book club with Lexie then cross the hall to talk with Justin while we played *Overwatch*. But the visitors kept coming anyway. They kept a sort of watch downstairs while I watched over Adam upstairs.

Courtney was the only visitor I admitted into the bedroom, but she carried up messages from downstairs, well-wishes and nuggets of news. Mr. Sealy the science teacher came with her every night, and he kept the kids entertained with puzzles and projects and board games. Todd and Bruce frequently joined in. The neighbors popped in with more food to add to the groaning buffet table.

My own team dropped by regularly. Though I could hardly call them that anymore, not since I surrendered my law license. My friends and colleagues had urged me to contest the disbarment. They were sure I could win. But I was tired of fighting.

I wouldn't miss the law, not the way I'd practiced it, and I definitely wouldn't miss Harry Leahy, with whom I had a brief, sour negotiation over my withdrawal from the firm. The final buyout amount was less than I was entitled to, but severing that relationship was compensation enough for the discount.

Anyway, cash flow wouldn't be a problem, at least in the short run. Todd and Bruce wanted to stay on in the apartment, as rent-paying tenants this time. That would help with the mortgage. Thanks to Courtney, the kids' education was paid for. The buyout money ought to take care of the rest. For the first time in ten years, I had the luxury of thinking about what kind of work I really wanted to do.

Some women's rights organizations made overtures. Time's Up asked me to join their board and help with fundraising, but I didn't want to be in the public eye anymore, even for a good cause. Rick Olsson wanted me to coauthor his book with him, but I refused that, too. Slapping my name on the cover would only be a ploy for sales and a pretty crass one at that. Kevin Trent offered me a job in his firm as a case manager, which was a title often held by disbarred lawyers who were still practicing on the sly. I turned him down flat. Only one offer had any appeal. A judge I knew approached me about serving as mediator, to help litigants reach out-of-court settlements. To facilitate a process in which nobody won and nobody lost—that might be the change I needed in my life.

I thought a lot about winning and losing during the days I spent by Adam's side, especially after Patti sent news about Tommy Wexford. Margaret Staley had dropped her case completely. Patti was baffled, but I thought I understood. Staley was never in it for the money, and once she realized that was all she was going to get, she abandoned her crusade. Which meant that Tommy had succeeded in doing what I thought was impossible: he'd kept his secret and still managed to win the case.

He'd won more than that, too. He'd just landed the lead in a new film version of *The Flash*.

I WOULDN'T MISS the law, but I would miss my team. I lined up interviews for Patti at several prominent law firms where I knew she would thrive. But she wasn't interested. She hoped to take over my practice, and Harry was dangling the promise of partnership in a few years if she succeeded. Cazzadee was going to stay on at Leahy & McCann, too, but only long enough to help Patti find her footing. Next fall she would start law school. She was going to do brilliantly.

Javier was already gone. He'd returned to the Suffolk County DA's Office, where we first met. He wasn't allowed to work on the

Benedict case—*stupid conflict rules*, he groused—but he kept himself apprised of every development and sent me regular updates.

Benedict had been charged with the rape of Rosita Vega. Mrs. Vega was a forty-year-old housekeeper, an undocumented immigrant with no formal education who nonetheless did everything right. She immediately called 911 after the attack; reported it to her manager, her husband, and three coworkers; went to a rape crisis center, where all the biological evidence was preserved; and gave a detailed statement to the officers who met her there.

Benedict's only possible defense was consent, and there was no hope of that in light of the video from the hotel's surveillance cameras; it showed him grabbing Mrs. Vega and dragging her into his room.

Videos proved to be his undoing. It turned out that there *was* a recording of my own rape. A search of the Benedict mansion by the Pennsylvania authorities turned up a memory card in Jane's jewelry box. The hidden camera, it seemed, was hers.

So despite the fact that I did everything wrong, there was enough evidence to charge him in Pennsylvania, too. He was back there now, alone in his mansion with an ankle monitor attached, cycling through defense attorneys in search of someone to replace me. There were lots of contenders but so far no winner.

It was video evidence that sealed Jane's fate, too.

Here's what Courtney told me afterward. After watching me on the news that night, she felt shocked and confused and suddenly full of doubt about her guardianship petition. She tossed and turned in bed and finally reached for her phone to open the app I'd sent her. She activated the CCTV camera, expecting to find her dad lying alone and inert. She expected to be reassured that she was doing the right thing.

What she didn't expect was to see a strange woman filling syringes while confessing to three separate murders. She made a frantic call to 911 while Mr. Sealy, her tech-savvy boyfriend, recorded the live-stream video and simultaneously sent it to the Weston police so that they could watch in real time, too.

The rest I learned from the police. The first officer to arrive on the scene tackled Jane to the floor while the second officer punched a dose of Narcan into my thigh. That triggered the geyser that brought me back to life and kept me there until the EMTs arrived.

Later the officer received a commendation for his swift actions that night, and I added my own profuse thanks for saving my life. Though, really, it was Courtney who did that. Courtney and the video.

Jane Benedict had been charged with attempted murder, along with a litany of lesser included crimes here in Massachusetts. But the locals were happy to ship her back to Pennsylvania to face the greater charges—for the murders of Reeza Patel, Tiffy Jenkins, and Emily Norland. Jane was now in a psychiatric hospital. Her lawyer was reportedly exploring an insanity defense.

ONE NIGHT COURTNEY came into my room with less welcome news. "Rick Olsson's here," she said.

"Again?" I was exasperated with his visits. We were supposed to be done with each other. Whatever I might owe him for trying to make him the patsy in my scheme, I'd more than repaid. I'd authorized him to air the heliport video, and I'd slipped him the video of Benedict's meeting with Reeza. That should have settled our account.

The problem was that he didn't use the heliport video in his broadcast, after all—*wasn't necessary* was the only explanation he offered. And he didn't break the virus fraud story either; he passed the thumb drive video on to Aidan Dunwoodie at the *New York Times,* who ran with the story and delivered the biggest bombshell ever to happen on the science and medicine beat. George Benedict, onetime savior of the world, was a fraud.

It was a nice irony, I thought: Benedict would never get his Nobel Prize, but the *Times* had a clear shot at a Pulitzer.

At any rate, it was Rick's choice not to use either video. I didn't owe him anything more. But still he lingered in Boston. He kept calling. He kept dropping by. He chatted up my friends and ingratiated himself with my children, and I'd finally had enough.

I left Courtney alone with her father and ran downstairs. I found Rick in the kitchen, washing dishes at the sink. "Why are you here?" I demanded. I planted myself behind him with my hands on my hips, though I doubt I looked very formidable, more than a foot shorter in my bare feet. "I told you I wasn't interested. No means no, right?"

He didn't turn from the sink. "You only said no to the book."

"What's that supposed to mean?"

He rinsed off a plate and added it to the rack. "I can't say."

"Why not?"

"Because it wouldn't be right." He reached for a towel and dried his hands before turning to face me. "To declare myself while your husband's dying upstairs."

I flushed so hot that my ears burned. My hands dropped from my hips. "It wouldn't ever be right," I said finally, thickly.

"We'll see," was all he said before I turned and fled upstairs.

THAT NIGHT AFTER Lexie was asleep, I crossed the hall to Justin's room for our game of *Overwatch*. I picked up my game pad and waited for him to turn on the screen. But he didn't. Our matches had been half-hearted at best these last few days, and tonight he didn't even bother to pick up his own game pad. I took that as his signal that he wanted to talk.

"How was school today?"

He shrugged. "Okay."

It was always a slow dance to get him to open up, about anything, and lately it was a snail crawl, ever since he learned the truth about his internet girlfriend. I hadn't planned to tell him, not yet, maybe not ever. But he was a smart boy, and he overheard enough conversations to piece it all together. He was embarrassed and ashamed and more than a little sickened when he saw her real photo in the various news feeds.

But tonight he wanted to talk about something else. "I've been, uh, thinking about what, uh, happened to you," he said.

This was something we'd been able to shield Lexie from, but Justin had watched my statement on the news. He knew everything.

"Okay," I said and waited.

"It just never occurred to me, you know, that something . . . like that could happen to my own mother."

I nodded. "I know what you mean," I said. "Except—it's not quite right to say it *happened* to me. Because the truth is somebody *did* it to me. And he did it to other women, too. Women you're not even related to. Women you don't even know. But they're just as real as I am."

"I get that," he said, but the look on his face seemed to say *What's your point?*

"My point is—this was done by somebody you admired—"

"Not anymore," Justin protested. "He's a total fraud. A thief!"

"But what if he wasn't?" I said. "What if he really was the genius who cured this terrible disease? But at the same time he committed these awful crimes against women? What would you think of him then?"

"Oh," he said, and his voice held all the uncertainty that the rest of the world seemed to struggle with, too.

Our talk that night lasted long past my allotted hour.

ONE DAY CAZZIE sent word that Ashley LaSorta had called. She had a new work number, and I called it immediately.

"You, too?" she said instead of hello.

"Me, too."

"Huh. You never let on. All that time we were working together, you never let on that it happened to you, too. You never breathed a word."

"I should have. I should have gone to the police. I should have told everyone. I thought I was protecting myself. But I was only protecting him."

"All our theories were wrong. He wasn't killing his victims, and he wasn't killing his avengers either. He wasn't killing anybody."

"We were wrong about everything," I said. "You know—" I hesitated. "You could go public now, too."

Ashley's answer was swift and flat. "Nope."

"You don't have to worry about the NDA," I said. "He wouldn't dare enforce it now. And no court would allow it if he tried."

"I don't care about the fucking NDA."

"Then why not go public?"

"Because it's nobody's goddamn business but mine! This happened in my private life, and I'm entitled to keep it private. I don't need to stand up at a meeting and have every UniViro board member trying to picture me naked and gagged instead of listening to what I have to say."

I took her point. But it was something else she said that grabbed my attention. "UniViro?" I repeated.

That was the other purpose of Ashley's call. She once again occupied the C-suite at the company. Benedict's ouster had cleared the way for the board to bring her back with the same title and even better perks. "I should get a T-shirt made," she joked. "*I survived George Benedict.*"

"Jane, too," I said quietly, and neither of us spoke for a moment after that, remembering the three women who hadn't.

Women like Ashley would always survive, I thought after our call ended. It wasn't because she was smarter than the others, and it wasn't her good looks either, though that certainly didn't hurt. It was that she was thick-skinned and hard-nosed. She was *lean in*, not *shy away*.

I knew that I'd been much the same. But now? I didn't want to lean in or shy away. I wanted to stand up straight.

AT THE END I was alone with Adam. He'd lost so much weight that he looked as if he'd collapsed into himself. A deflated balloon. His breathing came in shallow pants punctuated by long moments in which he didn't breathe at all, and I held my own breath along with him, wondering each time if this would be the moment. Then he'd gasp and suck in another breath, and I'd squeeze his hand tighter and resume the story of his life.

I'd taken him from his birth through his childhood adventures and higher education, professional triumphs, marriage and fatherhood, and remarriage and fatherhood again. On the last day of his life I reached the first day of Lexie's. I told him how cool and collected he was that day. How I marveled at the way he navigated the snow-covered streets to the hospital, all while delegating work and orchestrating childcare and timing my contractions while he cracked lame jokes. And how much I loved him, then and still and always.

He drew one long shuddering breath as his life story reached its end. I waited and watched for him to breathe again, but there was nothing left. His body had reached its end, too, at last.

I closed my eyes and let my head roll back, and I sat like that for a long time until his fingers grew cold against mine.

I finally opened my eyes and looked at the ceiling above me. I turned my head and looked over Adam and through the window beyond him. Snow was falling outside. It was the first snow of the season, and it fell thick and soft and silent.

Acknowledgments

I owe so much to:

Jennifer Weltz, my first reader and finest advocate;

Sara Nelson and her team at Harper Books, for all the effort and expertise they deployed in shepherding this novel to publication. It's been a privilege to work with them;

Addison Duffy and her team at United Talent Agency for guiding me through the headiest experience of my life;

Jean Naggar, who urged me to keep writing with three simple words: "Bonnie, make time";

My family, for their love, support, and wealth of arcane knowledge;

And most of all, my readers. I am deeply grateful.

Author's Note

If you or someone you know has been sexually assaulted, help is available. Contact the National Sexual Assault Hotline, a service of the Rape, Abuse & Incest National Network (RAINN):

Online chat hotline: https://hotline.rainn.org/online
Spanish online chat hotline: Https: hotline.rainn.org/es
Telephone hotline: 800-656-HOPE (4673)

The majority of sexual assaults are never reported to the police,[1] and the majority of their assailants are repeat offenders.[2] These two facts are not unrelated. Victims may have many compelling reasons for maintaining their silence, but the consequence is that their attackers are free to attack again.

For more information on the uses and abuses of nondisclosure agreements in settling sexual misconduct claims, see www.Cant BuyMySilence.com.

---

1 Department of Justice, Office of Justice Programs, Bureau of Justice Statistics, National Crime Victimization Survey, October 2021, NCJ 301775.
2 *Repeat Rape and Multiple Offending Among Undetected Rapists*, by David Lisak, University of Massachusetts, and Paul M. Miller, Boston University School of Medicine.

About the Author

BONNIE KISTLER is the author of *The Cage* and *House on Fire*. A former Philadelphia trial lawyer, she now lives in Sarasota, Florida, and the mountains of western North Carolina. Her website is www.bonniekistler.com.

DUE DATE	MCN	06/23	30.00

FAI